Jean Lorrain

FARDS AND POISONS

Translated and with an Introduction by

BRIAN STABLEFORD

CONTENTS

INTRODUCTION

FARDS ET POISONS by Jean Lorrain, here translated as *Fards and Poisons*, was published in Paris by Paul Ollendorf for the Société d'Éditions Littéraires et artistiques in 1903.[1]

As with the previous collection of Lorrain's works issued by Snuggly Books, *Errant Vice*, a translation of *Le Vice errant* (1901; 1902 in volume form), the material making up the present volume was mostly derived from the weekly items that he contributed to the daily newspaper *Le Journal* in the early years of the last century. They appeared there between June 1902 and May 1903 in three batches, the sequence being interrupted in the latter part of 1902 when two months were devoted to a sequence entitled *Heures de villes d'eau* and then again in the early months of 1902, when two months were devoted to a sequence entitled *Les Voies tragiques*. Lorrain presumably planned to publish volumes under those titles, and advertised the second as forthcoming in 1904 but it did not appear, although a few stories initially published under the heading were eventually reprinted in *Le Crime des riches* (1905). *Fards et Poisons* is, therefore, a thematic selection drawn from a well-stocked pool; even so, it a rather mixed bag, reflected in its division into four sections bracketed by a prologue and an epilogue.

---

1 Although Merriam-Webster only gives the Anglo-American "fard," with reference to facial cosmetics, as a verb, dictionary.com gives it as a noun, and there is no specific synonym, so I thought its use appropriate.

The work is representative of a distinct phase in Lorrain's work and an evolutionary development from the work contained in *La Vice errant*. The works of short fiction that Lorrain published in *Le Journal* gradually moved away from the standard narrative expectations of short stories, and although the groups in which they were organized did have overall plots of a kind, making them akin to novelettes or, in the case of the last section of *La Vice errant*, "Coins de Byzance" (also separately reprinted as "Les Noronsoff"), a novel, those cohering factors are rather loose. In *Fards et Poisons* they have virtually disappeared. Even when groups of items follow on from one another consecutively, often continuing the same reported dialogue, the aggregation has little or no trace of a story-arc, let alone a plot. Few of the items have any semblance of an ending, and many of them do not have a beginning either; they resemble fragments excised from a kind of endless series of conversations. The result is a strange kind of literary collage.

To some extent, the individual items resemble "character sketches" rather than stories, most of them featuring, and many of them being titled for, a particular character—almost always a woman—who is presented to the reader as an interesting specimen of a social phenomenon or a psychological quirk. Sometimes, a synoptic biography of the character in question is presented, but even when that happens it is usually a matter of setting the context for a single incident; a revealing "slice of life" that is supposedly a symbolic summary of the specimen's individuality or a tendency of modern society.

It is worth observing that Lorrain was not the only writer who developed and practiced that kind of narrative technique. While the stories in the present volume were appearing on the front page of *Le Journal*, usually as the lead item, the newspaper's editor had contracts with half a dozen other writers to deliver material on a regular—often weekly—basis: Edmond Haraucourt, Lucien Descaves, Hugues Le Roux, André Theuriet, J. H. Rosny (then the joint pseudonym of two brothers) and Paul Adam. On the rare occasions when a news item was reckoned important enough to take over the whole front page, leaving no room for the item of fiction even in the right-hand columns (of six), the editor made up for the omission by publishing two items of fiction in other issues. Those writers were not coming to the industry without prior examples to guide their practice.

Several French newspapers had begun running weekly items of short fiction in the 1880s and had continued through the 1890s, sometimes in the form of weekly "fiction supplements." That lively marketplace provided a golden opportunity for a whole new generation of professional writers, many of whom developed a particular expertise in the mass-production of items averaging approximately 1,500 words (reflecting the space beneath the newspapers' *feuilletons*, where they ran long serial novels) but ranging from a few hundred words to 2,000; those featured on the front page of *Le Journal* were at the longer end of the scale, sometimes stretching as far as 3,000 words. The technique of adapting fiction to such slots had been extensively explored by the prolific Catulle Mendès, and others who had followed in his footsteps with similar enterprise and artistry included Guy de Maupassant, Octave Mirbeau, Jean Richepin, Léon Bloy, Bernard Lazare and Jane de La Vaudère. All of them had been forced to develop narrative methods that permitted squeezing wordage into a narrow straitjacket that simply did not permit the construction of elaborate story-lines.

Many writers involved in that kind of work started out by constructing stories in a similar fashion to jokes, often in three phases aiming toward a "knight's-move twist" or a "punch line" of some sort, embodying an element of humor or cruel irony, and the newspaper slots also provided a useful outlet for what came to be called *contes cruels*. Mendès also found that brief fantasies of various kinds, especially fabular apologues, could easily be adapted to it, and Jean Lorrain was one of several writers who followed him in that direction—but such works alienated at least some of their readers, and editors became increasingly reluctant to use them, except as an occasional diversion. By the first decade of the twentieth century it had become clear that what most of the readers of Paris and the provinces liked best, and were prepared to consume most prolifically, were accounts of contemporary life in Paris, told with a scrupulously disapproving attitude to the presumed decadence and indecency of the city. All of the writers working steadily in the marketplace did that, coming at it from slightly different directions and filling a considerable spectrum of tones, but Jean Lorrain was perhaps the most extreme and the one who pushed the envelope furthest, so that his work became a kind of paradigm of excess, regarded by his fellows and competitors as both a shining example and a horrible warning.

Fards et Poisons is perhaps the Lorrain collection that least resembles an "orthodox" collection of short stories. It is not merely disorderly but deliberately so. The character who crops up most frequently in the conversation-pieces composing it is called "Maxence" but he is often left without a surname, and is never given the same one twice, even though his personality seems consistent. He is only one of several commentators evidently standing in for the author, but his interlocutors—most frequently Octave Vergy—are frequently other stand-ins, and he and they play the roles of storyteller and listener with equal ease. Often, Maxence says very little but merely utters tacit sighs as female informants show themselves off and show themselves up. Unlike his author, he is heterosexual—a necessary pose for the narrative voices of commercial fiction—but he is not much given to sexual relationships in the present; he and most of his peers tend to refer back to vaguely prolific past experiences while currently contenting themselves with a sadly cynical disapproval of everyone else's inability to resist erotic temptation. Precisely because of those marked eccentricities, however, *Fards et Poisons* is perhaps the most quintessential of Lorrain's works: the slice of his life that pins his own literary *persona* most precisely, like a lepidopterist's long pin.

Although it would not have been obvious to readers picking up the book without an elaborate knowledge of its provenance, *Fards et Poisons* was also a book whose contents had been severely disrupted in production and whose compilation was made in difficult circumstances, but in order to understand that and bear it in mind while reading the collection—which enables a fuller appreciation of its nature and ambitions—it is necessary to know how it fitted into the context of the author's life and career.

✳

"Jean Lorrain" was baptized Paul-Alexandre-Martin Duval in 1855 and spent his childhood in Fécamp, a small coastal town in Normandy. His father, Amable Duval, was a seemingly-prosperous but secretly profligate ship-owner whose vessels were involved in trans-Atlantic trade. Paul was initially educated at home before completing the initial phase of his education at a seminary, which he hated. The Normandy shore was a favorite refuge of English exiles who crossed the channel to escape scandal. Algernon Swinburne, who lived near Fécamp for some years, remained a model of decadent immorality so far as Lorrain's home town was concerned; the lurid decor of his house, and the scandalous things that were rumored to have gone on there, remained common gossip long after the poet's return to England, and the legend of his sojourn remained firmly fixed in Paul Duval's memory. Although he never met Swinburne, he did become acquainted with Lord Arthur Somerset, an Englishman of similar inclinations, who also lived near Fécamp for a while.

Somerset's influence might have been outweighed initially by another summer visitor to the Normandy coast, Judith Gautier, whom Paul Duval met in Fécamp in 1873, and by whom he was fascinated; she was then nursing the raw wound of her recent separation from her infidel husband, Catulle Mendès, who was later to become one of the pillars of the Decadent

Movement, and Jean Lorrain's principal literary model. Judith Gautier does not appear to have attached any importance to Paul Duval's brief infatuation—she made no mention of it in her autobiography—but he was later to comment on the change it had wrought in his life in such heartfelt terms that Edmond de Goncourt, Lorrain's closest friend and principal mentor within the literary community of Paris, became convinced that it had been the ruination of him. Goncourt came to believe that Lorrain's homosexuality was a kind of traumatic response to his doomed infatuation with Judith, and that everything he did and became thereafter was a kind of painfully-protracted moral and physical suicide. That is perhaps implausible, but what is certain is that almost all of Lorrain's longer works of prose fiction are graphic accounts of slow and painful processes of moral and physical suicide, and many of the vignettes in *Fards et Poisons* are accounts of similar evolutions, delivered with a curious kind of voyeuristic *schadenfreude*.

When he had completed his military service Paul Duval was sent by his father to study law, but he had no interest in that career, and when he announced his firm determination to follow a literary vocation instead, his father agreed to provide a modest allowance, on condition that the family name was veiled by a pseudonym. In 1880, therefore, Paul Duval became Jean Lorrain. He found lodgings in Montmartre, and launched himself into the stereotyped lifestyle of a literary Bohemian, hanging out in Le Chat Noir with the members of Émile Goudeau's literary club, the Hydropathes, and the most colorful future subscribers to the Decadent and Symbolist Movements. His first collection of poetry, published entirely under those overlapping influences, *Sang des dieux* (1882), had a frontispiece by Gustave Moreau, and Moreau's art became a very considerable influence on Lorrain's literary imagery. In 1883, he became a regular participant in Charles Buet's salon, where he made his most significant literary acquaintances: Jules Amédée Barbey d'Aurevilly, Joris-Karl Huysmans and "Rachilde"—Marguerite Eymery, who subsequently married Alfred Vallette, the editor of the most successful Symbolist periodical, the *Mercure de France*.

Barbey d'Aurevilly was a leading exponent of the philosophy of "dandyism," whose manifesto he had provided in *Du dandysme et de G. Brummell* (1845), and although Lorrain had neither the means nor the breeding to compete with such notorious homosexual dandies as Comte Robert de Montesquiou and Pierre Loti, he did what he could to keep up appearances, to the extent that Remy de Gourmont described him, by no means inaptly, as "the sole disciple of Barbey d'Aurevilly," not merely for his attire but for the plangent echoes contained in his work of Barbey's classic collection of misogynistic *contes cruels*, *Les Diaboliques* (1874; tr. as "The She-Devils"). Unlike Barbey, however, who was a thoroughgoing and cynical misogynist, Lorrain's portraits of women, although often savage and aggressive, are also tempered by a real and deep sympathy for female victims of a society massively weighted against them, and it is abundantly obvious in *Fards et Poisons* that he is far more appalled by and censoriousness of male brutality than he is of the wiles of *femme fatales*. Like many homosexuals, Lorrain had a quirky esthetic appreciation of women, especially extravagant women, and tended to place them on metaphorical pedestals; he adored Sarah Bernhardt, the Judy Garlandesque icon of the day.

When Lorrain met Huysmans, the latter author was working on his classic handbook of dandyism, *À rebours* (1884; tr. as *Against the Grain* and *Against Nature*), which became the prose Bible of the Decadent Movement. Lorrain's fourth collection of poetry, *Les Griseries* (1887), consists of material explicitly inspired by *À rebours*, and much of his fiction echoes the same inspiration, and his most famous novel, *Monsieur de Phocas. Astarté* (1901; tr. as *Monsieur de Phocas*), and the "Coins de Byzance" sequence in *Le Vice errant* are both modified clones of *À rebours*, providing elaborate character studies of aristocrats afflicted with all the manifestations of *ennui* and *spleen*, dying slowly of various physical afflictions and desperately seeking some kind of psychological remedy for their complex malaise. It is perhaps surprising that there is almost no trace of that in *Fards et Poisons*, where decadent ennui is more often the prerogative of female characters than males, and is more pose than affliction. Perhaps, having already done that, Lorrain had simply moved on, but it is also worth noting that by 1903 Huysmans was setting a very different example, dressing as a monk and living, in effect, as a penitent recluse. By then, too, Lorrain was seriously ill, partly as a result of the ether he had consumed, partly as a decadent affectation, and must have been thoroughly convinced that there is nothing in the least Romantic about the physical effects of an ulcerated lower intenstine.

Rachilde's literary career was yet to begin in earnest in 1883, although she had already started to cultivate a reputation as an *enfant terrible*, and an article that Lorrain wrote about her, entitled "Madame Salamandre," became the effective springboard of her reputation and public image—a calculatedly scandalous appearance that she cultivated carefully in public, and scrupulously belied in private. She shared Lorrain's fascination for masked balls, which were then in their last period of great fashionability, and he became her regular escort—with the blessing of Alfred Vallette, who knew that he had nothing to fear from Lorrain—competing with her in the outrageousness of their costumes. Rachilde was only the first of a series of women, mostly actresses, singers and artists, in the development of whose careers he took an interest, boosting them without ever expecting anything in return except the esthetic pleasure of his gaze. Most of them were initially grateful, but seemed to find it slightly creepy, and often dropped him when he was of no further use, inevitably seeming ingrate in consequence: an observation that provides a bitter subtext to many of the character sketches in *Fards et Poisons*.

While he cultivated those key acquaintances in Buet's salon, Lorrain was making a name for himself with the outspoken reviews that he wrote for the *Courrier Français*. His negative reviews were vitriolic, while his favorable ones tended to the opposite extreme, and their insistent flamboyance swiftly won him a reputation that attracted at least as much scorn and vituperation as admiration and praise, but which sold papers, and eventually helped to make him one of the highest-paid journalists in Paris—which was why *Le Journal,* then the most pretentious of the Parisian dailies, eventually commissioned him in 1901 to produce items on a weekly basis, in which he was naturally expected to live up to his reputation in spectacular style.

In 1885 Lorrain met Edmond de Goncourt, who was thirty-three years older than he was, but who swiftly took the younger writer under his wing, perhaps seeing him as a kind of substitute for his younger brother—who had died young in 1870. Lorrain became a regular at Goncourt's famous salon, the "Grenier." Goncourt's tutelage had its limits, however, and one can only imagine how distraught and disappointed Lorrain must have been in 1896, when he found out that Goncourt had left him out of the list of writers mentioned in his will as the recipients of the bequest that permitted the foundation of the "Goncourt Academy." It probably hurt him almost as much as the discovery he had made ten years earlier, when Amable Duval died in 1886, leaving nothing to his children but debts.

Lorrain's mother had kept control of her own money, and was not reduced to absolute penury by the posthumous consequences of her husband's hidden profligacy, but she could not maintain her son's allowance and became a dependent instead. His burgeoning career as a journalist thus became a matter of extreme urgency, but if he began to regret the many enemies he had made with his vicious reviews, it was too late for him to change course; his image was already formed, and could only be cultivated—which he did with great success, but not without personal cost. It was in order to maintain his rate of production that he had recourse to artificial stimulants, including ether. The ether kept him awake when necessary, and also provided him with hallucinations that he eventually mined extensively in his short fiction, but its long-term effects on his health were catastrophic.

When he left Montmartre in 1887 Lorrain installed himself in an apartment in the Rue de Courty, which he furnished in a calculatedly bizarre fashion that took aboard the lessons he had learned from Lord Arthur Somerset, Barbey d'Aurevilly and *À rebours*. Under the hallucinogenic influence of ether, however, the apartment came to seem direly discomfiting, and he began to refer to it as his "haunted house". He moved to Auteuil in 1890, telling his friends that he was doing so in the hope of recovering his health and composure. When he invited Oscar Wilde to dinner there in 1891 he thought the occasion sufficiently important to invite Anatole France as well, and the notoriously antisocial writer accepted. Marcel Schwob, who shared with Lorrain an enormous admiration for Edgar Poe, was also present.

Lorrain had given up taking ether by the time he moved to Auteuil, some time before he began producing the definitive series of *contes d'un buveur d'éther* that were reprinted under that subtitle in the collection *Sensations et Souvenirs* (1895). He was, however, already living with consequences that were to plague him permanently, and ultimately to kill him. He had always suffered health problems, manifest as recurrent fevers and gastric troubles, but the ether ruined his gut and eventually led to a part of his large intestine being surgically resected by the famous surgeon, Samuel Pozzi. It was in Pozzi's clinic in Paris that he eventually died, in 1906, from peritonitis consequent to an enema that blew a hole in his rectum, administered during a trip to the capital.

In 1893, Lorrain's mother moved into the house in Auteuil, and she lived with her son for the rest of his life; she had to be summoned from Nice when he was dying, and she raced to Paris in the hope of catching his last breath. In Lorrain's many stories echoing his childhood in Fécamp, his mother is always represented with the utmost fondness and respect, but there is no way of knowing what Madame Duval thought of Jean

Lorrain's work and lifestyle, or how the two of them got on while living together, first in Auteuil and then in Nice. There is no way of knowing, either, whether Madame Duval ever read the section dealing with "The Family" in *Fards et Poisons*, or what she thought of it if she did, but we can only hope that she did not take it as personally as some of his acquaintances took other items written in the same period.

The *fin-de-siècle* was winding down during the heyday of Lorrain's career, a prisoner of the calendar, and Lorrain, as the most outspokenly fascinated celebrant and most enthusiastic scourge of the mores of the yellow nineties, and the very archetype of its decadence in the eyes of some observers, would have been keenly aware of the countdown even if his health had not been suffering badly enough to motivate a removal to Nice at the century's end, initially temporarily and then permanently. It was not long after removing much of his literary activity to Nice that Lorrain produced *Monsieur de Phocas*, and not long after his permanent removal that he followed it up with "Coins de Byzance." *Fards et Poisons* shows him moving on from that, still evolving in terms of his distinctive narrative strategies, and still moving forward in his career in spite of the worsening of his physical condition. In 1903, however, he suffered a catastrophic setback when the artist Jeanne Jacquemin—one of the women whose career he had helped to launch by means of enthusiastic publicity—read "Victime," one of the items in a sequence of stories entitled "Femmes," which appeared in *Le Journal* on 13 January 1903. She recognized elements of herself in the character sketch of the central character, an alleged specimen of "hysteria" nicknamed Narcissa, took it very personally, and sued both Lorrain and *Le Journal* for libel.

The other stories in the "Femmes" sequence are reproduced in *Fards et Poisons*, albeit out of order and split into two groups in different subsections, but "Victime," unsurprisingly, had to be omitted. It is replaced there by a more elaborate "case study" of hysteria, from which the traces of Jeanne Jacquemin's biography have been removed, and which does not appear to have had any periodical publication prior to its insertion in the collection. Lorrain had to rethink his continuation of the series, and cuts were apparently made to the next item, which he had already written when the libel suit was launched; it appeared in *Le Journal* as "Ettiennette Staub" on 17 January, and was reprinted in *Fards et Poisons* as "Cordelia Staub." The central character of that story had borrowed elements from the biography of the opera singer Georgette Leblanc (1869-1941)—the sister of the novelist Maurice Leblanc and the lover of Lorrain's friend Maurice Maeterlinck—which had to be altered or excised for safety's sake. The sequence was suspended after a further two-part contribution—presumably already in hand—and Lorrain then switched to material of a somewhat different kind in his contributions to *Le Journal*. Maxence, prominent in the stories in the "Femmes" sequence, became a much scarcer presence in Lorrain's subsequent work.

I have added a translation of "Victime" to the text of *Fards and poisons* as an appendix, so that its "libelous" nature can be assessed and it can be compared with its replacement text, "Madame Holland." With the aid of hindsight, it is not difficult to see why Jeanne Jacquemin was upset by the notion that people might think that Narcissa was a representation of her, and the kind of mistaken inference she took from Lorrain's story is one that many other people have made, sometimes taking legal action in consequence. People who are acquainted with authors often think that the latter might "put them in their books"—and are not displeased if they think that the consequent representations might be flattering—but that is a misunderstanding of the creative process of constructing fictitious characters. Such characters routinely require sketchy biographies and revealing details, and authors have no other palette from which to take such colorations than their observations of the society in which they move. Usually, and wisely, when they are not actually writing *romans à clef,* they borrow from several sources to make up chimerical compounds, and add in a few extra idiosyncrasies, but when a writer is composing items with a tightly-restricted word limit to a punishing schedule, the complexity of such mosaics is bound to suffer. Lorrain presumably had no intention of offending and insulting Jeanne Jacquemin, and was certainly not implying deliberately that she was a hysterical erotomaniac, like the character in the story, but that lack of intention counted for little against the dire weight of appearances.

In the event, Lorrain and *Le Journal* were not only convicted of the libel, but the court imposed a massive punitive fine on the author, far out of proportion to the offence, and sentenced him to two months imprisonment. Not long thereafter he was summoned to court again to answer a formal charge of corrupting public morals by literary means, brought against *Monsieur de Phocas*. Similar charges and penalties had been successfully leveled in the past at Charles Baudelaire, Gustave Flaubert, Catulle Mendès, Jean Richepin and Paul Adam, to name but a few, but all of those writers had found strident defenders to protest the iniquity of the accusation and to argue stridently in their favor. Lorrain, much to his chagrin, did not find such support. Hardly anyone came forward to speak in his defense in the matter of the libel trial—the most notable exception was the ever-valiant Colette—and he seems to have been deeply hurt by the fact that even Huysmans, from whom he expected and solicited support, sided with Jacquemin and expressed the opinion that her alarm was justified. In the event, Lorrain convinced the artist that he had not intended to harm her and she ceased to pursue him, doubtless realizing that the punishment was entirely out of proportion to the crime; the fine and the prison sentence were overturned on appeal, but not until October 1903; in the interim, Lorrain had to live with the uncertainty of that outcome, and the fact that his relationship with Henri Letellier, the editor of *Le Journal*, had been somewhat compromised.

In the event, Letellier stuck by the author and continued to use his work regularly, probably not simply because his was still a name that could sell papers. In fact, *Le Journal,* faced with stern competition in the marketplace and a certain amount of legal harassment from *Le Petit Parisien* and *Le Matin*—which had begun to use short fiction in much the same fashion, but cast in a more populist mode—was already beginning to move downmarket in 1903, and it began to shift short fiction off the front page before the end of the year. Letellier's prestigious stable of writers began to drift away or to space out their contributions, although Lorrain showed Letellier the same loyalty that Letellier showed him while his declining health permitted him to keep working. From 1904 onwards, however, things were never the same again for the paper or for Lorrain as they had been in 1902. As the writer's health began to deteriorate drastically his work became less frequent and less potent.

Although Lorrain had already begun several series projects before writing the last items that he reprinted in *Fards et Poisons,* and although he published several more books thereafter that are by no means trivial, including the novel *Le Maison Philibert* (1904), it is not difficult to find signs in the present collection of a writer beginning to wind down, aware that the end might not be very far away, but also conscious that there are still many things that he wants to do and some that he feels an urgent need to do. There are several items in the collage that might have a hint of the "bucket list" about them, perhaps written with a consciousness of having certain things to do that might have to be done now in case there is no later in which to do them.

That is not a kind of consciousness that lends itself to elaborate planning and leisurely development; such virtues as urgency has tend to the brief and explosive, and the one advantage that *Fards et Poisons* has, even over Lorrain's finest works, written when he was at the peak of his powers, is that it has some fine rants, written with splenetic verve and force—but never simply or wholly vitriolic, always tempered with compassion for weakness. Few of the items are finished off with the kind of roundness that one normally expects an ending to supply; but their inconclusiveness is not mere carelessness; it is an honest reflection of something implicit in the "slice-of-life" methodology of narrative construction, which tacitly assumes that everything that happens is part of an ongoing process, which has no authentic endings, any more than it has any momentary beginnings: that everything is intrinsically partial, but that even the tiniest splinters of experience can contain, in a sense, the whole of life's tragedy, irony and occasional heroism—a heroism that is usually absurd, but not one whit less admirable for that.

This translation was made from the copy of the 1903 Ollendorf edition reproduced on the Bibliothèque Nationale's *gallica* website. That text contains numerous apparent errors of spelling and syntax, and several apparent misprints, often carried forward from the versions in *Le Journal*. I say "apparent" because Lorrain was a writer who often strove for unusual effects, and it is sometimes difficult to determine which eccentricities of implication are deliberate and which mere accidents. It seems to me, however, that many of the oddities are the kind of mistakes one would expect to occur on the part of an amanuensis taking dictation, who occasionally makes an error in elaborating his shorthand and sometimes puts the punctuation marks in the wrong places. I have done my best to try to figure out what the author must actually have intended, and can only apologize for any errors that I might have committed in the process.

—Brian Stableford

FARDS AND POISONS

PREFACE

AN ENCOUNTER[1]

For my friend Sem[2]

THAT morning, almost all of the petite women in long cloaks of pale fabric and waterproofs who got out of cabs or automobiles under the damp shade of Armenonville shrugged their shoulders nervously before penetrating into the moist stifling warmth of the halls.

It was lunch time. Behind the transparency of windows, in the midst of sparkling crystal and silverware, men and other women were already installed. And while green salmon sauce and slices of bloody beef, pink beneath their metal lids, circulated in the hands of waiters, the arrival of demoiselles from outside contin-

---

1 This preface was originally published in four parts in *Le Journal*, as "Le Revenge du pauvre; un recontre" (24 June 1902), "Sur les quais: Les Métiers qui tuent" (29 June 1902), "Sur les quais: Un Chaplin" (2 July 1902) and "Sur le quais: Quelques joies" (10 July 1902). It was followed in the newspaper by the two items making up the epilogue and then by the four making up the section entitled herein "Those Messieurs," which were separated from the items that they bracket in this collection by a considerable gap, as mentioned in the introduction.

2 "Sem" was the signature used by the caricaturist Georges Goursat (1863-1934), who published a large number of albums of caricatures. He lived in Bordeaux and Marseille until he met Jean Lorrain in the latter city; Lorrain convinced him that he ought to move to Paris, which he did in 1900. The first satirical album he published there, *Le Turf*, made him famous virtually overnight, and his career went from strength to strength thereafter. One can understand why people were often far from glad to see him observing them.

ued, all of them freshly tubed and newly recurled, the ravages of the night expertly repaired under the bright enamel of make-up. None, whether accompanied or not, could help pursing her lips or making a gesture of irritation before penetrating under the veranda. A few even hastened their steps, as if the shadow of an invisible creditor were on their heels; and all of them, as they penetrated into the glazed cage, betrayed the same impression of malaise.

Beneath the tall chestnut trees, which were dripping raindrops profusely, a man was seated before a glass of port and watching the entrance of the restaurant. He had a large album open on his knees and he was riffling through the pages—pages in color and devoid of text—which he was studying with a slow enjoyment: a large album bound in pale green and easily recognizable: *the* Album!

That album evidently embarrassed the mounting beauties. That game of illustrative massacre, in which a cruel artist stigmatized the faults and ridicules of the day, irritated them, like a mirror magnifying their defects.

The hostility of the stationed man was evident. He was installed at that table as if at a checkpoint, comparing and seeking resemblances. Worse, he took a malign pleasure in finding them, for his eyes sparkled when he recognized one of the women sketched by the artist, and beneath his long yellow moustache a mute laugh revealed the teeth of a carnivore.

The women were all the more exasperated because the curious man was a stranger. They could not attach a name to him; they did not know one of the dirty stories of the club, the boudoir or the public highway that satisfy unanimously the rancor and the laxity of crowds. There was no means of labeling that cowardly face with a scandal or a vice. Their impotent rage had to be content with muffled epithets, meager relief for their ulcerated vanity.

Some had gone green beneath their make-up. Léa d'Asti and Rosita Framboise had made the decision to turn their backs squarely on the stranger. It was the stupor of a henhouse watched by a fox.

Intrigued by the maneuvers, I ended up approaching the obstinate riffler.

The man raised his head.

"What! It's you? You, here!"

I had just recognized a comrade from the regiment, lost to sight for more than ten years: a very original, very intelligent, very artistic fellow whom I knew to be employed by a publisher of illustrated books. Confined in a studious street on the left bank, Paul Langlois lived far from the boulevard and the Bois, ignorant of the elegance and snobbery of the new quarters; for him, the Parc Monceau was a myth and he had surely not set foot in Auteuil since the death of Edmond de Goncourt.

It was there that we had met the last time we had seen one another. And it was that bookshop rat, that excavator of archives and obstinate lover of old books and fine prints that I found in the heart of gallant modernity, in the frame of the high life and elegance of a tavern in the Bois.

"You here, Langlois! But what are you doing here, then?"

Raising toward me the triangle of a faunesque smile, he said: "Research and self-education. It's quite a long way from the smiles of Reutlinger[1] to the exhausted rascality and professional usury of those mouths. It's in the brutal streak with which all these facial stockings are laddered, that the scathing irony of the artist is affirmed. The mouth of this one, for example, in the bloodless and chlorotic face; and that one, chipped like a chamber pot in a cheap hotel—how many oysters has that one swallowed to heap up so many pearls on her neck? And this other one, a macabre guignol doll, as if carved with a billhook, reminiscent

---

1 Léopold Reutlinger, who took over the photography studio founded forty years before by his uncle, developed new techniques for merging images that he marketed on a vast scale in the form of *art nouveau* picture postcards. In 1901-02 he produced a series featuring famous actresses and singers, which Lorrain must have loved.

of one of Veber's puppets, and the noseless and browless surliness of this slum-born face; and this one, finally, frilled, fluffed up, plumed, breasted and rumped in the extravagant luxury of a brothel-keeper. And that's what it is, amour; that's what it is, gallantry and Parisian fashion: the pretty women that Europe envies us, the elevated luxury that provincials come to gawp at in theater stalls and hippodromes; the blonde Imperias, whose sale, clarioned by all the papers, prepare a long and happy old age in the princely domains of Saint-Germain and Malmaison.

"In this Album, at least, the cracking of make-up and the butchering of masks allows the ignominy of lives and consciences to breathe . . . this Album delights and dilates me, it puts air in the lungs. It's balm for a wound, and I'd like the workers in all the night-schools to riffle through it at length. They'd see what mouths luxury and lucre make for all these people. This Album, you see, is the revenge of the poor."

"Anarchist!" I joked, patting him familiarly on the shoulder. "Where are you now? Still at your publishers?"

"No, they robbed me and then, naturally, they threw me out. I was employed; it's cost me sixty thousand francs, but I've gained my liberty. I'm publishing on my own account."

"Engravings?"

"Books too, I'm the boss."

"And you don't steal yet?"

"Not yet, but it will come, by virtue of lassitude or necessity. In life, you see, it's necessary to attack; it's not enough to defend yourself."

"And where are you living?"

"Oh, still out there in my old quarter on the river bank. Paris, for me, only commences at the Pont du Louvre; I couldn't live far from the quais. Oh, the pleasant strolls in the fresh morning air, past the displays of the booksellers of the Quai d'Orsay and Malaquais, the mazes of the little streets that run behind the Institut, parallel to the Mint. It's only there that I feel alive;

for me, it's the heart of the city; I can feel the arterial blood of studious and artistic Paris beating there, where I belong."

He had become animated while talking, and had almost closed the Album.

"All that doesn't tell me where you're installed."

"That's true. The Quai de l'Horloge, almost in the shadow of the Sainte-Chapelle. It's a pretty corner. You must come and see me. When I step outside I can see, to the right, the flow of the river all the way to the Pont du Change and, blue-tinted by rain and glistening with sunlight, the great mansard roofs of the Hôtel de Ville, the phantasmagoria of slate and smoke of tall houses running in a cliff to the Quai de Bercy. If I look to the left there's the Louvre, the colonnade and all the solemn décor of the palace and gardens. How have you been able to quit Paris? It's the unique city! To think that you prefer to that living and silky grayness of old stone, young verdure and water, where everything is gleam, sparkle and reflection, the raw skies and blinding tones of the Midi—you, an artist. You're preferring brutality to nuance! But do you even know Paris? You lived in Passy, that neatly-combed corner of an English park, where even the people you meet are from London."

I interrupted him with a gesture. "What are you doing here, then?" And, indicating the faces of the dolls caged behind the window: "They're neither portraits in the Louvre nor saints of Notre-Dame."

"What I'm doing here?" An abrupt release of the jaw projected his murderous maxillaries forward. "What I'm doing here is drinking hatred and vengeance. I've come to look at them with this Album in my hands. I'm getting drunk on their ugliness and feeding on their flaws; those grimaces and tics, charged and underlined by a deforming feature, relieve me, like a verdict finally rendered by equitable magistrates. If you know how I hate the lie that this is, the lie of consciences and mouths, consciences caked with principles, mouths smeared and reddened by lipstick; and the false candor of all those chemical tints. All that doesn't revolt you, doesn't sicken you and make your heart capsize?"

"Your mistresses have made you suffer, then? How you hate these women!"

"It's not the women I hate, it's their luxury: the thefts, the frauds, the crimes and spoliations that this frame of sumptuous vanity represents, and of which these creatures are the result. They're one of the manifestations of the monstrous injustice that the capital contains. They're the rare and futile flowers of a hothouse in which the nourishing compost-heap is made of blood and tears."

"Like all fertilizer, my dear—for, between us, you're rambling. Life can only be born from death, and it's from the fermentation of cadavers that saps springs: that's a law of nature."

"But not of humanity! To think that you admit—you!—this intensity of life developed to the profit of a few by the destruction of the masses. Life, for civilized men like us, ought to proceed by evolution and not be shored up by murders. That philosophy of the charnel house is unworthy of modern life."

"The eloquence of a public meeting, the utopian dreams of a young orator. These women are victims, as we all are, victims of laws of nature and social conventions born of our very nature. You're here to foam at their luxury; have you reflected as to how many drunken hiccups have made the pearls around their neck, how much saliva and how many tears they've had to swallow before obtaining the three rows of which every demoiselle who's *arrived* is proud?"

"And of how many blows and maladies the misery of others is made! No, you see, it's stronger than me: I hate injustice; the folly of its scales is a question of false weight. Woe betide the weak, woe betide the poor! That's the motto of our society. So the barbaric iconoclast within me roars easily in riffling through these pages—which are, hear me well, the preliminary symptoms of a terrible and perhaps imminent social upheaval."

"The revendication of the volcanoes! You talk like Mademoiselle Couesdon.[1] Your Mount Peleus will only give birth to a mouse. It doesn't matter, my good Langlois; I owe you an agreeable quarter of an hour; you're amusing to hear."

The publisher of art smiled bitterly.

"A flageolet solo in your concert of harps. You hypnotize yourself in your dreams, you see life and its real miseries from too far away. Come and look for me one of these mornings at my shop; we'll have lunch. I'll give you a tour of my quarter, my laborious and aged quarter of artisans of art and laborers; you'll see why I take a savage delight in the flaws of this high society. Telephone me; I live at 129, Quai de l'Horloge, remember. I don't want to compromise you any longer; your beautiful friends are looking at us."

The publisher got to his feet and closed his Album; we shook hands.

"Who's that wreck?" said the blonde Geneviève de Nyas as I passed her table. "He looks rather nasty. Some provincial sketcher?"

"No, from the Quai des Orfèvres, one of the moral police."

"*Merde!* One's no longer tranquil anywhere," clucked the frail child. "Moral police here! Come for you or for me?"

"Who knows? Perhaps for both of us."

"Hello! Hello! Is that you, Langlois?"

"Yes, it's me. Who's speaking?"

"Me, Jean Drag—don't you recognize my voice?"

"Oh, it's you. How are you?"

---

1 The celebrated clairvoyant and medium Henriette Couédon, or Couesdon (1872-?) became famous in Paris at the end of the nineteenth century, when she routinely claimed to be channeling the angel Gabriel, and issued numerous doom-laden prophesies in his name.

"And you? Are you free this morning?"

"Yes. Why?"

"I have a yen to come to ask you to lunch and visit your pad."

"That's a good idea; the weather's superb."

"That's the very reason. What weather, eh? It's not bad. I'll come to have lunch with you, then?"

"That's settled."

"When shall I pick you up?"

"Don't come to find me at the shop. We'll meet half-way at half past eleven. We'll have time to make a tour; the quais are delightful in the morning. One thing: do you mind having lunch at a wine-merchant's, a coachmen's wine-shop?"

"Is the food good?"

"You bet—better that Durand's. You can have entrecote Bercy and snails, as in Bourgogne; the owner's from Maçon. And a little wine . . . okay?"

"Okay. A nice view?"

"I think so. At the corner of the Rue de Beaune: all of the Louvre and the boats going past."

"Eleven-thirty, then, at the corner of the Rue de Beaune."

"No, the corner of the Rue du Bac, it's more cheerful; there's a café there. I'll wait outside and I'll take you to lunch from there."

"See you soon, then."

"Soon."

"Sales good this morning?"

"Yes, we've sold a few Van Dycks—three-louis engravings. See you soon. Good of you to have thought of me."

And that is how I found myself, that day at around midday, in the cool hall of a small restaurant on the corner of the Rue de Beaune, at table with my friend Langlois, the art publisher of the Quai de l'Horloge and ferocious seeker of defects, Langlois the amused riffler through Sem's Album, having a heart-to-heart with our elbows on the tablecloth, before the most odorous snails in wine sauce that I have ever tasted in my gourmet life.

Through the wide-open windows, at a slightly lower level than the quai, there was the décor of stone and water of the Valois' Louvre, the Louvre and gilded wrought iron steps of ornamental balconies; the light smoke of the verdure of the water's edge, so belated that year, the movement of the Seine, more divined than apparent; and, in the foreground, the coming and going of strollers idling over the displays of the parapets: all the gaily provincial and peaceful life of the Quais d'Orsay and Malaquais. And I lingered over that familiar décor, which had become almost new for me after so many months of absence, amused and charmed by the bourgeois bonhomie and the nevertheless artistic atmosphere of the quarter. In the next room there were the outbursts of coarse laughter and the chomping of jaws of a table of coachmen.

Langlois no longer had his carnivorous smile of the morning at Armenonville. In harmony here with people and things, he did not break the frame, as he had under the shade of the tavern, where his ferocity, lying in wait, evoked the evil thoughts of a barbarian spying on a Byzantine palace. Today his eyes were devoid of hatred and his words devoid of violence. We mulled over impressions of art and memories, memories of the regiment and the nostalgia of museums, museums in Spain and Italy. Langlois knew them in depth. The other day, Langlois had invited me to wander through that peaceful and studious quarter with him, to edify me visually regarding monstrous social injustice; he wanted to convince me, and win me over to his rancor, and we were talking about Tiepolo and Velasquez.

I was a little disappointed, but glad to see him calmer; and, slightly anxious about reawakening the sleeping hyena in him, I refrained from changing the subject.

We had coffee, and Langlois stood up.

We walked slowly toward the Pont Neuf. Antique shops are abundant on the quais, and our stroll paused, at various shop windows, before marquetry desks and groups of Saxe porcelain, retained here by the ingenious decoration of some upholstery and there by the archaic humor of a print. The quais of the left bank, from the Rue du Bac to the Pont Saint-Michel, and even a little further on, are a true museum of retrospective art offered to the joy of pedestrians. The prints! One, in particular, attracted my attention, a print from the end of the eighteenth century representing on a pond, perhaps at Versailles, a joust of beautiful women in formal court attire.

Frilled, their waists tightly corseted, springing like a stem between the cages of baskets, each beauty stood in the prow of her boat, falling one upon another, lances raised. The tall edifice of their powdered hair, crested with plumes, curly feathers and flowers, made them the little heads of dolls, violently illuminated by make-up. The combat was taking place around a monumental batiste bonnet garlanded with knots, reminiscent of fireworks beneath ostrich plumes, strewn from the height of a mast planted in the water. It was to obtain that gigantic trinket of honor that the beautiful jousters were fencing. In each boat, a red-faced rustic was plying the oars with all his might.

One of the beauties, touched by her rival's lance, was losing her equilibrium, and the pink of her knees appeared in the tumult of her underwear, her fall dragged down by the weight of her voluminous coiffure.

In another boat, the sailors were fishing out an unfortunate combatant who was drowning; in yet another they were bringing round a third, disheveled and in a bad way, vomiting up the water she had just swallowed, and over the entire surface of the pond there was a flotsam of plumage and wigs. Musicians installed on a stage were playing violins and flutes; on a platform, ladies in vast gowns with monumental hairstyles were playing with fans and looking on.

The Triumph of the Coquette was the title of the comical misadventures of those sumptuous dolls; humorous verses, in the taste of the epoch, attempted to underline the irony.

"A Sem of the day," smiled Langlois. "The Sems of today have more cruelty. Since you like satires in color, let's push on to the Rue Bonaparte; I know an amusing Rowlandson there."

I followed him; but when we arrived at the merchant's shop window, the print was no longer there.

"It must have been sold," sighed Langlois. "We can go back to the Pont Neuf, if you like, through these little cool and somber streets; the sun is beginning to beat down on the quais."

We took the Rue Mazarine and went along the Passage du Pont-Neuf, the dusty and dirty tunnel where Zola brought to life the anguish and ripened the adultery of Thérèse Raquin. How could the little shopkeepers make a living behind those yellowed windows, in the dull half-light of a Rembrandt painting? A popular patisserie was displaying cakes there that were visibly going stale! What contaminated air could the sick and gangrenous lungs of the poor devils relegated to that muffler be breathing?

"Yes, there are people who live here," Langlois thought aloud, in accord with my wonderment. "Committees of Public Health and Medical Congresses exist, with a view to combating tuberculosis, but such habitations still subsist. This passage isn't demolished, but they build schools—worse, they erect statues! Guillaume Dubufe[1] has commissions from the State, and in twenty years, these putrefiers of lungs will still exist—worse, they'll always exist!"

We were now in the Rue de Seine, entering into the Rue Guéguénaud, the narrow passage of which runs along the cold and massive buildings of the Mint: a studious and provincial street, animated at its extremity by the cinematograph of the life of the quai.

"Bonaparte once lived in this quarter, I believe," I hazarded, in order to break the silence. "Perhaps the house still exists. One of those mansards lost under the roofs surely sheltered the ambitious dreams of the First Consul."

"The visions of massacre and carnage of the little sub-lieutenant of Brienne. This street nourishes other crimes now."

---

1 The artist and decorator Guillaume Dubufe (1853-1909) decorated the Salon National des Beaux-Arts in 1896, as well as various rooms in the Élysée Palace, the Hôtel de Ville and many other buildings.

Langlois was seized once again by his obsessive mania of a moralistic administrator of justice, and, pointing to the high windows with heavy stone entablatures aligned on the first floor of the Mint, he said: "You see those windows? They're workshops. I won't insist on the harshness of the métier, but one of those windows shelters something monstrous. The worker toiling there is a man condemned to death; the work that is done there wipes a man out in eighteen months. He's the washer and scourer of old coins, the ones withdrawn from circulation: discrowned Napoléons, obsolete Louis-Philippes—in brief, wrecks soiled by the fingers of commerce and the lucre of recent commissions and the last reigns.

"Before putting all that metal back into the melting-pot, it's necessary to free it completely from the dirt incrusted in the designs of the faces; that's the work of the washer. A basin full of acid, which cleans the coin without eating into the metal, is confided to his surveillance; it's his job to heat and soak, when the time comes, the old coins awaiting melting down; but from that verdigrised copper, and the microbial dirt edged in the hollows of the relief, corrosive mephitic gases are emitted, which poison, twist and contaminate the lungs and entrails of the worker: it's short-term poisoning. The wretch leaning over that infernal cooking-pot for ten hours a day dies of disorders of the bowels, if those of the lungs don't get him first. Strangely enough, it's the healthiest and most vigorous temperaments that are used up most rapidly.

"In the faubourgs of Paris, as you know, it's the man transplanted from the fields who is the least defended. The Parisian son of a Parisian, degenerate most of the time, consumptive and chlorotic, resists the poisoning better, already poisoned as he is: a law of natural homeopathy, unless it's necessary to observe there, yet again, the frightful attraction of death for life, and her ironic disdain for weakness and suffering—everything that she knows belongs to her. But enough philosophy, I'll summarize: the man who works there, behind that window, never surpasses

16

two years of employment. The whole Mint knows that, it's not even unknown in the quarter, but the vacant employment always finds someone to fill it. Once dead, the man is always replaced. It's necessary to live."

"But that's frightful. The administration, the governor of the Mint, aren't responsible, then? The families don't have any recourse against them?"

"The administration is protected from any pursuit; it takes the lead. The washer of old money always dies by his own fault. Precautions are imposed on him, which he follows for a month, but which, by virtue of indolence, negligence or slackness, he soon ceases to observe. At the moment when the old money cooked in the acid exhales a murderous smoke, the cleaner ought to go into a neighboring room, in order to return to the workshop after a prescribed lapse of time, but those comings and goings soon offend the idleness of the worker, and it's necessary to take account of the insouciance of people used to living from day to day, the legendary 'There's no danger,' of the carpenter and the roofer. In sum, the cleaner of old coins has in common with his brethren the gilders with mercury and the employees of red lead and ceruse white factories, that life for him is doubly mortal; but the refounded and rejuvenated coins return to activate the folly of luxury and the fever of exchange, and that is worth far more than the life of a man."

A breath of wind rising from the river refreshed the quais. Fleecy wisps were fluttering in the air, fallen from the poplars; and beneath their moving stains, through the foliage of plane trees stirring in the sunlight, the landscape trembled, slightly ragged, like an Impressionist painting.

The trees in the bright sky, the Pont-Neuf linking its arches on a level with its equestrian statue, the two wings of the Louis XIII residence, brick and carved stone, of the Place Dauphiné, were all composed and nuanced in the delicate clarity of the Parisian midday.

"A lovely hour!" Langlois summarized. "There's good in life. Which doesn't prevent death, which is all around us, from pushing her cart a little more rapidly, alas, for some of us than for others. It's that brief agony, imposed on the poor by industry and the exigencies of métiers, which revolts in me the old fool of an honest man that I remain, for I'm not like you, my old Drag. I can still get indignant."

"And I've only come to hear you. Let's go, utopian, march!"

"I amuse you?"

"You interest me."

"Above all, I furnish you with copy. Well, listen, I talked to you just now about the washer and scourer of old coins, who takes eighteen months to die. I know more expeditious métiers . . . glass-polishers, for instance. Once, in the good old days— which is to say, ten years ago, for the dead go quickly—glass was polished by a wet method. The plates of unpolished glass were piled up in a large vat, like those used to wash photographic prints; each plate reposed between a double layer of pebbles and sand. The vat was agitated, for quite a long time; it was a little primitive, that fashion of polishing glass, but that's what they did.

"Polishers of glass wore away their muscles and earned their daily bread without anticipating their life overmuch; it was exhausting but healthy work. But there is progress, and one day, an American inventor found a machine to polish glass by a dry method. It was sufficient to think of it. Bellows project powdered sandstone over plates of glass that the worker causes to file past successively, because the blower is foxed.

"Isn't that ingenious? The pulverized sandstone falls on the plates in a shower, crackles there, and in less than three minutes, the milky opacity of the windows of jails, offices and bureaus extends there. The work is better done and there's an economy of time and manpower. But there's the atmosphere of those polishing chambers, an atmosphere of powdered sandstone and impalpable atoms of glass, a brilliant and cutting atmosphere that penetrates and perforates the lungs; thousands of broken needles prick the vesicles of the bronchi, hemoptysis arrives; every molecule absorbed inflicts a wound. The worker is condemned. He has six months; he dies in intolerable agony, vomiting blood clots. It's perhaps one of the most atrocious deaths there is, but its description is lacking in *Le Jardin des supplices*.[1]

"In the hospital, people are moved by those professional hazards; the American machine has raised protests from physicians; but the inventor, when challenged, justified himself. Once again, it's the worker who is at fault. He ought to be working with a mask over his face and cotton over his mouth. During the presentation of glass plates to the breath of the bellows, the respiratory channels ought to be protected, but as the cotton causes the man to suffocate and the mask stifles him, he takes them both off, and inhales in the murderous breath.

"Make these damned workers listen to reason, then! It's the American machine and the inventor who are right; these men of the people are all the same. You know the anthem."

We had arrived at the corner of the Place Dauphiné.

"I can show you one of those polishing workshops; it's sufficient to push on as far as the Rue Saint-André-des-Arts. It's at the back of a courtyard, and the place is almost tragic, because, in less than two years, the American machine has killed three men there. But at least, in the Rue Saint-André-des-Arts the worker is the boss and it's not so much a murder as a suicide. Every six months the business is put up for sale, and it always finds a buyer. The newcomer naturally hopes to get out of it safe and sound and to have more luck than his predecessor. Old human hope is there to lure him.

---

1 Octave Mirbeau's novel, *Le Jardin des supplices* (tr. as *Torture Garden*), was published in 1899.

"Fond hope, that liar
Smiles at us to deceive us,
The eternal youthful slut
Whose profession is dupery."[1]

And with a gesture of insouciance: "It's the métier that wants it. It's true that it brings in good money, but it nevertheless polishes off its man mechanically. The duration of resistance is even foreseen. An example: the owner before last had a brother, from the country, like him, half-employee and half-partner, who replaced him at the machine for four hours a day; the two men took turns for trips to the city. The younger was the first to fall ill; he started to spit blood and was sent to the country. The elder hired an employee and continued to divide his time between the machine and the outside. He only died at the end of a year; his predecessor had gone in six months. It was those hours of gadding about, of coming and going, that prolonged his life. The widow sold the business and went to find her brother-in-law in Lorraine, apparently recovered, but only for two years; his lungs were perforated. The present owner, who is not unaware of any of that, hypnotizes himself with his daily earnings and continues to polish his plates.

"You'll tell me that there's nothing to be done. These people are killing themselves voluntarily, merely hastening a little more rapidly toward death, in the fever or need to live . . . and there are the leaves, the trees, the breeze in those leaves, and the sunlit water . . ."

Langlois was leaning on the parapet of the bridge, his back turned to the statue of the Bearnais.[2] In front of us was the mirage of age-old stones, of high slate roofs, loggias, balconies and the heroic architecture that the buildings of the Louvre developed above the poplars of the banks and the plane trees of

---

1 These lines appear to be original to the text.
2 The equestrian statue of Henri IV.

20

the quais. At our feet the Seine flowed, shiny and silky, beneath the repeated arches of the bridge. Trams moving along the quais and boats on the river were going past, crossing paths, descending, coming back, hastening and stimulating, one might have thought, the life of the river, the artery of the city, always in movement; and that animation, becoming a joy in the sunlight, descended westwards with the river between two rows of palaces and gardens.

Langlois had fallen silent. He was gazing dazedly and passionately at the Paris of the Valois and Monsieur Loubet.[1] Did that Parisian love Paris enough? He became touching in his mute enthusiasm. Curiously, I examined his staring eyes, now troubled—imbued with tears, in truth.

"And there are people who are suffocating before the mephitic vapors of a bath of acid and verdigris, people whose lungs are bleeding under a shower of pulverized sandstone and needles of glass . . . and others, at this moment, slowly descending the triumphal avenues at the trot of their brown bays, returning from Armenonville, Madrid or some restaurant in the Bois. They've had lunch in the open air and are returning to Paris to attend to their affairs, affairs that represent for them three or four hundred thousand francs of profit, earned with a stroke of a pen, while, for those condemned to death in the workshop or the factory, the best day's work is worth ten or eleven francs . . ."

"What about you? What are you doing here, getting drunk on sunlight, architecture and utopian dreams, while the men you're talking about have already resumed their yoke of misery? Are you not stealing from them in your own way by lingering here feeling sorry for them instead of working? It's not so much over them as over yourself that you're groaning, and I know, you see, how long you've been having these fine crises of egotistical pity."

Langlois raised two rather glowering eyes at me. "What are you saying?"

---

1 Émile Loubet was the President of the Republic from 1899-1906.

"That perhaps there's a good deal of envy—unconscious, I grant you—in your social recriminations. Believe me, my friend, we're all wronged to some degree; we all have the right to think that we're exploited and frustrated; manual labor is undervalued, and so is talent. Can you tell me in what branch of the fine arts or letters the creator isn't at the orders of the editor, subservient to his command, domesticated to his caprices? What has become of the liberty of thought—worse, the liberty of inspiration—that the most obscure of primitives had under the worst tyranny of Italy? Interrogate any artist about that."

"Wellbeing has spoiled you," replied Langlois, sourly. "Whatever anyone says to you, you only ever consider your work and the public—not so much your work as the means of divulging it by means of newspapers or books, those procuresses. Man of letters!" He spat the epithet at me between his teeth, like an insult. "But then, after all, perhaps you're right. All those artisans that I pity are doing their job—a dangerous, murderous job, but lucrative—and they know it. With precaution, its perils would be diminished. Those precautions, they neglect; so much the worse for them. Modern society hasn't the time to pick up the soldier fallen on the road. Ideas are on the march, going forward; pity slows down and delays. The time of the good Samaritan has passed . . .

"But what about the victims who don't know, the ignorant and the innocent, the very young who have no suspicion of the danger that is crushing, strangling, choking them and tearing them apart, limb by limb and organ by organ, the horrible complicity of poverty and industry—women above all, young girls, almost children, the petty sacrificial victims of Parisian commerce? Nothing is done for them, and yet, millions are swallowed up every year by the famous committees on sanitation and hygiene! Oh, the sanitation of the city!

"Pardon me if I go back. A little while ago we passed through the Passage du Pont-Neuf, and you were suffocating in the rancid and jaundiced dust of an atmosphere in which the residents of the place live. Yes, Parisians of 1902 live in that unbreathable air; but there's worse still and not far away. The Rue des Grands-Augustins, which we passed along not long ago . . . the Rue des Grands-Augustins, you remember. There was the sunlight, with the bridge at the end, the trees, the blue sky, warm and intense life. Why didn't I point out to you a little sign on the left, at the corner of a door, bearing the advertisement: *Fashionable Pleats, Ruches and Boas?* I ought to have made you go in.

"What an alleyway—a sewer, rather, and black! You'd have refused to follow me. Dirty, stinking and oozing; an ignoble entrance to a ghetto! And the lassitude of the old stairway at the back, its tilted steps, their vanished backstops, as if collapsed under the footsteps of the Century, with all the filth of Poverty and Prostitution in its corners. The house is honest, though. It's a house of workers—better than that, of workshops. Let's go into the one on the first floor. In the asphyxiation of a low and airless room with no window—no window, you hear, without any opening but the door, the rarefied atmosphere of which is that of a tale by Poe, the tale of 'The Pit and the Pendulum,' where the mobile ceiling descends slowly and silently over the anguish of the victim—in that torture chamber of fine sewing, pretty, cheerful faces fifteen or sixteen years old, the very flower of the Parisian streets, work in a light that nacres the cheeks, illuminates blonde curls and refines profiles, as in Bail's *Dentillières* or Chaplin's *Dévideuses*: the light of an oil lamp.[1]

"It's midday. Outside, the sky is flamboyant, the sun burning, the wind blowing from the Seine comforting. Here, the oil lamp smokes and stinks. Ask a physician how someone develops tuberculosis, and what one does for workers in Germany! And the seamstresses sew and laugh, and under their agile fingers, those Parisian fingers unique in the world, the pleated tulles mount up, the ruches, plump up like feathers, and there are

---

1 The references are presumably to paintings by Antoine Jean Bail (1830-1918) and Charles Joshua Chaplin (1826-1891), although neither title is easily traceable.

boas, and whitenesses of woven air, frills of whipped cream, and champagne foam . . . still in the light of the oil-lamp.

"In winter, the lamp is the heating. It also warms in summer, but no one opens the window because there is no window.

"What do you say to that little Old Master painting? Doesn't it give you the desire to buy a ticket for the Tubercular Children lottery, the children of *Père Culeux*, as the vendors tenderized by absinthe cry in the streets? I'm sure that the little seamstresses of the Rue des Grands-Augustins also subscribe to buy a ticket. And yet, everything is for the best in the best of possible worlds, isn't that so, my dear Jean?"

✳

Leaning over a waxed walnut counter, Langlois and I leafed through the collection of Van Dycks.

We were in the little shop on the Quasi de l'Horloge. The light from outside, filtered through the foliage of plane trees, reached us softened, as green as the light of an aquarium, and in the studious and cool small room, reminiscent of a sacristy, with all its shining and silky walnut cupboards, the soul of the Muses stirred with the series from the Louvre and the Prado, for the Velasquezes and the Van Dycks, with the portraits from the National Gallery and the Hermitage, holding us attentive, emotional and grave to the extent of meditation.

Langlois' hand opened the boxes, turned over the sheets, and, in the supple deployment of parchment furnishing the silence with its creak, the haughty faces filed past: the favorites and the courtiers, the ladies-in-waiting and the amorous grand dames, all the great names of the English court, all the scandals and all the intrigue of the *Mémoires du Comte de Grammont*.[1] There was the ideal elegance of Lord Wharton, the melancholy young man

---

1 Lorrain has *chevalier* instead of *comte*; *Mémoires do comte de Grammont* by Antoine Hamilton (tr. as *Memoirs of Count Gramont*) was originally published in 1713.

with a crosier/trowel, as sexlessly handsome as a Shakespeare heroine in disguise. There was the sumptuously-costumed and turbulent Buckingham, the gleam of satins and velvets, magisterially rendered by blacks and whites, Lord Wharton, Buckingham, the lovers of queens and the mistresses of kings, sumptuous tight-fitting garments slimming the elongation of torsos further, beautiful curved and rounded breasts presented on Venetian *gros point* and perforated golden Cherusque lace, like the naked flesh of beautiful fruits in a basket; and pell-mell with the court of the Stuarts, there was that of the house of Austria, the grimacing masks of Velasquez madmen, the ugliness of dwarf *menines*[1] and the emaciated sadness of the Hapsburgs, the overwhelming ennui of their long eyes flexed behind their falling eyelids, the stigmata of their hollow temples and their narrow faces with such heavy jaws, the significant and legendary chins of degenerates, and the pallor and doll-like hair of powdered infantas, alongside the healthy flesh of the famous *Filandières* and the joyful faces of the *Buveurs*.[2]

The publisher's hand was still tuning the sheets, and a sad sensuality, a kind of serious and admiring lust, which seizes sensitive people at the entrances to museums, gradually penetrated us.

"The dust of centuries, the soul of the past," Langlois summarized, closing the Album on the *Reddition des Lances*."[3]

"The soul of the past, indeed. Your engravings embalm. One might think that a grain of incense was forgotten therein."

---

1 *Les Ménines* is a painting by Velasquez [*Las Meninas* in Spanish] also known in French as *La Famille de Philippe IV*; "menines" were attendants of highly-placed Spanish ladies; the Velasquez painting features one who is a dwarf.
2 By *Filandières* Lorrain presumably means the painting by Velasquez known in Spanish as *Les Hilanderas* and in French as *Les Fileuses* or *La Légende d'Arachné*, and by *Buveurs* the painting entitled *El triunfo de Baco* [The Triumph of Bacchus], popularly known in France as *Les Ivrognes*.
3 Actually *Le rendicion de Breda* [The Surrender of Breda], also known as *Las Lanzas* [The Lances].

"The vicinity of the Sainte-Chapelle. Here we're in the shadow of the Palais de Justice; the ambient air is solemn."

"I envy you, you know. You inhabit an ideal corner, almost a sanctuary in the middle of turbulent and modern Paris, and you, an artist, live in a permanent evocation of the past, in a rich atmosphere of masterpieces—what am I saying?—in daily contact with the most beautiful figures of art."

"Yes, I have some pure joys; but I also accord myself others."

I opened my eyes wide.

"I sometimes irritate my contemporaries. I publish unknown masterpieces that the organized juries would prefer to hide under the bushel, and which a benevolent critic neglects to announce between Félicien Champsaur's latest novel and the sublime rhymes of Madame de Noailles. I avenge the young painters for the reproductions by the gross of the likes of Chartran, Carolus and Bouguereau;[1] and the amusing thing is that the public bites. It's isn't only the likes of Henner's *Mater Dolorosa* and the colored statues of Jérôme that make a profit. Between a *Reître* by Roybet and a *Sainte Cécile* by Dubufe there's a good buyer for Maxence's *Sirène* or his *Annunciation* . . .[2]

"Maxence! The decorative sense and slightly Italian sumptuousness of his compositions! He's looked very closely at the Vivarinis and Primaticcios, but anyway, that's a little better than Galland;[3] I'm proud of having been the first to publish him. It's already five years since he was published in Germany, but in France, we only appreciate our painters when they return from

---

1 Théobald Chartran (1849-1907), Jean Carolus (1814-1897) and Wilhelm-Adolphe Bouguereau (1825-1905); the Academician Bouguereau was especially detested by the Impressionists and other *avant garde* artists of the *fin-de-siècle* as an archetypal representative of the old guard.
2 No record seems to survive of Jean-Jacques Henner (1829-1905) having painted a *Mater Dolorosa*, nor Ferdinand Roybet (1840-1920) a *reître* (reiter), but Dubufe's *Saint-Cécile* and a *Sirène* by the Symbolist painter Edgar Maxence (1871-1954) can still be seen.
3 Pierre-Victor Galland (1822-1892).

26

abroad. If Burne-Jones hadn't been English, would we have admired and fêted Burne-Jones? Maxence has all his qualities, and all his faults too, with personality as well; so critics have refrained from talking about him, from signaling him to the public; it's the public who got there by itself.

The old bonzes of the Institut only ever invent stillborn talents, unviable works: *one is a silversmith, Monsieur Josse,*[1] and that's all. A conspiracy of silence around the temperaments of the future, frantic publicity around runts of the pen and the brush. Ask Roinard[2] how many matinees at the Odéon have stifled poets. But the Minoses of the Dramatic Feuilleton know full well what they're doing."

"They ignore Régnier and discover Rostand."

"You said it. So, this year. I've offered to publish Mademoiselle Dufau's *Automne* and Moreau-Neret's *Aranjuez*. Look at this engraving."[3]

Langlois had just reached for a large album in one of the cupboards open behind him.

"They're not sketches, but is that blond and flavorsome enough? All the crimson golds of the landscape, all the rust of the foliage are as flamboyant as they are in the painting. Look at the lassitude of this beautiful woman's body. You'll remember the iridescent shadows of that russet nudity, the flesh that the veins tint mauve . . . and the transparency of grapes brightening the face of the young man! No photographer has published Mademoiselle Dufau, and yet the clarity of the dormant water

---

1 In Act I Scene 1 of Molière's *L'Amour médecin*, Sganarelle says "Vous êtes orfevre, monsieur Josse, et votre conseil sent son homme qui a envie de se défaire sa merchandise" [You are a silversmith, Monsieur Josse, and your advice reeks of a man trying to sell his merchandise] which became proverbial as a remark made to anyone offering interested advice.
2 The anarchist poet Paul-Napoléon Roinard (1856-1930).
3 *L'Automne* (1902) by Clémentine-Hélène Dufau (1869-1937) is now in the Musée d'Orsay. Lorrain misspells the surname of Adrien Moreau-Neret (1860-1940) with a double r, and there does not seem to be any surviving record of either of the paintings he credits to him here.

in the marble basin, like a fragment of a picture, already makes
the painting worthwhile. How it captures the sensual and calm
life, the joyful lust and ever-expansive desire of fabulous and
heroic Greece! What synthesis! Everything is here, including the
group of centaurs carrying away a consenting Dejanire, escort-
ing, exquisitely draped, a living Tanagra statuette.

> *"Autumn, opening her arms of appeal and weakness,*
> *Is dying of the crushing memory of amour*
> *And dare not hope for its impossible return.*
> *Her sensuous flesh in languid intoxication*
> *Implores the kiss of the mouth that wounds,*
> *And would like to harvest the sobs of amour.*[1]

"Those lines are also by an unknown, a woman who, being
neither a millionaire, nor Romanian, nor a duchesse, will have
no headlined article in the great dailies. And that is why I would
like to print them in Mademoiselle Dufau's engraving. For the
Petite Infante et les Camerera Mayor du temps de Philippe IV by
Moreau-Neret, it would require lines by Samain, but that would
necessitate a thousand and one steps with regard to publishers, and life is short . . . citations of poets of yesterday under
the works of painters of tomorrow, that would annoy both the
Institut and the Académie. I've already sold more than five hundred Dufaus and nearly a hundred Nerets. You can see that I'm
able to organize a few joys."

"At the expense of others."

"Naturally. There is always something in the misadventures of
others that consoles us for our own, and we can never have any
idea of the absolute happiness of people, even those we love."

"And you publish these works of young painters less because
of their merits than for the chagrined expressions of their older
and younger colleagues?"

----

1 The lines are from "L'Automne" by Renée Vivien [Pauline Tarn], from
Cendres et Poussières (1902).

"Adopted by fashion and the public. You said it. I like to disquiet the exultant intoxication of winners."

"A fine nature!"

"Very human, above all; but this corner reserves other joys for me."

"More!"

"And perhaps the finest and most profound of my life as an observer. Look."

Langlois had risen to his feet; he headed toward the window and, indicating the plane trees and the outline of their shadow on the causeway of the quai, he said: "It's there that I see them pass by."

And his voice was strangled by a little gasp of pleasure, a voice of amorous agony that had become wheezing in the clench of teeth. Again, Langlois' formidable jaw was projected forwards.

"Yes, it's there that I see them pass when they go to the Permanence."

"Who?"

"The demoiselles, the beauties of Paris; the registered prostitutes that the moral police don't release once they have them; the slaves of the *Lasciate ogni speranza* of the Prefecture. For you know the terrible law of fatality, said to be ancient, the monstrous slavery that weighs upon those unfortunate women. Once inscribed in the police registers—they have to be in order to follow the profession—nothing can scratch them out except marriage: nothing except marriage, do you hear, unless a political or ministerial influence intervenes, for they don't all marry former prefects of the Empire or men of letters. But I'm straying from the point. In brief, the entire tide, all the flux and reflux of sellers of caresses and brokers of moneyed amour, the boudoir and the street, the Acacias and the fortifications, the fashionable cabaret and the hovel, the brothel and the little private hotel, if the debut has been programmed, has to go that way to pay their visit. The Permanence is alongside; there's no other route; it's necessary that they pass my house. All the prostitution of the great boulevards and the noble quarters, Passy, Monceau, the Champs-Élysées, is obliged to file past this shop.

"And it's equality before the Law, as before Death. The same debuts make all those women similar. Choice frogs, mistresses of kings, as Bruant mocks in his terrible ballad of the *Bois de Boulogne*.[1] Gabrielle Bompard and Ninon de Lenclos, Casque d'Or and the beautiful Imperia,[2] the whore of the plains of Gennevilliers and the diamond-laden supper in gypsy restaurants, the streetwalker of the railway stations as well as the music hall stroller in furbelows, they all come here and they all go, the young and the old. They all come to display the defects of their trade and the shame of their sad flesh to the eye of the legal physician."

Langlois' eyes had become ferocious.

"And it's a joy for me, a joy of justice and revenge, when I see, passing in a victoria, in the new luxury of harness and the glint of nickeled steel, some pretty hussy of insolence and indolence, also going to make the visit, for acquired money and established income do not protect them from arrivals.

"The sea will dry up before the task is finished. The submissive whore remains submissive. A high-class tart who commands

---

1 *Au bois de Boulogne* was one of the most famous songs written by the cabaret singer Aristide Bruant (1851-1925), who performed at the Chat Noir before founding his own club, Le Mirliton.

2 Gabrielle Bompard was the accomplice of Michel Eyraud in a sensational murder committed in 1889, whose successful investigation made the Prefect of Police Marie-François Goron famous and marked a landmark in forensic science. She escaped the guillotine and was in prison when the present story was published. The writer Ninon de Lenclos (1620-1705), who was a leading figure in the Parisian literary salons, had a great many famous lovers, but was only imprisoned for attacking organized religion in her writings. *Casque d'Or* was the nickname of the notorious prostitute Amélie Élie (1878-1933), who became famous in 1900 or thereabouts as a subject of picture postcards, and even more famous after the present story was written; her memoirs became the basis of a notable feature film, *Casque d'Or* (1952). Imperia Cognati (1486-1512) was a notorious Roman prostitute immortalized in paintings by Raphael.

three chambermaids and belongs every morning to a masseuse, a hairdresser and a manicurist, is not dispensed of the formality for that; and twice a month, the English coachman harnesses the horses and brings Madame to the Quai de l'Horloge. And Madame waits her turn, she joins the queue, as at the theater— and as at the theater, she finds herself between a girl with Porte-Maillot hair and a pensioner of the external boulevards . . .

"And you don't find that a vengeance? That outrageous luxury, that shrill immortality of wellbeing and refinements exclusively reserved for a few, that injustice of chance and fate, which is not even a selection of beauty and breeding, since monsters of Sem's Album, the high life of the Acacias and the Café de Paris, are here reduced to the same level as the suburban mender in a skirt! You saw me, the other morning, lying in wait at the entrance to the tavern in the Bois . . ."

"You were trying to recognize them?"

"No, at that height of the situation, they all had respondents. But I imagine that I've already seen them."

"And you were drinking milk?"

"No more milk than blood."

THE THEATER

To Henri Letellier[1]

---

1 Henri Letellier (1868-1960) became the editor of *Le Journal* in 1899, having formed a limited company with several other investors to buy it. He was Lorrain's principal employer thereafter.

THE EMPEROR'S MISTRESS[1]

IT was at Foyot's, in the large hall that opens on to the Rue de Tournon. Maxence and Octave Vergy were finishing lunch under the immobile rain of enormous blooming chrysanthemums of the drapes. Twelve-thirty, which had just chimed, brought together all the lunchtime regulars: senators poring over brochures and printed sheets that were as many legal projects; professors from the School of Medicine who had come between lectures and whose hearty appetite did honor to the Faculté; a whole studious public whose voluminous briefcases and pockets stuffed with papers recounted ambitions and labors loudly; an entire ripe sheaf of talents and notorieties, whose physiognomies had been polarized by photography and the illustrated papers; here and there, a few artists: Widor, the musician, a neighbor; La Gandara, come between two poses from his studio in the Rue Monsieur-le-Prince to partake of a glass of water and a mutton chop; and, on days when the Institut was in session, Humbert, a nonentity of the excessively famous family.[2]

---

1 First published in two parts in *Le Journal* as "Les Débuts de Thérésine" (22 January 1903) and "Maîtresse d'Empereur" (27 January), the last of the "Femmes" sequence to appear under that title.

2 The first two references are to the composer and organist Charles-Marie Widor (1844-1937) and the painter Antonio de La Gandara (1861-1917), who painted portraits of Lorrain and his mother. The reference to "excessive fame" suggests that the family to whom reference is being made is that of the notorious fraudster Thérèse Humbert, whose pursuit and trial were the biggest long-running news story featured in *Le Journal*—the investigative journalism of which helped bring her to account—during the period when

All those diners, if not quotidian, at least regular, make Foyot's a kind of waiting room for the Faculté and the Luxembourg. Without speaking to one another, and without even exchanging a tip of the hat, each regular salutes there with a glance or a smile.

Like Maxence, Octave Vergy liked that tranquil and restful provincial corner, that tavern in the embalmed Rue de Tournon, in the shadow of the old stones and foliage of the Luxembourg, and, in spite of the electricity and the telephone, still very Louis-Philippe with its astonishing waiters with side-whiskers that one might have thought designed by Daumier, and its high old-style counter where, grave and smiling between two silver urns, a lively and stout lady in spangles presides. Only an English family, up for the treasures of the nearby museum, troubled the intimacy of the large hall that morning; and, impressed by the ambiance, those islanders had lowered their voices and were masticating almost silently.

Suddenly, in that meditative atmosphere, a door opens, orders are given as if from off-stage, there is a tumultuous descent from a fiacre and an entrance like a gust of wind: "Joseph, something fried, quickly, no matter what, and something grilled, a tisane and a demi-Evian—and be quick. I'm in a hurry . . . scarcely ten minutes . . . I have a rehearsal . . ."

And the lady comes in. All noses are lifted up above the plates, all gazes stare at the newcomer. Braced in a torsion that makes the most of her rump and her hips, the lady emerges slowly from an ample lynx-fur coat, parades a disdainful glance around her, and finally consents to sit down. She has placed a muff florid with hyacinths on the banquette, and then a minuscule greyhound bitch wrapped in a coat of white cloth spotted with gold; and

---

the items in the present collection were being published there; reference is also made to it in "Gilberte." The diner cannot be any of her actual relatives and is almost certainly the journalist Charles Humbert (1866-1927), whom Lorrain did not like and might have been seeking to insult slyly by suggesting a non-existent relationship between his rival and the fraudster.

the fur coat, casually dropped beside the young woman, allows a glimpse of the pink brocade of a splendid lining.

Now the newcomer takes off her gloves, and her fingers appear laden with heavy rings; there are pearls, opals, pink topazes and sapphires, especially huge pearls. She has taken the lap-dog on to her knees and puts on the table, clearly visible, a golden purse, a bottle of salts with a ruby stopper, a lorgnette, a handbag and all the apparatus. A violent perfume has made all nostrils quiver. Old messieurs, troubled, are no longer eating. Mirza, the favorite bitch, has stood up on her hind paws and is making a fuss of her mistress, but in her enthusiasm she deranges the boa of gray feathers and causes the Lalique pendant to swing. Mirza is a very well-trained beast, and Monsieur de Vermoustier, the right-wing senator, who does not take his eyes off the lady, remarks that Mirza is wearing a gold bracelet on her paw. Amour, that . . . !

The lady has started on the hors-d'oeuvre. She eats delicately, indifferently, her long eyelashes lowered, but one senses, beneath the eyelids, a watchful circular gaze that is inspecting the hall, recognizing her society and enjoying her effects. The sensational diner is, in any case, a very beautiful woman, perhaps a little massive, with the regularity of features that official sculptors lend to the Republic, but heroically helmed, beneath a bushy gray fur hat, by the copper and bronze of magnificent tresses. She has freshness, and the long and sinuous eyes are promising; there is a sure voluptuousness in their natural or artificial moistness.

Before so much simplicity Maxence had a moment of stupor.

"An actress?"

"You might say so . . . to the city, above all. Thérèse Evrard of the Odéon." And, sniggering over his plate, Vergy added: "Don't look at her; she knows me. If she sees us, we're stuffed. She'll come to talk to us and, you know, the barb, when she puts her mind to it . . ."

"Talent?"

"Talents. She puts on mourning for sovereigns the day after anarchist outrages."

"No!"

"She's a protocolary courtesan. For the moment, she's the mistress of Wilhelm . . . of Germany."

"Of Germany!"

"That's what she says."

"She's a woman at the pinnacle, then."

"That depends how you understand it."

"Let's say a picture-gallery woman. She has a museum beauty. Oh, well, she's recognized us. Here she comes."

Thérèse Evrard had, indeed, risen to her feet.

"I give up," she had said, crumpling her napkin feverishly. "There's no means of getting served here. Waiter, my bill!"

And, finally discovering the two men, at whom she had been squinting for five minutes: "Well, Vergy, you here! What luck!"

"My friend Maxence Vassenage. Mademoiselle Thérèse Evrard."

"I know Monsieur. Can you imagine, my dear Vergy, that I'm forced to take my meals here. There's trouble at home. I've thrown my cook out; twenty-five louis commission a month is a bit strong. I know that my coachman steals twice that, but horses are the most beautiful of human conquests; and to put the lid on it, I'm rehearsing here every day. That Ginisty is a torturer.[1] It's necessary to be at the theater at one o'clock."

"You're in the new play?"

"Yes, Bisson's piece,[2] which will come after *Résurrection*. But Bataille is holding the poster; that will put us off until the end of January, and I wanted to go to Monte Carlo! What a galley the theater is!"

---

1 Paul Ginisty was the manager of the Odéon from 1896-1906.

2 Alexandre Bisson (1848-1912). His comedy *Château historique* was produced at the Odéon in 1900, but no play of his seems to have followed any play called *Résurrection*, presumably supposedly based on Tolstoy's 1899 novel.

"Are you content with your role?"

"Ugh! A disaster. The author wants to give me the lead, the part of Sylvie, but I can't; I have such a complicated life." And, with a mysterious smile: "I might be called *out there* any day." She had pronounced *out there*, but we had heard *Berlin.* "Oh, I'm a poor slave, me."

"Grandeur attaches you to the shore."

"What do you expect, Vergy? It's a mission. I can't avoid it."

"Yes, we must always think about it, but never talk about it, isn't that so, Thérèse?"

The waiter had just put down the bill, discreetly, on a plate. Recalled to reality, the imperial mistress placed a louis thereon, negligently. "Keep it all, Édouard!"

Very gallant, Vergy had risen to his feet, and he aided Thérèse to insinuate herself into her lynx. He escorted her back to her fiacre. The doorman and a maître d'hôtel also thought they ought to accompany her.

Mademoiselle Evrard made a sensational exit.

Vergy returned to Maxence.

"She's entirely natural," the latter observed.

"Shut up. She's working seriously to have Alsace and Lorraine returned to us." And, laughing in his turn: "What a goose, eh? Unworthy of the chestnut, and also the cabbage, for she has never been the Emperor's mistress; all that is monstrous affectation, a montage of lies by a whore well aware of the stupidity of males. By that means she holds a few political men and all the theater directors to subsidy. She could sing tomorrow at the Opéra if the whim took her. In any case, she was very pretty once."

He interrupted himself to say: "Waiter, the bill . . . no, let me take care of it . . . you can invite me next time . . . and let me tell you the story; it's worth the trouble.

"Thérèse Evrard. I met her a dozen years ago—which doesn't rejuvenate her—in the Rue de Douai, at one of those famous lunches in which Sarcey[1] gave hospitality pell-mell to all the theater and all literature. The little hotel in the Rue de Douai was something of a Hôtel du Roule 'of the wings and of amour.' Everyone went there, the great and the small, the stars in quest of a good story for their new role to create, the debutantes in need of an engagement, a letter of recommendation or three lines in the Master's chronicle; comediennes, tragediennes, café-concert divas and operetta divettes, the consecrated and the unknown, the actresses and the theatresses,[2] ever ready for the sacrifice in order to obtain a paternal smile from Uncle, all devoured by the fever of publicity. What I saw strung along the staircase that led from the dining room to the library!

"The food wasn't exactly exquisite at Uncle's, but the table was wide open. How youth and fresh faces attracted Uncle's authority! It was an indescribable milieu; one rubbed shoulders there with girls from Montmartre who came with their corsets wrapped in newspaper and stalwarts of the Comédie-Française in hundred-louis dresses from Worth's and their coupés waiting at the door. That was where I encountered Thérèse Evrard. She was accompanied by her mother; she was fourteen years old—so her mother said—and wore her admirable hair in pigtails.

"A little tall still to be wearing a short skirt, Thérèse walked through that varied milieu with the freshness of a pink eglantine and the candor of Gretchen's eyes. She's kept their learned innocence under her long lowered lashes.

"All the old centurions of criticism, rakes more or less cooked by limelight and gallantry, quivered at little Evrard's advertised fourteen springs; there were the mewls of tomcats, the cooing

---

1 The prolific journalist and ultra-conservative dramatic critic Francisque Sarcey (1827-1899), abhorred by the *avant garde*, including Lorrain, but safely dead when the present story was written.
2 Because Lorrain uses the term *théâtreuse* [a pejorative term for an actress] in contrast to *acteuse* [a slang version of *actrice*, the orthodox French word that translates as actress] I have improvised an English transcription, which I have employed throughout the present translation.

40

of old pigeons and the bleating of old goats. Thérèse wandered through that menagerie like a young Christian martyr among the wild beasts of the circus; her innocence protected her. Her mother also watched over her, and the master of the house had taken her in affection. After lunch, Thérèse was admitted to play dominoes with Uncle.

"It was in the Rue de Douai that Thérèse and her mother had a stroke of genius. After a lunch attended by old Schlewitz, one of the richest financiers in London, Thérèse, seeing the old fellow lit up by port, and the sparkling eyes that gentlemen of that age don't normally have, contrived when they got up from the table to find herself alone with him in a little corridor leading to the servants' parlor—evil tongues have claimed that it was elsewhere. Suddenly, young Thérèse uttered a piercing scream, and Madame Evrard, come running with a few other mothers, found her child sobbing next to the bewildered old Englishman.

"'I don't know what's wrong with the little miss. I'd asked the domestic for the water closets and the damsel offered to guide me, saying that she'd show me *the little chapel*. And then, in the corridor, she started to cry.'

"Madame Evrard, her face scarlet, took the audience as her witness and talked about the police. Thérèse was a minor; she wouldn't be fifteen for another two days.

"Uncle intervened. Schlewitz was a great power; Madame was appeased and Thérèse consoled. The Master's protection was acquired. So she had a brilliant debut at the Odéon; the critics were unanimous in recognizing, if not the talent, at least the beauty and the simplicity of the debutante. Strongly supported by the management, Thérèse had all the plastic roles in costume dramas thereafter; her physique predestined her for them. She was the Florentine courtesan over whom the Guelphs and the Ghibellines fought, the Roman Empress whose litter traverses the stage in the third and fifth acts, and, heavy with brocade and dotted with precious stones, the favorite of all the tyrants of

Padua, Parma, Palermo and other petty Italian states. As a good actress, she ended up taking her role seriously; the *little chapel* is now the Emperor's mistress!"

"The mistress of . . ."

"Precisely, of . . ."

"But how did . . ."

"How did she become his mistress? Oh, that's a whole other story."

The two men were walking along the Rue de Tournon; a dry cold made the pavement hard and sonorous. Octave Vergy stopped to light a cigar.

"Yes, a whole other story; what's more, I heard it from Thérèse herself. You're listening to me! This is her version.

"By virtue of seeing Thérèse Evrard parade in the sumptuousness of Venetian corteges and the archaism of processions in Rome or Byzantium, the caprice came to me of the flesh of the beautiful girl. One doesn't see a plasticity like Thérèse's on offer with impunity, when heightened by the spice of legendary costumes and historical adornments.

"I knew that she was easy. She supported her success on adroitly distributed favors and was reputed, not without reason, to buy the favors of feuilletonistes with the generous alms of her body. Why should I not sit down at that open table and why should I, too, not dig into the feast of a beauty so generous towards and against everyone?

"I disposed then of a great morning paper and, without being the theater critic, I could unleash perfidious darts or telling eulogies in all directions. On several occasions, without a hidden agenda, I had burned incense to the real beauty of the artiste and her incomparable science of costume. Like anyone else, I was cultivated, and the welcome that Thérèse gave me every time I went to see her in her dressing room proved to me how much she valued me. There were *my little Octaves* here and *my good Octaves* there, affectionate taps on the neck, promising brushes of the hips, and all the small seductions with which actresses tease the dispensers of glory, great or small.

"Thérèse was then playing, in an Odéon revival of Dumas père's *Caligula* under Porel's direction,[1] some Palatine courtesan, a friend and confidant of Messalina, and, alongside the tragic and black beauty of Aimée Tessandier, a terrible female in the role of the Empress, she obtained a true success of blonde flesh. I allowed myself to be captured by that apotheosis of freshness. I redoubled by visits to Thérèse's dressing room, accompanying my court with gifts of flowers, and one evening, I invited her to visit my bachelor apartment the next morning, and to stay for lunch.

"I was then living in the entresol on the Quai d'Orsay where you met me, amid a clutter, often popularized by the illustrated papers, of nicely-bound books of art and Japanese prints. Thérèse was curious to see the bindings; all women are curious about entresols where it is in their interest to fall. She consented to come to see me as a friend, to riffle through my Elzevirs, my goffered leathers, my pigskins and shagreens. I had just received a tub of caviar from Riga and some choice smoked salmon from Holland. Thérèse was madly fond of zakuskis. It was a taste she had brought back from Russia; like every self-respecting actress Thérèse had done a season at the Théâtre Michel in Petersburg, and had been loved by a Grand Duke.

"She had no rehearsal at that moment. She would come to lunch the next day, but she would be sage . . . naturally. What that lunch was, you can guess. Chypre wine in the carafes, tea in the ice-buckets, zakuskis in the old China boats and mauve chrysanthemums on the tablecloth. Thérèse affected a child-like gaiety. There were girlish remarks and foolish laughter, but fundamentally, she was only thinking about *that* . . . and so was I, since that was what I expected, and for which she had come. The heady opoponax in her hair and the very fashion

---

1 Paul Porel (1843-1917) persuaded Gabriel Fauré to write the music for an 1888 production of Dumas' *Caligula* (1837), when he was in charge of designing stage-sets at the Odéon; Aimée Tessandier played Messalina in that production. Porel was appointed director of the Opéra-Comique in 1898.

of her bodice, buttoned over the shoulder, which a flick of the thumb was sufficient to open, indicated well enough that she was prepared for all sacrifices.

"We got up from the table; the coffee was served in the little Japanese drawing room you remember: piles of cushions of all hues and forms, propitious half-light filtered by a rain of pearls from a store in Yeddo, immense sprays of white chrysan-themums in Carriès stone, the walls hung with yellow silk, the frieze of grimacing masks and hilarious monsters, the fear of which added to the sensuality—a refined decoration in which the naïvety of my sadism still took pleasure.

"We took our places on a divan 'as profound as a tomb.' An Oriental cigarette authorized the abandonment of our attitudes; two glasses of kummel illuminated Thérèse's cheeks a little; we maintained a dangerous silence. I took possession of her hand, which was playing negligently with a flower, and I raised it slowly to my lips.

"Now there's a rapid rain of kisses that rise from the fingers to the wrist and from the wrist to the nape of the neck. The inconvenient button of the bodice has popped, Thérèse's cleavage appears, white and firm in the whiteness of batiste. That cleavage, I don't so much see as respire; a violent odor makes my head spin; from the nape, my mouth has reached the white and delicate flesh of the neck and seeks to reach the lips, which are still refused to me. Slackly abandoned on the cushions, Thérèse is only resisting for form's sake and punctuates the resistance with little chuckles. Those chuckles restore my composure; they irritate me, those chuckles. They're unnecessary, and have come too soon. I sense that I'm ridiculous. I fall upon her mouth and kiss it solidly . . .

"Then, in a quavering voice: 'It's bad what you're doing there, Octave, you're abusing me. It's bad, what we're doing. We're deceiving the Emperor!'

"A cold shower falling on my back wouldn't have chilled me more. 'You're right, Madame, let it be as you desire.' And I got up, coldly and adjusted my false collar . . .

44

"Thèrèse had stood up, chagrined. 'You're annoyed with me, my friend. I believe that I was wrong to come; I've been coquettish. The sentiment of honor, however . . . I'm not free; I'm his mistress!'

"I sat down tranquilly beside the comedienne. 'Let's not talk about it any more, Thérèse.'

"The actress had neglected to button her bodice again, and the nacre of her shoulders still emerged from the gap in the gray fabric. I pointed it out to her. Thérèse readjusted it with a febrile hand. 'And now,' I said, contriving a familiar tone, 'tell me your little story. You mentioned the Emperor; I didn't understand what you meant. There's a legend regarding Madame de Béthisy, the wife of the ambassador to Vienna under Napoléon III, who, at the psychological moment, demanded that her accomplices cry 'Long live the Emperor!' and thus gained partisans for the Empire. Fifteen years ago, during the Boulangist movement, all the grand dames of Paris demanded that their lovers cry: 'Long live the General!', and during the Last Affair, therefore, how many times must the cry 'Long live Colonel Picqart!' have rung out in the alcoves of the Monceau quarter?[1] Oh, our beautiful cosmopolitan bankers' wives were ferociously devoted to the great Cause and did the work of proselytism. But my dear Thérèse, I can't see you as Judith, except in the theater, and I'm wondering what the Emperor of Germany has come to do here.'

"The beautiful face of the comedienne was veiled with tears. 'You don't believe me, my friend?'

"'I'd like nothing better than to believe you.'

"'No, you're holding a grudge against me, and you're right. You don't have the composure necessary to listen to the story.'

_____

1 Georges Picquart was the army investigator who discovered the evidence that Alfred Dreyfus had been wrongly convicted on the basis of forged documents, and defied all the pressure put on him to keep quiet, blowing the lid off the famous Affair—with the result that he was deprived of duty and sent to Tunisia before being maliciously accused of fabricating evidence, although he was eventually exonerated along with Dreyfus.

"'I can't ask you to verify it, but I've never been calmer. Tell me. It interests me.'

"And with a long sigh, the actress, having laid her head back on the cushions, said: 'After all, it might be best. When I've told you everything, my attitude will be justified.'

"And then she commenced the most implausible story. It was, intercut with anecdotes from old feuilleton romances and patched up with theatrical clichés, the most fantastic Russian salad that the reading of Alexandre Dumas père, Eugène Sue and Octave Feuillet had ever been able to inspire in the brain of a milliner. I recognized and saluted the scenes and stage-sets in passing. The sets were from Feuillet, the scenes from Sue, the romanticism of the intrigue came from Dumas. The Emperor appeared there by turns, under the features of Monsieur de Camors and Prince Rodolpe of Gerolstein.[1]

"She had met him in a forest—a forest in Swabia!

> "*It's deep in the woods of Norway*
> *And of Swabia that Schiller*
> *Made the snow-elves dance*
> *Beside the clear water of springs.*[2]

"Their first conversation could have been set to music. It was during an imperial hunt. How did Thérèse Evrard, a fixture at the Odéon, come to be in that Swabian forest? A mystery!

"The Kaiser appeared to her, young, robust and proud, molded in the ribbed green velvet of a hunting costume. Naturally, he had strayed a long way from his retinue. Thérèse didn't recognize him; only his beauty impressed her, and his nobility; for, by his appearance alone she had divined the great lord. Their gazes met, an emotion gripped them by the throat . . . tremolo in the

---

1 *Monsieur de Camors* (1867) is Octave Feuillet's masterpiece; Rodolphe of Gerolstein is the hero of Eugène Sue's monumentally successful *Les Mystères de Paris* (1843).
2 The lines appear to be original.

46

orchestra, electric projections in the wings, the distant sound
of horns . . . and that same evening, a hunting-lodge sheltered
their amour.

"It was thus that she became his mistress, instinctively, having become irresponsible in the grip of passion, Yseult at the
sight of Tristan—these heroic and princely amours require the
music of Wagner.

"Yes, my dear, she had the aplomb to tell me those howl-
ers, and a great many more. The Kaiser, dazed by amour and
recognizing that he was loved for himself and not for his rank,
identified himself at the third rendezvous. That liaison had been
going on for three years. They were still as infatuated as on the
first day. He wanted to install her in Berlin, but she had refused,
because of the Empress—and then again, she feared the intrigues
of the court. Ready for the slightest signal, she lived in Paris; a
coded telegram, and she went running. Their rendezvous had
always taken place in forested and mountainous solitudes, on
the shores of lakes shaded by fir trees, and there was always a
feudal ruin above the treetops, moonlight in the ravine and a
swan on the lake. The stage was set as if by Carré himself, with
a side court and garden.

"In those settings the Kaiser turned into Ludwig II of
Bavaria. He loved to forget with her the cares of the Empire
and the annoyances of government. The socialists were giving
him a lot of trouble and his brow was often sad, but then he
became a child again with her. What a charming and delicate
nature! One day, when they had been picking edelweiss on the
mountain, he had wanted to send them himself to Madame
Evrard, who was still in Paris in her third floor in the Rue
Cardinet. He often consulted her about affairs of State; he had
confidence in her French common sense. 'You see things from
a distance,' he often repeated to her. In fact, she did see a long
way, and never ceased thinking about the lost provinces. Oh,
that Alsace-Lorraine! And Thérèse, suddenly in profile, directed
a long gaze eastwards . . .

"She eventually concluded: 'Well, what a fine drama one could write with all that, if they knew it!'

"'A drama! Say an opera, my dear. But Wagner is no more." And as she looked at me, a trifle anxiously: 'I see it above all as a fine novel. Consider this opening: *I was seduced in a forest!*'

"'That's not nice, Octave, you're making fun of me. I was wrong to tell you. You'll never forgive me.'

"And, biting my lip in order to remain serious, frowning and cruel, I said: 'No, I'll never forgive you.'"

"And you've kept your word."

ILLYNE YLS[1]

MAXENCE went back to the hotel; the elevator took him to the third floor. He went to his room, switched on all the electricity—the chandelier and the bulb at the head of the bed—and opened the window. The warmth of the long corridors heated by steam had taken him by the throat; he was choking. After the chill outside, that sensation of warmth became a malaise. It was only three o'clock, but a sky of soot was already making the room dark. Over an ocean of mansard rooftops, sections of wall and chimney-pots, there was the distress of Parisian Decembers. Maxence was seized by a coughing fit.

A glacial damp was rising from the street. The young man closed the window again and drew the curtains. Isolated from the twilight, the room was immediately illuminated comfortably, with its hangings of yellow silk. Maxence spotted his correspondence on the table, deposited there by the maître d'hôtel. Pell-mell with pneumatiques there were envelopes bearing the postmarks of theaters and publishers. Maxence collected two armchairs at the Comédie-Française, a box at the Opéra-Comique and a forestage box at the Cigale, two accounts of sales from Marco Bruner and a proposition from Egelmann, the art publisher in the Rue de Tournon. The pneumatiques were invitations to dinner.

Then he deciphered the back of a postcard: *Bonjour Maxence. Write to me. I often think about you; I'd like so much to see you*

---

1 First published in *Le Journal* on 25 December 1902.

The text was accumulated, in delicate handwriting, beneath a figure of a semi-naked woman; the postcard was illustrated. Maxence examined and recognized that slimness, the pure lines of the nape and the body of a young nymph in a Greek tunic with loose pleats. He also recognized the pose; it was that of a photograph that the artiste had sent him the previous year, with great mystery, a unique photograph, taken for the princely heir to a great European power, and of which she had made a print for him, Maxence, alone; but it was necessary for him never to show it to anyone or mention it to anyone; the slightest indiscretion might attract the worst inconveniences to Illyne.

It was that intimate photograph whose reproduction was now running around the world, hanging in the shop-windows of stationers and printed on postcards by the thousands. Maxence recognized the pretty gesture of frail arms lifted behind the head and two hands, laden with rings, placing a heavy crown of flowers thereon. A good commercial stamp, seven rows of pearls—Maxence knew their provenance and the donor, a rich Viennese banker recently killed in an automobile accident—completed the vulgarization of the exported Tanagra. The postcard had a London postmark; London was where the passion of a royal lover retained and confined Illyne. Maxence could not help smiling as he thought about the face that the royal lover must have pulled before the portrait of the idol, specially made for him, put into circulation.

Vulgar publicity and affectation: all the character of Illyne was there. It was also the program of her life. She had always lied, unconsciously at first, and then knowingly, uniquely preoccupied with her attitude and its effects, unhealthily avid for publicity, incessantly posing for the gallery, incessantly obsessed with creating around her an atmosphere of deception, and truly happy once that atmosphere was created.

Had Prince George even been her lover? Maxence hesitated to believe it. Certainly, the handsome Hanoverian might have had a caprice for the pretty girl that Illyne was, but that the whim had become a liaison, of which the courtesan wanted to convince the world, that was something else. For two years Illyne had been showing him telegrams in support, laconic and passionate dispatches from Cowes, Brighton, London, Vienna and even Florence, all triumphantly signed "Georget," but Illyne was the kind of woman to send those telegrams to herself; there are agencies for that sort of thing. A profound knowledge of Illyne authorized Maxence to all suspicions.

That mania for lying, which had become as necessary to Illyne as water to a fish and air to a bird, that joy in deception which transfigured her and rendered her truly prettier, that need to make a mockery of everyone and treat humankind as a vast flock of imbeciles—a system somewhat offensive, at length, for the little circle of her friends—that deep-seated falsity and perpetual rage for play-acting, had ended up diminishing Illyne; her personality was reduced by all the slightly base dishonesty, spiced, it is true, by all the willful ingeniousness of the perverse little being.

All those reflections Maxence made as he studied, feature by feature, the delightful face of the actress: the exquisite form of the chin, the elongated oval of the cheeks and the sinuous design of the eyelids over the large candid eyes: the flowery eyes of a child. That little nymph with the irises, which Watts might have signed, that delicate and aristocratic creature with the profile of a duchesse, was the insatiable and cunning Illyne Yls, of whom, at twenty-six years of age, the columns of a certain press could no longer count the jewels or the lovers.

And Maxence's eyes shone, for, in all that comedy played in cities and courts, had he not been slightly complicit? At one time, had he not guided the pretty girl's first steps with his advice? In some of the fires of anarchism to which the futile stupidity of the rich had accustomed him, had he not incited Illyne to debauchery and lucre, unleashing the cruelty and covetousness of the girl upon the bleak imbecility of the high life? How many times had he represented her career as a courtesan to her as a mission of justice—even better, as a revenge of Amour and Beauty against the oppression of capital? All the deceptions of the métier, therefore, Maxence had excused; more than that, he had indicated them, delighted by the good tricks that she played thus upon a caste he detested. But that Illyne was now employing those deceptions, all those duperies and lies, against him, he thought quite bad, and he had looked hard at himself in the mirror, and, bruised as he was by passing forty, he had not yet seen the face of a mug.

Maxence could not swallow the insult of the postcard. One does not conduct oneself thus with an associate—for had not the beginnings of their liaison been a true association? Maxence recalled the details of it, and the phases of that morose delectation were not without pleasure for him.

A character assassination of the pretty girl in a petty boulevard daily had initiated their relationship. Maxence was then dabbling in journalism. Illyne Yls, deceived by a London manager and a few business publicists, had just had a resounding failure in a boulevard music hall. All Paris was still talking about that unfortunate debut. The liaison the girl had contracted with the Duc de Maistre had put her in the public eye; the owner of a music hall, a good sniffer of scandal, had decided to put the lovely creature on the boards. Illyne had appeared as a magicienne sitting on a crescent moon; she made rabbits disappear there. The debut had been a flop; the gallery had not had enough whistles and gibes for the gaucherie of the debutante, decked in a wig, blinded and bewildered, and who, in her panic, was making the gesture of a conjurer to the right while the rabbits disappeared to the left. Maxence had devoted a column to that astonishing debut; he did not spare the new star any more than the old comets heaped up that evening in the hall, all the centenarian old cosmopolitan gallantry who had come to look the young person up and down and display their ill-acquired jewelry once again.

The article had created a stir, Illyne, maltreated, had wanted to know the author. Maxence had been slightly reluctant, but, one morning, he had allowed himself to be taken to see the courtesan. Oh, the décor of that first meeting! The journalist had found Illyne lying in the sumptuousness of a large Louis XVI bed, decked in plumes, shining with lampas and clouded in lace. In the huge chamber, hung with white watered silk, Maxence had no longer recognized in that supple and frail little girl with the eyes delectably ringed with blue and the hesitant and delicate voice, the gauche and clumsy magicienne of the other evening.

All of Maxence's literature had gone up in flames before that creature with the pride of an infanta and the fresh charm of a dauphine. The theatress had welcomed her detractor with a forgiving grace; the journalist had compared her by turns with a princess of legend, a unicorn and an item of Venetian glass. It is true that there was nothing in Paris then more fragile and precious than the nudity of Illyne Yls. Maxence had thought that it was an atrocity to have made that delectable girl make her debut as a conjurer. Since she wanted to be in the theater she ought to have appeared as the heroine of a féerie. If she consented to that, he would write a piece expressly for her; he had a heartfelt desire to repair the injustice he had committed, and wanted to impose Illyne Yls on All Paris.

They had become friends.

The association had succeeded. Maxence had introduced the courtesan to directors; Illyne's beauty and the subsidies of her lovers had imposed the author and his plays. Illyne had appeared successively in three ballets by Maxence, still as gauche and rigid with emotion in the theater as she was supple and clever in the city, but surrounded by such a luxury of figuration and scenery, sustained by such an ingenuity of special effects and devices, supported by the vogue and snobbery of clubs and boudoirs, and in such dazzling jewelry and costumes, that the awkwardness in question became a charm; people went, in part, to see Maxence's friend miss her cues and prance awkwardly on the stage.

In any case, when public curiosity waned and the receipts began to decline, Illyne had sure means of causing both to rise again. Maxence had found a marvelous pupil in Illyne. She had an unequaled instinct for publicity. It was thus that she lost successively her horses, an eighty-thousand franc necklace, was menaced with acid by anonymous letters, etc. etc. . . . until the great tom-tom of the final suicide.

The horses, stolen on Saturday, were recovered on Sunday; the necklace was returned by a nabob, a fleeting lover who had added two rows to it; the anonymous letters, published in full in the newspapers, were the work of a grand dame of the English aristocracy . . .

And her private life aggravated the mystery, its horizons crimsoned by the flames of Lesbos. As for the suicide to the full orchestra, which was to entertain society, they had staged it themselves and drafted the sensational bulletins.

In order to keep the public in suspense, had she not imagined one day simulating a quarrel between the two of them? Jealousy had furnished the motive, and in a violent scene in the wings of the Alhambra, she would fire a revolver at her author—and would miss him, naturally. Maxence, a trifle anxious about his friend's skill, had utterly refused that final maneuver, but had nevertheless admired the genius of his accomplice.

Since then, life had separated them. He was living in the Midi, she in London, and it was to him that she was addressing postcards aggravated by portraits and declarations.

As it is necessary to make the decision to laugh at everything in order not to cry, Maxime insinuated the card in the frame of the mirror, and wrote beneath it an alexandrine already consecrated to another queen of the theater:

Princess of drumbeats and queen of humbug![1]

1 Lorrain applied this description to Liane de Pougy, with whom he had once been closely linked, and whose career he had played a significant role in launching; he wrote the pantomimes *Rêve de Noël* and *L'Araignée d'or* for her, the latter staged at the Folies Bergère in 1895. Pougy must have seen echoes of herself in the fictitious character of Illyne when the story was published in *Le Journal,* and must have known that other people would make the same connection, but she did not react as violently as Jeanne Jacquemin three weeks later and does not seem to have held it against him. She did not attend Lorrain's funeral, but she did send a wreath.

CORDELIA STAUB[1]

"OH, the hysteria and the affectation that it always engenders; unless—for the inverse is also true—the two states of the soul complete one another, and when the hysteria does not precede the affectation, it succeeds it. All the neuroses want to appear on stage; they are haunted by the boards, tinsel and costume; they are obsessed, most of all, with the public and hence publicity! As for actresses, from those of the subsidized establishments to the most infimal theatresses, you know the state into which overwork and prolonged late nights put their nerves. One might say that, in them, one looks into a storm, and the hypertrophied vanity of that entire society; those women, eternally quivering like leaves after a squall, are hypersensitive to the slightest attack, the slightest allusion and the slightest criticism, sick with jealousy, rivalry and publicity . . .

"Hamville is the land of nervous crises, scenes, tears, scandals and slaps, and also suicides.

"Naturally! Oh, Hamville, the realm of storms in teacup and dramas in a washbasin, dry bandages and fainting spells."

"A fine opening, but a little long," said Vergy, going to take a little statuette of green bronze from the mantelpiece, which he turned over and over in his hand. And, returning to the other three men sprawled at hazard on the divans: "Where are you going with it, Maxence?"

------

1 First published in *Le Journal* 17 January 1903 (four days after "Victime") as "Ettiennette Staub."

"A story, naturally. Are we not practicing experimental psychology? I'm going to lay my foundation-stone. I have my supporting proof."

"Oh, really? And what's the name of that proof?"

"Cordelia Staub."

"The tragedienne?"

"Oh, tragedienne, singer . . . above all, she has a plastic talent. She's a cantatrice for men of letters and a tragedienne for musicians."

"A talent apart!"

"Yes, one of the glories of great auditions of *Tristan and Yseult* and the *Damnation*. There are three or four in Paris who fill the hall of the Casino de Paris for her performances, and perhaps extend to ten a success in the Théâtre Sarah Bernhard in Monte Carlo."

"Pardon me, but Cordelia Staub has had a real success in Germany."

"And in Belgium too, of course, and in Toulouse. There are stars of the provinces, and above all of the frontiers, suburbs of Munich and Brussels—but England and America don't know them. Theatrical glory doesn't pass over the straits."

"When you've abused the woman enough, Maxence, perhaps you'll tell us her story?" And Vergy, who had just replaced the little statuette on the mantelpiece, leaned his elbow on the shelf while caressing his moustache mechanically. "I don't share your opinion of Staub. I saw her in Pierre Louÿs' *Aphrodite*. She had an incomparable plasticity and displaced grace in each of her movements; one couldn't be any more Greek."

"What! A Greek, her, with that square Flemish face?"

"Yes, I know, the face is a little heavy. That's the proof of her artistic science. That Teutonic beauty, by means of the drape of her tunic and the simplicity of her coiffure, found the means to evoke a Tanagra."

"A Tanagra *de foie gras*."

"You're stupid, Steinberg. I have photographs at home."

"What does that prove? Now that all photographs are re-touched, all women revert to the same type. Fanny Chimère has just sent me one; in it she resembles closely the *Cruche cassée* by Greuze[1]—and Fanny is fifty."

"Idiot! It's absolutely idiotic, what you're saying. Cordelia Staub, at twenty-eight, has magnificent silvery blonde hair, the hair of an Infanta, white and firm flesh and the eyes of a Nereid, green eyes, strangely troubled, between long golden lashes."

"Very pale gold."

"No matter! Cordelia Staub is young, healthy and fresh, and Fanny Chimère is an old music-hall smoked shark, cooked and fluffed up by all the stage lights and all the nocturnal cabarets. Try to see her elsewhere than under the lights, and give me news of her."

"The fact is that Fanny Chimère's morning awakening . . ."

"The resurrection of Lazarus, a subject for the competition for the Prix de Rome."

"Of Saint-Lazare, you mean—but, with all that, we're not hearing Maxence's story. The floor is given to Maxence Sassengage.[2] And you, go away."

And Maxence, having nestled in his cushions, began:

"This goes back ten years or so; I was the theater critic for the *Revue Latine*. In the world of the theater no one was talking then about anything but the arrival in Paris of a new star whose acting and beauty would revolutionize the stage, a star from beyond the Rhine, since Mademoiselle Cordelia Staub was born in Cologne. A lyric tragedienne, she had voice and diction, gesture and register, mime and middle C; and with that, as beautiful

---

1 *Le Cruche cassée* by Jean-Baptiste Greuze (1725-1805), which shows a young woman holding a broken pitcher, was popularized by an engraving made in the 1770s that was widely circulated.

2 Maxence's surname was previously given as Vassenage. It is possible that he is not the same character as the Maxence Chottard in the Epilogue, which appeared in two parts in *Le Journal* prior to the present item and its immediate predecessors.

as a Thorvaldsen goddess[1]. She was simultaneously the Erda of
the *Nibelungen* and the undulant whiteness of a Rhine-maiden.
Materna, Duse and Langry for plasticity—those were the names
cited in her regard. Staub had thrilled Munich in *Siegfried*, the
Die Walküre and the *Meistersinger*, and all Berlin in Schiller's
Brigands.[2]

"She was to make her debut in Paris in Georges Hüe's *Circé*[3]
at the Opéra-Populaire, and all the directors were disputing her
at a price of gold. Think of it: a woman who had all the strings
in her lyre—and 'all the strings' was the phrase, for a strange legend preceded her. It was said that Cordelia Staub was absolutely
pure . . . or, rather, defended against all enterprise by a passionate affection for her uncle, a very young uncle only ten years
older than his niece, Hermann Staub, the painter, who traveled
with the young woman and never quit her. He was the one who
had discovered her, had pushed her into the theater in spite of
the opposition of the family, and had extracted from the *petite
bourgeoise* of Cologne the admirable artiste that Cordelia had
become. The young woman had avowed an exalted gratitude
to her creator, a kind of religious cult of an enthusiastic fervor;
she was not known to have lovers, and no adventures were attributed to her.

"Hermann Staub was thirty-seven and was a dark-haired
version of the type of his niece. That tells you the nature of the
whispers generated by the couple. In the world of the wings,
people accept no matter what monstrous implausibility rather
than the virginity of a woman of the theater. There are atmo-

---

1 The Ollendorf text renders this name Thorswalden, but Lorrain must
mean the Danish sculptor Bertel Thorvaldsen (1770-1844), who produced
a great many statues and busts named for characters in Greek and Roman
mythology.
2 Jacques Offenbach's *Les Brigands* is a French comic opera that parodies
Giuseppe Verdi's *I Masnadieri*, based on Friedrich Schiller's *Die Rauber*;
Staub is surely more likely to have sung in the Verdi version.
3 The composer Georges Hüe (1858-1948) did not write an opera called
Circé.

spheres that soil like mud. La Staub had too much success not
to be her uncle's mistress; that was the revenge of her rivals.
Calumny is the other side of the coin of glory, a perfume of
incest preceded the couple.

"It would be to misunderstand Paris to think that that legend
harmed La Staub. Far from being diminished by it, the tragedian was magnified by it, hoisted up as if on a pedestal by a hint
of horror and a great deal of curiosity. Those who denied the
liaison lent the young woman compromising amities:

"*Like cattle lying pensive on the sand . . .*[1]

"You know the beautiful line by Baudelaire and, some said,
La Staub's lyre was that of Sappho, that other lyre-bearer.

"The Staub uncle and niece were staying at a family hotel in
Passy, on the Boulevard Beauséjour, and they were not encountered anywhere; the young woman only went out for rehearsals
at the theater. Her debut, announced for the end of the current month, had been postponed to the tenth of the following
month, and curiosity, ignited by beautiful photographs of the
tragedienne exposed in all the shop windows, exasperated so
much mystery even further.

"Indifferent as I am by nature, I shared the state of mind created in all Parisians by the attitude of the Staub couple. So, on
the morning when little Marthe Féry of the Odéon, and above
all of Les Escholiers,[2] came to see me at home in a great tumult
of silk underwear and, alarmed and excited, made me party to
the violent desire she had to introduce me to her friend Cordelia
Staub, and the visit she had requested to make to me, Maxence
Sassenage, I welcomed Marthe Féry like a Messiah, and, instead

---

1 The line is the opening line of "Femmes damnés," initially removed from
Les Fleurs du mal after its prosecution, but subsequently restored.
2 Les Escholiers were a troupe of amateur actors who supported professionals in putting on shows in private houses.

of treating her as a negligible person with a packet of Khedive cigarettes and a glass of white port, I gave her lunch.

"I was firmly determined to extract from the little actress a confession regarding the tragedienne. Marthe did not make me beg. The Duse from beyond the Rhine treated her as a friend; she had a great heart, a soul of such nobility . . .

"Marthe had devoted a cult to Cordelia Staub. She had seen her perform in Berlin, she had written to her, the tragedienne had replied, and better than that, had received her. When Marthe returned to France the correspondence between the two women had continued, an amity had followed, passionate on the part of the little actress, quasi-maternal and tutelary on the part of the great artiste; and, when I risked a sharp-eyed wink at the story of that feminine amity, 'It's an infamy!' Marthe cried, rigid with indignation. 'Cordelia is above suspicion; she's spring water in rock crystal. Cordelia is impeccable, do you hear, Sassenage, impeccable!' and she hammered the syllables through clenched teeth. And, at an allusion to the grand amour of the uncle and the niece: 'That's too stupid. Hermann Staub is married to an adorable young woman, as brunette as Cordelia is blonde, and younger than her by three years, a pair of turtle-doves.'

"Marthe Féry demolished all the objections. She only quit me having convinced me of Mademoiselle Staub's purity. We had agreed a day for my visit and introduction.

"The little actress brought the uncle and the niece to me the following Thursday. I was then living in the right wing of an old Louis XVI house between the courtyard and the garden, in a street in Neuilly, a former folly of the eighteenth century in which the great seigneurs of the time had the custom of sheltering their amours. On the day in question, at five o'clock, I was under arms in the apartment with renewed flowers, white chrysanthemums, in all the vases and the oak mantelpiece ornamented with holly branches. A hired coupé stopped outside the gate. A tall dark-haired young man got down, then Marthe

Féry, then another female silhouette bulked out by a long sable mantle, the head swathed by veils. I presumed that it was Cordelia Staub.

"There was the sound of a bell, and then voices in the antechamber, and the door opened to the visitors.

"'It's her, here she is'—and Marthe Féry precipitated forward and knelt down before the tragedienne, standing and smiling.

"Mademoiselle Staub had kept her mantle; underneath it she was wearing a long white velvet dress, crumpled in places by golden embroidery, but she had taken off her veil, and, beneath an immense ermine beret there was the dazzle of blonde skin, healthy youth and the hair that you know. 'I desired so much to make your acquaintance, I like what you write so much, isn't that right, Hermann?' And she held out an ungloved hand to me. The uncle, a very young uncle, had remained to one side, muffled in furs. I stammered a few admiring phrases. So much aplomb disconcerted me.

"'Isn't she beautiful, my friend Cordelia? Show your figure, I want him to see you, and show your hair too . . .' Marthe Féry forced her friend to emerge from her sable.

"'What a child! She's a child!' said the tragedienne, allowing her hair to be removed.

"Cordelia Staub made herself at home; she approached my desk and, spotting two or three photographs of her that I had placed there, negligently: 'That's very polite,' she said to me. Then, suddenly discovering my packet of *petits bleus*: 'Oh, I have a heap of people to inform, with your permission . . .'

"And, installing herself in my armchair, she drew from my collection of telegram forms and began to write on them; 'To Francisque Sarcey, Rue de Douai; to Henri Fouquier, Avenue de l'Alma; to Henry Bauer, Rue de Prony; to Catulle Mendès, Rue Boccador; to Gustave Larroumet, Quai de Conti; to Félix Duquesnel, Rue Boissy-d'Anglas; to Émile Faguet, to Camille Lemonnier, etc., etc.'

"Mademoiselle Staub wrote her correspondence in my home. It was necessary to inform the critics. 'And now, quickly, someone to take these to the nearest post office; it's very urgent.' I rang for my valet de chambre, astonished that she hadn't demanded a porter.

"'That's done,' she said, getting up. 'You'll forgive me? Now, I'm all yours.' And she held out both hands to me, smiling tranquilly.

"Marthe Féry had approached the window. A carriage had just stopped outside. 'Oh, my God!' she said, taking the tragedienne swiftly by the waist. 'Madame Staub is getting down and traversing the courtyard; she's coming here.'

"'My aunt! Your wife, Hermann! Who could have foreseen that? Go and meet her, quickly, avoid a scandal. Oh, Monsieur, excuse me, it's a poor madwoman.'

"A violent blast of the bell made us jump; negotiations were engaged at the door, and then a quarrel burst forth, dominated by the shrill voice of a woman Hermann Staub had gone out.

"The tragedienne had let herself fall into an armchair, and was wringing her beautiful hands convulsively . . .

"'Oh, it's horrible, and it exhausts you, and kills you in the end, these infamous suspicions—for these odious calumnies, it's my aunt who propagates them and puts them into circulation.'

"I pretended not to understand. Hermann Staub had just come back in: 'Excuse me, Monsieur . . . my niece must have told you . . .'

"He took the tragedienne to one side. 'Cordelia, Thecla is demanding that you go on ahead with Marthe. I'll take her back to the hotel; she's already calmer; it's her jealousy that has taken hold of her again. My wife is ill, Monsieur, she imagines things.'

And the trio left, as that had come.

"I saw Cordelia Staub and Marthe Féry traverse the courtyard and climb back into their hired coupé, and a minute later, it was the turn of the brother, accompanied by a young woman in black; they both climbed onto a fiacre.

"I only saw the tragedienne again on the stage; but the finest comedy was the one she played in my home, for the aunt's jealousy, the pretended scandal she had come to cause, the coincidence of their presence, all three, in my apartment, all of that had been planned, organized and agreed on in advance between them. The Staubs were anticipating a journalistic indiscretion and a sensational article in the newspapers, which would be seized by the publicity organized around them. But as I was still a gallant man, I refused them that pleasure."

MADAME HOLLAND[1]

"WHAT terrible eyes!"

It was at the Ritz, stuffed with Englishmen attracted there by the passing of Edward VII. Curious to see the elegance of the other side of the Channel, Steinberg, Mornard and I had come to dine there, also avid to contemplate and admire a few of the English beauties, miraculous type-specimens of splendor and freshness, sensational professional beauties, that London imposes once or twice a year on the snobbery of other capitals.

A woman came in and, followed by a man in a black suit, made her way with some difficulty to a small table encumbered by pink carnations. In full dress, all embroidered white tulle decorated with gray pearls and black jet, her shoulders bare, she was a statue of living snow, the nacre of which was brightened in places by vivid pink, at the ear-lobes, around the breasts and at the elbows; the face retained an admirable pallor. She was tall, slim and supple, as thoroughbred as a greyhound, with none of the British stiffness that, surrounding them with a nimbus of haughty grace, gives so much charm to the aristocratic women of that country. Hair of a mat solid gold helmed a petite head, but the prestige of the foreigner was in her eyes, large eyes of

---

1 As noted in the introduction, I can find no evidence of this story having been published prior to its appearance in *Fards et Poisons*, although it seems to have been designed for publication as an item of the sort he was contributing regularly to *Le Journal*. It is possible that Letellier, recognizing its relationship to "Victime," declined to use it.

green-tinted liquid enamel, which had caused all three of us to exclaim when she came in: "What terrible eyes!"

They were the eyes of dreams and portraits, those eyes of sky and sea that drink light and whose irises dilate, irradiated like wheels, invading the face, devouring it, so to speak, inhaling you and sucking the soul: hallucinating and hallucinated eyes, the violent and yet candid intensity of which is reminiscent of staring flowers. You know: those April cornflowers whose dew-pearled blue seems to be watching you from the slopes of embankments. In Normandy, children call them 'fay's eyes.' The woman who was dining a few tables away from us had those eyes.

> *Ardent eyes, distant and cold,*
> *Eyes of flesh and yes of souls*
> *With gleams as cutting as blades.*[1]

Steinberg was carried away.

"Hysterical eyes," Mornard concluded.

We protested,

"Hysterical! I maintain the word; I've known a few in my career as a physician, and they all had those eyes. I wouldn't want to be the husband of that pretty woman."

"Of that ideal creature! What! You suspect her of ardors?"

"I'm not supposing anything. In any case, nothing is less justified than the fiery temperament attributed to hysterics; there are very cold hysterics, even chaste ones; convents of women are full of them, and that might be the case with our diner this evening, but I feel no less sorry for her husband, and, delightful as that creature might be, I don't envy his happiness at all . . ."

"Why?"

"Because I have a horror of lying, and deception is the atmosphere and *raison d'être* of that woman. I've already been

---

1 Apparently original. Lorrain had published several previous stories making much of strange and fascinating eyes prior to "Victime," and this is not the only one in the present collection.

observing her for ten minutes; I'm convinced. She doesn't give the impression of suspecting our presence, but nothing seems to exist for that distant and inaccessible person; she is only preoccupied with us. She has seen the impression she has produced quite clearly; she isn't looking at us, and yet she isn't taking her eyes off us. Preoccupied with us, did I say? What an error: she's only preoccupied with herself, with the curiosity she awakens in this hall. Observe her: she only has one idea, to light up gazes and desires and concentrate them all on her.

"It's that exasperation of the personality that is the basis of neurosis—whence comes in afflicted individuals the need to interest others in their fate by means of dramas and chimerical adventures, to move others to pity or terrify them with the story of a past imagined by them, a mania for lies and inventions, an unhealthy need to compose and create stories wholesale and then export them, embellished and surcharged with such a variety of details that the patient ends up believing them herself—and that's the very character of hysteria, that thirst for strong emotions and extraordinary adventures, always lived in imagination, which the invalid strives to impose on the credulity of others.

"Hysteria is avid, above all, to share its folly and contaminate others with it. That need for dramas and intrigues in existence, that morbid appetency for the implausible and the extravagant, I've always observed in these invalids, for I did three years of medicine in Charcot's service, and then I was attached as an intern to the Laennec hospital, in the service of Bauchard,[1] the famous gynecologist, and God knows how many of the maladies that are treated there develop hysteria in women! How many fanciful tales I was obliged to endure, and sometimes marvelous fabulations that might make the fortune of a Ponson de Terrail or a Jules Mary. To hear them, all those unfortunate women had the pasts of heroines of the assize court, historical dramas or feuilleton novels."

Mornard put his elbows on the table, familiarly.

---

1 The Hôpital Laennec is real, but Bauchard is fictitious.

"Among all those neurotics, one interested me in particular; her case was rather rare. She was the daughter of a botanist at the Jardin des Plantes, an exalted and charming creature who had deserted the parental dwelling in order to go and live with a teacher at the Lycée Janson de Sailly. She had a diaphanous pallor, almost transparent, by virtue of thinness, could have played a pure spirit in one of Allan Kardec's séances, so otherworldly was her silhouette. Her musical voice, the heavy and fluid silk of her magnificent hair, and its pale gold hue, made her a sort of dream princess, but the stigmata were within her: the mobile mouth, incessantly bitten by the tips of the teeth, a disquieting red mouth, and, beneath the straight eyebrows, the violent and blue water of terrible eyes.

"She was at Laennec for a fibrous tumor on which Bauchard operated three days after her arrival. The operation succeeded marvelously, but the after-effects were long-drawn-out and the invalid remained with us for nearly three months. We nicknamed her Ligeia, she had such a supernatural and Poesque appearance.

"Strangely enough, that creature of dolor and the beyond, who had appeared to us as a soul, the day after her operation, still bloody and bound with bandages, made coquetries to the interns. There were sidelong glances under the long eyelids, the friction of hands lingering in ours, attitudes and effects of her hair. We would have been stirred by less.

"After a month, the Nélaton ward was in revolution; Ligeia had excited the pity of the Sisters by the tales of her misfortune and the spectacle of her resignation. It was to escape the pursuits of her father, a monstrous father smitten with her, that she had thrown herself into the teacher's arms. At the college, where she had sometimes gone to ask for her lover, she had been the object of the obsessions of professors and pupils; life for her had been very hard, and once, in the deputy head's study . . .

"The poor Sisters listened, terrified, to that disconcerting odyssey, but the patient reassured them quickly by the fervor of her prayers. She also edified them by the piety of her reading; the *Lives of the Saints* and the *Imitation* were permanently by her bedside. I even think that Ligeia, toward the end of her convalescence, had a few crises of ecstasy. The entire hospital, and Bauchard, were interested in that young woman, so pale and transparent, whose eyes fluttered, and revulsed so easily, while her frail body extended in the arc of a circle.

"The novel *Là-Bas*, which had just been published, put an aura of equivocal prestige around the actions of gestures of the patient; interns fond of literature—and I was one of that number—thought they saw in her a sort of Madame Chantelouve—Huysmans' terrible heroine.

"Before addressing herself to surgery, the patient had had recourse to occultism. Ligeia had been exorcized—at least, she said so. A defrocked canon, a thaumaturge well-known to the police for the illegal practice of medicine, had attempted to cure her by means of the application of precious stones; the applications were preceded and accompanied by prayers, ceremonies and affectations vaguely recalling the rites of the Black Mass. That therapy had only exasperated the patient's suffering. It was then that, desperately, she had come to address herself to Bauchard. Now she was returning to health, slowly but surely, in his care; but the stories whispered at the bedside and spread from ward to ward had created a legend around the convalescent. For some she was a saint, for others she was possessed; and when Ligeia quit the hospital, abominated by all the other patients and regretted by all the service, it was a personality, perhaps encumbering, but very curious, that Laennec lost.

"Scarcely had she returned home than the young woman repaid the cares of which she had been the object by telling the worst stories about the surgeons and the interns. She had been the object of the obsessions of all of them. Still bleeding, scarcely having begun to scar, there was not a single intern who had not solicited her, pressed her and harassed her, and Bauchard himself had not escaped the contagion of the endemic madness developed around her in the manner of a bewitchment.

"Ligeia recognized thus the kindnesses and the illicit favors that people had done for her; she slandered for the sake of slander, perhaps less culpable than another since it was unconscious, and she was surely convinced of her insinuations.

"Naturally, there was no truth in what she advanced. Memories of her reading had furnished her with the details of the intervention of the defrocked canon, the rest was pure imagination; the adventures of her childhood were also imagination, her father's abominable amour that had forced her to desert the family home, the exception made of her liaison with the teacher; imagination again, the obsessions of which she had been the object on the part of the personnel of the college; hallucinations, finally, the covetousness that she ignited everywhere she went—for, to hear her, her charm of lust extended over everyone, of both sexes. Even the women did not escape.

"It was Bauchard who furnished us with these details a month after the patient had left, his whole body shaken by laughter, in the operating theater. 'The most curious case of hysteria that I've ever seen, Messieurs, and yet God knows whether . . . she truly believes herself to be a witch, and that no one can resist the fluid emanating from her eyes. With that, all her desires become realities for her. Hallucinated, the hyperesthesia of her sensations gives her the carnal illusion of being truly possessed, but she experiences the desire instead of inspiring it.'

"If, on to that special state, you graft the love of lying, the mania for the romantic and the poison of literature, you can judge what abominations might emerge from that infernal cuisine, and yet, the malady of that unfortunate woman can be summarized in the unique formula: the Horror of the Simple."

The couple had just stood up. Preceded, this time by her husband, the woman passed close to us again; she passed by, sheathed in the somber and luminous scintillation of her dress embroidered with pearls and jet; a wave of perfume bathed us in passing, and in that atmosphere, for a second, all three of us felt stirred and moved, as if something had brushed our knees.

The Englishwoman had not looked at us, but we had shivered under the current of her liquid pupils, on watch beneath her long eyelids. She was now installed in the garden, and while her husband lit a cigar she fanned herself gently, with an abandoned and charming lassitude, her bosom offered, her nape and profile exposed. A waiter served coffee.

Mornard had not ceased to observe the woman.

"Disquieting resemblance . . . the more I look at her, the more I rediscover in her the beautiful Madame Holland. Madame Holland wasn't as tall, however, and didn't have that appearance of an English millionairess . . . nor did her hair have that splendid and solid golden color, and yet . . . and yet . . ."

"Madame Holland, yet another story," we said, impatient at his distraction—to which Mornard replied, pensively:

"Not another story, but the same story, or, if you wish, its sequel. I told you just now about Ligeia, the visionary patient of the Laennec hospital, the mistress of a petty schoolteacher. She quit the service and I lost track of her, but I was to rediscover her five years later, married and installed at Saint-Raphael, in the sunlit and picturesque amphitheater of the Chaine des Maures. Ligeia was known there as Madame Holland.

"I was taken to her home by a rich perfumer from Grasse. I was spending the winter there, attached as a private physician to a consumptive multimillionaire, whose vast fortune and the climate of Grasse didn't prevent from dying; he passed away there in April, as the almond trees were shedding their flowers. An enlightened art-lover and possessor of a few beautiful drawings by Fragonard, Ariste Sacoman—violets from Nice, carnations from Menton and tuberoses from Grasse—talked about nothing but that Holland, a prestigious potter newly installed in the region and discovered by him in Saint-Raphael.

"To hear him, that Belgian's metallic ceramics, as prismatic and iridescent as the skies of Provence and the sunsets over Estérel, were even more beautiful than those of Vallauris. Sacoman uttered endless eulogies regarding the work and talent of the husband, but he seemed even more enthusiastic about the wife. She was the Muse inspiring the fired stoneware and the translucent glazed clay that the winter visitors snatched for pots of gold. A match for the likes of Massier and Tiffany, Holland would not have been a peerless practitioner without the quasi-divine and tutelary presence of his young wife; Madame Holland was a saint, a soul. A creature of abnegation and devotion, it was from herself that she drew the mysterious power of evocation by which her husband's work was illuminated. It was her frail undulating silhouette of an elf of the meadows, her pliant grace of a nix of the Rhine that Holland modeled and caused to surge forth from the flanks of his vases, half-drowned in the precious and coruscating substance of his stoneware.

"Where did that perfumer find the epithets and images with which he enameled the tumult of his speech to describe the figurines and the metallic reflections of the potter of Saint-Raphael? They had 'tresses as heavy and tentacular as octopodes, bodies, bodies as long and flexible as kelp.' The substance of certain ceramics 'undulated like algae,' the golden sand of certain others was incrusted with beryls,' and there were 'all the nuances of nostalgic gems . . . the glittering venom of emeralds, the mourning-dress of mauve irises and the bloody pride of rubies.' And in all those flames and all those gems one rediscovered the hair and the eyes of Madame Holland.

"Stunned by the jargon, I allowed myself to be taken to Saint-Raphael; a telegram arrived too late to inform us that Monsieur Holland was in Nice. We found the young woman alone at the workshop. Imagine my amazement: Madame Holland was Ligeia, the possessed woman from the hospital! I found her even more charming; marriage was successful for her; her simplicity disconcerted me and her aplomb too, for she pretended not to recognize me.

"White and supple in an ash-gray dress devoid of any ornament, she welcomed us with a reserve and an absence of coquetry that was the very negation of her legend. She had become another woman; she was no longer Ligeia. Only her eyes remained the two cornflowers of intense light, simultaneously liquid and flower, that had enchanted the entire hospital, the eyes of tender candor about which Sacoman had been talking to me for a whole month. In that woman, however, what seized the soul and the senses much more abruptly was the timbre of her voice: a musical and grave voice to which I could not weary of listening in the arbor of Virginia jasmines where Madame Holland received the perfumer and me.

"There was the enveloping and luminously gray charm of Saint-Raphael in April. On the terrace where we were sitting, overlooking the mountain and the sea, heavy and heady pink stocks were aligned, and at the foot, fields of buttercups extended endlessly, laying out a primitive flower-garden between the bright summits and the blue of the gulf. Blossoming under the sun, the entire murmurous countryside entered the arbor with the pink flowers.

"Oh, that slumbering and humming landscape, all frissons of bees and vegetal exhalations, above the great fresh breath of the sea! A blue-tinted landscape, dotted in the foreground by flowers, of which the resinous odor of nearby pine-woods, warm and dominant, seemed to me to be the orchestrated perfume.

"And it seemed to me that I had always known those sunlit and vaporous peaks, that entire circle of mountains, already familiar, of which I had been ignorant the day before. Always! It is the same with landscapes as it is with faces; when they are truly beautiful, one already carries them within oneself; the surge of sympathies is only based on unconscious and very ancient memories. One recognizes a soul in the limpidity of the gaze, and in Madame Holland's eyes, and above all in the timbre of her voice, I had rediscovered a harmony already dreamed, a woman resembling her soul.

"I quit Saint-Raphael delighted with my visit; now I shared Sacoman's enthusiasm. I refrained carefully from disabusing my Provençal by revealing his idol's past to him; one does not enlighten a man in love, and the tales once circulated now appeared to me to be calumnies, the base vengeance of rejected lovers. Madame Holland's charm had operated. We returned to Grasse and made out eulogies mutually. We had not even seen the ceramics, we had only looked at the woman, we had forgotten the husband.

"I did not return to Sant-Raphael. Sacoman did not appear to want that, and I did not want to cause the worthy man chagrin. I did not see the Egeria of the Holland workshop again, but six months later, having encountered Sacoman in the Salon de la Nationale and asked him about the potter's beautiful wife, he cried with a comical alarm: 'Madame Holland! Oh, she certainly put one over on us, that one, and I passed through the Inquisition because of her, a woman who resembles an angel. Oh, the trouble I've had, but also those rascally eyes, lying and villainous and full of stories . . . and lying for the pleasure of lying! She had me quarrel with my best friends, and worse, nearly made me fight a duel. Didn't she tell my friend Bernède that I was his wife's lover? Madame Bernède, an honest mother who has four children—and he believed it, the imbecile! But fundamentally, what cunning! Hadn't she persuaded Madame Bernède that I was in love with her, and she told me that Madame Bernède looked at me with a kindly eye, and very gently, she pushed us into one another's arms. Was that Machiavellian enough? And all that for vengeance, because I'd refused to buy two fired ceramics for ten thousand francs.'

"'Five thousand for stoneware?'

"'Oh, he doesn't give his products for nothing, Monsieur Holland; it was Madame who hoisted the price. I'd already spat out three thousand for an aventurine plate and one little time in the pine grove.'

"'Ah! The plate was paid for in surplus—and Bernède also bought ceramics."

"'Bernède and all the rest. She maddened us all.'

"'And the husband?'

"'Holland? He went bankrupt, poor fellow.'

"'With a woman of that intelligence?'

"'And then he blew his brains out. Madame Holland had left him; she left on a yacht with an American from Cannes. The slut, eh—would you believe it? With such eyes!'

"'Yes, but we didn't look at her mouth enough'—and, glad to place my erudition—'remember the Arab proverb: Look at the eyes to know what it is, look at the mouth to know what it will become.' She had a very disquieting mouth, the beautiful Madame Holland, that red, supple mouth, continually bitten.'"

The Englishwoman and her husband had just stood up; they traversed the gallery and went up the monumental stairway that leads to the rooms.

Mornard could no longer hold still. He got up in his turn and we saw him go into the hotel office. He negotiated there for a good ten minutes and came back to us triumphant. Joy illuminated his emphatic and intelligent Basque face.

"It's her," he proclaimed, letting himself fall into a rocking-chair left vacant between us. "It's her, it's Madame Holland, I wasn't mistaken; it's Ligeia too, but how much more beautiful . . . I read the names in the hotel register: Mr. Arthur Humphrey and Miss Cecilia Nepherston."

"So what?" we protested.

"How can you not know the name of Arthur Humphrey, the famous thought-reader, the spiritualist magnetizer of Great Britain, the Donato of the far side of the Channel. Cecilia Nepherston is his subject, his Lucile. Ligeia was bound to finish thus; everything predestined her for that career as a seer. It's her latest avatar; I wasn't mistaken, I wasn't mistaken—one doesn't encounter such eyes twice—but she's taller, embellished: with an aura of astral light, an adept would say. I have spoken."

MONSIEUR SMITH[1]

"**Y**OU don't believe that it's a suicide, then?"

"No; I knew the dead woman too well. She was crazy, a neurotic, even more a victim of her milieu than the milieux from which she had descended, than the atavism that was evoked in her. She was the daughter of a Slav father and an Egyptian mother, but not all foreigners are consecrated to suicide. People have tried to make that poor Comtesse de Tremères a Baronne Maria Vetsera. The drama of Mayerling is in the air since Aderer's fine article.[2] To begin with, there's no Archduke Rodolphe in the death of the woman with whom we're concerned."

"And you don't admit a crisis of despair, a depression of the will leading the feeble creature that every amorous woman is to a final catastrophe? Oh, I know that you're a partisan of

---

1 First published in *Le Journal* in two parts, "M. Light" (1 January 1903) and "L'Araignée rouge" (5 January 1903)—i.e. directly after "Illyne Yls" and immediately before "Victime," thematically bridging the two. It will be remembered that the spectacular performance piece that Lorrain wrote for Liane de Pougy, staged at the Folies Bergère amid a blaze of publicity in 1895, was *L'Araignée d'or*, in which she played an arachnid fay. The pantomime in question is caricatured in Jane de La Vaudère's *roman à clef* stigmatizing Lorrain, *Les Androgynes* (1903; tr. as "The Androgynes"), which makes interesting reading in juxtaposition with the near-simultaneous *Fards et Poisons*.
2 The French journalist Adolphe Aderer (1855-1923) included in his book *Chez les rois* (1903) a fanciful hypothetical account of the apparent double suicide in 1889 of Archduke Rodolphe, the Crown Prince of Austria, and his mistress Maria Vetsera, at Mayerling. Lorrain is presumably referring to an excerpt published in advance of the book.

energy, obstinate in preaching the duty to live even before the right to die, but think: a woman's soul, the poor little brain of a sentimental milliner that they all have—fortunately, otherwise they'd be monsters. Remember that there was talk of a rupture, a lover who left her; large losses of money, bad operations on the Bourse, had spoiled everything. It needs no more to push a poor woman to suicide who has lost her footing and, perhaps also losing her head, feels herself falling into the gulf."

"Yes, I know the anthem, but what gives me reason to believe that it was an accident and not suicide is the very simplicity of the death: no flowers on the bed, no lit candles, no stage-setting. No flowers in the land of flowers, in Nice. If the little comtesse had wanted to end it all, she would never have resigned herself to quitting our veil of tears thus, without noise. All day long she's coming and going with her sister, as usual. The ladies are seen in the morning on the Promenade des Anglais; they have lunch at the Westminster hotel, invited by a friend; during the day they go to Monte Carlo, but the Comtesse de Tremères doesn't play, she only goes into the gaming rooms in the evening, when she has a sensational new dress to exhibit; they're seen taking tea at the Hôtel de Paris, returning to Nice by the six o'clock train. The ladies return to their boarding-house at seven and part in the hall, each going to her room . . . the time to dress for dinner . . . the Comtesse is late and when her sister, Baronne Smolenska, becoming impatient, goes to find her and goes into her room she finds her lying on the bed, with a chloroform-soaked pad under her nose, still warm . . . and dead.

"Well, that fashion of escaping life doesn't resemble Comtesse de Tremères at all. That death is the English exit of a very practical American miss or a young Frenchwoman brought up in a girls' school and edified regarding the superfluity of conventions and appearances. Comtesse de Tremères would have died on stage, beautifully, like an Ibsen heroine. She was complicated, the little comtesse. Alive, she cared too much about her entrances and exits to treat her friends so rudely. Oh, certainly, sufficiently unhinged to slide into suicide, but far too literary not to declaim stanzas from Sappho beforehand. Can you believe that she wouldn't have graced us with a single couplet?

"Besides which, all women who attempt their lives, escape death—I mean women of the world and the demi-monde; the burnishers who light stoves never fail. Apart from an income of twenty-five thousand francs, one has obligations to the gallery; one gets up again from a suicide as one gets up again from a bed; it's a pretext for pretty poses and luxurious peignoirs. Let's not forget that, in society, women learn how to die from the fifth acts of dramas, they all have the obsession, to some degree, of the consumptive languors of *La Dame aux Camélias*.

"In any case, Comtesse de Tremères was a fervent user of all anesthetics. I knew her when she was an etheromaniac; from ether she went on to morphine and cocaine as one passes from Annunzio to Tolstoy and from Dostoyevsky to Ibsen. We find her again at chloroform; chloroform has done her a bad turn.

"That, Messieurs, is why I don't believe that it was suicide."

Maxence and Pierre Steinberg had their elbows on the tablecloth, and, while drawing slow puffs from their cigarettes, stared attentively at Octave Vergy. The latter, sitting facing them on the other side of the table, appeared to them in the manner of a Carrière portrait, fuliginous and vague in the imprecision of his features, blurred by the tobacco fog of a smokers' dinner.

Slowly, Vergy poured himself a third glass of kummel.

"Did you know Comtesse de Tremères well?" asked Steinberg.

"Yes and no. I'd lost sight of her, but it was given to me to get close to her in particular circumstances. I even mingled in her life a little. Anyway, judge for yourselves. It was about ten years ago, before the *Sancho* had entirely disappeared from the boulevard. I was doing the exhibitions there, in the Champ-de-Mars and the Champs-Élysées, including the little chapels open in the vicinity. Nowadays I talk in the revues about the Uffizi in Florence, the Academia in Venice and the Prado in Madrid, but debuts are always difficult.

"So, the *Sancho* was employing my talents then. I had just described, or, rather, verbalized, the Salon de la Rose-Croix, a mystical, erotic, catholic and also esthetic exhibition opened under the auspices of the Sâr, the Sâr and Magus Péladan, the one and only.[1] It was situated, I believe in the Rue de la Paix, among drapes of peacock-blue plush, much more favorable, believe me, than the paintings. What was seen there was rather bad, but the intentions were excellent. I've retained a few of the names. Schwabe was rife there, alongside Armand Point; Marcius-Simons, graduated like a stained-glass window, fulgurated there alongside Séon; Séon caused Séailles to pale there, and the fantastic recklessness of compositions was only equaled by the alarming excess of the titles.

"Visiting those phantasms of art was aggravated by religious music and the accompaniment of invisible organs; odors of incense floated in the rooms, footfalls were muffled by thick carpets, and at the back of the last room, the portrait of the Sâr in a black velvet doublet, like Hamlet, glowed like an apparition under the jets of three reflectors, draped in red velvet and framed in green gold. It was puerile, comical and charming.

"I consecrated to that Rose-Croix the ironic and emotional article that it merited; I harvested a good number of insulting letters, a few enthusiastic letters and a duel. On the very morning of my encounter, as I was climbing into a carriage to go to the terrain, I picked up a rather strange letter in my correspondence, still regarding my ill-fated article on the Rose-Croix. The signatory rendered homage to my critique, which he approved

---

1 Joséphin Péladan's Salon de la Rose+Croix was held from 1892-97. Among the artists who exhibited there was Edgar Maxence, cited in the prologue, and other Symbolist artists were extremely prominent there, including those cited: Carlos Schwabe (1866-1926), Armand Point (1860-1932), Pinckney Marcius-Simons (1867-1909) and Alexandre Séon (1855-1917); Gabriel Séailles (1852-1922) was a critic. It is perhaps surprising that Lorrain does not mention that one of his favorites, Jan Toorop, was also featured, along with fellow Belgians Fernand Khnopff and Jean Delville. Gustave Moreau and Odilon Redon, by contrast, disapproved of Péladan, and did not contribute.

point by point, appealing to my artistic competence to flay the injustice and partiality of the Sâr. The Sâr had dared to refuse his submissions. The sacrificed modeler invited me to come and see his works in his studio at number eight, Rue de Caulaincourt, and declared that he would be very happy if I would accept the dedication; the artist knew in advance that I would admire his craftsmanship and composition. He was in haste to enable me to admire his *Araignée en pleurs* and his *Marguerite des Mauvais Vallons—sic*. The artist's name was Smith.

I replied to Monsieur Smith that I was just about to fight a duel over the article that enthused him so much. If I came back safe and sound, I would certainly come to see his *Araignée* and his *Vallons*.

I came back from the pond at Villebon with a sword-thrust in the groin that kept me in bed for three months. During the three months that my convalescence lasted, Monsieur Smith sought conscientiously to obtain news of me. Twice a week, *petit bleus* addressed to my mother enquired very tenderly about my condition, and when the newspapers announced my return to health, Monsieur Smith, in a pressing letter, solicited the honor and the favor of coming to see me in my domicile.

I was better, but still restricted to a complete immobility. I was far from the moment of going out, even in a vehicle, and my days were dragged out, monotonous and slow, on a chaise longue, where I yawned recklessly, bandaged and bound as in the aftermath of surgical operation, with only my upper body and arms free.

I wrote inviting Monsieur Smith to come.

I regretted it almost immediately, for in response to my invitation I received a letter in which Monsieur Smith declared that he was not Monsieur Smith but Comtesse Nadia de Tremères, a German Pole, Slavic by birth, the divorced wife of the Comte de Tremères, young, pretty, desirable, very fond of literature and art, a sculptor herself, a fan of my talent and well-known in the most various esthetic milieux. Sâr Péladan called her his little mystic urchin; she had posed for archangels and ephebes in Séon's studio. I would adore the absence of her hips and breasts; she was entirely my plastic ideal and 'something akin to a black philter swam in her green eyes!'[1] A madwoman! I was dealing with a madwoman! All it needed was the irruption of that Péladanite into my convalescence.

"I wanted to cancel the invitation, but curiosity held me back. I was so bored! In brief, on the appointed day of the rendezvous, I did not forbid my door, and at half past five, Comtesse de Tremères made her entrance into the half-light of my study, lit by two lamps.

"Nothing was more delightfully pretty than Joséphin Péladan's 'little mystic urchin,' nor anything more artificial and willful. Between the gold of violently dyed hair and the redness of lips brutally emphasized by lipstick, were eyes molded by kohl, nostrils touched up with pink, earlobes gently carmined, cheeks nacred with veloutine: the most fabricated and most delicate enameled figurine of gold, coral and jade that ever emerged from the hands of a jewel of Chrysopolis. Artificial! How adorably artificial she was! Thin, spare, molded in a long green velvet dress scintillating with blue-tinted jet, with gestures of a studied languor and hieratic attitudes studied at length in museums; she was simultaneously a Dampt *Mélusine*,[2] an Alexandrian Tanagra, an androgynous Muse of the Théâtre de l'Oeuvre and a Willy *Maîtresse d'esthètes*.[3] With all that, an alarming transparency of complexion and strange liquid green eyes: the only true thing in her entire person, the liquid green of her eyes illuminated by the false gold of her hair!

---

1 The supposed quotation is not specific, but the imagery is all drawn from Baudelaire's *Les Fleurs du mal*.
2 The Sculptor Jean Dampt (1854-1945) produced a group in steel, ivory and gold entitled *Le Chevalier Raymondin et La Fée Mélusine* in 1894, which was greatly admired, by Joséphin Péladan among others.
3 *Maîtresse d'esthètes*, signed "Willy" but written by Jean de Tinan, was published in 1897.

"Word of honor, in the solitude of my barely-lit study, I was slightly scared of her. Monsieur Smith was colorless and spectral.

"Comtesse de Tremères was tender, compassionate with regard to my health, anxious and quivering on the subject of my wound. Then she told me her story. Monsieur de Tremères was a wretch, naturally. He had deceived and ruined her; she had divorced him in time to save an income of thirty thousand francs. She lived with her sister, Baronne Smolenska; her misfortunes had rendered her Polish again. She only lived for art now—and her green eyes scintillated strangely in the shadow—she loved my nature, my way of seeing and saying things, the bravery of my opinions and the independence of my criticism.

"Finally, she came to sit down on one of the arms of the chaise longue, where I was listening, hypnotized, spoke to me with an ardent voice, leaned over me, and suddenly, passing her arm around my neck, planted her lips on mine.

"I was so nonplussed that I did not make a movement. In any case, my bandages paralyzed me. Monsieur Smith prolonged her kiss.

"Comtesse Nadia reeked of ether, opoponax and fever.

"The arrival of my surgeon delivered me; he came in like a gust of wind and the visitor got up. Having come to the neighborhood for another patient he had come up in passing. Comtesse de Tremères and he were acquainted. After a rapid handshake and an exchange of a few words, the young woman withdrew, saying: 'You'll permit me to come again, won't you?' And her undulating silhouette disappeared, in a wake of perfumes.

"'You know Monsieur Smith?' said Doctor Haimien. 'You didn't say anything to me, secretive as you are. Beware, fortunate man—she's a dangerous woman, especially for a convalescent with a wound in the groin. As a friend, I'm warning you, but as a surgeon I forbid you her visits completely until further notice. I don't intend her to demolish my invalid; you're recovering too well.'

"I told him the truth about the Comtesse's letters, her visit and the final incident. 'And you know her, Doctor?'

"'Certainly, I know her! She's one of my clients; I've operated on her.' And, after a hesitation: 'Yes, I took them out . . . she no longer has them. But that doesn't prevent anything; on the contrary—nature abhors a void. I warn you, my dear Vergy, she's a terrible woman. She knocks a man down like a ninepin. She might look thin and delicate, hardly able to stand up, but she's rabid; oh, she's insatiable. She's already demolished clients of mine! That doesn't distress you, at least, what I'm telling you, my dear? They don't call her the Red Spider for nothing. Perhaps I'm trampling on your flower-bed somewhat by telling you all that!'

"'Me? Not at all. She scares me slightly, the beautiful Comtesse—and then, that odor of ether and fever!'

"'An etheromaniac, of course. And tenebrous with it.'

"'No?'

"'Or bound to become one. So, it's understood: you'll close your door to her. Now, let's have a look at your wound.'

"The next day, I informed the Comtesse de Tremères by means of a *petit bleu* that I could not be disturbed. The emotion of her visit had given me a fever, and I could not receive anyone at all until further notice; I would notify her as soon as I was better. The better in question never came, of course, and from tender, Monsieur Smith's letters became insulting. For two months I was harassed by her vehemence and her threats. I had passed up happiness; I was a wretch, and sooner or later I would know that one did not insult a woman of her character with impunity. Doctor Haimien was also pursued by fulminating letters; then, one day, the correspondence ceased and the next Salon informed us that Comtesse Nadia was the mistress of Jacques White.[1] The English painter exhibited a sensational

---

1 I have left this name as the text renders it, on the assumption that it probably does not refer to the actual Scottish painter John White (1851-1933), or to the American John White Alexander (1856-1915), a regular exhibitor at the annual Paris salon after 1893.

portrait of her. You've all seen it, anyway, that portrait, as you've seen the others. Every year, Monsieur Smith changes painter and lover; Monsieur Smith has the folly of the palette."

"And the brush."

"No wordplay. Be sure that this year's—for there must be one—will have a great success with his painting. The portrait of a suicide. What an advertisement, and what a scandal for an exhibition!

"Alas, it's necessary to live."

✳

"There's a portrait of her; I told you so. We can admire it next fifteenth of April at the Salon of the former Champ de Mars, unless you prefer to come and see it at the painter's residence. I've just come from his studio—it's Reynaldo Forlinari. The worthy fellow has put on mourning, but he's sweating joy from every pore. Just think—success is within his grasp, the portrait of the suicide, a woman whose death and adventure filled the press for four days running. What an advertisement, what a scandal!

"The worthy Italian rolled his big moist eyes, saying to me: '*Quanta bella, quanta amabile, quanta simpatica*; the day of her death was the saddest of my life,' but I read in his tear-varnished eyes: 'the best day of my life.' Anyway, as he showed me out, moved by my eulogies, he had a fine tone of sincerity. 'This portrait, Monsieur Vergy, I shall send to Milan, Livorno, Florence and even Rome, if necessary. I want my whole country to know the image of my dear Contessina. I shall also send it, if necessary, to Germany . . . yes, I shall send it to Munich and Vienna, *povera piccolina*; I want *ma dolore et ma picture* to fill the world with her memory.'"

"The tourney of portraits, what."

"It's the year of heritages, a wind of fortune is blowing for artists. Our Reynaldo has lost his lover and inherited glory."

And Vergy concluded, silently: *it's necessary to live.*

Our dear ironist had just sat down at the table in the club and we were gambling insolently on a game of écarté at a hundred sous a hand; it was five o'clock and the footmen had just brought candles hooded with little lampshades, the reflection of which reanimated the exhausted pallor of the players.

"Is it good, the portrait?" asked Steinberg, marking the king.

To which Vergy replied: "It's very Italian, and modern Italian, but that has a certain piquancy. All trickery, naturally, over-refined in places, finished with minute care, almost in miniature, alongside sections executed with a truly extraordinary fury, brush-strokes like strokes of a whip, paint lashed and lashing, which gives a singular life to the fabrics. The white satin dress in treated in that fashion."

"Bellowing Boldini; I can see it from here."

"No, its better than that, but the face is too contrived, the flesh is enameled."

"Like the model."

"Poor little Comtesse!"

"Yes, *povera contessina*, as Reynaldo put it so well—but the color sings, and the hieratic attitude is certainly hers."

"It is?"

"That of a sphinx, naturally, a fatal androgyne, a blood-drinking and marrow-sucking ghoul. Forlinari has painted her standing, as if petrified in the white satin of her dress, a white stain that shines and breaks, and which, striped by great gray shadows, makes her even taller and even thinner: an unreal and spectral Comtesse de Tremères, whom one might believe naked under the fabric, whose uncovered shoulders are almost those of a cadaver, so livid are they; but the green of her wide, anxious eyes, is that of a cat's eyes, the red of her lips is that of a wound, and the ardent russet of the hair, dotted here and there with emeralds—matching the eyes, the emeralds—makes one think of a blonde Salome. Anyway, it's anything you wish, that portrait, except a woman of today. It's Circe, Cleopatra or Semiramis, a creature of perdition, the accursed *phâme*,[1] the sorceress of painters of the soul and etho-poetic Mages."

"The bodice has no sleeves?"

"Need you ask? Simple stone shoulder-clasps."

"And no other jewelry than the emeralds in her hair?"

"Have you seen it, then, the portrait?"

"No, but I know the dress. It was last winter's combat costume. I encountered her in two or three salons in that outfit; she attracted a pack. And one thing that proves to me that she died by accident and that there was no hint of suicide is that the poor creature died in a dressing-gown, a poor pink flannel peignoir from a Printemps store. Surely she would have put on the beautiful white satin dress with the stone epaulettes, and wouldn't have forgotten to strew the emeralds in her hair if she had wanted to kill herself. She wouldn't have failed to give that fine publicity to her portrait and her painter. The *contessina* lived for the gallery, above all, and would have planned her apotheosis carefully. That portrait is the very proof of the accident. Comtesse de Tremères must have miscalculated the dose of chloroform. Chloroform doesn't madden like ether or morphine. It's necessary to go and see it, then, this portrait?"

"Yes, all the more so as Forlinari has every audacity and every unconsciousness. He's made the portrait symbolic."

"Oh, symbolism is your school! And how has he symbolized the Comtesse?"

"Oh, trivially. He's simply placed an enormous red spider in the pleats of her dress."

---

1 This word crops up occasionally in late nineteenth-century French re-portage, and was presumably familiar then, but it is no easier to deduce its precise meaning from other contexts than it is here. It might come from the Greek *pheme* [fame, or rumor] rendered into Latin as fama and applied to a goddess bearing disguised messages from the gods, but the old French *fame* was an early spelling of *femme* [woman], so it might be a fancy synonym for *femme fatale*.

"No!"

"As I tell you. A species of monstrous crab, bloody and sticky. It gives the impression of following her and simultaneously participating in her life; it's hallucinatory. It's the atmosphere of the compositions of Jean Veber,[1] that red spider in the train of that ball gown. It's the green gnome of Mélusine and the knock-kneed dwarf of the princesses of tales, *La Dame à l'araignée rouge*! Remember that that was the Comtesse de Tremères' nickname in certain studio milieux. Forlinari couldn't be unaware of that, since it was his friend who . . ."

"What friend?"

"Yes, I'm becoming confused; it's a whole other story. I'd rather recount it to you.

"It's Haimien, the surgeon who cared for you, Maxence, who took me to Forlinari's studio. He was curious about the portrait, firstly because he knew the Comtesse, on whom he'd operated, as you know, and secondly because the Chevalier Minuti, the famous fencer who died last year, and whom he had treated, also died somewhat because of the Comtesse."

"How?"

"Yes, Minuti was the lover of the Spider Lady before Forlinari. Forlinari was his friend, and inherited Comtesse de Tremères after his death."

"A fine inheritance!"

"All the more so as the lady is rather dangerous. Minuti only received his famous sword thrust at the assault on the Grand Hotel because he was extenuated by the pretty creature. *Lassata, sed non, satiata.*[2] In the times of the Roman decadence that little woman would have flattened three gladiators a night. In brief, it was at the death-bed of his compatriot and friend Minuti that Forlinari met Madame de Tremères. It was at that same bedside

---

1 Jean Veber (1864-1928) began his career as a caricaturist and that reputation stuck, but as a painter in oils he was a Symbolist.
2 "Exhausted, but unsatisfied"—an oft-quoted phrase used by Juvenal in his fanciful character-assassination of Messalina.

that he heard her baptized with the name of the Red Spider in a fit of the dying man's delirium—which didn't prevent him, on the return from the cemetery, from becoming the lady's lover."

"Wait a minute—I can't make head nor tail of your story."

"Yes, I know, it's a little complicated, formed like an aggravated Italian intrigue in the modern style."

"Minuti, Forlinari, the Comtesse de Tremères, alias the Red Spider—that's Gaboriau retouched by Annunzio: Florence and Montmartre."

"No, it's simply one of Doctor Haimien's stories. I'll tell it to you as he told it to me; that's much simpler.

"Last March, Haimien was summoned to a consultation with Minuti, the Milanese champion. During the famous assault at the Grand Hotel between the Italian masters and the French masters, Minuti had received a nasty thrust of a foil from the celebrated Sérignac. The foil had broken and the blade had penetrated his right side. The case of the Italian fencer was grave; the lung had been perforated and the wound was triangular.

"Haimien found the Comtesse de Tremères installed at the wounded man's bedside, lavishing upon him the cares of a lover or a sister. Madame de Tremères was Minuti's mistress and made no mystery about it; she was at home in the Italian's apartment and spent the nights there.

"Haimien had operated on the Comtesse three years before and was only partly astonished by her presence in the home of the fencing master. He even admired the effrontery of the woman, still in society, who quit the maternal domicile so willingly in view of the danger to her lover, and, scornful of gossip, came to play nurse at his bedside. There was a bravado in that and a challenge to ordinary hypocrisy that pleased Haimien. Nevertheless, the wounded man, although surrounded by all cares and who seemed to be on the way to recovery in the early days, did not recover. His condition even appeared to deteriorate; he lost weight and fever soon no longer quit him. With his cheeks on fire and his eyes hollow, after crises of a disquieting excitement, he fell into long prostrations and strange torpors. The surgeon was alarmed, for there was fear of phthisis.

"Comtesse de Tremères, still faithful to her role as nurse, showed an untiring devotion.

"One day, Haimien, who had come to visit during one of the young woman's rare absences, talked to his patient in private and thought he ought to lift his morale. 'It's not good sense to agitate thus. You'll never be cured with this nervous overexcitement; you're nurturing your own illness. It's necessary to aid one's physician—and yet, if anyone is in good conditions for a cure it's you, my dear Minuti. You're young, endowed with a marvelous muscular strength, sound, and cared for by the most tender, the most attentive and the most faithful friend . . .'

"To which the wounded man suddenly propped himself up, with a strange smile. 'The Comtesse! Oh, you judge her well, but it's her who is killing me and preventing my cure. She's a ghoul, rabid, a man-eater. Scarcely have you departed that she throws herself upon me, sick as I am, and demands my caresses. You think that my wound and my condition should stop her? On the contrary, one would think that she's taken it upon herself to exhaust my weakness. Yes, by the Madonna, one might think that she's thirsty for my blood, she's *una creatura di perdicione*, Doctor. I've never known such ardor, and yet . . .' And with eyes dazed by fear and a feverish tremor shaking his entire body, Minuti entered into the path of confessions.

"It was the Comtesse de Tremères who had killed him. In the unfortunate assault at the Grand Hotel, if he had defended himself so poorly, and a bad parry had broken the foil that had perforated his lung, it was because he was extenuated by that terrible woman. Emptied of strength by a three-month liaison, which he wouldn't wish on his worst enemy, his legs buckled and he could do no more. Sérignac's thrust he owed to that human leech, that vampire with the head of a Byzantine virgin, installed in his life for three months, who was pumping out all his blood. Oh, that was because she had a particular science of amour, that culpable comtesse, and he could no longer do without the taste of her skin or the savor of her kisses. He was bewitched, ensorcelled, as if by a philter, *una vera strega*[1]—and the language of his childhood came back to him with the natal superstitions!

"Haimien listened with amazement to that disturbing confession. 'And I've done everything to break it off, Monsieur le docteur. When I sensed that I was losing my footing, that I was drowning with that woman, I told her that it was all over. With death in the heart and a frenzy of kisses on the lips, I threw her out and I forbade the concierge to let her come up. She came to wait for me in the street, she followed me without addressing a word to me, like a good dog, and also like a witch; I felt her eyes boring into my back—and then, I had forgotten one thing; at one time, I had given her a key to my apartment, and one night, when I came in, I found her nestled in my bed. And then it began; she had such a genteel fashion of passing her pretty arm around my neck. It recommenced, and Sérignac skewered me like *uno vero pollo . . .*[2]

"'And then I was bought here, and she cared for me very well, the *contessina*. Oh, it couldn't have been better; she's so attentive, so amiable and so pretty; but as soon as I could move a little, she passed her arm round my neck, and when I felt her skin against mine and the silk of her hair against my cheek, then I no longer knew what I was doing, Doctor! And as she likes caresses—and me too, alas—I'll never be cured; she's a demon, that woman, and I can't hold it against her; she loves me, it's for amour. I can't do without her—impossible. What do you expect? It's destiny; I'll die of it.'

"Haimien took it upon himself to reprimand the Comtesse. Madame de Tremères opened her liquid green eyes wide, and listened to the surgeon speak with amazement. Minuti had said

---

1 "A true witch."
2 "A true chicken."

90

that? But it was delirium! His fever had increased, then! Minuti had accused her—her!—when it was him, the unfortunate maniac who solicited her and obsessed her day and night. There was no hour when he didn't require amour, and as soon as they were alone . . . feeble as he was, she often had to struggle against him. She suffered enough from the erotomania that the fever that had developed in him; she avoided approaching the bed and took a thousand precautions to limit him to it . . . and it was her that was suspected! And the emerald of her eyes was obscured by tears.

"Haimien sensed that he had offended her, and, as he still hesitated, Madame de Tremères, with an adorable gesture of modesty, took Reynaldo Forlinari as her witness. He could speak, the man who had helped her to care for poor Minuti . . .

"Haimien withdrew, making his apologies. Minuti had deceived him. However, on the eve of his death, Haimien had to yield to the evidence. During the frightful death-throes of the fencing master, which lasted two nights and a day, he never ceased to abuse Madame de Tremères, and with his fist extended toward her, half-emerged from the sheets, where Fortinari and the nurse retained him, he wouldn't consent to lie down again until the wretched woman had finally gone. 'The Red Spider do you see it? The hideous beast lurking under her skirts, over there, under the armchair? That's what has pumped my brain, emptied my bones and drunk the marrow. Oh, its viscous and hairy tentacles, it's my blood that makes it so red. How it stares at me! Oh, the monster. Oh, put out its eyes. It's going to leap upon me and bite my neck; it's lying in wait for me, waiting to kill me when you've gone. Don't leave me! Don't leave me! Chase her away. The monster will go with her. Can't you see that it's her soul, that it has her splendid green eyes?'

"And he choked in a gasp.

"They made Madame de Tremères leave.

"A nightmarish agony, which, you see, inspired the model and the painter!

"Is it edifying enough, that portrait of the little comtesse baptized with the same name with which her other lover insulted her? Quite convincing, the detail of that red spider posed in the pleats of her dress? Does it resemble sufficiently a little woman disequilibrated by haunting a Péladan and dying of an error of dosage of chloroform or ether?

"Mysticism and affectation! I contend, personally, that the Comtesse didn't commit suicide; she would have done that quite differently."

SOCIETY

For Henri de Régnier.[1]

<hr>

[1] Henri de Régnier (1864-1936) was one of the most prolific Symbolist poets and prose writers of the 1890s, but the Symbolist element in his work became far less flamboyant over time.

A SALON IN DANGER[1]

"DECIDEDLY, there are only cosmopolitans. Just look at this salon.

"The mistress of the house is Hungarian, the husband is Russian, the lover Italian. The cousins, flowers of Austria, are flirting with England, America and Spain. Only the two of us are French. Pardon me, there's also old Colonel Bridge, but he's so stupid that he compromises the nation.

"That beautiful blonde with the eagle eyes is from Venice; that pretty brunette with the mobile and supple body is from Budapest; her flirt, the pure-bred Andalusian type with the eyes of a gazelle, is Brazilian. People are cooing and wooing here in all the idioms of Europe and the two worlds, and yet the tone is sovereignly Parisian. All the women here are young, pretty and elegant, and only walk around in a silky rustle of fabrics for the sake of the desire to please and to be even prettier; the amiable, nickel-plated, varnished men, all with the air of grand seigneurs, only appear to be preoccupied with seducing the women. What do all these people live on? A mystery. No one ever talks about money. Amour seems to be the sole concern of this society of luxury and pleasure.

---

1 First published in *Gil Blas* in three parts: "La Riviera: Un Salon en danger (14 February 1903), "La Riviera: Une Cour d'amour" (21 February 1903) and "La Riviera: Quelques nobles dames" (5 March 1903). It was the first of two brief story series that Lorrain published in *Gil Blas* in the immediate aftermath of the libel suit, possibly in order to help with his legal expenses, although he continued making regular contributions to *Le Journal*.

"There's a hothouse atmosphere, a heady intoxication of tropical plants in a chirping of birds of paradise; the drapes in the splendid and fresh rooms are a caress for the eyes, the hair and shoulders of these women; the excessively new works of art, symbolically fragile, in profusion of green plants, have the temporary aspect of a hotel room, but that ephemeral luxury fits in very well with the excessively benign sky and the magical vegetation of the Riviera. It's a theatrical figuration in an *ad hoc* décor; one always expects the whistle of the stage-manager, and to see the friezes, the supports and the backcloth rise up; but the consciousness that all this is only temporary augments its charm strangely; it's their brevity that makes the splendor of apotheoses. At length, even their splendor becomes fatigued.

"It's the same with this society; it's only pleasurable because one is passing through—what am I saying?—because one is among migratory birds here."

"A flock of tall cranes," sniggered Bergues.

"Oh, no boulevard wit here; you'll decompose the atmosphere. These women are young, bold, welcoming and brilliant; what more can you ask of them? Where do they come from? What imprudence! Where are they going? What sadness. *Carpe diem*; let's seize the moment and pluck these women like the flowers they are, ephemeral and intoxicating, and let's find in the mystery of their existence and their luxury—the luxury that we suspect to be condemned—one excitement more to enjoy. Remember, my dear Bergues, that the thought of death has always doubled pleasure, and true lovers are only ardent in cemeteries. Great sensual pleasures are sad."

"What are you two plotting in this corner? I'm sure that you're speaking ill of us."

That was the cheerful voice, a trifle hoarse and drawling, of the mistress of the house. Baronne de Méplonoff had just insinuated the nacreous charm of her shoulders between our two frock-coats.

"Speak ill of you! What do you mean by that, Baronne?"

96

"Yes, of us, the rest of us, the cosmopolitans—you're a little scornful of us, you Frenchmen; you've remained very Latin; you're like the Chevalier de Tigra, my incorrigible friend. For him, as for you, foreigners are always barbarians."

"You're right, Baronne, and you have the science of propriety—oh, you can boast of having the gift of divination!" exclaimed my friend Bergues. "My friend and I were just making the vindication of your salon."

"Of my salon?" The young woman did not quite repress a movement of joy. "Only my salon?"

"Of salons of the foreign colony in general and yours in particular. Where can one find prettier women?"

"I'm not here for nothing," cooed the Hungarian, and drawing us both to a pouf in the falling shadow of a clump of lataniers. "Oh, you were saying nice things about us? I'm curious to hear the couplet. Would you like to give me an audition, and consent to repeat it for me?"

And, stopping the couples passing by with the tip of her fan: "A moment, please, Comte! A minute, Princesse! Deign to pause, Marquis. Duc, you listen too. Highness"—for they were all titled, as is fitting on the Riviera, where the passage through the Var ennobles—"stop a moment, for the curiosity of the fact, stop a moment. Monsieur Jacques Duthil is going to speak well of us. Yes, this Monsieur who doesn't speak ill of anyone has finally decided to eulogize!"

"As well say lie," sniggered Bergues.

A tap of the fan whipped his fingers, but the Baronne had attained her objective. A whole audience of frock-coats and bright dresses had gathered around us. It was terrible: Madame de Méplonoff had improvised a lecturer of me.

I got out of it very poorly. I do not have the gift of preparing effects, and then again, all those ignited curiosities, all those eyes aimed at mine, all those nervous women expecting a prodigy, along with, masked by good will as it was, the malevolent attention of males, always hostile to the success of one of their own, paralyzed me. I fished up, with great difficulty, a few phrases of my conversation, but my memory failed me, I lacked aplomb. In brief, I was pitiful. Bergues looked at me, astonished.

"Decidedly, you lack conviction, my dear," concluded Princesse Adriani.

"What one conceives well can be expressed clearly," sniggered Baron Poukine, mangling Boileau.

Bergues came to my aid. "I assure you that he was quite brilliant just now; I don't understand it myself."

"First night nerves, no doubt," fluted the shrill soprano of Comtesse Sylvane.

"*Bis repetita non placent*,"[1] remarked Princesse Adriani, impertinently.

And the Hungarian, a little chagrined, ended the session, but added, by way of consolation: "Improvisory natures are the most generous."

My attempted lecture was a disaster.

Marquise Smotti, always compassionate, sat down next to me—the Marquise has always been kind to me—and men complimented me. I could no longer doubt that I had been detestable. The other women, with the unconscious cruelty of their sex, had turned their backs on me; it was a complete defection. Baronne de Méplonoff had given the signal for that herself. Bergues saved me. I had remained collapsed on the divan, vanquished; in the blink of an eye he stood me up, pushed me in front of him in the direction of the mistress of the house, and, with an inclination of the upper body, said: "We're taking our leave of you, Baronne, never to return."

"What are you saying?"

"As soon as your salon is literary, Monsieur Duthil and I no longer have any reason to frequent it."

"Literary? I don't understand."

"You've just made Monsieur declaim. It's the end for your house. You're going to be invaded by old women; your salon

---

1 "That which is repeated does not please." The quote is from Horace.

was the only one where one encountered young ones. Yesterday, it was still the only place where poetry was made without being spoken, since the napes here were fresh and the gazes brilliant; but we ended up laughing. There's a crack in your wall, Baronne; intellectuality has penetrated your home."

"You're mad, Bergues."

"No, that's the way it is. You're going to be besieged by requests; the entire Riviera is a postulant of talent in quest of expression, the opportunity is too good. Think about it: a salon where the guests don't perform, a salon where one listens, a salon in which no poet has ever deflowered his work—but don't worry, verses will put an end to it. Oh, you don't know the terrible and murderous vanity of this promised land of all the demi-glories and all the influences of the coast: the Côte d'Azur, the coast of grace, the coast of refuge too—but you've entered into the dance."

And, shaken by mad laughter, that animal Bergues let himself fall into an armchair.

Baronne de Méplonoff listened, terrified. People had formed a circle around us; we now had an audience; a hedge of breasts, palpitating in expertly fissured bodices, leaned, a trifle anxiously, over Bergues' hilarity.

"But yes, that's how it is, Mesdames; you'll no longer flirt, whatever our friend Madame de Méplonoff does. Her hand will be forced, and we shall no longer see the trains of your dresses moving freely here. You'll be parked in a row of chairs, all the women together, condemned to listen in silence to the thirty-five numbers of the program. That's the way it is in literary salons; I know, I've frequented them. Out of fifty guests at those intellectual jousts, ten are listeners and forty performers, that's the average. And the listeners—one might as well say those condemned to the pillory—have no means of escape.

"The artistes keep watch on the door, more preoccupied with cutting off the flight of the victims than waiting their turn and yet, what a fever they have to be heard, to be admired and to produce themselves—what preoccupation, this one with his diction, that one with his gesture, and all of them with their profiles; and what cordial jealousy of one another; and what struggles over the program! You know that, Baronne: the pianist incrusted to the piano, the poet stuck in the fireplace like a caryatid, the cellist clinging to the cello and the harpist, arms entangled with the strings of the instrument like an octopus in its algae, refusing to cede his turn: the harp does and does not yield. Yes, you'll have that horrible spectacle."

Bergues became epic; his speech was Apocalyptic. Baronne de Méplonoff had collapsed on a sofa; her pallor, her attitude, everything in her, begged for mercy. Bergues took pity on her.

"I had to signal the danger to you, Madame."

And he concluded with a courtly salute.

"What's this? Do you know these people, Giffart?"

The Baronne, extending her hand toward a side-table, in a pretty rotation of the upper body that made the most of her neckline, reached for an invitation card placed on a tray among the letters, and handed it to Pierre Giffart.

Pierre Giffart and I were in the home of the charming Méplonoff, Bergues' friend. Giffart is a well-known sportsman who combines the profits of three garages, cleverly distributed between Cannes and Monte Carlo, with a fearful passion for automobiles. We had become three flirts attached to the fascinating Hungarian. It was the exquisite hour between three and four when the flux of visitors still belated on the roads or in the torpor of social matinees leaves the leisure of amorous strategies to sigisbeos.

All three of us were there in the vast drawing rooms of the Villa Marpha, with the Venetian blinds closed. Outside, the flowers were languishing in the intense heat; the dark room was brightened by a spray of stems and enormous calices, tall arums and broad yellow irises, in large expansive Sèvres vases. In the four corners of the room, clumps of white azaleas were stifling in gilded baskets. Sitting at the piano, Eva Waston, the daughter of Lord Waston, the billionaire promoter of Beaulieu, was playing Grieg's sixth sonata quietly, and her small, energetic and proud head helmed by her auburn hair—at least five louis a bottle—put on top of the Erard grand the amusing note of a pricey trinket. The décor was rather cosmopolitan.

"Don't know," said Pierre Giffart, passing the invitation card to us.

> *Villa Corrine, Last soirée of the* Cour d Amour.
> *Madame la Comtesse and Monsieur le Général Comte Villy de Koetmuken beg Monsieur et Madame de Méplonoff to be kind enough to honor with their presence the Medieval soirée that they are giving at their home on 15 April 1905.*
> *Recitation of rondels and chansons de gestes:*
> The Princess and the Camel, *a farce in the taste of the eleventh century, played by the Comtesse de Koetmuken and Monsieur Jackson.*
> *Coronation of Troubadours.*
> Nota Bene: *Gothic headgear is* de rigeur.

Bergues read the card attentively. "I foresaw it; you've been classified in the clan; you made Monsieur declaim in your home, you've become literary; they're inviting you; you're theirs. They don't often have a recruit like you, young, pretty, elegant, rich—especially young; one generally waits until later to make one's debut in the Maecenat, the entire camp of Agramont must be celebrating; you no longer have the right to disappoint their expectation. It's necessary to go, Baronne."

And he handed back the card.

"What! But I don't know those people. Who are these Villy de Koetmukens?"

"Worthy people, very honest, above all, the Koetmukens—which is rather rare on the Riviera—the most united of households, the Comte in admiration of his wife, neither of them young, the Philemon and Baucis of the Côte d'Azur, about whom there would be nothing to say without their innocent mania for literature, for literary fame above all, and their unhealthy obsession with the Middle Ages. Their invitation card is a whole document: *Villa Corrine, Last soirée of the Cour d'Amour*. The Comtesse takes herself for both Marguerite de Valois and Madame de Staël; she writes, she composes, she is first-rate on the piano, prevalent in prose and verse, encourages poets, judges, discusses and crowns their works, discerns renown, discovers talent, and with that, a fury for costume, the cult of the Middle Ages, an obsession with historical finery, a mild folly of disguise, a need to dress up things and people.

"Her soirées are *Cours d'Amour*, the guests are troubadours, she presides over Decamerons. No account is ever rendered of a dinner at the Villa Corrine—there is no local paper that spares us its receptions—without mention of the surcoats of *menu vair* and the heraldic skirts of the mistress of the house. She's belated in life; in the twentieth century she goes around coiffed in a chatelaine's hennin with a *ferronnière* on her forehead.

"Like the late Duchesse d'Hangomar, who believed that she had the soul of Mary Stuart, had once lived in Holyrood House and still feared the rancor of Elizabeth, and the famous Duchesse Théosophe, whose still-living son was once Cleopatra, Madame de Koertmuken is firmly convinced of having lived before, under Charles VII and at the court of the Valois. However slightly you know her, she will tell you straight out, lowering her eyes, that she has known the amour of Charles VII and also that of Henri IV, Agnès Sorel under the first and Marguerite de Navarre under the second—hence her predilection for all rhymers and singers of ballads, and her unconscious attraction toward poetry and art.

"With that, dried up and filled out by her fifty years, a tomato on a melon and the melon on a milestone—that's her silhouette: you can see that dwarfish figure in an armoried skirt, coiffed with a hennin. As for the husband, the chevalier in perpetual adoration, thin and bony, he gives the impression of being cut out of old parchment: a small upper body perched high on the legs of a heron; physically, he's Don Guéritan, the Don Guéritan of Marie-Anne de Neubourg[1]—what's more, the nicest people in the world."

"You certainly give me a desire to meet them!" And, cha-grined, Madame de Méplonoff got up from the divan and closed her fan abruptly. "What would I do in the home of such people?"

"Educate yourself, Baronne. You'll learn there, by sight, how a salon, even in honest society, can easily become comical. Oh, the dangers of literature! Because a woman turns easily to the burlesque by surrounding herself with failed authors and mili-tant bluestockings; nothing gains ground like the ridiculous, and, bizarre as the Koermuken couple might be, they would pass almost unperceived without the legion of pretentions and incongruous vanities grouped in a circle around them. They're the hub of the wheel, the kernel of the fruit. It's the law of na-ture. Once the heart of vanity is lit, all the other vanities cluster around it in order to warm themselves there. Their salon is the refuge of all obstinate and disappointed ambitions, the sanctuary of all the beautiful souls that have difficulty emerging: *Refugium peccatorum*,[2] and what a museum collection . . . for fossils are worth as much as old portraits.

"You ought to go there, Baronne; it's a unique opportunity, all the more so as the opportunity is rare and they aren't prodigal

---

1 "Don Guéritan" is presumably an eccentric spelling of Don Guritan, a character in Victor Hugo's *Ruy Blas* (1838), set in 1699. Maria Anna of Neuburg (1667-1740), Queen of Spain at the time, is also a leading char-acter in the play.
2 "The refuge of sinners"—usually used as an appellation for the Virgin Mary.

with their invitations. The Comte and Comtesse are suspicious. That salon of conserves is conservative, and has no confidence in youth, the youth of women especially. Those ladies render themselves justice; by way of compensation, ephebes abound there; the house is in the tradition of Talleyrand: women of the past and men of the future. You'll find a lot of young centenarians there, of whom you owe us a description. Since you're being admitted into the lair of the sibyls, your regulars have a right to an account of your visit."

"Yes, Baronne," Giffart interjected. "You owe us the story of your descent into Hell."

"You're scaring me!" cried the Hungarian. "I don't want to go."

"Yes you'll go," said Bergues, returning to the charge. "You'll go because you'll see curious things there that one doesn't see anywhere else: all the livery, the valet de chambre, the groom and the cook dressed in the Turkish style and polished in advance."

"What are you saying?"

"The way it is. The Koetmukens only have an income of fifteen thousand francs and are forced to count their luxuries. On the evenings of costumed fêtes it's negroes who provide the service and are stationed in the vestry; those negroes are economical; the glance gains by it, but exits from the ball suffer."

"I'll go in black, then," riposted the Baronne, finally amused. "What else will I see?"

"A thousand-and-one marionettes and a phantasmagoria. Colonel Mégard, whose imprecise profile is reminiscent of the arabesques of a fritter left in the frying-pan too long, and the Colonel's wife, the oracle of the Society, who deprives of their *particules* the friends who have ceased to please her, as one deprives children of dessert."

"No!"

"Yes, it's thus; she strips people of their titles; she alone decrees the nobility of someone; in addition, she's above suspicion, and with good reason."

104

"That's funny."

"You'll also see her son, the suave Anatole, a young ephebe with a deep voice, who is said to make his mother's bonnets and wears a coachman's checkered cravats, Anatole and his green waistcoats, the work of those ladies, and who has also never been suspected."

"The lily of France," sniggered Pierre Giffart.

"You'll also encounter old Trompe la Mort, an octogenarian tragedian, who gets into his wife's old corsets in order to declaim *Le Cid*'s speech."

"And gets into them without difficulty," I couldn't help saying.

"Corsets transformed into armor by clever applications of leather carried out by the local cobbler."

"You'll hear in her works Madame du Donjon Lorinette, who signs her poetry with her maiden name, Ophélie Rabaud, the grand-daughter of Jean Bart and the niece of Lady Tollental, who died in the Great Indies in the seventeen hundreds, also related to the Calas family."

"An entire history of France."

"You'll also see the worldly baritone Jacques Callot, by no means young but endowed with a voice that's still fresh, marvelous in the *Air de la Calomnie* [1] and the duet in *Roméo et Juliette*; General Linière, who turns a madrigal agreeably and embroiders like a fay, on the drum, poetry and ladies' needlework, myrtle and laurel—they're all fond of it—and Abbé Plumet, Monseigneur's secretary, who puts the verses of the Gospel into Latin distichs and cultivates epigrams successfully; the salons fear his malice. He's also a furious embroiderer; there's no one like him for repairing chasubles and mending altar-cloths; he's an abbé of the old school."

"But it's a menagerie!" said Madame de Meploniff, laughing.

---

1 The familiar French title of *La calunnia è un venticello*—an aria from Rossini's *Il Barbieri de Siviglia* [The Barber of Seville].

"And finally, if you arrive early, you might surprise the master of the house perched on a stepladder in the process of lighting the chandeliers, and if he puts on the Palikare costume that he wore at his last ball, the tarlatan fustanelle tailored from one of Madame's old dresses, over cotton underpants that are poorly-closed—for good reason, three-francs fifty liquidation sale items don't button up well—you'll make agreeable discoveries."

"What are you saying? You're going mad, Giffart!"

"The pure truth; one can't make these things up. At his last Cour d'Amour the Comte had put on the embroidered jacket and Greek bonnet of the *Roi de Montagnes*. All of that had been found at Runiori's, the costume hirer in the Rue Victor, but, the fustanelle being lacking, the Comtesse had the idea of genius of cutting it out from the tarlatan of an old ball gown; and old pair of underpants dyed carmine completed the outfit. The long-johns corkscrew from the knees to the ankles, the fustanelle sticks out like a dancer's tutu, and on the evening of the ball that's the grotesque get-up that the first arrivals surprised, perched on a ladder, armed with a rat's-tail, under the crystal of the chandeliers; the women shivered. In the effort of hoisting the whole body up to the candles, the underpants had slipped and gaped . . ."

"What horror!"

"Don't worry, they're superfluous fears. The absent are always wrong."

"It's necessary to go, dear friend." That was Miss Eva Waston, who, leaving the piano, her sonata and her attitudes, had crept up quietly to join the group.

We all raised surprised eyes at the American.

"Yes, it's necessary to go," the imperturbable young woman said. "You must tell my father; he'll be so glad, he likes the ridiculous French—I mean, French ridicule—so much."

"All right, I'll go," the Barronne declared.

Leaning toward her ear, faithful to his role as demonic tempter, the laughing Giffart whispered: "You'll also see the Marquise de Beauconteur, whose name is an entire program . . ."

"Well, Baronne, what about that Medieval soirée? You've come back from it; tell us about the *Cour d'Amour*."

We were at Princesse Adriani's in the little pale blue damask drawing room, where the refined taste of the mistress of the house only admitted biscuit porcelain groups and white Sèvres vases, great Louis XVI urns on marble tops of lacquered tables and rounds of plump cozy amours, of a milky candor, reflected in the polished pewter of long mirrors: an entirely sober, elegant and bright decoration, emphasized that day by bunches of white irises and luminous yellow chamomiles, thrown in profusion in the openings of vases.

Princesse Adriani is reputed, rightly or wrongly, to be sumptuously maintained by Sir Herald. It is true that one never encounters Sir Herald at the princesse's house, but she spends six months a year aboard the American billionaire's yacht, the *Washington*, the largest pleasure-boat in the world, after Edward VII's. The princesse then goes with him along the coasts of Sicily, Greece and even Asia Minor. Three times a year, the *Washington* moors in Nice, in the three months of the year—March, April and May—that the Princesse spends in her villa at Saint-Maurice.

Twice a week there are violins and chamber music at the Villa Orphée; artistes from the Opéra and stars of Monte Carlo can be heard there for fees that are never haggled down. Those auditions and one grand dinner a week form the social routine of the Princesse. Apart from a few men, she only receives foreign women, never French women, in her drawing room; their futility, she says, fatigues her silent gravity.

Princesse Adriani is from Palermo; the Prince was from Naples; I say 'was' because no one has ever seen Prince Adriani. Widow or divorcee, beneath a slightly haughty reserve, the Princesse is nevertheless a delightful and welcoming creature.

Although *déclassée* by virtue of her situation as the maintained friend of an American, she has found the means to have the most exclusive salon on the Riviera; her house is the Ivory Tower of cosmopolitan society

It was in that salon that we were to find Madame de Méplonoff again. We searched for her as soon as we arrived and finally discovered her in the little blue Sèvres boudoir, sitting on a narrow jonquil silk sofa with Eva Waston, very vaporous that evening in a cloud of slivery silk gauze garlanded with large mauve clematis flowers.

"Take the migrainine,[1] dear friend, since antipyrine hasn't succeeded for you, or even quinine bromal hydrate, two hours before the fit," the Englishwoman insisted, "because it's the fever, a little spring fever, that you're suffering from. My father employs strychnine arsenate, but that's a little violent, the bromal hydrate should suffice."

The plaintive Baronne, her eyes hollowed out by the migraine, as her cheeks were colored by the fire of the fever, said: "It's this perfidious climate, this perfidious climate."

"And your automobile excursions along the dusty roads, and this mistral," Miss Waston replied.

We arrived in the middle of that consultation. We finally had the guest of the Villa Corinne, escaped alive from the *Cour d'Amour*. In the large drawing room next door, Princesse Adriani's other guests were pressing around Duc d'Hangomar, returned from Ceylon; his stories seemed to be impassioning the audience.

"Well, Baronne, what about the Medieval soirée? You've come back from it; tell us about the troubadours." That was Pierre Giffart, who posed the tendentious question in an insidious voice.

The Hungarian made an exhausted gesture.

---

1 "Migrainine" tablets were widely marketed at the turn of the century as a treatment for headaches. They contained the analgesic antipyrine and caffeine citrate.

"It made you ill?" insinuated Bergues.

"Not even that. It was so ridiculously dull."

"Dull—why?"

"You'd exaggerated, Messieurs. Imagine a public of old subscribers of the Conservatoire and a few door-openers, decked out at Bon Marché, with paste jewelry. It was poor and sad, all those of men and women piled on chairs forming the five rows of the audience, all coifed in Isabeau de Bavière's hennin or Buridan's toque. They seemed so bored, stood there, as immobile as old figurants."

"The seigneurs of the Tour de Nesles. I can see it from here," Giffart sniggered.

"A soirée costumed at Sainte-Périne," Bergues added, "or the anniversary celebration of a laundry-boat."

"Don't mock; it was much more distressing than that. My heart sank. I thought involuntarily of very old parents fallen into poverty and constrained to parade in a fairground booth. They all gave the impression of being ashamed of their outfits—the men especially, for the women had more aplomb. Among others, one was frightfully thin and plastered with make-up, with the profile of a cormorant with an impressively long beak. Imagine a tunic of blue gauze folded like an accordion, over meager shoulder-blades and long, frightfully naked arms, necklaces and bracelets of blue Egyptian scarabs; and with that, a blonde wig childishly curled. She was going green under the blue of the gauze and the blonde of her curls, and the enamel of her flesh was cracking in the hollows of the shoulders, the corners of the lips and the wrinkles of the temples; it was nightmarish. A Marquise Ubelli, I was told. She was costumed as Thaïs."

"The Thaïs of the Musée Guimet," laughed Pierre Giffart. "Very droll, your mummies' reunion!"

"And the other escapees from the Pyramids?" Bergues interrogated.

"Oh, I don't know, I didn't notice. That Thaïs hypnotized me."

"I can imagine," said Miss Waston. "God, that's amusing; how I wish my father was here. I want to go and fetch him—no, I'll tell him tomorrow at table and he'll give me the beautiful pigeon-blood ruby from Morgan's."

"You haven't seen anything else, then? But that's cerebral anemia," Bergues persisted.

"I was annihilated by disappointment."

"What about the master and mistress of the house?"

"I don't remember."

"You spoke to them?"

"I don't know."

"And the marvels announced in the program, the *rondels and chansons de gestes* and that farce in the taste of the fifteenth century: *The Princess and the Camel?* And the *Coronation of the Troubadours?*"

Madame de Meplonoff sketched a vague gesture of discouragement.

"What, not one little verse? You haven't remembered anything?"

"Yes, I do remember, for the incident struck me: suddenly, a little woman, svelte, lively and unconstrained, a charming little old woman with a high powdered coiffure, her figure tightly clad in a long frock-coat of multicolored taffeta, launched herself with gliding steps into the middle of the room, a true portrait of the time of the Revolution, for she had a top-buckled hat with long black plumes."

"I recognize her," sniggered Pierre Giffart. "The lady has aplomb."

"Oh! Who is she?" asked the Hungarian.

"Go on—I'll tell you afterwards."

"It was charming, that Louis XVI apparition in the midst of the Middle Ages, that Middle Age in particular; and the lady was dolled up delightfully, a true Hoppner.[1] So, she launched into a gavotte, advancing furtively, her gestures garlanded, one

---

1 The English portrait painter John Hoppner (1758-1810).

110

arm here and one there, her entire body following the movement of the verses, she declaimed:

> "*'Is it a flower? Is it a dart?*
> *Is it a whole? Is it a part?*
> *Gaze so pert and waist so fine,*
> *Libertine laugh, it's Columbine!'*"

"Oh, how I would have liked to be there!" exclaimed Miss
Waston.

"And everyone applauded; I couldn't believe my ears," observed Madame de Méplonoff. "But the singer had something
about her. Who is she?"

"She was known in Bordeaux as Madame Mélanie Taffard,
of Taffard, Bordenave and Son, herring-smokers. Widowed,
she came to seek refuge in Nice, and calls herself Madame de
Grandchamp—Var nobility. The lady was once pretty and is
still a sly one. As artful as intrigue and as knowing as a circum-
stantial gambler, she has social graces and urbanity. She had an
unfortunate adventure; a gentleman who wished her well died
in her bed."

"No!"

"It wasn't very long ago, and the worst thing is that he wasn't
doing anything in that bed; he was seventy-five years old."

"And the lady? But she must be at least sixty."

"He died of boredom, then."

Mad laughter saluted Eva Waston's sally—the Englishwoman
had thought aloud. Only her earlobes were a little pinker; Miss
Waston was decorative even in her modesty.

There was a silence.

"And the incident of the Comtesse de Tressacq, with the
master of the house, you're not telling us about that?" insinuated
Pierre Giffart. "You're keeping secrets from us, Baronne."

"The Comtesse de Tressacq? I don't even know the name. I
assure you that I haven't seen or heard anything."

"I'm better informed than you are, then."

"Are you with the police?"

"Perhaps in the service of the Ministry of Foreign Affairs—but these are the facts. The Comtesse de Tressacq is an old lady as curious as a gallant chronicle, on the lookout for all gossip, all acts and deeds, and mad for masks and disguises. Although a septuagenarian, she doesn't miss a *Veglione*, is at all the *Redoutes*, witnesses while masked all the intrigues of Vogade, Corso's Sundays and, if she doesn't battle in the street on confetti days it's because, prudently, she fears slaps. But she's only seen during the Carnival. At least she has no illusions before her mirror, and doesn't afflict people with the spectacle of her decrepitude. Comtesse de Tressacq was once very beautiful, much courted, much loved, and now, resigned by experience to the kinds of homage that her income of two hundred thousand francs attracts, she lives for the rest of the time confined to her splendid Villa des Baumettes. She takes a malign pleasure in making her heirs languish. She only receives them when she's feeling well; when she's ill, her door is pitilessly closed to them. She opens up to them often enough to demolish their hopes, although they sometimes reanimate. She's a figure from another century.

"Now, the other evening, at the Koëtmukens', once the effervescence of the recitations had calmed down, a penitent in black satin was remarked, sitting discreetly apart, who hadn't removed his mask. A few Buridans informed the master of the house; there was an impoliteness in that incognito, retained in the midst of all the uncovered faces. Monsieur de Koëtmuken decided to go and interrogate the penitent. He asked the veiled figure to lift his hood or name himself.

"The mask got up, and an irritated female voice said: 'My name? But you only have to look at the blazon embroidered on my cape and you'll see it there in armories.'

"And as Monsieur de Koëtmuken, confused at having to deal with a woman, stammered: 'But I'm not sure, I can't make out . . .'

"'Comtesse de Tressacq,' emphasized the little whistling voice. 'The name is well-known enough. Tressacq: *s, a, c, q* . . .'

"And with that *s, a, c, q* . . . the penitent stood up, traversed the salon rapidly, and left the Comte dumbfounded."

"No! That happened?"

"Just like that.

"There was amazement, but great joy when it was discovered what the Comtesse de Tressacq had been sitting on all evening: an intimate item of furniture that Madame de Koëtmuken, because of the shortage of chairs, had brought down from the toilet cabinet and covered for the occasion with a velvet dust-sheet from Liberty."

"Tressacq, *s, a, c, q*," remarked a hearty reiter, stressing the final consonant. "One always has the seat one merits."

"But the charming thing," concluded Bergues, always well-informed, "is that when he was alive, the Comte de Tressacq was the Ministre des Cultes."[1]

---

1 Literally, Minister of Religion, but the first syllable of Cultes, in isolation, would mean "bum," hence the joke; whether bearing in mind the term *cul-de-sac* makes it any funnier is a matter of opinion. Tressacq can also be interpreted phonetically as *très sac* ["very rich," in argot], and the emphasis on the letter *q* when it was spelled out for the final time in a guttural German accent might have made it sound like *que*? [what?]. French humor doesn't always export well.

FIVE O'CLOCK CONVERSATION[1]

"THE DUCHESS OF GLOCESTER,[2] a Peruvian bride. Millions and millions, and one would have the further advantage of I know not what story of a testament torn up as a fine gesture under the noses of the Duke's family. The Duchess has the blood of the Cid in her veins. The son, very English, tried to blackmail his mother. When she refused to pay his debts for a third time he went on the boards and gave all America the spectacle of a duke and peer hamming it up. The Duchess is still beautiful. The woman accompanying her, that tall, thin, supple brunette molded in pastel blue cloth, is Miss Rowenna, her sister.

"She's one of the finest catches in Buenos Aires, but will never marry. She's an esthete, a lover of Dante Rossetti, the Carpaccios

---

1 This item is adapted from a story series published in *Gil Blas*, consisting principally of "La Riviera: Propos de Cinq heures" (15 April 1903), "Histoires de Paris: La Case de la Monti" (26 April 1903) and "Histoires de Paris: Agonies de riches" (6 June 1903), but reordering them and also absorbing the text of a book review previously published in *Gil Blas*, "*La Confession de Nicaise*" (1 August 1902). The item features characters that had been introduced—much more elaborately than they are here—in an item in *Le Journal*, "Fleur de Luxe" (1 February 1903), which might have intended to be the first of a series, other material of which was recycled in the *Gil Blas* series.

2 I have given this name as Lorrain renders it; he might have employed it precisely because there was no Duke of Gloucester (and hence no Duchess) in 1903, the title having been allowed to lapse since its last employment in the eighteenth century (it was recreated in 1928).

114

of Venice and the Botticellis of Florence; she possesses in her town house in London the chamber of Saint Ursula, reconstituted in accordance with the painting in the Accademia. At Fiesole, where she spends the spring, she's had the famous mosaic of Ravenna reproduced in her hall. She's one of the most original figures in Cosmopolis. What a pity that Jacques Snydaure isn't here. He could document us regarding the two sisters. He spent last summer with them on the London Riviera, for they also have a Riviera over there. What can he be doing? What an individual! He was supposed to come at five o'clock, and it's half past. He's polite, your poet!" And Madame Hocheuse consulted the minuscule watch on her bracelet.

It was a five o'clock tea in Monte Carlo, in the Hôtel de Paris, in the hubbub of an exasperated aviary rumor of all the idioms of the world, sung, chirped and twittered at the same time by all the women, of the Riviera, young, mature and old, for the sake of flirtation or vanity.

Whether they descend from dusty automobiles, swathed in furs and drivers' dust-covers, caps pulled down over the hideous goggles of Hoffmannesque physicians, or emerge, all sails aloft, from the hands of their chambermaids, occupied for hours in repairing the clarity of complexions and furbishing the metal of hair, they are all there, the tendernesses and the most legitimate wives, making the assault of luxury and elegance, under heavy hats encumbered by Lewis flowers, all displaying amid their costly embroideries and ruinous cleavages monstrous Morgan pearls, Lacloche diamond necklaces and translucent Lalique enamels.

The men, appearing between two spins in Panhard machines[1] or two spins of the roulette wheel, circulate, indifferent and hurried, come under orders to organize dinner and the employment of the evening; and they are the greatest names of

---

1 Automobiles manufactured by Panhard et Levassor were ground-breaking in the 1890s and regularly won races, continually setting new records amid a blaze of publicity.

Europe and the two worlds, the trusts of New York, the mines of Massachusetts, the London peerage, Hungarian magnates, the noblest families in Austria, the heaviest German crowns, the oldest fiefs in Bavaria, the oldest palaces in Italy and the most heavily-mortgaged patrimonies in France, with the prettiest Parisian girls: the chasers of large dowries, lovers of parchments and hunters of quail and grouse.

"Madame de Nodge, a Parisienne of the Monceau quarter staying at the Hôtel des Plumes had promised her friends, Mesdames Avril and Hocheuse, the presence of the novelist Jacques Snydaure, and Jacques Snydaure had not arrived.

"Finally, and not without harm," said Madame de Nodge, holding out her gloved hand to a tall young man who had suddenly surged forth behind her. "We've been waiting for an hour, and it's now that you arrive! You're quite insupportable, Syndaure." And, turning to her friends: "Monsieur Jacques Snydaure, the advertised phenomenon."

The other two women inclined slightly over their teacups, and two pairs of eyes gazed at the young man.

"What bad place have you been lingering in, to be so late?" Madame Nodge's clear voice attacked.

"A very bad place, in fact, for there were even more fleshy foreigners there than there are here. I've come from the Agence Stick; I waited there for more than an hour, it was full of cosmopolites."

"The Agence Stick! You're leaving again?"

"Yes, I have a nostalgia for Sicily. I want to see the Latomies of Syracuse again, and the gardens of Palermo."

"Will you be gone long?"

"At least two months, April and May. The older I get, the more the Latin soul is revealed in me. Florence in September, Venice in October and great Greece in spring, that's how I want to organize my life henceforth."

"In the meantime, you're disrupting our days. We were here at five and it's almost six."

116

"Our plans always disrupt those of others," the young man concluded, with a vague gesture.

"Look, Monsieur Snydaure isn't wearing his rings today," little Madame Avril observed blushing.

"The famous rings," Madame Hocheuse emphasized.

"Indeed," replied Snydaure, darting a long glance at his bare hands. "It's sometimes necessary to belie the legend. Exaggerate it today, demolish it tomorrow; that's the way to keep opinion breathless. It's the system of the Scottish shower applied to publicity. Publicity is everything, for daughters of the theater as for men of letters. It's necessary to live."

The novelist had taken his place at the table and was piling slices of lemon into his tea. Madame Hocheuse who had only hazarded one remark thus far, absorbed in the examination of the young man, said: "Pardon me Monsieur Snydaure, but why don't you give lectures? You'd succeeded in that marvelously."

"Why? I've never thought about it—and then, speaking in public, recounting to an entire audience one's impressions and petty affairs implies a dose of self-confidence and conceit of which I haven't yet attained the measure."

"And yet, modesty doesn't stifle you," mocked Madame de Nodge. "In fact, I believe Monsieur Snydaure to be rather vain, but I understand his hesitation before lecturing. It's regrettable; some people make a lot of money out of it."

To which the novelist, obstinately stirring with his teaspoon, replied: "Yes, I know, the tourney of great tricks, the departure of Monsieur Montesquiou's great orchestra and the skimming of the two Americas, the French nobility going to enlighten the New World, which has been enlightening the armorial of France for twenty years with dollars and trusts. Monsieur de Montesquiou wants to pay the debts of the faubourg like that, but his tourney doesn't envisage heirs; he isn't married, as everyone knows; he's an Evangelist of art."[1]

---

1 The *New York Times* reported on 12 October 1902 that the famous dandy Robert de Montesquiou would receive 175,000 francs for his lecture tour of

"In the land of salt pork," sniggered little Madame Avril. A severe glance from Madame de Nodge recalled her to order.

Snydaure went on: "But that torch-bearer is also a collector emeritus, and I have neither historical knick-knacks nor an art gallery to supply between two conversations on esthetics. Boldini hasn't confided any of his paintings to me, nor Helleu any of his pastels. What would I do in those tourneys of the Stock Exchange, having neither ancestors at Bouvines, prestige among painters, nor credit with second-hand dealers?"

The three women exchanged thin smiles.

"And there's Monsieur de Serpigny, painted and established from top to toe! You have almost as much talent as Henri de Régnier, Snydaure. You could have written *Le Mariage de minuit*."[1]

"Perhaps, but I would have been very embarrassed to sign *L'Inconstante*. That's a work that affirms a very personal experience."[2]

According to you, then, Snydaure, *L'Inconstante* is the book of the season?"

"Better than that; it's the prettiest woman's book that has appeared in ten years."

"What about Madame de Noailles, what do you make of her, then?"[3]

America. Lorrain loathed him, because as long as he existed, Lorrain could only be reckoned the second most flamboyant homosexual dandy in Paris.

1 Henri de Régnier's *roman à clef Le Mariage de minuit* [The Midnight Marriage]—in which the character of Jacques de Serpigny, misrendered as "Serpignies" in the Ollendorf text, is clearly modelled on Robert de Montesquiou—was first published in 1903.

2 *L'Inconstante* [The Inconstant Woman], signed Gérard d'Houville (Henri de Régnier's wife Marie, the daughter of José-Maria de Heredia) was also published in 1903. The marriage seems to have been somewhat unorthodox—Régnier took Pierre Louÿs with him on his honeymoon, apparently to substitute for him in his conjugal duties, and that might explain Snydaure's catty remark.

3 Anna de Noailles (1876-1933) was a Rumanian princess who married a French Comte and became one of the three leading female writers in France during the last phase of the Belle Époque, along with "Gérard d'Houville"

118

"Madame de Noailles remains the unique poet of *L'Ombre des jours*, but in prose, Madame Henri de Régnier remains the magisterial, exquisite and disconcerting writer of *L'Inconstante*."

"By the way, do you know that a new book by Mademoiselle de Pougy has been announced: *Ecce Homo*?"[1]

"*Ecce homo*? It's her memoirs, then, dedicated to Monsieur de Max."

"Liane de Pougy is a delightful ironist. *Ecce homo* after *Idylle saphique*. There's also a tale dedicated to Reynaldo Hahn. The book was due to appear on Good Friday, but the author hesitated at the last moment, Pougy is a Bretonne."

"And has the right to all pardons."

"What wit!"

The Duchess of Glocester got to her feet.

"Snydaure, you must have gossip about her. You spent the last season at her home."

"Is that her sister, Miss Rowenna, with her?" interrogated little Madame Avril.

"No, that's Musidora Smithson, the dancer from Boston who is making her debut at the Théâtre Sarah Bernhardt next week. Two years ago they tried to launch her in Paris; all the salons of estheticism hitched themselves to her glory without being able to force the threshold of the music halls; our great Sarah has just generously offered her theater to her. Miss Smithson will still make as much money as Monsieur de Max in *L'Aiglon* or Mademoiselle Parny in *Théroigne*, or Sarah herself in *Werther*, or Brandès in *Clarisse Arbois*."

"Don't be nasty, Snydaure; you're talking like a boulevard news item."

---

and Colette. Her second collection of poetry, *L'Ombre des jours* [The Shadow of the Days], was published in 1902. She published her first novel in 1903.
1 *Ecce homo: d'ici, de là* [Behold the Man: From Here to There] (1903), dedicated to the actor Gaston de Max, was Liane de Pougy's fifth book, following her fictionalized account of her relationship with Natalie Barney, *Idylle saphique* [Sapphic Idyll] (1901).

"In truth, this tea has a taste of Neapolitan absinthe, we're stirring so much theatrical gossip into it. You want to know about the Duchess of Glocester?"

"Everything. You know it all."

"Everything! You're greedy. Unfortunately, there's nothing to tell. The Duchess of Glocester is the most honest woman in the world."

"And honest women have no history?"

"Similar in that to happy people."

"Pardon me, I haven't said that the Duchess of Glocester was happy. She was, on the contrary, the most deceived, the most mocked and the most robbed of all women. As pretty as a blonde South American Spaniard can be, and madly in love with the Duke, she became a widow after six years of marriage—for six years, read six centuries, of jealousy, anguish and despair. The Duke deceived her royally."

"But why, if she was so pretty?"

"Why? For one very simple reason: Glocester only had debts, and Dolores Rowenna brought him forty millions."

Then Madame Hocheuse, very interested, said: "According to you, then, Monsieur Snydaure, money kills love, as it kills gratitude, pity, and all good sentiments, and if the Duchess was deceived by her husband, it's because she had brought him millions and millions; if he had married her poor, the Duke would have been more faithful?"

"At any rate, he wouldn't have deceived her as quickly. One doesn't enslave a man by purchasing him. The instinct of independence that is in us drives a slave to all revolts. Every liberty alienated in exchange for money always ends up liberating itself in a scandal or by a treason. Whether it's a matter of a wife married for her beauty or a man married for his name, adultery will always be a liberation for them. They prove in the sun their right to be free; the yoke only subsists when accepted; it breaks when it's only endured."

"You're an anarchist, Monsieur Snydaure."

"No, I'm only a philosopher, and I observe the revenge of the poor every day."

"So, according to you, the Duchess of Glocester merits her unhappiness?"

"You're making me say monstrous things. No one merits unhappiness, but certain situations attract it; exceptions of fortune, talent and beauty are most under threat. Lightning strikes summits. The Duchess of Glocester was born too rich to be happy."

"She's pretty, though."

"Certainly, but see how isolated she is; no one pays court to her."

"You're contradicting yourself, Syndaure; she must have all the flirts."

"Pardon me, but she's known to be in love with the Duke; schemers don't have time to waste. Barring financial catastrophe, the Duchess is consecrated until death to interested sigisbeos, parasites and the complaisant."

"But it's a matter of going through the street in rags; personally I'd only go out any longer in cheap dresses," objected little Madame Avril.

"You'd be even prettier." The writer looked from the corner of his eye at Madame Hocheuse, who had not said anything.

Madame de Nodge paraded her lorgnette over the audience for a long time. Snydaure's theories exasperated her; she was looking around for a living argument that could belie them. A slight quiver ran over her face and, putting her hand on the young man's arm she said: "You who find explanations for everything and can disentangle effects and causes so well, tell me why that fat woman over there, that thickset mass with a common square face, whose solitaires gleam so brightly, is enthroned surrounded by young men and pretty women. What charm can that one exert?"

"No charm, but the certain empire of a large fortune denounced by her jewelry. All that youth comes to warm itself in the fires of her jewel-case for she possesses one that is famous in Paris; it's Michael Emmaus who brightens it."

"What, that woman is La Monti?"

"In person."

"The superintendent of the pleasures of the great Emmaus, the petty Pompadour of that fat Slav enriched by bankruptcies? But she has neither youth nor beauty."

"But she's an admirable stage-manager. She's the person who organizes the fêtes of Celle-Saint-Cloud. All the youth aspires to figure in them. Emmaus gives a serious cachet, and the pieces put on there aren't too difficult to play. All they demand of actors is impetuosity and conviction, and in the duets, the singers are left the choice of roles. *Trahit sua quemque, voluptas!* Everyone takes his pleasure where he finds it.[1] Emmaus watches, and pays rubies on the nail once the performance is over."

"Very eighteenth-century—and it's that fat slattern that regulates the ballet. Emmaus never throws the handkerchief to one of the dancers, then?"

"It's a long time since Emmaus blew his nose. He's a witness; he watches."

"You don't say."

"Which it's necessary to believe. All those young women, then . . . ?"

"Yes, theatresses without an engagement."

"And the young men?"

"Flautists, Italians, velodrome racers, jugglers and acrobats, the fine flower of suburban music halls and hippodromes."

"Then, that Monti has never been Emmaus' mistress; she's a procuress?"

"That's where you're mistaken. La Monti is still Michael's mistress, and has been for thirty years."

"But she's never been pretty."

"Never."

"She's even rather ugly."

"Rather."

---

1 A more literal translation would be that everyone is drawn (or even dragged) by his particular pleasure. The quotation is from Virgil.

"Common."

"Certainly; she was a laundress."

"No!"

"As I tell you, but a beautiful skin; a russet freshness, bulging eyes, a sniffling nose with open nostrils, the jaw of a mastiff, a mouth as squashed and pink as a puppy's, and low on her feet, massive and thickset with golden down from the nape to the heels, a back for Jordaens, a true fauness."

"You've seen it, Syndaure?"

"You're harsh, Mesdames; there's a generation between La Monti and me."

"How do you know, then?"

"Hearsay—and then, La Monti's physique counts for little in the empire she's acquired over Emmaus. The psychology of that liaison is very interesting; it's a whole story, and this is it:

> *"Lord, I bless you in spite of the immense error*
> *Of being the frightful rich man that no one can love.*[1]

"That's a verse of Monsieur de Montesquiou's. The adventure of Emmaus and La Monti is a paraphrase of it. Emmaus is, as you know, one of the Croesuses of Europe. For nearly a century the family name has been synonymous with billions. At twenty-five, that stirrer of fantastic numbers found himself sentimental. Sickened by seeing all the pretty women rushing at his millions like wasps at a honeycomb, repelled by offered kisses and extenuated by good fortune, weary—abominably weary, above all—of the facility of both, and mutedly irritated by all the covetousness ignited around his name, Michael came to search for a personal adventure, a woman who, addressing the man and not the banker, would flatter and caress the most secret fibers of the individual. *Passers-by go in search of brief adventures . . .*

---

1 The lines are not by Montesquiou; the attribution is malicious; a feminized variant appears in a later story in the present collection.

"So Michel Emmaus, the lover for whom women lay in wait in the foyer of the Opéra and the boxes of the Comédie, the most sought-after lover in the Marboeuf quarter and the Avenue du Bois started prowling the exterior boulevard in the evenings. There, his incognito preserved him from unfortunate recognitions. Wrapped up in a large overcoat, his nose in a muffler, with a bowler hat pulled down over his eyes, looking like a clerk, the man who wore much-admired blue fox pelisses on the evenings of premières went to ask the gigolettes of the Butte for anonymous spasms and a few minutes of forgetfulness. In their arms, at last, he was a passer-by, and ceased to be Michael Emmaus.

"It was on one of those nocturnal hunts that he encountered La Monti, then Honorine Frespin, laundress by day, streetwalker by night . . . it was necessary to pay the bills. The pink face of the whore stimulated the banker; he followed her to the furnished hotel where Frespin took her clients. How did Emmaus' card-holder fall into the girl's hands? Michael was a cautious man, but anyway, La Frespin quickly deciphered the name; it wasn't unknown to her. Who in Paris was unaware of Michael Emmaus?

"The streetwalker had a stroke of genius; she put the card-holder back in the overcoat and served the banker the spiciest dish of her métier, and when Emmaus wanted to settle up the half-louis agreed in advance the cunning creature said: 'Keep that for yourself, darling. I've never met one like you. Whenever you want, I'll always be there, and it won't cost you anything; I'm yours for free, that's a promise.'

"Michael couldn't believe his ears; someone loved him for himself, someone was treating him like a little man. Two days later he went back to find La Frespin. The girl played a tight game. She had him under the skin; he stirred her giblets; she would have liked to be rich in order to add him to her furniture and keep him all to herself. Michael, moved, became profoundly smitten with the laundress. The comedy lasted six months. For six months Emmaus was the lover of the heart of a streetwalker on the Boulevard Rochefoucauld, but by the seventh month he couldn't stand it any longer; he named himself and installed his mistress in a little house in the Rue Monceau. She still lives there today. Emmaus made a fine feast giving the worthy girl a surprise and enjoyed her bewildered gratitude frenetically, moved to tears by her feigned amazement.

"After thirty years of liaison, Michael Emmaus still believes that he's recompensing in La Monti the only passion that he has ever inspired, and is convinced of her disinterest."

"To the innocent, full hands," concluded Madame de Nodge.

"To the innocent, full hands; you have good ones, Madame," said Jacques Snydaure, bowing. "We ought to say instead: to millionaires, empty hands—we don't have enough pity for the poverty of the rich."

"The poverty of . . . ?"

"I mean the moral poverty, the distress of a soul in infinite solitude, toward the sixty of our most envied millionaires."

"Is it you who are saying that, Monsieur Snydaure? And I thought you were an anarchist!" As Madame de Nodge smiled with her beautiful fleshy and promising mouth, the red of her lips moved like a jewel-case over the enamel of her teeth.

"That's where you're mistaken. Personally, I know of nothing more heart-rending than the agony of our great movers of money, nothing more atrocious and sadder to see than the covetousness and intrigues lying in ambush around their death-bed, and the ignominy of such families—the near and distant relatives falling on the cadaver like a flock of carrion crows. Oh, the family, those enemies given by nature, and, when there isn't any, the criminal maneuvers of employees, all that base cuisine of interests and competitions swarming around successions.

"To be sure, I feel sorry for people getting old, but my pity goes most of all to those growing old immured in a great fortune, immured and isolated, for around them, cupidity kills all good sentiment, any hint of tenderness; their death is awaited as the term of a settlement. They perish in a desert, weaned from all affection, in an atmosphere of lies and grimaces, and when, by chance, they're alert individuals who have drawn some profit from experience, they die in a frightful skepticism, having penetrated with daylight the comedies of their entourage, their hearts dolorous and dry, perhaps even more at the end of illusions than suffering . . .

"Oh, the state of soul of those old pirates of banking and industry, in whom the sweat of the workers—to talk anarchist—has maintained the arthritis and blistered the unhealthy flesh, with what terrible fear they must look into others and themselves when the hour comes to end it all! Oh, their reentry into nothingness is preceded by a few rather morose reflections, those potentates of capital and share-dealing!

"That frightful solitude of the aging millionaire, a novel of ferocious psychology has been marvelously staged in the agony of the banker Otto Treutberg. You've all read, Mesdames, the jolly *Confession de Nicaise*, in which Pierre Valdagne has a petty bourgeoise, sensual and unprincipled, but so intensely amorous of life and so childishly fearful of poverty depraved so logically and so delicately by a modern Valmont, that one even forgives her the murderous act that closes the book.[1] Nicaise Chavée has become, in exchange for a large sum, the mistress of Otto Treutberg. Treutberg is sixty, coarse, ugly and obese, and for the first time, the young woman, who has rolled around the bachelor pads a little, is obliged to overcome physical repugnance, but she has the retinue of a royal mistress, and lives installed in the Château de La Varenne. Her husband, exiled as an engineer to the Urals, has a salary of sixty thousand francs a year, and the amorous financier does not abuse his visits.

"On one of his trips to the château, Otto Treutberg is seized by an attack of angina; the frightened young woman summons

____

1 *La Confession de Nicaise* by the prolific novelist Pierre Valdagne was published in 1902.

her lover, Doctor Naudet, who does not hide from her that the situation is grave: Treutberg might die. Then he leaves Nicaise alone with the invalid. Now, the banker has not made a will and cannot make one. He had confided two millions in bonds to Naudet to put in a bank, and Nicaise knows that she only has to say a word to Naudet for those two millions to be hers, but it is necessary for Treutberg to die before the next day. Nicaise, who witnesses the banker's agony and sees him choking in the pangs of angina, does not break the little tubs of amyl nitrite that might prolong his life for a few hours, and coldly watches him die."

"Pooh!" interjected Madame de Nodge. "That's just a variant on the trick with bolsters or pillows of housekeepers standing to inherit from old men."

"Oh, housekeepers don't have a monopoly on that trick, there are honest wives who use it successfully on certain husbands who are taking too long to die!"

Syndaure regretted his words immediately, for there were two widows there, Madame Hocheuse and Madame de Nodge; but those ladies had not flinched.

"When they have too much intelligence, children don't live long," remarked Madame de Nodge. "The fact is that duly drawn-up testaments never appear to have prolonged the existence of testators."

"That's because the testaments have been communicated," the incorrigible Snydaure replied. "Wise individuals who want to enjoy an opulent and tranquil old age, only ever admit to an income for the term of their lives. Two years ago I lost an aged relative who deceived her heirs thus; she claimed to have invested everything in life annuities and only reserved a hundred thousand francs to leave to her domestics; she changed them every six months, but for six months she ensured their devotion and zealous service by skillful promises of a legacy.

"Thanks to that fortune, which she claimed to have alienated, my old cousin Bradschaere—for her third marriage had been to a Scottish lord[1]—was able to dine with her friends for fifteen years without the slightest anxiety, and risk the most varied vacations on the edge of Italian lakes and Oberland stations, accompanied by charming and needy persons whose hotel expenses she defrayed, without fear of abrupt gusts of wind on the lakes, or experiencing vertigo on the edge of precipices. Oh, she was able to have a happy old age, my cousin Bradschaere." And Snydaure added: "She was an experienced woman."

"Indeed."

"Yes, she had rolled around a great deal, and her jewel-case represented several intermarital stages."

"She had a jewel-case? What imprudence!"

"Don't worry, she left it in the bank and only wore imitations."

"She was a woman of genius."

"As I told you. And Valdagne's banker was a nag by comparison. To confide two millions to one's physician—no one is infantile to that degree."

"Notaries have been so much maligned."

"And with reason. Moral: one can only confide one's money to the earth and one's soul to God."

"We're rather jovial, but your Treutberg was an imbecile," concluded Madame Hocheuse.

"Who only got what he deserved," overbid Madame Avril.

"Yes, the poor man had had a moment of confidence," said Snydaure, with a melancholy sigh, "and he paid dearly for it. He believed in the honesty of others, although he had never had any himself, but remember that he was on the brink of death, he was sinking. Intelligence had already quit him. Who knows whether the novelist did not want that failing to highlight the force of evil in the old man In any case, it isn't that agony hastened by a slut that is the interesting feature of the book; the characteristic and heart-rending detail of the isolated distress of the million-

____

1 The surname that Lorrain probably has in mind is Bradshaw, although that originates from the north of England, not Scotland.

aire is the chapter in which, already irredeemably afflicted and sensing that he is doomed, Treutberg confides to his mistress the keys to his writing desk, and, indicating a drawer to her and an envelope in that drawer, makes a sign to her that she can keep its contents for herself.

"Now, in that envelope are two hundred thousand francs in banknotes, and a note saying: *For the woman who will be there when I die.* The multimillionaire had foreseen the hour of his death, but had not foreseen what woman would then be with him."

"More and more cheerful, what you're telling us, my dear Snydaure, but I suppose that it isn't for nothing that you're entertaining us with these funereal subjects? I've known you for a long time. You're a man of preparations."

"Indeed; it's necessary that I burn my ships, since I've been unmasked. If I've talked to you for such a long time about *La Confession of Nicaise*, it's because there's a little Madame Chavée here."

"A Madame Chavée, maintained by a banker. Where?" The three women all looked at the same time, with their faces behind their hands, in all directions in the restaurant.

"In the corner on the left, the tall young woman in chinchilla, with the toque of orchids."

"A long branch, indeed—but very, very pretty," said Madame de Nodge, prolonging the examination, "and she has pearls, that's all I'll say."

"And look at the emeralds in her ears."

"And the ones on her fingers. She has a complete outfit: pearl necklace, emerald clasp, emerald pendants and two on every finger."

"A fortune, then, that little woman?"

"A fortune, no, but two years ago she had one of the great gamblers of Paris in her skirts; that's Madame Brocke."

"Madame Brocke! The mistress of Isaac Abraham!"

"Isaac Abraham the Pole, the grain-merchant of Odessa?"

"The same."

"She's ravishing."

"It's Abraham who was killed, however, six months ago, in an automobile, and that's why she's wearing mourning, in emeralds and flowers in fashionable tea-rooms."

"But Abraham was only her financial backer; one doesn't wear mourning for one's banker."

"A financial backer who managed his capital forcefully, so I hear."

"But while giving himself such interest, at least two hundred—what am I saying?—three hundred per cent. Anyway, she's not unemployed; do you know who's with her?"

"No."

"Rospiglieri, the banker of Livorno, and MacFerney, of the copper trust."

"She's devoted to capitalists, then, that little woman!"

"Everyone specializes nowadays. One is the mistress of sovereigns, of jockeys, of bankers; she moves in her milieu, and is right to stay there. The milieu is profitable."

"Married?"

"Naturally. I told you about a Madame Chavée. The husband is employed at a large salary in one of the branches of those Messieurs. When the couple have four or five little millions, you'll see that they'll be the most honest and most perfect household in some sunlit station of the Riviera."

"Villa des Mimosas, between Cannes and Antibes. I can see it from here—or between Nice and Beaulieu on the Villefranche road."

"Balls at clubs and great dinners at the Reserves, Madame Brocke will be at all the charity sales and will receive Archdukes."

"But I don't see the agony of Isaac Abraham in all that, Snydaure, the solitary agony of the old man."

"Abraham's was rather short. He was killed instantly, crushed, pulped, between his machine and the embankment. He had the folly of speed and was traveling at a hundred kilometers an hour. The auto swerved and went into the ditch. The driver was found gasping on a heap of stones; peasants overtaken half an hour before, observed the disaster. The machine was there, still wheezing and shaking over the pulped cadaver of the banker but there had been a woman with them, a woman swathed in veils and mufflers, masked with goggles—unrecognizable, in sum, and that woman was never found. Completely eclipsed and disappeared, the masked unknown—and that woman was the pretty Madame Brocke. She had breakfasted that morning with Abraham at Pithiviers and had left with him in the automobile.

"Having jumped out before the machine overturned—Madame Brocke has agility—the delectable egotist had not wanted to be compromised. Enquiries, inquests and death certificates were only formalities, Abraham had died under his machine, and what did the agony of a chauffeur matter to a high-flying woman like that? With admirable sang-froid, she had continued her route, had sought information from the first peasant she met about the nearest railway station, had consulted the timetable there, and the first train had taken her back to Paris. She had been able to go home for dinner and appeared the same evening at the Opéra, for the accident had happened on a Friday. It was in her box that she learned the news. The Prefecture of Police only received a telegram late in the evening from the Mairie of Escrenne, in which the identity of the dead men was recorded.

"I promised you a Madame Chavée."

THE FAMILY

For Jean-Baptiste Forain[1]

---

1 Presumably Lorrain means the Impressionist painter Jean-Louis Forain (1852-1931), with whom he was certainly acquainted.

CHILDREN'S GAMES[1]

"WHY don't I like the family? My God! Because I've seen my own and others at too close a range. I wouldn't go so far as to say that relatives are enemies given by nature, that would be to exaggerate matters, but it's certain that, making an exception for the father and the mother, a kind of protective and malevolent hostility is the atmosphere that we find around our other relatives. Attentive to our slightest faults, unjust to our rare qualities, brothers, sisters, aunts and cousins appoint themselves as judges of all our actions, criticize what we say and do without mercy, decree our careers and our aptitudes, and without paying the slightest heed to our tastes and our instincts, assign us the role in existence that pleases them and fixes us. We are theirs, every moment of our life belongs to them. We owe them all deference, and in exchange for a little acrimonious advice, we are held, with regard to the most senile uncles and the most peevish aunts in the position of the soldier standing to attention with his head still and silent in the rank. No rights, but all obligations. At the slightest deviation, all recriminations, and at a hint of recidivism, all the maledictions of the family, with threats of being scratched out of the testament."

And Roger, waving his hands comically above his head, sketched the customary anathema of the "noble father" in boulevard dramas.

---

1 First published in *Le Journal* 11 February 1903.

"What a tableau! By how many uncles have you been disinherited, my dear?"

"None. Nature has endowed me with a long string of cousins; I even owe them a rather dolorous childhood, for, misfortune having determined that I was one of the youngest, the priority of age conferred on the others the right to rebuke me and pull my ears. Not only was I the one most often punished on the reports of bad jokers, who were subsequently given to me as examples, but in games of blind man's buff or hide-and-seek organized by those turbulent little creatures, the most fatiguing roles always devolved to me. It was always me who was *it*. The worst injustices were committed every day at my expense; my weakness made their joy, and, jostled and beaten by the boys, abused and slyly pinched by the girls, I was always accused of bad behavior and rendered responsible for the worst misdeeds. It was me, me, *the mangy one, from which all the evil came,*[1] and I still have at heart the frightful cunning of my cousin Hermance, a little Saint-Touch-me-Not with the voice of a shrike, whose rascally imaginations, if she hasn't changed, must greatly inconvenience her husband . . .

"I retained that trait. In a charade in which I played a heretic conducted to the pyre—for it was always me who was hanged, quartered, tortured and decapitated—didn't my cousin Hermance have the idea of coiffing me, in the guise of the bonnet of the condemned, with her own bloomers. She had demanded that I walk barefoot. I had only been left my chemise, like a penitent, and, with that chemise lifted over my loins, my face blackened with soot, I was pushed while being whipped—for I was an infidel—and while the legs of the wretched bloomers dangled over my face, the entire band, excited by evil scapegraces, uttered cries of joy and lashed my buttocks with hazel switches. My cousin, who was playing Queen

____

1 The quotation is from Jean de La Fontaine's fable in verse "Les Animaux malade de la peste" (tr. as "The Animals Sick of the Plague").

Isabella the Catholic, strutted behind, draped in an andrinople curtain; her two little sisters, Totote and Germaine—the older was seven—played two Moorish princesses destined for the strappado. They had been tied by the foot to a tree, and their weakness consecrated them to the worst treatment. The spectacle of those I endured penetrated them with such terror that they started to scream; the youngest princess forgot herself. The emotion of the royal captives attracted their parents; a rain of slaps descended on Isabella's cortege; the Inquisitors were dispersed and the captives freed.

"As for me, the unfortunate heretic, I was convicted of indecency. My cousin Hermance, who had the gift of the gab, proved as clear as day that I was the instigator of the entire masquerade. I alone had regulated the details and the accessories; it was me who had wanted to be whipped.

"'But that's sadism,' exclaimed my Aunt de Ponvielles. 'That child will deprave the others.' And, turning to my mother: 'Rosalie, it's impossible to keep Roger with our children; he has an unfortunate imagination. My poor Hermance'—for my Aunt de Ponvielles was the mother of that young person—'how were you able to resolve to figure in such a horror? How were you able to allow your sisters to be tied up by the foot?'

"The little liar had tied them up herself, but that didn't prevent her from crying hot tears and protesting her innocence loudly. All the other kids joined in the chorus; they feared Hermance's perfidy. Madame de Ponvielles, tumultuous and red-faced, withdrew, taking her daughters away. I remained alone in the garden with my mother. That evening, all the aunts and uncles met in the drawing room to settle my fate. It was decided that I would be sent away to school; my presence was a danger for the other children. I might contaminate with my bad example that troop of urchins and vicious little girls.

"It was thus that I knew injustice, the taste of which made me heart-sick, and that I appreciated for the first time the equity of family councils. It was also my first contact with the hypocrisy of society, for that of children reflects exactly that of humans, and all the infamies that I discovered at school affected me less profoundly than that first misadventure of my life as a small boy.

"My schoolfellow appeared to me to be neither less cowardly nor more villainous than my cousins, and in truth, I found less prejudice and stupidity in those bitter pariahs known as junior teachers than in my noble Aunt de Ponvielles. Thirty years after that incident—the poor woman is dead now and God has her soul—for her I was still the fellow who had removed her daughter's bloomers to put them on my head."

"All right, but you had an unfortunate aunt."

"She nevertheless incarnated for me the malevolent iniquity of the spirit of family, as my aged second cousin Fromentier personified its tedium. Oh, the families of the old bourgeoisie and the extraordinary specimens one finds there: old spinsters with manias, sententious and finicky old boys similarly stuck in another epoch and a special eccentricity of which modern progress has destroyed the mold. It required the quiet, as if quilted, provincial life that certain quarters of Paris had then, and the respect of outdated habitudes faithfully observed and transmitted, to prolong into our day touching and comical fossils of those sorts. My cousin Fromentier was one of those types.

"She was seventy-five years old and possessed some wealth. She was a stout woman with heavy legs, her figure deformed by a commencement of hydropsy; the pink and shiny skin of her face was cracking gently, like old porcelain. A tower of blonde hair gripped her temples, her mouth was moist and slack, and her nose still thin between the puffiness of her cheeks. Always aureoled by extravagant bonnets with yellow ribbons, Cousin Fromentier, dolled up like a superannuated coquette, retained the ragged freshness of a hollyhock. Mittens on her swollen hands, enormous rings on all her fingers, and a brooch with a miniature of Colonel Fromentier in the ruche of her collaret completed the lady's harness. The colonel was also depicted full-length in an oval frame hung up in the drawing room above a piano that was never opened.

"Cousin Fromentier had buried two husbands and three daughters, but she had retained an income of twenty-five thousand francs, and that solid fortune in landed property guaranteed her the assiduous deference of a host of little cousins. I was one of them, brought there by family, counting—quite mistakenly—on the facile expansion of the senile tenderness of an aged egotistical sensuality.

"My cousin Fromentier lived in Montrouge, in a large house between a courtyard and a garden, which resembled a branch of the Petits Ménages,[1] it was so crowded with old people. All the sexagenarians in Paris seemed to gather there. It was a succession of small four-room apartments, narrow and neat, the most sought-after of which overlooked, in full sunlight, the chestnut-grove of the garden. The ground-floor apartments opened on to narrow parallelograms of arbors and flower-beds, the outmoded flowers of which testified well enough to the age and taste of the inhabitants. My cousin occupied two apartments combined into one on the first floor; her means permitted that.

"Her six windows, draped with imberline, which the sun bathed in winter from ten o'clock in the morning, overlooked the wallflowers, in spring, and the sunflowers, in autumn, of Mademoiselle d'Etiennevent, who lived below her. She was the only person in the house that my cousin Fromentier consented to see. Mademoiselle d'Etiennevent was noble; my cousin had the dignity of her twenty-thousand-franc income. That exclusivism in the choice of her relations earned her the respectful consideration of the other tenants.

"My cousin Fromentier received every Sunday. We found ourselves in the midst of the family there, variously distant cousins from the four corners of Paris, and as soon as the threshold was

---

1 L'Hôpital des Petits Ménages was a retirement home for aged couples in Issy-les-Moulineaux, on the site now occupied by the Hôpital Corentin Celton.

crossed I felt sick, so rarefied and insipid was the air of the old lady's room. My cousin was always afraid of catching cold, and the windows were only opened for half an hour a day, the time to make her bed, and in that room, as sunny and overheated as a greenhouse, where the stout woman simmered all week wrapped in an enormous shawl and thick woolen skirts, the atmosphere was further aggravated by the reek of mincemeat, the food of Coquet, my cousin's beloved pug and the nasty odors of that animal. As fat and shiny as a lump of lard under his short fur, which was falling out, Coquet was an object of disgust for all of us. His tail stiffened by age, hairless and paunchy, Coquet dragged himself over the floor with the slowness of a sick beast, and his strong breath made us laugh and pinch our noses. The wretched animal breathed everywhere . . .

"All those infirmities did not prevent my cousin from being excessively fond of her dog. She wrapped him in her skirts all day long, and, when he was not in his basket he dozed and snored on her knees, only waking up to show us his teeth. The pug was the *bête noire* of our visits.

"Oh, my cousin's insipid room and the interminable pauses that my parents thought they ought to make there every Sunday, attentive to the slightest caresses that she seemed to take pleasure in inflicting on me. The cousin received us sunk in a large arm-chair with wings, her knees higher than her loins, with a gold chain around her neck, clad in shiny silk, its creaking muffled by her woolen underclothes.

"'How are you, cousin?'

"'So so, so so. And how is the child?'

"And the ordeal commenced. There were sticky kisses of her slack mouth on my cheeks, then pats of her moist hands, and then it was necessary to embrace Coquet, but not too hard, in order not to do him harm; and under the severe eye of my father I had to submit to the putridity of the old dog's rotten teeth.

"That was one of the rituals of the visit to Cousin Fromentier, a veritable family institution. The ceremonial was regulated in advance, as at the Escorial, and none of us would have dared to fail in it. Once at Montrouge, all the children were obliged to embrace Coquet. But I was the favorite, and another torture was reserved for me. Cousin Fromentier had a box of English toffees placed permanently on a small table set beside her. She took one out of it at intervals without offering them to anyone, and her greedy old lady's fat lips were always in the process of sucking. As I said, I had the honor of her preference, and in that quality, it often happened that my cousin took one of her half-sucked toffees out of her mouth and stuffed it into mine, saying: 'Finish that, my child; it's very good, it's orange-flavored.'

"And under the imperious eye of my father, I had to swallow the frightful sweet, all sticky with saliva, that had been granted to me . . .

"'Oh, cousin, how good you are, how you spoil him!' cried my parents.

"And I also had to say: 'Thank you.'

"That ingurgitation of sucked toffees in an old lady's hot and stuffy room, under the gaze of an icy and authoritarian father has always remained with me as a symbol of familial ennui. I haven't forgotten that repugnant chore of my childhood Sundays, after thirty-five years."

THE PLOMIGNON HEIRS[1]

"IT'S necessary, however, not to think that I base my holy horror of the family uniquely on the impressions of childhood. If I live like a wolf, prudently distant from my relatives and put several hundred leagues between my residence and the town where my parents live, I have other motivating factors than the memories of a small boy.

"I've witnessed a few death-throes . . ."

Roger had quit the divan, where he had been sprawled among the cushions, his elbow on a Scutari square, a cigarette between his lips, and came to stand in front of the fireplace with his back to the fire, in the pose of a drawing-room lecturer, offering the soles of his feet alternately to the flames.

"Yes, I've witnessed a few deathbed scenes, and the interest I've seen brought to the dying has enlightened me definitively regarding the place held by those who are departing in the hearts of those who remain. It's then that one sees becoming manifest—what am I saying? developing in all its beauty—the famous human egotism, and, at the same time, the very particular solicitude that the death-throes of rich relatives awaken in the soul.

"The most notoriously indifferent individuals suddenly discover a tender sensibility for the sufferings of the dying person; the most hardened old ladies and the quadragenarians most

---

1 First published in *Le Journal* 17 February 1903.

desiccated by experience set records of sensitivity around the bedside. 'How he's suffering! It's atrocious to see him agitating thus!' It's a spectacle of which they cannot bear the sight, and with all their prayers they summon the death that will liberate the patient. 'It would be better if it ended!'

"And, in fact, they're in haste to see it finished. Under the handkerchiefs with which they are dabbing their eyes one glimpses strange gazes and singularly attentive pupils. The heirs are on watch, making an inventory of their dolor, without prejudice to the other inventory. And from the Boule clock, valued at twenty-five thousand francs, to the feverish hands of the invalid, which are clutching his sheets, all their sharp and taut covetousness goes back and forth in the room, impelling the gasping unfortunate with all their strength toward the final annihilation."

"Aren't you exaggerating a little, Roger? In truth, I suspect you of lyricism."

"Lyricism, me! I'm attenuating. In any case, I've seen, and I'd rather tell you what I've seen. Firstly, the false joys of the Plomignon heirs. I'll proceed as in feuilleton novels: sensational chapters and titles in large type.

"Madame Plomignon was dying, and her family thought that it was really about time. Gathered in the beautiful apartment in the Avenue du Boise-de-Boulogne that Madame Plomignon had occupied for twenty years, her son and her two daughters, the issue of three different marriages—Madame Plomignon had been thrice conjoined—were resigned from the first days of her illness to the loss of their mother.

"All three were married and provided with children. At the beginning of the illness they had invaded the old lady's domicile and installed themselves in the beautiful apartments. The father-in-law and the two sons-in-law were there, all taking turns on night-watch; and during the day, the Plomignon grandchildren, four of whom were already married themselves and founding stocks, for God blesses numerous families, and between twenty and forty years of age the dying woman had conscientiously occupied herself with repopulation. Between her three marriages, the great grandmother of today had lost a few little Plomignons.

"The woman that I called Mère Plomignon, seventy-five years old, apartment in Paris, château in Limousin and villa in Cannes, was an amiable woman, highly-colored, luxuriant and robust, and, great-grandmother as she was, she had not disarmed. I had met her ten years before in Nice, where, during the Carnival, she followed all the vegliones and brought back prizes and banners to the redoubts of the Casino. The costumes she sported there preoccupied her for six months in advance; their luxury was extravagant. All the family's ostrich plumes were requisitioned for her head-dresses; Mère Plomignon's Louis XVI dominos and Watteau shepherdesses revolutionized the juries; furthermore, she was the best woman in the world. She had not moldered for thirty-five years in the province to end up cloistered in a convent! 'I have a right to a happy old age,' she said. 'I had enough boredom when I was a young woman.'

"Married for the first time to a notary, she had lived in Pont-à-Mousson for fifteen years. Her second husband, a commandant and then a colonel of cuirassiers, had dragged her from one garrison to another for ten years. She had only known a few good times in Orléans, once she had become the *première presidente*, thanks to Monsieur Plomingnon. Once Plomingnon was liquidated, the amiable widow had ceased her matrimonial experiments; she had a right to retirement.

"It was those memories of the notariat, the regiment and the magistracy that shook Madame Plomignon joyously. She loved luxury, pleasure, the sumptuousness of three residences, ran around the spa towns in summer, filled the Riviera with her presence in winter and only returned to Paris in spring. She received everywhere with an open table, only granted what was necessary to the family, and acquitted herself toward it with beautiful gifts to her grandchildren. Madame Plomignon understood life; at least she had profited from her experience of it. Madame Plomignon lived in accordance with her tastes.

"Her children criticized her. Her son, daughters, sons-in-law and daughter-in-law did not approve of Madame Plomignon's lifestyle. Her expenditure was exaggerated; they considered her travels, her winter stations, her attire and her plumage to be so many inroads into the family patrimony. That crazy ancestor was compromising the future of her descendants. It is true that the stout coquette, among so many prodigalities nurtured an almost culpable liking for boas, plumes and down-feathers. She also liked flowery lampas, shiny satins, crackling watered silks and the tumult of colorful silk embroidery. She was also fond of jewelry, and, violently bedecked, plumed in eruptions of ruches and furbelows, paraded from Aix to Trouville and from Dinard to Monte Carlo the most astonishing carnival of loud dresses and rocketing hairstyles: an innocent and lavish masquerade, the augmentation of the expenses of which her natural heirs saw fearfully.

"'She's a living scandal. It'll be necessary to have her locked up. She's dilapidating the wealth of our children,' Maître Rocadour, Madame Plomignon's second son-in-law had already insinuated several times. But as the worthy woman only spent her income, was adored by her suppliers and her domestics and also had numerous friends ready to defend the benefits of her table and her hospitality, the good Madame Plomignon found herself sufficiently protected against the good intentions of her children, and Maître Rocadour had had to resign himself to living on his advocate's practice, on which he lived rather poorly with Madame Rocadour, née Hortense Plomignon, and the three demoiselles Rocadour, all three married into the army between Toulon and Draguignan.

"So, on the evening when Madame Plomignon, who had been running around clothing stores and milliners' salons all day, was obliged to go to bed with a thirty-nine-degree fever, the news was welcomed by the family with a certain relief.

"All the Plomingnons resident in Paris raced to the dwelling in the Avenue du Bois-de-Boulogne. They installed themselves by the bedside of the invalid, firmly determined to care for her until the last sigh. Maître Rocadour, informed by telegram, immediately quit his province, confiding his studio to his head clerk, and took up residence, with his wife, in his mother-in-law's house, to the great scandal of the other Plomignon children, who only came to spend the night there.

"'We finally have her,' declared the implacable ministerial officer. 'At her age and with the life she's led, it's impossible that she'll escape.'

"'Poor mother, the organism is well used up in her,' sighed Madame Himoulet, Madame Plomignon's elder daughter. 'She had such an agitated existence, she didn't listen to anyone. Her winters in Nice have advanced it!'

"'Every evening at the restaurant! She led the life of a courtesan. My mother-in-law is dying of excess,' concluded Maître Rocadour. 'She's killed herself.'

"'Poor mother! We loved her so much,' said Madame Himoulet.

"'Our mother lived as she pleased,' Monsieur Plomignon junior, having become the head of the family by virtue of the old lady's comatose state, felt obliged to put in. 'We don't have the right to criticize her conduct. She could certainly have put a little bit by every year, and thought a little more about her grandchildren, but in sum, our mother is seventy-five, and dying at seventy-five is a beautiful death.'

"'Less dissipated and calmer, though, she might have lived for a few years more,' objected Monsieur Himoulet, who rather liked his mother-in-law. The silence of his brothers-in-law warned him that he had said too much. The hypothesis of Madame Plomignon's prolonged existence had caused significant glances to be exchanged in the assembly.

"'Shut up; you only say stupid things,' Madame Himoulet, née Adèle Plomignon, whispered in her husband's ear.

"In short, the good Madame Plomignon was dying, extenuated by the usury of pleasure. That was also the opinion of the three physicians summoned in all haste to her presence—for there were three, each household having brought its own. The Himoulets, like the Plomignons, only had confidence in their own doctor; Maître Rocadour, who had not been able to displace the Faculty of Draguignan, had interposed an intern and, after a long discussion of diet and treatment, Madame Plomignon's death-throes were organized . . . and it was a beautiful agony.

"From one day to the next the apartment took on the appearance of a hospital; the interested parties no longer cast off, and amid the muffled footfalls of the comings and goings of watchers, each incomplete household spent the night in the drawing-room, attentive to the sounds of the sick-room with one eye on the knick-knacks in the display-case, some of which were quite valuable; and every morning, a Rocadour flanked by a Himoulet relieved a Plomignon flanked by a Rocadour, who had previously relieved a Himoulet flanked by a Plomignon; and the dying woman did not die, prolonged, one might have thought, by all that confidence.

"I had known Madame Plomignon on the Riviera and had consecrated a veritable amity to the amiable woman. As soon as I was informed of her condition, I went to obtain news of her. Every day, I was introduced into the drawing room where the family was sitting, and my solicitude elicited the response of contrite expressions: 'Not dead yet! Not yet! She's very low, and surely won't last the night.' Or there were variants of this sort: 'We don't understand it; the physicians can't get over it. It can't go on like this; it's too painful. My wife can't stand it any more.' Or: 'We thought that it was all over; she nearly passed away last night. It's atrocious, these false alarms.' And in the meantime, the moribund was given extreme unction pitilessly. Twice a week there were processions of curés, last sacraments and *Asperges me*, amid *Oremus* and genuflections. The old lady was confessed and reconfessed repeatedly . . . but Madame Plomignon didn't die.

"Her soul riveted to her body, she resisted all those funereal preparations.

"One evening, however, I thought the supreme moment had come. When I called in at about seven o'clock, on my way to dine in the Bois, to obtain news of the dying woman, I found all her descendants in tears. All and sundry of the Plomignon grandchildren had been summoned to grandmother's bedside. 'Oh, Monsieur Roger, this time it's really the end!' And I was taken in to see the agonizing woman.

"Madame Plomignan was black. Her eyes were bloodshot and blood was decomposed in violet patches beneath the skin; she had the swollen and earthen face that one associates with plague-victims; her tumefied lower lip was slack; her haggard eyes no longer recognized me. Madame Plomignon was breathing with difficulty and her breath was whistling like a death-rattle; the poor woman was really doomed. I looked at her one last time and I followed Madame Himoulet into the drawing room. Part of the family was gathered there; two grand-daughters were drawing up invitation-lists for the funeral under the dictation of their father, Monsieur Plomignon. The daughter-in-law was checking the suppliers' bills that had already begun to rain down on the domicile of the not-quite-dead woman. They got up to greet me with desolate expressions and handshakes.

"Maître Rocadour, in the process of making an inventory of the paintings in the room, took possession of me and drew me into Madame Plomignon's dressing-room. I found Madame Rocadour there and two little Himoulets emptying the old lady's cupboards and drawers; there was a strange display of dresses, lace and furbelows.

"'I wanted to show you,' said the advocate. 'Is this the wardrobe of an old woman? They're theatrical costumes, and these hats . . . what a masquerade! The headgear of performing dogs.'

"Monsieur Himoulet, who came in on tiptoe, took his brother-in-law back to the drawing room. I took my leave and Himoulet escorted me to the threshold of the apartment. There the worthy man unburdened himself to me. 'My brother-in-law is frightful. He wants to open the safe and wants Plomignon to take away the share certificates in order to avoid declarations to the Registry. He simply wants to steal the money—a ministerial officer! He's been well received by Plomingnon.'

"I never saw that astonishing family again. Madame Plomignon cheated her children by not dying again that time. The worthy woman escaped. Nowadays she spends her winters in Cairo and puts straits and seas between herself and the expectations of the Plomignon heirs."

AUNT DE QUINSONNAS[1]

"OH, the family! We haven't finished laughing and crying if we start on the chapter of heritages and successions. The family cost me nearly five hundred thousand francs."

"Disinherited, my poor Quinsonnas?"

"Absolutely, everything was radically taken away from me by an old provincial aunt, the most incorrigible old spinster that the unhealthy exercise of high and low devotions has ever produced."

"Of five hundred thousand francs?"

"Exactly; at four per cent that would have been a good twenty thousand francs of annual income, which passed under my nose, and for a carnival prank. An entire heritage, of which I've been robbed for a studio joke, the succession of my Aunt Aménaïde de Quinsonnas, my father's sister. You know how much I like masques, and the haste I have to disguise myself. The worthy lady has left everything to convents and churches: pious donations and foundations, and all because of an unfortunate misunderstanding in which my aunt was, in fact, slightly maltreated—but she also wears such extraordinary fashions."

---

1 Adapted from an item published in *Le Journal* before any of the other items in the present collection on 24 April 1902 as part of a sequence of "Histories de Masques." The newspaper version begins with the narrator refusing to go to the Bal Gavarni in spite of the promise of seeing "Caroline Otero" and "Liane de Lancy" there; that passage is cut in order to link the story to the preceding two items, which might have been intended to begin a story sequence that was abandoned, although that operation leaves the final line of the item a trifle stranded, deprived of its initiating parenthesis.

"But this is a whole story. Why haven't you told us before?"

"I'd bore you."

"On the contrary. If *Peau d'ane* were told to me, I'd take an extreme pleasure in it, and we'd have had no doubt that Mademoiselle de Quinsonnas, as soon as she was your aunt, was full of interest."

And after a few vigorous taps on the cushions of dear Roger's divans, once nicely nestled between the Venetian velvet squares and his pink Turkish silk pillows, we set ourselves to listen to him dutifully.

"I'm not telling you anything, my friends, in saying that I was brought up in the provinces."

"That's obvious even in your works," insinuated that bad penny Jacques Baudran.

"My father, soon a widower and very smitten with a liaison that weighed upon my life, was scarcely occupied with his son, and the orphan I was would have risked moldering and etiolating in the Jesuit college where my author had deposited me without the solicitude and vigilance—I won't say maternal, but scrupulous and finicky—of my Aunt Aménaïde. Mademoiselle de Quinsonnas had not approved of my father's marriage, but she appreciated his mistresses even less. On the death of my mother, of whose prettiness and elegance she had always been jealous, our Aunt de Quinsonnas, who had not wanted to receive us three months earlier, descended upon us like a whirlwind, with perfect expressions of contrition, already in full mourning for the dead woman before the corpse and been removed, demanded to see her dear nephews, intimidated the domestics and, taking possession of my sister and me, said: 'Oh, my poor children! Fortunately, you still have me.' And, my father having come in at that moment: 'Monsieur,' she said, looking at him haughtily, 'a misfortune never comes alone.'

"'Indeed,' Monsieur de Quinsonnas replied, never caught at a loss, 'here you are again, my sister.' That was the usual tone of family reconciliations.

"My father didn't remain surly with his sister for long. He was only too glad to discharge the education of his daughter and his son on to her. My sister was placed with the Ursulines of Laon, and I was imprisoned with the Jesuits. A year after his widowhood, my father went to live in Reims, a city of luxury and resources for a man of his tastes, and my aunt de Quinsonnas was triumphantly installed in the old family house. My mother's presence had driven her out of it; she had never been able to accustom herself to the presence of a young woman; death reopened its doors to her. She returned to it as the absolute mistress, as the elder, and as head of the family, since my father, her younger brother, left the place and the care of his children to her.

"My Aunt Aménaïde had the vocation of criticism and investigation; it is for love of despotism that she had remained an old maid, and yet, Mademoiselle de Quinsonnas had been pretty. Unsuspectably virtuous, she had prided herself on it, above all, in order to be scornful of people, and devotion was for her, a right of criticism. She had the soul of the Inquisition.

"My aunt de Quinsonnas was a veritable power in the society of Laon; her large fortune, her functions as *presidente* of the Enfants de Marie, her affiliation to all the fellowships of the town, her gifts to churches and her ostentatious alms, the sumptuousness of her temporary altars at the Fête-Dieu and her practical attachment to bigotry put her on a pedestal above the common and made her a sort of Jesuit general in a crepe hood and black merino dress—for, out of hatred for fashion, my aunt always wore the mourning for my mother that she was unable to feel, and for a further ten years paced the solitary streets of Laon in hooded bonnets and rigid crinolines.

"My aunt de Quinsonnas! But there'd be a whole book to write about her. What a childhood we had, my sister and I, in the hands of that peevish and tyrannical old spinster! A few details cited at random will establish her better for you than a long story. My sister and I arrived at dreading the days of emergence, and God knows the terms in which she had recommended us to the superiors of our respective schools, Père Anselme and Mère Angelique. 'Be very severe, Father; don't let anything pass, Mother. Children aren't raised sternly enough. See how my brother turned out, who was spoiled so much!'

"There were incessant recriminations on the subject of the author of our days, punctuated with laments regarding our future and sudden effusions of tenderness, especially before strangers. 'Those poor children, what would have become of them without me? I've devoted myself to them, will they remember it later? Life has already overwhelmed me with so much bitterness.'

"Already anticipating a future for which the present gave us horror, our father, neglectful of us as he was, had become the object of our affection. We saw him in passing, between two adventures or two pleasure parties, but his brusque good humor and his fine insouciance made us feel more cruelly the punctilious and despotic character of his sister.

"My aunt de Quinsonnas! Two or three of her manias will establish her better than a whole portrait. Had she not demanded that my weekly linen be laundered in her house; it was brought to the school every Monday; she intended to keep a check on my conduct by the examination of my sheets. 'Boys lie, but sheets speak,' she affirmed, with an experience disconcerting in an old spinster.

"On our days of leave she took us for a walk in the cemetery, and, stopping us between the tombs, she told us in detail the stories of the dead, which were always disastrous. Adultery, fraud and usury demolished in her mouth the most laudatory epitaphs of the heirs of the dead; she took the pleasure of a hyena in tearing apart the pasts of the defunct; and with that, she had the pride of a peacock in believing that she was honoring God with her pious practices; a little more and she would have distributed places in Paradise.

"What we endured with her! We had arrived at dreading her visits to the parloir. Her endless recommendations, the willful extravagance of her attire, half-nun and half-lady of the parish, made the other pupils roar with laughter; and no treats, in order not to develop our evil instincts. In the weeks when she came to visit us we were ragged for three days by our comrades because of Aunt Aménaïde.

"Now that you know the lady, imagine her discomfiture and her fury on the day when, by virtue of an irreparable error, my aunt de Quinsonnas, having disembarked in Paris on the Monday before the beginning of Lent in order to surprise the conduct of her nephew there, came to my studio, in the midst of a masquerade of artists and models gathered there in costumes before going to tour the nocturnal restaurants and dance-halls.

"My studio in the Boulevard de Clichy had been chosen as the general rendezvous. It was the year of my medal at the Salon, and my father, who had allowed me to follow my vocation as a painter, to the chagrin of my aunt, was jubilant in his pride in the inanity of her predictions. My aunt had not yet been able to adapt to my success. 'But he's working,' my father said, 'he's collecting medals like flowers, and commissions are flooding in. What more do you want?' My aunt Aménaïde was nourishing an idea at the back of her mind; she intended to catch me at fault and convict of debauchery that laborious nephew and receiver of medals.

"So there she was, having departed surreptitiously for Paris and taken the Odéon-Clichy omnibus from her little hotel in the Rue Saint-Sulpice, which deposited her two steps from my door. Her Inquisitor's flair had inspired her well in bringing her to me on a day of the Carnival. We were in full effervescence, already lit up by champagne and above all, intoxicated by youth, a whole band of young painters and apprentice sculptors, disguised at random, decked out with the fantastic whimsy of artists, as toffs, coal-heavers, mamelukes, wild men and tramps, along with half a dozen beautiful girls with figures generously offered in short skirts and provocative disguises. The band was almost complete and we were only waiting for Pégomar, a

154

Biterrois student in pharmacy in the Latin Quarter, whose verve and whimsy were priceless.

"At that point, my aunt de Quinsonnas arrived. On the strength of her crinoline and hood, my domestic mistook her for a masque and let her in. A charivari, a volley of hurrahs and animal cries saluted the entry of the lady in curlers, her nose sporting spectacles, under the outmoded shade of a hooded bonnet. 'Vive Pégomar! Oh, the good Pégomar, has he succeeded!'

"So my aunt, grabbed, jostled and embraced in passing, is seized by the legs and hoisted on to the shoulders of a eunuch and a tramp. Suffocated by stupor, she feels frenetic hands exploring her underwear and foraging in her closed bloomers. The laughter redoubles, a saraband of lunatics spins and howls around her, women roll on the floor, overcome by laughter, unable to do any more.

"Choked by wrath, pinched and jeered, she finally finds the strength to scream: 'I'm Quinsonnas' aunt! My nephew, I disinherit you!' I jostle my friends in vain; no one wants to believe the truth; everyone continues dancing and demanding applause for Aunt de Quinsonnas.

"Too late! My aunt Amenaïde had fainted. A drunken musketeer poured a glass of champagne over her in vain.

"Mademoiselle de Quinsonnas was jaundiced by it and never wanted to see me again; she died having disinherited me and my sister—who was, however, quite innocent of anything. Her fortune went to the congregations. That's why I don't like masques."

AMOUR

To Doctor Robin[1]

---

1 Albert Robin (1847-1928) treated Lorrain for his intestinal disorders; he was also a noted art collector. His other clients included Stéphane Mallarmé, Octave Mirbeau and Marcel Proust.

MANINE[1]

"YOU'RE making a fuss of me and welcoming me . . . with songs! When I'm not there, I'm sure that you never think about me."

"Never! That would be too difficult for me."

And, looking boldly into the young man's eyes, the brunette seized the young man's hand and, with an abrupt gesture, placed it on her bodice, over the heart.

The express was traveling at seventy kilometers an hour. The long series of carriages, shaken on their brakes, undulated unsteadily, a strange iron snake in the morning mist. An autumnal aurora set the countryside ablaze, igniting mirror gleams in stagnant ponds and pale golden smoke in the reddening foliage of the poplars. The dew-soaked pink and gray landscape, moistened by light, was framed in rapid Corots in the vasistas of the door, and in the compartment crowded with sleepers; Maxence, numbed by the thick atmosphere of the carriage, had raised the blind in his corner. With his nape plunged in the pillow obtained in the station at Marseille, he watched the marvelous tapestry of yellow silk and silver thread woven in the meadows by the autumnal sunrise.

"Laroche! Halt of ten minutes! Buffet!"

Having swallowed the traditional milky coffee, he had reinstalled himself in his compartment, in the atmosphere rendered

---

1 First published in *Le Journal* 29 November 1902, the first item in the "Femmes" sequence.

insipid by the odors of leather and human respiration; the train
had pulled away; the interrupted spring had resumed almost
immediately, and, huddled in his corner under his blankets,
Maxence hypnotized himself in the contemplation of the external scenery . . .

The enchantment of the sky continued there, attenuated with
every passing minute by the diffusion of the light which was
tarnished as the sun climbed; and in the gradually extinguished
coloration of the countryside, it was neither the rust of gilded
wood, like some sumptuous golden cloth, nor the pale gold of
dried reeds on the edges of pools, nor the luminous streak of
the Seine in long silky tremors on the edge of the horizon that
retained his thoughts, but two eyes evoked, two violet blue irises
in the lustrous shadow of long black lashes: the two Provençal
eyes of the little grisette from Toulon rediscovered the previous
evening in Marseille.

Less than a brief fling, an encounter already two years old
. . . a sway of hips and the amber of a downy nape remarked
one morning in April in the hubbub and the sunlit tumult of
the Allées La Fayette . . . Manine's gaze, alarmed at first, and
then smiling, once she sensed that she was being followed. The
display of a flower-seller had permitted them to meet; the girl
had stopped there. Maxence had offered her a posy of pink carnations; it had been accepted without him having to beg.

That evening, they dined together, and three hours later, they
were lovers.

The girl had given herself without reticence, without complications and without bargaining, as if it were the most natural
thing in the world. In that blessed land of sunlight, people make
love as one breathes, or as one plucks a flower; it is a familiar
gesture, an ordinary function of existence. Maxence pleased
Manine, and Manine had pleased Maxence. They had not
needed three days of flirtation to give one another the pleasure
that they incarnated mutually; and it had been just as well for
the young man, who was leaving the following day.

In memory of the night's embraces he had only prolonged his sojourn until the evening. He had been due to leave in the morning by the first train; he had only left at eight o'clock, after dinner, and the same hotel room that had been witness to the stammer of their first astonished and curious kisses and ardors sheltered the languor of their adieux and the transported sadness of their spasms.

The little Toulounnaise had proved to be a marvelous instrument of pleasure. Where had she learned that wild science of emprise, those passionate surges that made her hurtle and bruise herself against the breast of the beloved and, after the slow savor of kisses drunk and drunk again by a devouring mouth, that fashion of nestling, her head on his shoulder, in her lover's arms and sobbing there softly and slowly?

"Oh, if I'd known you were leaving so soon, I wouldn't have been with you. You're going to be lacking to me now!"

And Maxence, amused by that confession, had not dared to respond to her that a pretty girl never lacks lovers, and that she would find others . . .

In her violet and violent eyes the young man had read that Manine was not a girl to confuse her memories and that for that passionate creature, Maxence would remain Maxence. Slightly emotional at that thought, he had kissed her one last time, climbed into the carriage and would not have been the egotist that we all are if, once the train had pulled away, he had not thought aloud with a sigh of deliverance: "It's better that I'm leaving; I'd be capable of attaching her to me."

Would he ever see her again . . . ?

And he had seen her again. He had rediscovered her, the following autumn, in Marseille, and, by a singular coincidence, in the same sunlit and animated décor of a crowd of idlers and a flower-stall.

She had recognized him and come straight toward him.

"You here! That's a stroke of luck—I ought to be working today! I haven't been to the workshop. Why? I don't know. Something told me . . . it's the good God who wanted it."

And in the evening, they dined and slept together. This time, Maxence gave three whole days to Manine. She was still the insatiable creature of pleasure, rushing to the caress like a young animal to nourishment, and, the initial hunger appeased, lingering and delighting in teasing, of a savor unknown in other lands.

What a hunger for amour and what abruptness in the resumption of embraces! He had been grateful for that, for the ecstasy and the dolor in the impulses and kisses of that astonishing mistress.

Was she like that for the others? That was the question Maxence asked himself. That voluptuous girl could not be chaste, but was he not the one she preferred to all others? And, internally flattered, Maxence took her address.

Now he found Manine again in all his trips to the Midi. Every time he went to Italy or the Riviera, he stopped in Marseille. He gave three or four days to his little friend from Toulon, and there were also halts accorded to his sensuality and his vanity as a refined and fond male.

During one of those halts, in the course of a conversation, when the girl was exalting to Maxence the joy she had in seeing him again, to the young man's skeptical remark: "You're making a fuss of me and welcoming me . . . with songs! When I'm not there, I'm sure that you never think about me," the Provençale had made that unexpected and charming reply: "Never! That would be too difficult for me."

Maxence had carried that sublime response away, preciously. It had amused him for more than three months, and then, in his last passage, Manine rediscovered had, in her slightly animal unconsciousness of an amorous woman, emitted an even prettier phrase, of tenderness and languor.

He had arrived in Marseille on Saturday and, exhausted by a journey in a carriage crammed from Genoa to Toulon, had arranged a rendezvous with the girl for the following day. They would have lunch together and then take a siesta. Impatient to seize one another again, they had expedited the traditional shellfish, fish soup and ravioli of a Provençal lunch and had only taken a leap from the restaurant to the hotel; and, in the room with the shutters closed in advance, before the dancing light of a great log fire, lit since eleven o'clock, there had been the frisson of the first kiss, the arms around the waist and lips fastened to lips. She had thrown herself on the bed like a young beast and, her hands knotted over the nape of his neck, she drank his breath avidly for a long time, no longer letting go of his head; and when the suffocated Maxence made a backward movement, she gripped him even more forcefully and drank more avidly, as if from the neck of a bottle. Half-strangled, Maxence fell, dragging her down on the bed.

The girl, lying on him, weakened, continued her obstinate caress, and as Maxence, stiffened by desire, strove to engage himself, and, in his impatience, tried to undress her, leaning all her weight on the young man's body, she held him captive, and, in a voice as soft as a plaint, said: "No, not yet." And with a reprise of frenzy: "You please me so much that I'd like to sleep like this, on top of you, all day long."

And Maxence had shivered delectably, moved in the utmost depths of his being.

In the mouth of the little grisette, so warm and so ardent in pleasure, that imploring request, had not that thirst for a quasi-chaste embrace been the most conclusive confession of amour?

"You please me so much that I'd like to sleep like this, on top of you, all day long."

It was Manine, the supple and lively little creature of lust from Toulon, who had uttered that plaint and that phrase, and they were the violet and violent eyes of the ecstatic brunette that Maxence evoked.

The train was still traveling.

What was he going to find in the Paris of mist and melted snow, the low dull sky of unpolished glass, where ardent and bleak life mark all actions and all sentiments with an artificial character? Maxence was apprehensive in advance of the made-up faces, the obsequious and lying smiles, the contrived attitudes and the bruising politeness; and before that war of knives that he was about to resume, in the midst of intrigues, ambitions and traps of a whole host as needy as him, civilized men brought back to the barbaric state by the struggle for existence, it was the supple and brown silhouette of Manine and her puerile soul that the traveler evoked . . .

And before the smoke of factories and the suburbs that had already appeared, Maxence huddled beneath his blankets, feeling chilly, and he regretted the sun.

GILBERTE[1]

ON stage, the battalion of figurantes, packed into flesh-colored leotards, exhibited a series of defective anatomies.

It was a lamentable flock of out-of-work boot-perforators and burnishers, brigaded in the rifle-fire of rehearsals in the faith of tucked-up underclothes and moved by the clumsy hands of the assistant director—which is to say, in the direction of the newcomers, the acid thinness of children, yesterday still in penury, whom prostitution had not yet replumed, flat chests and thin ankles, anemiated necks of little girls whose gracility would make the bloodshot eyes of quadragenarians leer; then there were the knock-kneed legs and ballooning stomachs of stout women, the old guard of the paunchy women of the cho-rus, all rubbed with rouge and sprinkled with fard, and, under the green-tinted yellow of the same shocks of hair parading the same faces of plaster with smiles like wounds and black eyes.

They were putting on a revue; the wit of the authors was poured there into cock-and-bull stories and dirty equivocal quips about the bleak banality of the scandals of the day and all the current affairs. And the oldest and most bedraggled would come in their turn, dolled up with spangles, undressed to excess or frightfully ridiculous, to spout stupidities or rhymed obsceni-ties, whose facile allusions would draw gross belly laughs from the spectators.

---

1 First published in *Le Journal* 2 December 1902, the second item in the "Femmes" sequence.

And there were couplets on Rostand and rondeaux of Willy as a seamstress, Willy skirted to the waist and coiffed nevertheless in the famous sideburns, in the midst of a battalion of Claudines in short skirts, Claudine in Paris, Claudine at school, Claudine at home, Claudine in bed, Claudine in Marseille, Claudine in Lesbos, Claudine at Saint-Lazare. A Willy more natural than Willy was making a whole seraglio of vicious kids with flamboyant eyes maneuver under his orders.[1]

There was also the scene of the Shah of Persia, a cat with three tails, naturally, run adrift of the divans of a brothel, and that of Casque d'Or, already a trifle used up, the chorus of Apaches and allusions to the Humbert family. For that the entire troupe had performed, with the principal comic of the house as Thérèse Daurignac, and a great gangling fellow, a kind of bellowing candlestick, as Eve Humbert.[2] And all the rabble of an audience of bourgeois and petty clerks would applaud, tickled by the equivocation of the travesties. The grotesquerie of men and women excited them as much as the buttocks of beautiful girls crammed into the leotards of hussars.

---

1 "Willy" was a "house pseudonym" attached by Henry Gauthier-Villars to books he commissioned for his brother's publishing company, and under which four quasi-autobiographical novels by his wife Colette, featuring the adventures of "Claudine," were initially published. When public opinion discovered their actual authorship Gauthier-Villars was pilloried as a thief, although it is not obvious that he had ever intended to suggest that he had actually written all the books published under the Willy name. By 1902 the topic was fair game for the satirists and revues of Montmartre.

2 Thérèse Daurignac became Thérèse Humbert by marriage to a well-connected but not wealthy man, and attempted a notorious fraud when she tried to pass herself off as the designated heir of an American millionaire, Henry Crawford, whose life she claimed to have saved; she obtained loans on the basis of those fictitious expectations; the fraud ran from the early 1880s to 1901, when her creditors sued her and the scandal broke; the Humberts were arrested in Madrid in December 1902, after huge publicity in the press, especially in *Le Journal*, which claimed that its investigations had led to the Humberts' arrest. Their daughter Eve was judged at the subsequent trial, somewhat controversially, to have been a victim of the fraud rather than an accomplice.

And over all that flesh offered in the costumers' finery, over the tufts of blonde armpits as over the amber napes of brunette tomboys, the pitiful flock of figurantes passed, increasingly undressed from one scene to the next, increasingly naked from one act to the next, a moving display of lard and thinness, paired up under the gaminess of sweat and fard.

And amid the cigar-smoke and the insipid odor of beer, Maxence, run adrift in that café-concert of the exterior boulevard, thought about the little constructed heads, the expressive masks and the violent napes of the race among whom he had been only yesterday.

Maxence had once lived the artificial and unhealthy life of those girls. Like all the men of his métier he had had the curiosity of the music hall and Montmartrean dives. He had had playlets performed at the Mathurins or the Cabaret de la Purée,[1] and ballets staged at the Folies Bergères. He knew to what penurious childhoods, what poor hygiene, what deplorable diets and what precocious falls the dolls exhibited here owed these unhealthy bloatednesses, these exanguinated gracilities and these sad pallors. Oh, the professional suppers, the days of hunger alternating with nights heavy with nourishment, the lobster bisques following lunches at the pork-butcher's, the chaudfroids of grouse mingled with oxtails. And the chlorosis contracted in the maternal lodge, cultivated in the stink of the wings, and the hereditary tuberculosis maintained by the draughts of the stage. Voluntarily, Maxence forgot the defects and wounds due to the brutality of males.

---

1 The Cabaret de la Purée, founded by Léopold Stevens and the singer Eugénie Buffet, only had a brief existence in 1902-3, which is incompatible with the chronology of the story; by then the latter had been famous for many years, singing in numerous café-concerts, including one on the Boulevard Rochechouart, often costumed as a streetwalker. It is unlikely that Gilberte is modeled on her to any significant extent, but she did know Lorrain in her early days and mentioned him in passing in her diplomatically discreet memoirs. She became even more famous after 1903 as a singer and film star.

Meanwhile, mauve, pink, green and violet under the electric projections, the lamentable heap of flesh for pleasure, and also flesh for suffering, continued to maneuver to the ferocious applause of the crowd.

And over a red firework setting ablaze a Trocadero more hideous than nature, out of place at the end of a minuscule Pont Alexandre, the curtain fell. It was the entr'acte.

Through the eddies of the crowd precipitated toward the exit, Maxence reached the little door communicating with the wings. Maxence was there, above all, for Gilberte de Noyelles, a beautiful girl of the gallantry whom, a few years before, had mimed a role in one of his ballets. He was the one who had almost determined her debut. He had noticed her at the Acacias and the small tables of the Café de Paris. Gilberte de Noyelles, a Landaise freshly disembarked, had an amusing precision in her eyes, her teeth and her gestures. Her elegance contrasted with the tormented slackness of the other whores.

Maxence had indoctrinated her, and with the touching unconsciousness of boulevardiers, procurers much of the time without suspecting it, he had taken the Landaise from the pathways of Armenonville and the halls of Maxim's to the boards of the Rue Richer; he had exhausted her gamut artistically. He was the one who had found the name de Noyelles more elegant than that of Dhormoy, which had decorated her present avatar. The incomparable plasticity of the debutante had aroused enthusiasm. Gilberte wore travesty with the effrontery of a woman sure of an outline still intact.

Since then, the mime of the Folies had slipped into morphine and the worst adventures. Maxence, exceeded and burned by Parisian life, had exiled himself to Provence. On his return he found Gilberte a revue commère in this little café-concert on the Boulevard Rochechouart. Curiosity regarding the once-adored arms and shoulders had brought him into the heavy atmosphere of the theatricule, and on the strength of the poster, a large polychromatic image in which Cappiello had dislocated the silhouette in an extravagant arabesque, he had attempted the voyage to the land of memory.

The name of Gilberte in the program and those of a few other subsidized women, engaged by the management for the publicity of their jewel-cases, put an atmosphere of a general rehearsal into the corridors. There was the prattle and barbed perfidies of little friends come to denigrate the play of the theatresses, their physique and the play. It was simultaneously All Montmartre and All Marbeuf; the Rat-Mort rubbing shoulders with the elegance of Chez Paillard. Only the presence of Noyelles filled the fore-stage boxes every evening. It was a special clientele of high-flying whores with abundant diamonds, in the company of socialites in tailored costumes: arrivistes, déclassé mondaines, and fans of travesty. An excessively well-known marquise was triumphing that evening in the forestage box to the left; a braided Grand Duke was on parade in the one to the right. Cythera was sizing up Lesbos, and in the entr'actes, the Highness and the divorced marquise were receiving the same visits. In the corridors, petty journalists, posted there to glean news-items for the evening newspaper, were trying out last words.

"What's new, Chochotte?" said one of those gentlemen to a little clean-shaven friend, like an actor, under a heavy headband of dyed hair.

Maxence frayed a passage through that special crowd, with difficulty. Saddened to the point of feeling ill—for he too had once taken pleasure in the putrescence of this milieu—he made his way through the corridors to the dressing-room of his friend Guilberte. A few gibes from the scene-shifters and a minute of negotiations with the dresser, and: "Ah! It's you, Maxence," jeered the voice of the great artiste, a rascally and thick voice. "Come in then, you old hack!"

The star's dressing-room was crammed with women. There were five-hundred-louis otter-fur pelisses and little overcoats in Belgian cloth: an entire court of passionate admirers was watching Gilberte undress. At the entrance of the young man a few women exchanged black looks. Her torso bare, her chemise pulled up over her loins, her thighs still sheathed in her leotard, Gilberte de Noyelles was being made up for the third act. A large bowl filled with soapy water occupied the entire dressing-table. Leaning toward a mirror, the artiste was painting her eyes carefully with greasepaint

"Are you well, old friend?" she asked, without turning round. "How do you like me? I'm in progress, eh? And yet, this role, what a disaster! I don't even have a single good couplet. Nice, eh, my costume of a modern-style cyclist? It's Choubrac who designed it for me. But you're going to see me in the third. I'm in 'Bouncer at Maxim's' and I pack a drunken punter into a fiacre. You'll see; there, I have one of these gestures; I've been taking lessons from Sulbac. I get my audience on their feet! But it's at the end that it's necessary to see me, at the apotheosis, in 'Gallery at Chauchard's.'[1] Ask these ladies. Marguerite de Nelles and Zizi Patoche come here every evening. That's friends! They're true fans . . . and you, what's become of you, my little Max? You're not getting too bored in your new home town? I've heard that you're living in a pine wood. That's a fine place for you. Show me your mug a little—you've thinned down, but it suits you."

Maxence was examining Gilberte attentively; his eyes contained both sadness and alarm. Oh, the hoarseness of the voice, which he had known vibrant and warm, the thickening of that pretty face, still pert and charming, but the oval of which was heavy. The swelling of the shoulder-blades, and, strangely enough, the apparent thinness of the legs—legs that seemed to have melted. It was not yet deformation, but it was the blurring of the lines of a maturing body.

The depressed Maxence counted the defects and flaws, but what he could not take his eyes off was the cleavage, where, under the white greasepaint and rice powder, a tattoo appeared, a frightful tattoo in blue ink, which dishonored the torso and

---

1 Alfred Chauchard was the co-founder of *Les Galeries du Louvre*, which became the massive department store *Les Grands Magasins du Louvre*.

170

invaded the lobes of the breasts. It was two hearts pierced by an arrow, surmounted by the words: *Yours, Victor!*

The actress perceived the young man's gaze. "You're eyeing my tattoo. You haven't seen it? That's true. There was enough talk about it in the papers. That's how one gets publicity! I was fond of that one—almost as much as you, it goes without saying. What a passion! I nearly committed suicide for him . . . and the stab-wound he gave me! What a scandal! He was a scene-shifter. Measure the scar." She indicated a little red mark, still visible, under the right armpit. "Oh, it's not worth the trouble of getting bad-tempered, you little kittens. So what! I loved a man; I've even loved several." She suddenly pushed her dresser away. "What are you giving me there, Adèle. Are you crazy? My 'Bouncer at Maxim's'—you're sticking on my 'Exposition.'" With the swooning laugh of a turtle-dove and a wink addressed to the young man, she went on: "My scene-shifter, word of honor, had a noggin like yours, you resembled him." All the women amassed in the dressing-room sniggered. "Go on, clear off, the rest of you. Decamp, Get out of my sight. You, stay."

And when she had slammed the door on the stampede of the women: "Hey, Adèle, my Pravaz syringe. Quickly, a prick!"

And while the kneeling dresser insinuated the poison into the flesh of the tranquilly offered thigh: "You know that I'm still fond of you. Come to my place tomorrow. Six o'clock. I'll come back from the Bois. I dine here, at the theater . . . oh, no, not to-morrow, I can't; I have a fitting at the dressmaker's. Two o'clock, then . . . no, business meeting. The day after, then . . . damn, I'm going to Versailles. Thursday, then, come to lunch with me, we'll have an hour and a half to ourselves, until three o'clock. You're always quick. Adieu, my wolf. Adèle, give Monsieur my address. And don't come back to say *bonsoir*, I'm having supper with the princess tonight."

And Maxence withdrew, thinking about the little amorous women of the Midi, who wanted to sleep all day with the 'fondler,' without attempting anything else but a kiss on the lips, so much did they love the friend for love's sake!

CONTESSA BOROSONI[1]

It is not for your neck, whose iridescent vein
Stands out more blue in the shadow of San Marco,
Nor for your laugh, as thin and taut as a bow
That my dream of your city's canals is entrapped . . .

I love you, O Venice, for the soul of old parks
Of verdure and dead water which your gaze provokes.
I have drunk in your slow eyes the poison of Venice,
And like a Byzantine censer in San Marco

I am burning and dying for the plaintive gray water
Of your green-tinted eyes where ancient parks dream.[2]

THE poison of Venice! Had that madman Henri Steelman bored Maxence enough with the death of Venice since returning from his voyage to Italy? Having traveled from Switzerland to the Italian lakes, after a week divided between Bellagio and Garda, Steelman had reached Verona, and, without lingering over the tragic melancholy of the city of the Scaligers, had gone to the lagoon and the city of the Doges. The sumptuous and morbid agony of *Della Regia del Mare* over the feverish water of its canals had impressed that artistic soul violently.

---

1 First published in *Le Journal* 9 December 1902, the third in the "Femmes" series.
2 The lines appear to be original.

Steelman was seeing Venice for the first time. The enchantment of an architecture of dream in the softness of a silken atmosphere, the treasures of the centuries amassed there by a race of pirates and merchants, the magnificence of the Orient and ancient Byzantium miraculously allied to the grace of Italian art, the mosaics of San Marco, the roseate exterior of the ducal palace, the grandiose solitude of so many deserted palaces, the nostalgic rhythm of gliding gondolas, and, in the pearly colorations, rosy at dawn and black at dusk, the charm of sorrow and splendor that is the very poison of Venice had taken possession profoundly of the young man's soul and had penetrated it with a strange and unhealthy enthusiasm for all that sublime putrescence.

It was not so much its museums as its narrow flagstoned streets and the slow water of its canals that Henri Steelman had loved. To the flamboyance and rutilance of the mutedly brilliant vaults of San Marco and the gemmed chiaroscuro of its chapels he preferred the eloquent abandonment of little churches in outlying districts. He had become fervent for ancient wells, the rims of which, worn away by the elbows of women, lent their crumbling marble to sculpted rounds of archangels and amours: the old wells of the small squares of Venice.

Most of all he had loved the piazza of the Ospedale, not far from the epic statue of Colleoni,[1] the Colleoni outlining the increased pace of his horse against the nacreous sky of the Adriatic, and if he preferred the distress and the monotonous horizon of the Fondamente Nove to the variegated crowd of the Riva degli Schiavoni and the Piazzetta, it was in the Arsenal quarter most of all that he prolonged his leisurely strolls, for it was in those narrow and populous alleyways encumbered by ragged children and *facchini* lingering before merchants of calamari that he had always encountered the prettiest girls.

------

1 The equestrian statue of Bartolomeo Colleoni (Lorrain renders it as Coléone) by Verrocchio.

It was there that the Venetian type flourished most purely, conserved, it was said, in the age-old negligence of a mariner people and maintained by the rut of males.

Then, her shoulders narrow and drooping, draped from head to foot in the long black shawls that refine her silhouette even more, willingly sweeping with the hem of a trailing dress the steps of *escalettas* and the worn pavements, the Venetian woman, with her excessively frail neck and her excessively heavy hair, the sway of her body and the glide of her step, easily imposes the vision of a slender sea-swallow with clipped wings in slow flight. There is malaria in the transparency of her pale face and the rings around her widened eyes. She is as attractive and as feverish as the lagoon, and beneath the pretty five-pointed forehead that Veronese had given to all his women, she offers the expressive and slightly dolorous face of difficult convalescence and impoverished races.

Venetian women have also drunk the poison of Venice, and it is that poison that they carry in their veins, the blue of which stands out too apparently in the grooves of the wrist and the temples.

> *It is not for your neck, whose iridescent vein*
> *Stands out more blue in the shadow of San Marco,*
> *Nor for your laugh, as thin and taut as a bow*
> *That my dream of your city's canals is entrapped . . .*
>
> *I have drunk in your slow eyes the poison of Venice.*
> *I love you, O Vanina . . .*

Steelman would not have been the poet and dreamer that he was if he had not incarnated that magnificent and plaintive soul of the centuries and the Adriatic in a woman. First of all, there was a flood of ecstatic letters sent from Venice and Florence, to which he had followed the couple. Contessa Vanina Borosini was married.[1] Of the authentic nobility, descended from the Veniere family, which furnished several doges to the Republic, the contessina, whom Casanova would not have failed to mention in his Memoirs if he had encountered her in the previous century, appeared through the enthusiasm of Steelman's letters as the worst kind of adventuress. She lived alone in Venice in a palazzo on the Grand Canal—a historical palace, naturally—while the Conte, her husband, was delayed in Florence, where he led the great party of the Circle of officers.

Steelman had met the woman at the Austrian consulate, at a soirée offered to the Austrian colony; Steelman was a little Hungarian on his mother's side. On seeing her come in, the young man had had the lurch of the heat of a sensitive man who sees a portrait suddenly become animated and step out of its original frame—and what a portrait! A museum masterpiece. "That woman is Venice entire," declared one of Steelman's inflamed letters to Maxence.

Staying at the Hotel Danielli for three weeks, Steelman had remained there for three months. Contessa Borosini had within her all the burning fever of true Venetian women for their city; she had the religion of its churches, its museums and its palaces, dolorous regret for its past and an obsession with its decadent splendors; and in the long and heavy black velvet dresses that sheathed her like a sword, it was not a sea-swallow but a supple and smooth swallow of ruins that the young noblewoman evoked.

Touched and flattered to find in a foreigner her own enthusiasm for the city, the contessa had welcomed Steelman like an old friend. Delighted to develop in him the religion she had in

---

1 The discrepancy between the title and the story is carried forward from the original publication of the story in *Le Journal*, where the title is given as "Le Comtesse Borosoni" but the name is spelled Borosini in the text. The latter is presumably intended, the mistake in the title probably having been made by the newspaper's typesetter, but as it is retained in the book and numerous secondary references thereto, I have retained it as well.

herself, she had spontaneously offered to show the young man the pearl of the Adriatic in detail and become his guide through the elect city of his dilettantism and his amour.

"The Beatrice of a new Dante," the young man had replied.

That was going before Steelman's desires, and the work of initiation commenced: slow excursions in gondolas, long stations in museums, matinal visits to churches, rendezvous arranged before some Madonna in a little-known chapel or a piece of architecture lost in some distant and populous district, trips to Torcello, the Chioggia or some island in the lagoon, from which the young man came back overwhelmed by a happy sadness and intoxicated by all the opium of the melancholy of the past and the water.

The contessa and Steelman no longer quit one another. Introduced by her to a few families of the aristocracy, Steelman had quit the Hotel Danielli and taken a little palazzo. From a *forestiero*, he had become a citizen of Venice. In one of his letters he even talked about settling there permanently. His correspondence never ran out of eulogies regarding his new friend. Oh, yes, he had drunk the poison of Venice in the beautiful eyes of that Vanina Borosini. The whole city accepted him as her sigisbeo, but he had never obtained anything from her, even in the languor of their belated excursions by gondola under the smiling and complicit moon—nothing but a handshake, or a brush of the elbow perhaps slightly prolonged. The contessa disconcerted audacities by the innocence and the tranquil boldness of her limpid and nacreous eyes.

Those eyes wider than innocence . . .

And Steelman quoted Maeterlinck, entirely infatuated.[1]

And Conte Borosini was playing dead. He was still in Florence, where he gambled and lost a lot of money. From

---

1 The quotation from Act IV, scene 2 of Maurice Maeterlinck's *Pelléas et Melisande* is not exact.

certain letters, in which Steelman asked Maxence to visit his stockbroker and activate the sale of some rather large bonds, Maxence judged that his friend was not indifferent to the gains and losses of the dear Conte. He concluded that the delicate and troubling Borosini was a rather perilous creature for the purses of *forestieri*.

With that, Steelman had announced his departure for Florence. They were going to find the husband. Then, no more news. Maxence could have believed that his friend had fallen into the *in pace* of some convent in Florence, or was simply sequestered in some Tuscan palace by relatives of allies; he was despairing of ever seeing him again when a letter postmarked Paris defeated all his anticipations.

She's here; we're here; I've brought the soul of Venice to the quais of the Seine.

Steelman had returned to Paris, and this time it was the couple who had followed him.

Henri Steelman invited Maxence to come and join him the following evening in a facing box at the Opéra-Comique. He would introduce him to the contessa . . .

Maxence rendered himself free.

That evening, *Pelléas et Mélisande* was being performed; he arrived for the fourth act.

It was the fountain scene, in the crepuscular park of the Château de Golaud. Maxence, entering on tiptoe, only saw and only looked at the contessa. A whisper introduced him; a religious atmosphere reigned throughout the hall; the contessa, intent on the play, scarcely turned round, and held out to the young man, over her shoulder, a strangely long and heavily ringed hand.

She was a slim woman with a narrow and passionate face that further emphasized a willful chin; the parallelism of the mouth and the extraordinarily straight eyes gave the thin face a character of eternity; thick black tresses framed a prominent forehead; a violent perfume of Chypre emanated from her, a fe-

line languor slowed all her gestures; but the greatest eccentricity
of the bizarre woman was the fine black down by which her lips
were blurred, and the shadow of which rendered the flat chest
of an adolescent disquieting. It was a true torso of an ephebe
that the contessa offered, set in the blue spangled tulle of a dress
evidently cut by Doucet.

On the stage there was the adorable dialogue of the two lovers: "One might think that your voice has passed over the sea
in spring; I feel closer to you in darkness," and all the pearls of
a poetry naïve to the point of quintessence. And every passionate phrase, Contessa Borosini underlined with a gaze, and her
bright eyes stared slowly, for a long time, at Steelman's.

That modern Hebe of the poison of Venice was maneuvering
with a frightfully sure hand.

Cost: ninety thousand francs that, two months later, the
unfortunate Steelman admitted to me that he had lent the
husband.

The couple had flown, leaving a few debts to suppliers and
the costs of their installation to the charge of the sigisbeo.

And Steelman confessed to me afterwards that he had never
possessed the contessa; that superior woman had only let him
take her mouth two or three times, between two doors or behind
a screen, in a savant surge of frightened modesty and contained
passion, but at least Steelman retained from her a note of rare
manufacture:

> *Adieu; I'm leaving, taking away an immortal
> memory of you; my husband is taking me away, and
> that is life. Have you not had the best part of me: my
> lips and my desire?*

A STAR'S CHAGRINS[1]

"LEFT DANGLING! Yes, my little Maxence, that's where I am. Left dangling, like a pearl, like an evening breeze. Don't be alarmed if I'm using slang, it calms my blood a little. You see, there isn't a cat in my dressing-room and if you hadn't come up this evening in Montmartre I could have mistaken myself for Aimée Asler, known as the Pneumatic Bell-Jar because she makes a void in the hall. Those ladies have gone to transport their vice elsewhere; it's little Ida Verteuil who is all the rage. When you came a fortnight ago, it was packed with women. I couldn't turn round. Word of honor, I had to throw them out, it reeked of fur. They were like bitches after a bone. You saw them when I changed costume; their eyes were eating my skin. But *Eurydice* reappeared on the posters of the Folies-Plastiques with that little nag Ida Verteuil in the role of Mercury . . . Bonsoir, adieu, no longer anyone, you'd have thought it was the Place de la Concorde at two o'clock in the morning . . . oh, women, women, what camels! Word of honor, I believe I still prefer men! It's nice of you to come, my little Max."

And the beautiful girl, packed into her travesty for the third, strode back and forth furiously in the four square meters of her dressing-room. A vague recurrence had brought Maxence back there: a caprice of idleness or unconscious nostalgia for low

---

1 First published in *Le Journal* 18 December 1902 as "Chagrin d'étoile," the fourth in the "femmes" series, immediately preceding "Illine Yls."

dives and worse milieux had brought the young man back to the music hall on the Boulevard Rochechouart. Having arrived at the end of the second he had come to spend the entr'acte with his old friend. He had found her quivering, beautiful with a crimson anger that transfigured her, and, in her costume as a bouncer at Maxim's, a red dolman as low cut as a ball-gown that left her cleavage and arms bare, she was veritably reminiscent of some tragic Fury.

Everything exasperated Gilberte that evening: the torpor of a half-full hall, the somnolence of the claque, which had missed three cues, and, which she considered the worst insult, the desertion of Royal Lesbos, being released by those ladies, passed over to the enemy. Furthermore, the revue was only flying on one wing, the receipts were falling, the stage-manager, encountered in the wings, had just been punctiliously polite to her; as for the director, he had been frankly gross; he was making himself invisible and didn't even reply to the letters she sent him.

Oh, if she didn't have her forfeit, she would have chucked it in, but she was tied down by that forfeit of twenty thousand francs. Twenty thousand francs, and she was touching two louis a night.

Maxence had stumbled into the middle of a volley of insults and recriminations addressed by the actress to her dresser. Gilberte was relieving the overflow of her wrath there. Passion had rejuvenated her; her doughy features had recovered the precision of old; and Maxence, stirred in his secret fibers, could not help admiring the spark in the gaze and the expressive profile of the stormy young woman.

"Théroigne de Méricourt went into the dressing-room, exaggerating her salutation."[1]

"Try to be polite, you," Gilberte riposted. "I'm in a bad mood."

---

1 The singer Anne-Marie Théroigne de Méricourt (1762-1817) was a prominent figure in the French Revolution who attempted to speak for the rights of women before being judged to be insane and interned in the Salpêtrière.

And without interruption, without leaving him the time to get a word in, she had unloaded the baggage of her grievances, her frustration and her rancor. She had experienced cruelties in this den of prostitutes—Gilberte de Noyelles used a different term—and if she had known she would never have come into such a factory. The claque no longer even remembered the artistes, everything was adrift in the bazaar, the reprise of *Eurydice* had dealt them a blow, it's true, but that wet blanket Bordenave—the director—had thrown in the towel after the punch. No initiative, no vigor. He ought to have beaten the big drum, flooded Paris with posters, placed notices in all the papers, opposed publicity to publicity. See whether the director of the Folies-Plastiques was asleep at the wheel. He passed news items to the press, and clever, enticing news items, true teases for the public; and, pinched in the right place, the public came.

That Bordenave hadn't even renewed her name in large letters in the program, while Ida Verteuil's was on the Morris columns—one could see that name from a league away. It's true that she was the friend of the director, an old adherence of five years, and if it had been necessary for her, Gilberte, to do that with Bordenave, no, she would rather have gone to a laundry-boat . . .

Maxence listened to that flood of mud splashing with an amused amazement, slightly disgusted but even more amused. He recognized the epithets and the argot terms in passing, with the professional emotion of a sewer-worker on a stormy day. Now the resentment of the woman and the artiste turned on Ida Veteuil, the execrated rival who had stolen her friends.

"What does she have going for her, that one? She's as thin as a fishbone, she has no hips or tits . . . the face of a vicious kid and the hollow eyes of a consumptive, a hospital beauty, Parisian chlorosis for the usage of old men. Necessary to see her in the morning in the Boise without make-up; she looks like Tom Kinley, the English jockey. Those ladies think she had pretty legs; that's easy of course, with a stuffed leotard." She had seen Verteuil's at her costumer's; there were three kilos of cotton in each leg, one in the calves and the rest in the thighs; only the belly was really hers, because she was beginning to get a paunch, the divine. She was made like a frog. "It's like her lisp, that ends up making you . . ."

And Gilberte reeled it off; they had heard too much of it, and they had understood that in the reprise of *Eurydice* they were making her play an entire act in pantomime. Oh, it was necessary to see Ida Verteuil in that; she was non-existent. She had seen her at the general rehearsal, and Séverin had said to her—and he was a master—"Ida Verteuil's performance was the very negation of pantomime."

Gilberte had become pretentious again; Maxence liked her much better vomiting insults and ordure than as a priestess of the art.

"On stage for the third." There were two raps on the door. "Madame, it's you."

"All right, I'm coming. I'll see you here again. I'll be back in ten minutes."

The bouncer at Maxim's withdrew. Maxence breathed out. Gilberte's theories of art oppressed him like an illness.

Left alone with Madame Adèle, the dresser, Maxence heard her confession.

"Mam'zelle Verteuil's success has dealt Madame a blow, for sure, but Madame also takes things too much to heart; she hadn't got two sous' worth of simulation and she thought she'd arrived, and went at it full tilt. It was the same in her affairs; she misfired with all the serious lovers and only went for infatuations. It's true that hers, until now, got a lot of publicity, especially the one with the scene-shifter, when Madame threw all her friends out and went gallivanting off with her Victor to spend a week in Le Havre. Monsieur knows about that: Victor Béju, the scene-shifter with the tattoos and the dagger-thrust.

"Oh, that affair got a lot of publicity, and the flowers and visits came in after that event, and Madame had opportunities then, they were all after her like dogs. My word, that had excited them. It was then that Bordenave came to propose the engagement to Madame and Monsieur le Baron gave her the fifty-thousand-franc necklace, and we had a full hall, and if Madame had wanted to, at the beginning, she could have filled a jewel-box—because, between us, the most beautiful diamonds aren't those that men offer; they let themselves be rolled over by the merchants, whereas women . . ."

"A basket of flowers for Madame Desnoyelles; should I take them to the stage?"

"No, leave them here, Mathis," the dresser said to the errand boy. "There's no one in the hall."

It was an immense tall sheaf of white lilacs, florid with large Niel roses. Madame Adèle plucked the card out delicately.

"Wladimir Morajef, embassy attaché. Don't know him. Finished, the time of the boyars. This comes from Vauillant's. A ten-louis spray, and he's perched, the cossack. Rue de Villejust, a good quarter, but you'll see that Madame won't respond. Oh, she can tell say she's spoiling her life, that one. A man who begins with two hundred francs' worth of flowers is always good to catch. It's better than going to make faces in town for twenty-five louis, for I can tell you, Monsieur Maxence, you being a friend, that funds are low—that's where we are."

"Quickly, my *Galerie de chez Chauchard*, I'll miss my entrance."

Gilberte hurtled in; she was radiant. The hall had been garnished since the commencement of the act. The two forestage boxes on the left were occupied, one by the newlywed Duchess of Gainsborough herself, with the Duke and her brother, Edward Switson, the American oil millionaire, and the other by the rich Maurice Marchand, the joyous party animal, and an entire band of jokers like him. He had shouted to her throughout the scene and had put the public in joy; the whole hall was electrified by it, and her too. Even better, who had she just met in the wings? Grand Duke Albert himself, who wanted to compliment her and asked her for the number of her dressing-room. It was the third time he had come to applaud her. This time, he had bought the embassy personnel, but she had received him behind the scenery, not wanting to let him in. She had left her Rue de Ponthieu casket at home, figuring that her Lére-Catelains were good enough for that public of mugs, and now the grand quarters were finding the way to her dressing-room again. The Russians were great connoisseurs of stones and Gilberte didn't want the Grand Duke to see her wearing fake gems.

All this news Gilberte dispatched while changing costume, if one could call a costume the armature of jewelry that she was sticking directly to her skin. Extended over an imperceptible flesh-colored gauze, it was a stream of diamonds with emerald pectorals over her breasts and a long pendant or rubies descending into her cleavage, the central motif of which oscillated in front of her pubic region.

The apparent nudity of the beautiful girl was illuminated under that moving rain of diamonds.

"With regard to Ida Verteuil," she said, while attaching one of her shoulder-clasps, "the Grand Duke told me a good one; it appears she's become a success by tucking up her tunic and showing *it* to the gagas in the orchestra stalls. It's the nail of the evening; they only come for that—and nail is the word, for she's rather thin. The Grand Duke told me that he found *it* insufficient."

"You're on, Madame Desnoyelles," called a voice through the keyhole.

"All right, I'll be there. What's that!" The beautiful girl spotted the spray of lilacs. "Who sent that? Madame Adèle, chuck out that card and stick in one of the princess's; there are plenty in my card-holder." And, turning toward the bewildered Maxence: "It's like this, my lad, the Baron is only jealous of women—that excites him, the old fellow. When he comes to pick me up after the spectacle, he needs a little stir, the brave fellow; it gives him his little thrill. It's necessary to do something for these old men!"

A CONQUEST[1]

YOU all know Charles Franchard, the novelist whom twenty years of the high life and ten years of overwork have prudently exiled to the Riviera. The Faculty having made him understand that it was time to stop, he preferred to slow down under the sun rather than in the rain, and Franchard has become Provençal. Nice is the port of refuge of all the aged beauties and a few old beaus too—a rather dangerous port, because the bright light there slows up the artificiality of make-up and the treason of dyes cruelly; it emphasizes wrinkles and goose-feet terribly, the radiant sun of the Midi, and the auburn tresses of patched-up and repainted princesses, whether they're from Finland or Silesia, don't contend well with its radiance. If the climate of Nice prolongs existence, by way of revenge, it seems to hasten old age, for nowhere else do the women seem as decrepit.

So, Franchard retired to Nice, a little, I think, because of that millenarian entourage; forty chimed is still youth by comparison with so many centuries amassed there under Lewis hats.

Although mature, Charles Franchard hasn't renounced pleasure; proud of a profile divulged by photography and the illustrated dailies, he has retained his silhouette; a severe diet, cold showers and a good masseur still permit him an arched and flexible back. Alerted by the ridiculousness of others, he

---

1 Another story published before the material making up the prologue and epilogue, from *Le Journal* 24 May 1902.

wears his gray hair forthrightly, and parades in the port with an evident pleasure the head of an ancient court and the swagger of a musketeer; he won't be truly grotesque for another five years.

Naturally, Charles Franchard wouldn't be a man of his time if he missed a veglione or a blue or white dance. Those masked fêtes are the last hope and ultimate resource of coquetry *in extremis* and belated conceit. There is no age under the mask; the mask is the father of all illusions; it deludes the person who wears it and it deludes those he encounters; and then too, all covetousness, all inadmissible sentiments and all desires for adventure escape in full liberty behind the mask.

Nice has that folly more than any other city in the world. There's a crush at the veglione of the Carnival, and the crowd flocks, ardent and bleak, to those fêtes of lies and equivocations. Think about it: a city of schemers and aged beauties; the rendez-vous of all the lusts in the world, and all the base appetites come to exploit them.

What attraction could that old rogue Charles Franchard, cooked and recooked in the fire of all Parisian prostitutions, find in those open markets of all duperies and all lies, those balls in which any adventure is sold at a bargain price, if the prey slips away, out of disappointment, if one makes advances? But there was an aged child in Charles Franchard. Vanity, which never disarms in him, even under the snow of white hair, destines the worst surprises for him.

Merely by the modest and mysterious air with which Charles Franchard smoothed his blond moustache, the day after the last veglione, at about six o'clock, at the Club, we were fixed as to the state of mind of the ex-beau. Charles Franchard had had an adventure, and was burning to tell us about it. We didn't let him languish for too long. To a few jokes about the employment of his night, and a few discreet allusions to the rings around his eyes, he opposed a few shrugs of the shoulders, sketched a semblance of resistance, and then, as if exceeded and making his decision, he said: "Well, yes, I had an encounter, and a delight-ful encounter; God is good to me."

"He still sends you dreams?" asked little Aiguades, impertinently.

"Dreams? Never at night, but sometimes, at this hour, night-
mares about the state of the city."

And the novelist looked the little oil-manufacturer straight
in the eyes.

"A woman, truly?" riposted the latter. "What age? There were
well-conserved cadavers at that ball, the same ones there were
two years ago."

"Indeed; you were even parading one on your arm last
night," replied Franchard, indifferently—and then, standing
up: "It's too hot in here; don't you feel the need, Messieurs, to
change room?"

Little Aiguades took that as read. He left. The novelist had
touched him with the allusion to his fixed liaison with an old
and celebrated courtesan. Aiguades, very snobbish, appreciated
women primarily by the publicity of their jewel-box.

Nevertheless, Franchard was no longer talking; the skirmish
had chilled him, and he replied to our questions: "What's the
point of giving you details? These encounters live, and aren't
recounted; it's a quasi-retrospective adventure, the passionette
of a girl, married today, who dared to talk behind the mask in
the overexcitement of the ball. Yes, a young woman, with thirty-
year-old shoulders, which could only be accused of twenty, so
luminous were they, and who as a girl, had quivered for old
Franchard and his work, his work above all! Yes, Messieurs, I
had once made that little heart beat, and filled it with its dreams
at fifteen. It's flattering, all the same, to have been the man with
silver spurs, brilliant in the dew of *A quoi rêvent les jeunes filles*.

> *"My heart has its secret, my life has its mystery,*
> *And the man I loved knows nothing about it.*[1]

---

1 The first line is the first line of the famous "Sonnet d'Anvers" (1833) by
Félix Anvers; the second is improvised.

"Last night, emboldened by the occasion, she found it piquant to make me her confidences; she even admitted having bought my photograph one day. She read all my books!"

"You were her poet."

"You said it, my dear Saint-Helier. Have you ever been anyone's poet? And I listened to her, simultaneously consoled for my forty-five years and regretful of no longer being thirty."

"Ruy de Gomez loved by Doña Sol![1] Was she a good affair, at last?"

"You're filthy, Saint-Helier. We flirted in all honor, and at four o'clock in the morning, I returned her to her door. I don't deflower my memories; experience has taught me to respect little blue flowers. She told me her name, but I don't even know her face."

"What! She didn't unmask?"

"She'll unmask tomorrow, at my Thursday tea, and I invite you all, Messieurs to come and see my unknown woman. I want to convince you that old Franchard is no joker."

Franchard did, in fact, receive on Thursdays. At five o'clock we met up there, always some ten friends, amused by the coming and going and the unexpectedness of visits, feminine visits especially, the tendernesses of Monte Carlo coming to shake the hand of their old Charlot—an excuse for an excursion to Nice—and a few beautiful ladies with the fever of literature and manuscripts to place, all happy to make contact with the old glory of the writer.

The following day, at the appointed hour, we all made our way to Saint-Lambert, to the Villa Ophyre; a rather mature Russian princess was doing the honors of the tea.

"Madame Essonnes," announced the valet de chambre.

"That's her," Franchard whispered.

A young woman had just come in.

---

1 Ruy de Gomez and Doña Sol are characters in Victor Hugo's *Hernani* (1830).

"Dear Master, how emotional I am, in penetrating into the sanctuary. What joy! I've been waiting for it for fifteen years!"

And there was the usual anthem.

The master welcomed the disciple with the gesture of a Pope giving a blessing.

She was a young woman of about thirty, a little stout but still desirable under wavy tresses of beautiful blonde hair, a Bengal rose complexion, a witty nose, nicely turned up and a slightly wide mouth furnished with lovely teeth; the eyes were lovely too, in spite of the forced naïvety of their astonishment.

Madame d'Essonnes made a suggestive shrug in order to rid herself of her furs, and entirely clad in white under her sable, installed among the cushions a rump more soliciting by virtue of its resilience than its contours—and what effluvia of Chypre from that incarnate trefoil! Madame d'Essonnes' timidity had fallen away; she was talking now like a little madwoman, rambling on and on. She recounted her admiration for the master, which had once been a true passion, and her immense joy at being received by him; she spoke about his talent, his work, cited morsels of prose and tirades of verse. Franchard had been the god of her youth, and how beautiful he had been!

Franchard assumed an indifferent expression, and we expected to see a manuscript emerge from all her dithyrambs, the fatal manuscript of the woman of the world in quest of good advice.

Now Madame d'Essonnnes talked about herself; she was married to a great Parisian physician; Monsieur d'Essonnnes earned sixty thousand francs a year, but, absorbed by his clientele, he had not been able to accompany her to Nice, where she had come for the carnival. She was occupied with medicine there, having serious tastes and not the frivolity of other women; she had qualified as a doctor but only occupied herself with the medicine of the face. She had the cult of beauty; certain human faces were true masterpieces; to allow them to age was a crime. A celebrated man or a beautiful actress didn't have the right to grow old. For ten years she had been studying the matter! as a practitioner, passionately, and by means of savant massages, applications of unguents of which she had the secret, and incisions, if necessary in the little blood vessels, she triumphed over wrinkles, swellings and blotches; she made flesh firmer again and rendered freshness to the most ravaged complexions.

"So, you, Master"—she approached Franchard—"whom I knew to be so handsome fifteen years ago, at the première of *Germinie Lacerteux*[1] . . . oh, that première, I still remember it . . . you, who wouldn't appear on stage at the première of *Izeil*[2] . . . I saw you in Madame Sarah's box . . . you were still very good but you were filling out . . . well, if you want to entrust your face to me, in ten sessions, not one more, I can take away your jowls, make them retreat into your ears again, like that! A few sacrifices in the cheeks will take away your blotches . . . it's nothing, minuscule suctions . . . I'll make your fat fade away. I'll disengage the wings of the nose; three applications of unguent will erase your wrinkles, and I'll render you your beautiful profile of the thirtieth year, and that for nothing, for the glory of having cared for Charles Franchard. And I don't work for less than two louis a session. My address here: 27 Rue Vernier."

Franchard's jowls, Franchard's wrinkles, Franchard's fat!

In the midst of our consternated silence, Madame d'Essonnes had launched herself upon the master, and had taken possession of his face. Combining action with words, she palpated his cheeks, rubbed his temples and kneaded his nose. Franchard, hallucinated by horror, did not say a word or make a gesture.

Now, Madame d'Essonnes distributed her cards to us: *Madame d'Essonnes, Professor of Beauty.*

The last conquest of the author of *Cydnus* was a masseuse![3]

---

1 Edmond de Goncourt's dramatization of the 1865 novel that he had written in collaboration with his brother Jules was produced at the Odéon in 1889. Lorrain was present at the première.

2 *Izeil*—more often rendered as *Izeyl*—by Eugene Morand and Armand Silvestre was first produced in 1894, with Sarah Bernhardt in the lead.

3 The best-known work with this title is José-Maria de Heredia's poem "Le Cydnus" (1893), featuring Cleopatra.

YOUYOUTE[1]

IN the chaos of costumes, between two eddies of the ecstatic and enthusiastic crowd, acclaimed, applauded and greeted by cries, cheers and clouds of confetti, to the hysterical and frenzied music, the rabble of the studios filed past.

It was the latest Quat'z-Arts Ball.

A halo of luminous dust misted the overly narrow hall; there was a crush in front of the boxes, where assorted groups of enticing models and young painters were parading, decked out in multicolored costumes and theatrical jewelry. There were Gaulthiers d'Aulnay and Buridans, Hamlets and Romeos, peasants of the Jacquerie and Knights of Malta, the Round Table and even the Doleful Countenance, Templars and Don Quixotes, Louis XIs and Olivier le Daims, all the Tristans and all the Tannhausers; and all the Elsas and all the Marguerites of Provence and Bourgogne, including Faust's, and all the Beatrices and all the Isabellas, and all the Princesses of Italy, Germany and Scotland, and all the Dulcineas of Toboso and all the vagabonds; and the Shakespeares and the Tassos, Ronsards and Commines, Cervantes and Dantes; and the Court of Miracles and the Esmeraldas and all Notre-Dame de Paris. And amid all that Romanticism illustrated by a picturesque crowd there was the file of splendid nudities offered in the ingenious decors contrived by each studio.

---

1 Published as "Les Pudeurs de Youyoute" in *Le Journal* 6 May 1903, perhaps intended as an item in the "Femmes" sequence, although not labelled as such.

191

And there was the Black Mass, and its naked woman with the ecstatic face, laid out on a black velvet cross amid the vacillating light of candles, with a bewildered bishop kneeling at her feet, swinging a sacrilegious censer toward the idol.

And after the penitents and inquisitors of that accursed parade, there was the triumphant *Femme au paon*,[1] and her savant illumination of Venus crouching in the radiant ultramarine and emerald tail of a monumental peacock.

And the final marvel, perhaps the most esthetic, conceived by the Jean-Paul Laurens studio: the *Livre d'heures*,[2] and the proud nudity of a woman standing, a living bookmark, in the middle of a gigantic open missal: the same woman of the famous illustration by Rops surging forth, shameless and smiling, from the leaves of a holy book; the very nudity of the famous etching, aggravated by the scaffolding and the monastic envelopment of the hennin.

And the whole crowd stamped its feet and howled, arms extended toward that offered flesh, further esthetized by the magnificence and bizarrerie of the frame.

As I risked a few appreciations of the modesty of those demoiselles: "What an error you're making," said Jacques Harel, the man of the wax masks awarded medals by all the Salons. "Those young women are very capable of scruples, and it's necessary not to draw offensive conclusions from their facility in exhibiting themselves. Anyway, with women anything is possible; the most unexpected turnabouts, the most improbable contradictions—all that enters into the feminine domain. Look, let's go have a beer; the atmosphere here is unbreathable. Oh, they put on a show, our young future Raphaels!"

---

1 This title seems to be used generically, as none of the various works of art to which it is applied seem to match the description. Lorrain would certainly have been familiar with Louis John Rhead's 1898 *art nouveau* poster *La Femme au paon*.

2 The Academic painter Jean-Paul Laurens (1838-1921) had many students, but is unlikely to have encouraged any of them to imitate Félicien Rops (1833-1898). The Rops painting that Lorrain has in mind might be *The Temptation of Saint Anthony* (1878).

And when we were installed at a table in the temporarily deserted buffet, all the crowd having rushed toward the parade of flesh: "Five years ago, I was at Vaucottes, a little artists' hole between Etretat and Yport. I'm a great walker, a burner of kilometers, and nothing is worth as much for me as the pleasure of the road. Nothing is worth as much, either, as the high plateaus of the Norman cliffs, especially in July, when the fields of oats close at hand and the fields of rye further away, the whole green and dappled sheet of the young crops, is undulating like a sparkling and glaucous green band between the shiny blue silk of the waves and the luminous blue of the sky.

"That morning, I had set off at dawn, ballasted by a bowl of milk, warm and fuming milk, that I had seen drawn from the cow in front of me, but I had already been walking for five hours, and a bowl of milk, when one already has twenty-five kilometers in one's legs, a thirty-year-old's appetite and my height, and when one has been walking for five hours in hot sunlight in the stimulating sea air, is meager. And my stomach was protesting loudly: vain protestations, for there was not the slightest habitation on the horizon.

"I must have gone astray. To the left and in front of me there was the line of cliffs, the motionless Chanel, which had become a sea of blue gems with the rising heat—lapis, one might have thought—and to the right and behind me there was a heath and gorse, no longer any crops: flat calm and solitude; a great silence murmurous with the hum of insects and the crackle of dry grass. Even the skylarks had shut up.

"I was desolate; was it going to be necessary for me to retrace my steps and swallow again, in that health, the thirty kilometers covered so briskly in the fresh blue air of the morning?

"Suddenly, the sound of little bells and that of two wheels screeching on the gravel of a country road made me lift my head. A hundred meters away, level with a field of oats a little teak-wood English cart was traveling, with nickel-plated ironwork as shiny as razor-blades.

"It was salvation. I launched myself across country, taking the shortest route, and arrived just at the bifurcation of a road, which the providential cart was taking. A woman was driving it, a woman in a bright dress, alone in the tinkling of the bells, with a gigantic white lace hat on her head, with an immense peak.

"'But it's Harel!'

"'But it's Youyoute!'

"It was her, Youyoute, the model from Montmartre, even more appreciated by painters than sculptors: such a pretty shade of ash-blonde hair, such luminous nacre and roses in her blonde complexion!

"'Youyoute, here!'

"'But I live here.'

"An hour later, we were finishing lunch in the little drawing room of her chalet, brightened by bunches of gladioli in stoneware vases, and now that I had repaired my strength, a tenderness and a desire gripped me on finding her so plump, reposed and embellished, with round arms, which I had known pointed at the elbows, and a dimple in her chin, which I had never seen, that little good time girl, previously as thin as a gutter-cat. Her bosom had developed, her hands were now manicured, with nails trimmed into almond shapes, and in her hair, brighter and more gilded, in all her flesh, whiter and more refined, there was an odor, a perfume of elegant woman, which I inhaled with full nostrils, while discovering in the gap in her bodice a roundness and pinkness that my improvised hostess had not had in 1896, when I had known her in Veules, with the painter Haybert and the Seymour band

"Youyoute, or the Little Lampshade, we had nicknamed her, because of her precise and frilly elegance, a fashion she had of dressing herself cheaply, which made her resemble, in her fluffed-up, brightly colored dresses, her extravagant dancer's skirts under her immense hats—gauze and tulle then, lace now—a delicate and fantastic little lampshade, an animated lampshade, of which her pretty thin and transparent body of an anemic little girl was the mild milky and rascally light, the illumination of amour.

"Youyoute trailed around the studios of Montmartre then, where the line of her neck and her charming slenderness allowed her to be retained days in advance and elevated the sittings of the skillful model to ten francs an hour—but by night she posed the ensemble.

"She had belonged a little to everyone, the pretty Youyoute, in order not to cause anyone pain. Why sadden someone? It cost so little to let herself go, and it was so hard to refuse herself, so, she had been everyone's, to some extent—except for me.

"I was very young then, twenty-two at my debut in the capital, without much money and without much hair on my chin; and then, I had always had a repugnance, because of Hayberts, Youyoute's lover in title, a tall American who did portraits and who, not very delicate, was reputed to send his mistress willingly to borrow two to ten louis from friends, whom Youtyoute had obliged . . . It's true that he sometimes returned the louis, and treated the band royally at the Rat-Mort and even at Père Lathuile's when he succeeded in hooking a lucrative commission for a portrait in the Étiole quarter from a successful compatriot—but people said that Hayberts had always forgotten to settle the bill.

"He did worse, however, that great bandit Hayberts.

"During their season at Veules, in phalanstery, in a house rented at common expense near the watercress beds, when the whole band was installed, didn't he take it into his head to pass Youyoute off as his sister, Miss Ellen Hayberts, and produce her under that false name at the Casino in Saint-Valery, and didn't he link up there with bourgeois married couples, hooking confidence and commissions in an honorable milieu. 'Give me the money, for I love my sister very much.'

"Youyoute's dress for the regatta ball at Saint-Valéry-en-Caux! The entire studio—no, the entire band—worked on it. A Japanese robe in gray and ash crépon, thirty francs at the

Mikado, that Hayberts had tucked up and adapted himself with twenty meters of tulle, which we had all decorated with yellow hollyhocks with our finest brush-strokes . . . arms bare and virginally coiffed, without any other jewelry than two watch-chains in her braided hair . . .

"She was divine that evening, little Youyoute—the Daughter of the Regiment, as we called her. So, to send her to the ball we all chipped in . . . 'Master and Miss Hayberts' carriage is here!' And Hayberts, clean-shaven, insolent with freshness with his Anglo-Saxon complexion, installed himself, well gloved, in a suit and white cravat in the caleche for which we had all paid with our deniers . . .

"How long ago that was!

"Hayberts had sold her, more or less, that summer, in Saint-Valéry, to the owner of a spinning mill in Rouen, a charming fellow encounter by the seaside, who paid two thousand francs for a water-color of Miss Hayberts. Fortunately, he hadn't promised marriage; Hayberts was a man who might have risked the big coup and tried blackmail . . . but all that had finished. Thanks to God, she had 'got out of the soup,' as she put it, while she was leaning out of a little window overlooking an orchard; she had finally found the amour of a man, not very young, not very handsome, not very clever, but who adored her, had furnished her an apartment and installed her in it that year in this farm-chalet. She liked it a lot, thanks to her cart and her little horse; it amused her greatly to drive it. He left her there, moreover, quite tranquil. He had gone away the previous day and wouldn't come back before the twentieth. It was the twelfth, so . . .

"And, as if intoxicated by the fine odor of blonde hair and jasmine that exhaled from her, tempted by the solitude and the opportunity, I leaned on the window sill next to her and put my arm around her supple waist, sniffed first along the nape of her neck, and then, approaching my lips to her cheeks and chin, I reached her mouth, a moist pink mouth as flavorsome as a fruit.

196

"'No, no, not that,' she said, straightening up with a sudden sadness of her entire face, her eyebrows straight and hard. 'I'm faithful to him, not that, not that.'

"And as, unhappy and crestfallen, I persisted in gesture and gaze, my hands joined, desperate, Youyoute said, quite naturally and unconsciously: 'With an old one, I don't say, but with a new one who never before . . . no, that would be too bad; that would be deceiving him completely . . .'

"You can see that, with these creatures, there can be bizarre scruples and unexpected modesties."

Around us, the buffet hall, invaded by costumes and naked models was thunderous. The screams of women, pinched or tickled, who were almost forced, finished maddening the males; the ball degenerated into an orgy.

We got up and reentered the bacchanal.

GILETTE NOINTEUIL[1]

THIS goes back a long way, to the epoch when I was living in Passy. In the mornings at the end of April and the beginning of May it was a joy for me to stroll in the round paths along the fortifications, in the quasi-solitude of the underwood, gray splashed with green and gouached with violet for the emergence of young shoots, and in that frail and tentative décor of new verdure, I sometimes encountered Jacques Nointeuil and his son.

Jacques Nointeuil lived in Auteuil; my apartment was in the Rue du Ranelagh in Passy, and our common strolls through the brushwood rejuvenated by glaze were our only true encounters.

I only had a mediocre sympathy for Nointeuil; he was a vague colleague. Lively and intelligent, busy, resourceful businesslike, patching together and accumulating articles and affairs in more than twenty periodicals and dailies, he was one of those indefatigable producers of copy who get paid by the line and who chronicle by the meter, a great follower of burials, fêtes and literary banquets, a great punter in clubs and ever-present at premières—one of those fellows that one sees everywhere. We

---

1 From *Le Journal* 12 May 1903 as "Frolements d'âmes", but the story is a slightly revised version of "Au-délà" (tr. as "Beyond"), which had been reprinted in the collection *Buveurs d'âmes* (1893). In the earlier version the interlocutor with the sick wife is named Saintis, and his wife's name is Marthe. *Le Journal* also reprinted "La Verre de Sang" (tr. as "The Glass of Blood") from the same collection on 20 May; Lorrain might have been ill and having difficulty producing new material to maintain the weekly supply.

exchanged hasty handshakes in the corridors of theaters and on the stairways to editorial offices, and, in our matinal encounters along the fortifications, brief banalities regarding the weather and the previous day's events. Our relations were limited to that, because I had scant esteem for Nointeuil.

I knew that he was married to a delicate and sickly young woman, rarely glimpsed in the half-light of a ground-floor box at general rehearsals, and that dolorous creature, condemned by the Faculty in the wake of childbirth, and nailed to a chaise longue for five years in isolation and immobility, Nointeuil deceived brazenly, cynically and casually, overtly leading a life of prostitutes and gambling dens, parading his caprices of an evening and liaisons of a month in the places where ennui is abused, from the galleries of music halls to the dining-rooms of Maxim's, picking up his mistresses in the wings of petty theaters and the tables of nocturnal cabarets—and the poor isolate adored him, it appeared. She had consecrated to that rake, it was said, the exalted worship of an amorous schoolgirl, a worship whose devotion was exasperated by the chastity imposed henceforth on her young amour. Afflicted and damaged by marriage in the very sources of life, that cripple of maternity perhaps cherished the author of her suffering, the unconscious and maladroit male, all the more because of the defect of which she was going to die.

Nointeuil had in his favor—and it is necessary to render him this justice—that he surrounded that agony with a great comfort, and even a semblance of luxury, Madame Nointeuil was slowly fading away in an elegant frame of choice furniture, rare plants and bright silks. The Nointeuils were installed in the pretty Villa Montmorency, isolated by the clumps of bushes and irrigated and florid lawns of a veritable park.

On sunny afternoons, between one and two o'clock, I sometimes encountered Madame Nointeuil in the Bois, lying in a hired victoria, her feet placed on the front banquette, but under blankets heaped round her, so slender and so pale with her thin face so desperately weary.

Did the poor woman know what kind of life her handsome Jacques was leading? The existence of men of the press has such exigencies that he could, in sum, conceal his faults from her, but did he save the appearances? Did he take that trouble? Nointeuil was away from home four or five nights a week. How many times had I encountered him, even in the depths of winter on the sad and lamentable six o'clock train, a train of overalls and blouses in the second-class compartments, black suits and fur wraps in the first-class compartments: a train of workmen's departures and party animals' returns.

In brief, I had got it into my head that the pretty invalid of the Villa Montmorency was dying less of her illness than the infidelities of her husband, and my increasing antipathy for Nointeuil—an antipathy into which a little scornful hatred also entered, for the insouciant mass-producer of copy, indifferent to letters and all artistic effect—aggravated all the sympathy, the sympathy of all the most compassionate sentiments, that attracted me toward his frail young wife and caused me to pity her fate.

That morning, like every other, I had taken the newspapers and periodicals that had come in the post, in order to read them in the sunlight.

Nointeuil accosted me, long enough to exchange the customary banalities and for me to enquire about his wife's health; he had sat down beside me on my bench, and while striking the hair of his little boy mechanically, he had taken from the heap of papers I had brought a small periodical that I had just set down on it, open.

"The *Chimère*, ah! a revue of the young," he mocked, impertinently. Then, spotting a passage: "This is what pleases you, isn't it?" And in a mordant and grave voice that I had not suspected in him, he intoned these verses by Griffin: "*Here among the oaks, the shadow is a strange mirror of dreams, and it is as if all the flowers are living old, pensive lives* . . . old pensive lives," he repeated, as if dreaming . . . "*and when I think, as I gaze at the plains out there, which unfurl behind the branches, that corteges are passing of forgotten hours . . . go on, poet . . ."* And he interrupted himself, in order to resume, in a changed voice: *"of forgotten hours . . . or almost forgotten, for now I am old. They go toward the sunlit hills like girls and youths, singing, and I close my eyes . . . and I smile in thinking that I was once one of them.*[1]

"Yes, pre-existences, the anterior lives of Baudelaire: *I lived a long time ago under vast porticos.*[2] Perhaps, after all, poets are only souls who remember, souls endowed with memory, which evoke through present realities, and above all are able to evoke, old evils suffered and splendors lived beyond, in olden days.

"They are in the movement, these young ones," Nointeuil concluded, closing the revue. "Sincere or skillful, they have scented the wind. It's certain that Naturalism is dying. We are weary of photographic renditions of low morals, and the public is finally sick of a literature of the sink and the sewer . . .

"Romanticism, which had sublime flights, had become out-moded in its trinkets and gewgaws, and yet there is certainly something else . . . perhaps the study of mystery, of the ungrasp-able and the foreshadowed, which surrounds us and yet always escapes us! But the frissons of the soul, these brushes of the invisible world, which literature makes tangible . . . oh, to know what there is before us, and what there is beyond . . .

"It astonishes you, what I'm saying? Yes it does, because I'm a man who is always out on the town every night, a hunter of low dives, you imagine . . . Listen, I know that you don't like me much"—and to a gesture of protest—"and that's entirely under-standable. With the literary work you do, and the temperament that I believe you to have, you must find the person you see in

---

1 This early experiment in free verse by Francis Vielé-Griffin (1864-1937) would have seemed much more contemporary when quoted in the earlier version of the story. It appeared in his collection *Les Cygnes* (1887) and might well have appeared in a periodical before that, but not the short-lived *La Chimère*, which was founded in the early 1890s.
2 The quotation is the first line of "La Vie antérieure," in *Les Fleurs du Mal.*

me—the copy-merchant, the restaurant idler—quite odious . . . and then too, I flaunt my infidelities in public, with whores, and what specimens, eh? And an interesting little wife, heart-broken and ill, who adores me and whom you must love—for Madame Nointeuil is the very model of the kind of woman to captivate you, a man sensitive and cold at the same time . . .

"But I, too, adore my wife. I adore her, I tell you—and the proof of it is that I married her for love, without a sou of dowry, despite the opposition of all my family, and that I grind out three or four articles a day in order to provide the welfare that she has. But I had the bad luck, having married for passion, and being sensual and sanguine, that my wife is no longer a wife . . . you understand? Since giving birth, four years ago, since the birth of this scamp"—and, pushing away gently the child that he had been grasping a trifle brutally, saying: "Go and play, my boy," with a slight tremor in his voice—"since the birth of that child, I have a sister at home, a friend, if you prefer, a comrade . . . and what a comrade! An unhappy and miserable creature condemned to death: what a ball and chain!" The phrase escaped him with a cruel snigger. "But nothing more between us . . . nothing for her but death, and not long delayed . . . and my wife still loves me and desires me, alas, poor thing . . . oh yes, she loves me."

And after a silence:

"Now, I have senses, I'm thirty-two years old; I'm not a dreamer and a neurotic like you. I'm a sanguine fellow, ardent and dancing . . . and then, it's so sad at home, that unhappy young woman who suffers and dares not complain, always lying still on a chaise longue, that silent martyrdom racking and rending that incurable wound . . . and it's so unjust, above all! So I take my hat and I go out. I go to Paris, no matter where, the first low place . . . and I forget . . .

"I forget . . . I try to forget.

"Those whores are comfortable mattresses, in sum, and when one can sleep with one, it's as much gained over old age and the dreary daily grind. Nowadays, as I have a thin and emaciated invalid at home, I take for preference lovely, robust and sturdy girls. A month ago I was with one of them—you know her, anyway, Margot Shicler. At about two o'clock in the morning, my senses finally calmed, I found myself suddenly sitting up, my heart in my mouth, seized by an immense disgust, for the girl and for myself, as if an odor of human putrefaction were rising from the sumptuous and banal alcove of that five-louis whore.

"Leaning over her, I watched her sleep. Sprawled across the bed, her face buried in the pillow as if crushed in the disorder of her heavy hair, she was snoring, her legs parted, on her belly, and the roundness of her enormous rump was cynically ballooning under the sheets.

"I admit it, the flesh that I had just possessed brutally filled me with horror. Thus wallowing, it released into the rarefied atmosphere of the room such a terrible stink of human animality, such an overheated reek of female, that I jumped out of the bed and, faint with an abominable distress, with my heart afloat in my breast, and a taste of dead meat in my mouth, I quickly slipped into my clothes, emptied one of my pockets on to the mantelpiece, and left.

"When I breathed the fresh outdoor air it was half past two. There were no cabs. In despair, I went to terminate that frightful night in Les Halles, to try to drown the sickening taste that was still in my mouth in the salt water of a dozen oysters and the effervescence of soda . . . The animal odor of that girl seemed to have impregnated my skin and my clothes. Oh, that odor! So I went to carry it back to my invalid, to the sweet and plaintive woman abandoned out there.

"The market traders were beginning to arrive. The florists were setting in the blue-tinted dawn, in the passage between the butter and fruit. Instinctively, I bought bouquets of narcissi and white gillyflowers perfumed with vanilla and pepper, and at quarter to six I was at the Gare Saint-Lazare, on the workingmen's train, my arms laden of flowers.

"I arrived home at Auteuil at half past six. Gilette was asleep. She didn't hear me come in and I was able to undress myself carefully and go to bed in the room I occupy next to hers, without disturbing her sleep, the precious morning sleep that restores the blood and the strength of invalids . . . And, about ten o'clock, it was her voice that woke me up, asking me from the other room: 'How did you sleep? You were dreaming aloud. You called out my name twice.'

"'Me? It's you who were dreaming, my love.'

"'Not at all. I couldn't sleep. I got up to pour myself a spoonful of chloral. You called my name twice, quite distinctly. *Gilette, Gilette.* Then I asked you what you wanted, but you didn't reply . . . so I thought that you were dreaming, and I let you sleep. I even looked at my watch and at the clock on the wall of my room. My watch showed two o'clock, the wall-clock ten past two. I wasn't asleep, you see.'

"'Then it must have been me who was dreaming,' I concluded, not wanting, for fear of frightening her, to know that I had not been home that night.

"Two o'clock in the morning! Admit that the coincidence is at least strange. At the very moment when I was fainting, seized by an abominable moral anguish, in a whore's room in the Europe quarter of Paris, my wife, in bed at Auteuil, distinctly heard my voice call out her name twice. *Gilette, Gilette.* Are there, then, secret affinities that extend across space, or simply correspondences and contacts of souls?

"Yes, these young writers have lifted their noses and scented something in the wind."

And Nointeuil placed a finger on the little revue.

"There's certainly an unexplored thread in the unknown, a whole mine to exploit, in medicine as in literature, in the world of the Beyond."

CRI DE COEUR[1]

PHILOSOPHERS, for centuries, and psychologists, for a hundred years, have been getting lost in confusion trying to write about the eccentricities of women and their inexplicable scruples.

Women! I know a charming caprice that one of them had, the coarseness of which proves to me, more than all the protestations in the world, how passionate she was and how violently smitten with the man she loved.

She was a theatress like so many others, with neither more nor less talent, a beautiful girl with an abrupt profile, a nose that was too short, blue eyes perhaps a trifle prominent, but an insolent health, red ears, and under the heavy tresses of chestnut-brown hair, as splendid and robust as a nasturtium.

I had met her several times, in winter, in amateur circles where pantomimes were being produced. Supple and lithe in the floating blouse of Pierrot, her forehead barred by a black skull-cap, I had found a very odd figure in her floury make-up, like a grotesque baker's boy. I found her again at Trouville, during the week of the races, in the process of revolutionizing the beach with her costume and her abrupt manners of a hearty

---

1 From *Le Journal* 15 May 1903. As with the previous story, this one includes an element of recycling, albeit a much more modest one, the passage dealing with the encounter on the beach in Trouville being largely appropriated from a passage in "Le Bûveur d'âmes" (tr. as "The Soul-Drinker"), the title story of the collection from which the previous item and "La Verre de Sang" were taken.

matelot—a matelot with ten-thousand-franc pink pearls in her ears, and whose great sport was to run in the morning with two Scottish griffons, with a serge skirt stuck to her hips, yellow brodequins soaked to the ankles, paddling in the waves under the pretext of bathing the dogs.

A blue sailor's jersey, which molded her free breasts, un-coupled her like a novice and made her the friend with hips of which all Romaticism dreams after reading *Mademoiselle de Maupin*.

I had last seen Edda Effister in a Pierrot costume on stage at the Mathurins; I found her again bathing her griffons at Trouville; the recognition was quickly accomplished. As we both went back over the sand, before separating, she to return to her little racecourse villa and me to go back to the Roches-Noires, we went to have a vermouth at the little wooden bar opposite the casino. The dogs, streaming with sea-water and shaking their tails, gravely sat down on their hindquarters two paces from the table; Miss Effitser avidly consumed five cakes.

The pleading eyes of the two dogs touched me, and I signaled to the stallkeeper. "Two cakes for my dogs?" said the beautiful eater, divining my intention. "Cakes for dogs when there are people who have no bread? You shouldn't do that!" And she got up abruptly, giving the signal to depart.

That remark, in the mouth of a young woman, astonished and charmed me. Instead of quitting her, I took a few more steps with her, seized by a sudden curiosity.

"Oh, it's because I know poverty myself," Miss Effitser added, looking me straight in the eyes. "I'm the daughter of a mason, or rather a manual laborer, for he followed all the métiers, my father, and when he was brought back to us, half dead, at the house, there were seven of us dancing before the bread-bin, four boys and three girls, the eldest of whom was sixteen, with no mother. I had killed Maman in being born."

She had said that frankly and simply; perhaps her great limpid eyes shone a little more brightly, with a sudden redness in the cheeks and ears, which made the two ten-thousand-franc pearls in the lobes a little rosier.

"Indeed, the poverty of London . . ." I said stupidly.

"London? You're joking," Miss Effitser interrupted. "I'm as English as you are. My name is a *nom de guerre*, a caprice of my second lover, the one who launched me; I have no need to make my brothers blush if I've turned out badly. English! You think I'm English, that's a good one. I'm from Montmartre, from the Rue des Abbesses, between the Moulin Rouge and the Moulin de la Galette. Ought I to end up badly enough? But my father was from Criquetot, on the other side of the Seine, between Le Havre and Etretot. I haven't even had the idea of going there in the three years since I've been coming to spend the summer here. Do you know it, Criquetot? Etretot's said to be so pretty—there are true cliffs that way."

And that beautiful frankness made Edda Effitser and me two friends. We saw one another in the evenings when she wasn't occupied by professional obligations. She often dined aboard yachts in Deauville harbor, and didn't sup any less often in the Hôtel de Paris, where the incomparable brightness of her complexion, the health of her young flesh and her strong musculature made her dearly appreciated by rich owners and important trainers. Edda Effitser was just the woman for sportsmen, not reluctant for any fatigue; she was crazy about yachting and automobiles, rode a horse like a centauress, and, as neat as an eyelet and as straight as an osier in her tailored costumes, which molded her, adequate to her figure, she was not so much a flirt as a pretty companion for excursions, records and the road, ready to become, at nightfall, the ideal mistress, full in flesh, healthy and flowering well, devoid of caprices or vapors.

Very practical and avid for gain, endowed with a fine business sense, which she certainly owed to her Norman atavism, that mason's daughter possessed, in addition to her little house in the Rue de Prony, a few houses to let in the sun, and solid life annuities. Edda Effitser was no more than twenty-six years old and, already rich, she did not neglect any opportunity to round out a fortune, of which she had fixed herself the ambitious figure of two millions.

"Yes, two millions, my lad. On that day, I'll become an honest woman. I'll only have a lover, and a lover of my choice, for I'm not stupid enough to imprison myself, bound hand and foot, in marriage and fertilize a handsome fellow with my money who won't care about me. I'll have a salon of painters and men of letters; one has All Paris when one has a good table, and a few clubmen, a few old friends that I'll conserve in order not to fall into the cenacle and the little chapel, daubers and versifiers. I'll place fifteen hundred thousand francs in loan-funds and only keep five hundred thousand in capital. Who knows, perhaps I'll adopt one of my nieces, for it would amuse me to make an honest woman of her. I have the choice; we were seven children. Of the four boys, two are married; of the two girls, my sister Angèle is dead.

"I send twenty-five louis every New Year's Day to each household. Of the two unmarried brothers one is under the flag in Africa, a spahi. He costs me rather dear, but he's so well-built . . . as a kid I had a kind of crush on him; he's often hard up. The other went entirely to the bad, but he hasn't succeeded as well as me; I no longer occupy myself with him; do you know, he's gone so far as to make threats . . ."

I listened with a delighted interest to that instructive story of the family of a mason in the year 1903, full of admiration for that beautiful practical girl and her flavorsome cynicism.

With that, Edda Effitser doubtless owed to her peasant origin, that famous father from Criquetot, a touching love for the countryside and a facility for tenderness before the beautiful spectacles of nature. There was a contemplative soul inside that cunning businesswoman. Her greatest joy was dining in the fields, sitting down at a rustic farm table and guzzling dairy produce, fresh eggs and hastily plucked birds. She frolicked like a young animal in the long grass of orchards, was passionate for ducks and chickens, enthusiastic for their broods, and I had all the difficulty in the world preventing her kissing calves on their sticky muzzles and rubbing her cheeks on the velvety noses of foals. I even found that little girl's antics a trifle ridiculous in a creature with the brain of a notary. She didn't have the physique for those follies, and when I saw her climbing apple trees, laughing, I couldn't help biting my lips in thinking about the pages consecrated by Guy de Maupassant to the expansive joys of the boarders of the Maison Tellier.[1] They all have those childish amusements on the eve of their first communion, in the carpenter's shed.

Who would have thought that that girl, so shrewd and so cheerful, that arriviste, preoccupied before anything else with the large fortune to make, had a corner within her in which she cultivated the little blue flower. That was the way it was, though.

Edda Effitser was in love, but she hid it like a flaw. She only made me the confidence on the tenth day of our friendship, which is enormous for a woman's secret, but in the end, she could no longer hold on to it. Her lover made her too unhappy; she suffered too much because of that scoundrel Henri Thénard, a great gawky sculptor she had known in Montmartre, and who, the monster, had only written to her twice during the month she had been at Trouville.

He claimed to be retained in Paris by commissions, a fine joke that she didn't swallow; she knew him too well; she guessed that he was idling all day in the cafés of the Boulevard de Rochechouart, at table in the window with bands of artists like him, a heap of bad acquaintances, and from the Nouvelles-Athènes to the Delta, looking for little women and taking them up to his studio on the pretext of seeing whether they posed well.

---

1 In Guy de Maupassant's oft-reprinted "La Maison Tellier" (1883) the keeper of a brothel in Normandy takes her inmates for a day out to attend her niece's first communion.

That was how she had met him. He had accosted her, and then followed her, one day when she had gone to Montmartre to see an old friend. He had named himself as Henri Thénard, sculptor, and struck, he had said, by her sculptural beauty, he had solicited the favor from her of serving as his model. And when she had jibbed, slightly shocked . . . oh, it wasn't smooth talk; she had only to follow him home; it wouldn't cost her anything to visit his studio, and, mostly out of curiosity and a little for the attraction of Thénard's short, thick, curly beard and large misty eyes with long lustrous lashes, she had allowed herself to be conducted to the Passage Pigalle. Oh, what a coaxer he was, and how he knew how to talk to women, how he knew how to take them, above all. The same day she had become his mistress. Edda's defeat hadn't taken long, and the liaison had lasted four months now. She had the sculptor in her blood, and yet, how he's cheated on her! He wasn't even embarrassed about it; she couldn't go to his place without finding women's clothes dropped in every corner. "Models," he replied, and went on smoking his cigarette.

She had had to renounce being jealous, but couldn't resign herself to the absence of her Montmartrean Hercules—for, muscled like an athlete, he didn't disdain to wrestle in fairgrounds sometimes. At Montmartre, and then at the Trône she had seen him fell professionals from Marseilles like dolls stuffed with bran on several occasions. Oh, he had women, that one; she accepted everything; but what she couldn't resign herself to was his absence and forgetfulness. That Henri refused to come with her to Trouville and install himself with her in her little villa, nothing was simpler; the sculptor didn't eat that bread; but that he couldn't find the time to come and see her one Sunday with a ticket valid from Saturday to Monday, and hadn't had a minute to write her one of the little letters that seductive men know how to write to their little women, no, that was too much.

And the lovely girl recounted her pain to me with eyes almost shiny with tears. So I shared her joy on the morning when she

210

accosted me on the beach and shouted to me as soon as she saw me: "He's coming, he's coming . . . he'll arrive on Saturday."

She had received a letter from him; only another for days to wait; he had finally decided to come.

Those four days Edda Effitser lived in a quivering emotion, as feverish as a fiancée and as joyous as a spouse.

On Saturday afternoon, at five o'clock, I was in her home, in the dressing-room adjacent to her bedroom. The beloved sculptor was due to arrive on the nine o'clock express. Miss Effitser couldn't keep still. There were roses in all the vases to celebrate the friend's return; the chambermaid, harassed by contradictory orders, was turning over the bed. Suddenly, the doorbell rang and the cook appeared on the threshold, holding a telegram.

Edda had gone white; she took possession of it, read it, and said in a hoarse voice to the chambermaid: "Don't change the sheets . . . it isn't worth the trouble . . . he isn't coming . . . he isn't coming."

And the poor creature collapsed, sobbing, kneeling, bewildered and prostrate, against the base of the bed.

THOSE MESSIEURS

To Jérôme Doucet[1]

---

1 The journalist Jérôme Doucet (1865-1957), "editorial secretary" of the *Revue Illustrée* from 1895-1901, in which he published work by Lorrain. His *Princesses de Jade et Jadis* (1902), a lavishly illustrated collection of three *contes*, echoed the title of Lorrain's *Princesses d'Ivoire et d'Ivresse* (1902).

THE STREET[1]

IT was in the ardent moisture of the last fortnight in July, on the Boulevard Sebastopol—or Sebasto, as the rabble of newsvendors and louts of the Châtelet and the boulevard abbreviate it—at the corner of the Rue Turbigo, at half past three, the hottest part of the day, in the middle of the crowd in alpaca and twill trousers of the local stallholders and petty shopkeepers taking a breather outside their shops, still decked with the flags of the fourteenth.

The asphalt was burning, the airless boulevard opened wide its interminable luminous causeway, as if ablaze with flags; heavy trucks coming down from the Gare de l'Est crossed paths with trams packed with people. On the sidewalk there was the coming and going of weary pedestrians, dragging their feet, hats in hand and sponging their brows. In front of the cafés, the steam-bath temperature accumulated market haulers at the tables, bare-breasted and sweating, shop-assistants paled by anemia and errand boys with fuming tunics. Moloch descended upon the city, making it boil like an immense vat, and the weariness and bitterness of that hot humanity was mingled with the strident bellowing of the nearby cattle-market, the infamy of the rotten cabbages of the Vegetable Hall and the greasy nausea of the Butchers' Hall.

The hour was sickening and heavy.

---

1 First published in *Le Journal* 17 July 1902.

Posted at the street corner, seemingly defying the heat-wave, one passer-by was contrasted with the open necks and congested or defeated faces of everyone else, by virtue of his neat attire, clean linen and the clarity of his complexion. He was a man of about thirty, robust and thickset, with the pink and square face of a Saxon and an abrupt nose, almost the crushed profile of a pug, but with a gleam in his gray eyes and the russet fleece of his moustache.

He had an arrogant expression and, sure of his muscles, he gave the impression of a solid conceit; in any case, his ostentatious elegance denounced him as a fop of the quarter, one of the most swarming haunts of urban prostitution. His white flannel trousers, the silken waistband tightened around the torso devoid of a waistcoat, the colored plastron and the boater with a Scottish ribbon established well enough what the man was: too handsome to do anything was his métier.

The man was smiling with an advantageous air and darting his little gray eyes in the direction of the boulevard; he was evidently expecting someone, better than someone, an affair, for he was dolled up; the thick gold chain displayed over the blue of his waistband was almost that of a licensee.

The man had paid his bill at the café where we were sitting and was pacing the asphalt, preoccupied with holding his stature and his waist braced for when *She* or *He* arrived—*She* or *He* because all game, fur and feather, is good for the skimmers of the Parisian street.

The ruffian's conduct interested us.

A closed fiacre stopped, the lowered window-blind was raised and a gloved hand waved a handkerchief; the man hastened to the door.

It was a woman, a woman masked by a thick beaded veil. The bright silk blouse and white serge skirt were those of a bourgeoise; a whiff of incarnadine trefoil animated us with its fresh odor. The woman was dolled up too. The man scarcely tipped his hat, seized the little gloved hand and, leaping into the fiacre, installed himself next to the unknown woman.

216

"Driver, Gare de Vincennes, quickly."

The carriage drew away.

"Voyagers for the pleasure train," sniggered my friend Gromentz, "en route for Cythera. I'll wager on a Marne fry-up and an idyll at Convert's."

"Also en route for blackmail, suicide and tears. Didn't you see what a bird of prey the handsome lover is, and what a tragic adventure that numbered carriage is ferrying? For that woman is neither a whore nor on a spree; it leaps to the eyes that she's on her first adultery. A whore would have come in an open carriage, all sails aloft, proud of affixing her caprice and her choice. That thick veil, all those precautions and the closed fiacre recount loudly enough that the lady is watched, has to take every care, and is making her debut in crime. She's a bourgeois adulteress, some married woman, perhaps the mother of a family, who's taking that Pranzini[1] of the Faubourg Saint-Martin to dinner to a guinguette: the wife of an established local merchant, still honest yesterday, unhinged by turning thirty and the excessive heat. Women go mad under the sun, and that one's no longer very young. By the opulence of her cleavage and her hips, one can bet on a good thirty-five years.

"Poor woman! Perhaps she has a paunchy or skeletal husband, worn out and exhausted by office life, and the solid stallion that that fellow is will have bowled her over in the intimacy of her being. They're legion, who have kept themselves impregnable and faithful for years of marriage, and whose virtue suddenly cracks and capsizes in a fit of folly, a surprise of the senses before the temptation of masculinity and muscle; Messalina wakes up and revolts against Lucretia, and there's one slut and one cuckold more in Paris.

"The gigolo knows that kind of woman well; he catches her scent and lies in wait for her, he recognizes her, accosts her, follows her, obsesses her and tracks her like a prey, because for him,

---

1 The notorious *souteneur* [gigolo] and triple murderer Henri Pranzini, guillotined in 1887.

the married woman is the prey of choice, the sure and remunerative affair. He has everything to gain, since she has everything to lose; and, strangely enough, when the sexual hour has chimed in those women, it's to the pimp, to the whores' 'little man,' to the lover—worse, the professional of amour—that they go, fatally and irrevocably; the brutalities and the caresses of which they divine the gigolo to be the dispenser, madden them; he symbolizes for them all forbidden lusts.

"The gigolo! He emits for those unfortunates the same perverse and promising attraction that the gigolette with dyed hair, the base streetwalker, exerts on the libertine.

"Poor creatures that the enervating odor of vice, finally sniffed and inhaled, has intoxicated! They're doomed henceforth. No matter what they do, the gaze of those men ripened them like fruit; in two or three encounters they're overripe . . . but woe betide them. Once the sin is committed, they'll be followed and tracked down. The gigolo will soon have discovered their real name and their domicile; and the demands for money will rain down, imploring and tender at first. Monsieur has lost at the racecourse, an inconvenient settlement, a protested bill. Then the letters change their tone, from pressing they become menacing; the man will evoke the name of the husband and the mother-in-law; he will terrorize the unfortunate woman with notes left with the concierge and stations himself outside her windows; and the fear of the scandal, the anguish of the truth revealed, the fault finally known, will make her spit out to the wretch all the money she can divert from the household and even the maintenance of the children. In order to delay the frightful moment she will pawn her jewelry, even steal from the husband, cash the bonds stolen from his safe, and, the pitiless, insatiable man always demanding more and more, the sad creature, at the end of her tether, will arm herself one day with a revolver, lose her head and shoot herself or her persecutor: suicide or murder. That's where the gigolo will lead her.

"You can see in what joyful pleasure train that handsome redhead from Les Halles is taking away that veiled woman . . . Mesdames les voyageuses, all aboard for the Court of Assizes, Saint-Lazare or Saint-Ouen."

"You're cheerful."

"I see things as they are. It has been given to me to observe these messieurs at work and to appreciate the manner in which they operate. I've mingled in one of those atrocious bargainings of reputation and honor, and I've prevented all of a family's façade of honorability and peace from sinking in a chance liaison.

"The name of the unfortunate woman who was its victim doesn't matter. Only know that she was the wife of a prosperous businessman of the Marais, of a good family, with a morality above suspicion, the mother of two children, a pretty enough woman, although rather stout. Her conduct had never given rise to the slightest criticism.

"How had the poor creature ceded to the obsession of the man who exploited her? In what circumstances or location had their encounter taken place, and how had that honest bourgeois wife been able to descend to a liaison with a pimp—worse, a master blackmailer?

"I spared her the shame of confidences—confidences that dishonor, and always make you slightly complicit—on the evening when, pushed to the limit, terrorized and trembling, she came to take refuge with me and ask my advice.

"Why had she come to me rather than another of her husband's friends? She didn't know, but an obscure instinct had told her that I would take pity on her and wouldn't reject her.

"She couldn't do any more; for two years the liaison had lasted . . . or the penal servitude . . . and what slavery! Oh, yes, there was no worse misalliance than that of the heart!

"The abominable man—how she detested him now!—had stunned her at first with passionate protestations, transports and caresses. She knew the tariff now. His demands had always increased, grown, and when, sickened and revolted, she had tried to break it off, the man had uttered ambiguous phrases with an equivocal smile, allusions to her husband, to her children, to her household, and every effort to escape the net had only tightened its mesh more narrowly.

"He no longer pretended now; he no longer took the trouble to give pretexts for his perpetual demands for money; his gambling losses and his overdue debts to suppliers had been good for the early days of their liaison; he wanted cash because he needed cash and it was necessary that the coin weighed and rang. And it was by ten, fifteen and twenty-five louis that the unfortunate woman paid out.

"It was in the sinister and mocking argot of the criminal that he talked now, like a pimp to a whore. He no longer addressed his letters *poste restante*, he came to deposit them with the concierge and waited downstairs for the response. Sometimes, he demanded that she come down to talk to him in the street. She saw him pacing back and forth under her windows, and sometimes she was at table with her husband and children, or in the drawing room with a visiting friend, and she knew that the wretch was waiting for her, getting impatient, outside. And what a wretch, capable of any slander and any scandal! *Don't oblige me to come up and don't leave your little man standing. You know that Bibi doesn't like to wait. Ernest* was the final threat of all his notes.

"In two years she had given him more than five thousand francs; she was indebted, she had pawned her jewels, realized her savings; she had even sold her string of pearls, her wedding present, and was wearing false ones. And of all that misery, all that ignominy, the lover was aware, and had perhaps advised, threatening to inform her mother-in-law, her brothers and her husband.

"Oh, the lugubrious and lamentable story, and her more frightful reticences, through what pallors and what tears!

"I took it upon myself to go and find the fellow. Madame G*** gave me his name and address. He lived in this very neighborhood. I went there one morning, at eleven o'clock. I found the handsome Ernest in bed. It was his mistress, some whore, who came to open the door. The handsome Ernest accumulated. At the first words, the man, his suspicions aroused, stopped me. 'Anna,' he cried to his companion, 'it's on account of Madame G***'—he said the name unthinkingly. 'Pass me my notebook; it's in my jacket pocket. Pass me the jacket too.'

"Propping himself up on his elbow Ernst rummaged through the pockets. He took out his notebook. Monsieur Ernest was officially certified in the racecourse enclosures; the notebook, drawn out like a cash-book, bore to the debit of Madame G*** fifteen thousand francs of bets in various hippodromes. Madame G*** had a passion for gambling, and Monsieur Ernest punted for her at the courses. Madame G*** had an open account with Monsieur Ernest H***, bookmaker; nothing was simpler. Monsieur Ernest had taken his precautions; the visits with which he obsessed his client had no other objective than recovering his advances.

"With regard to the police, Monsieur Ernest was covered. It was the very cunning of the role that permitted me to save the poor woman; it was the notebook that established the debt that aided me to get Madame G*** out of the couple's claws. I took it upon myself to go and inform Monsieur G***. I told him about his wife's debt, occasioned by her passion for gambling. In order to pay off arrears to the jeweler and the couturier, Madame G*** had gambled but she had fallen into the hands of an equivocal bookmaker, and Madame G*** could not remain obliged to a Monsieur Ernest.

"Monsieur G*** was an honest man; he presented himself at Monsieur Ernest's home the following day, with me, and the bewildered Monsieur Ernest, intimidated by the presence of the husband in his home, exhibited the notebook and presented an invoice. Monsieur G*** paid out the fifteen thousand francs.

"Thus, one unfortunate and imprudent woman was saved—but for every one that is saved, how many are lost, like ewes carried way by a torrent!"

SUPPORTING EVIDENCE[1]

"**B**UT blackmail . . . it lies in ambush in every corner of Paris, and I'm only talking about the special blackmail that reposes on the exchange of fantasies and the friction of the epidermis. I'll spare you political blackmail and that of businessmen.

"I defy you to open a morning paper without finding one or two exploits of those messieurs therein, and you can be certain of discovering more in the evening papers. That very lucrative and not very perilous industry is imposed on our modern society; it is the sole means of existence of a host—what am I saying? of a population—of needy individuals, idlers and players. A third of Paris lives at the expense of the other two, and there is no need, in scanning the newspapers, to look for a special rubric. Blackmail, to an alert eye, transpires in the slightest news items.

"Madame X***, the wife of the well-known banker, has committed suicide in her beautiful house in the Avenue Marceau. Rich, pretty, admired by her husband, one of the rare faithful wives of the capital; she had no motive to end it all so abruptly. Everyone searches, racks their brains, to divine the motives for the suicide. Madame X*** had been suffering for a long time with atrocious pains in the heart; Madame X*** killed herself

---

1 First published in two parts in *Le Journal* as "Preuves à l'appui" (6 August 1902) and "Un denouement" (11 August 1902).

in order to escape the abominable anguish of the incurable and horrible malady of angina, that society is content with that explanation.

"Error: Madame X*** has poisoned herself to liberate herself from the persecutions of a master blackmailer of the true society, Marquis de C***. After paying his debts at the club several times, Madame X*** could no longer meet her lover's demands for money. It was necessary that the family find something. The correspondence fallen into the hands of the husband had finally enlightened him, and Monsieur X*** had wanted to protect the name of his children. And that's one!

"Eighteen months ago we learned one morning of the sudden death of Miss Ellen Huntry, and there was sadness and amazement from the Cascade to the Madeleine. Miss Ellen Huntry, of whom Helleu had exhibited such delightful engravings, had fired two pistol shots into her heart. She had done it coldly, in a fiacre, three days before her marriage to the Duc de Fredesborg, a marriage announced and acclaimed from Paris to London and from Fifth Avenue to every suburb. A card found at the time in a minuscule card-holder had saved that delicate cadaver from the horrible promiscuities of the Morgue; it had been possible to take the body of Miss Huntry to her home—yes, that lugubrious wedding present was returned to her mother.

"Public opinion went astray deliriously before the unexpectedness of that death, three days before the marriage at Saint-Pierre-de-Chaillot, forty-eight hours before the evening of the contract.

"People wanted to see in that tragic end a drama of amour; Miss Ellen Huntry loved someone else, and, her hand forced by her relatives, thwarted in her heart, she had escaped the marriage in the church by the door to the cemetery, and the whole American colony, and even the irony of the clubs, felt sorry for that Juliet of New York, sacrificed to an invisible Romeo. The gentry gave the funeral of a Shakespeare heroine to that daughter of an oil-merchant; all the white roses and white lilacs

that the poetry of two thousand years and more had shed over
the shrouds of virgins died for amour snowed in Père-Lachaise
around the monument of the immolated blonde.

> *"A strange and heart-rending grace*
> *Is in the white trespass of lilies,*
> *Shed over the transparent water*
> *Of overfull bouquet-bearers.*
>
> *"In their narrow coffin of glass*
> *Their beautiful gleaming cadavers*
> *Have the august and severe charm*
> *Of virgins dead at twenty.*[1]

"The silly remarks and dreams of sentimental schoolmis-
tresses and romantic little girls.

"Miss Ellen Huntry had put two bullets into her heart in
order to put an end to the menaces of a lover of the street—
worse, a lover of the stable—to which she had been subject for
three years. A weakness, a surprise of the senses, had overtaken
her one summer day as she dismounted from a horse, with the
stable groom, the employee who accompanied her to the Bois
every morning. It was the end of June and in the cool gloom
of the stable, after the blinding light and heat of the avenues,
amid the sweat of the animals and the strong odor of moist
rumps, their hands had met, and their eyes too. An animality
weighed upon the atmosphere, and there was the solitude and
the exhaustion of the hour, and the excitement of the excursion,
the warm season and the youth of the man and the fatal empire
of the occasion. Miss Huntry had not been able to resist the
abruptness of the embrace; the man had drawn her to him with
a violent gentleness, mastered her with a glance of his bright

---

1 The lines are from Lorrain's poem "La Mort des lys," published in the collection *La Forête bleue* (1882) and also quoted in *Monsieur de Phocas. Astarté*
(1901).

eyes, taken her lips and also taken her, abandoned and silent, indignant but simultaneously delighted.

"He had taken her again the next day, and for years, had taken her every day, but they saw one another now in town. In order to meet the man of the emprise, the man whose sex organ reigned despotically over hers, Miss Ellen Huntry, that jewel and flower, that blonde grace, so frail and so exquisite, for whom a white azalea had been the only comparison permitted in speaking of her, had rented a ground floor apartment at the entrance to the Bois at the Porte de Passy. The groom, in order to keep her to himself, demanded that she came there every day; she left it revolted, shivering and mastered, exhausted by sensuality, anger and caresses.

"Worse, the man now had other demands, and that was natural; Miss Huntry had money. That adorable creature paid, and very dearly, that groom, that stable ruffian, who was no longer content, the wretch, with the priceless lust of that twenty-year-old beauty. In spite of her pulchritude and her youth, Miss Ellen Huntry expiated the blatant injustice of being rich.

> *"Lord, I bless you, in spite of the immense wrong*
> *Of being the poor rich girl that no one can love*

"And that man, who would have given ten or twenty francs of his own to a streetwalker, extorted enormous sums from that delicate and elevated creature, because she was guilty of being a millionairess. And that blackmail, eternally lying in wait in the sexual relations of the penniless and the capitalist, is the revenge of the poor, the iniquitous and yet necessary vengeance of Indigence and Weakness against the strength and tyranny of Money. That is the harsh situation created by a society in which Money is everything.

"Exploited in his salary, subservient to the caprices of the boss who degrades him, oppresses him and imposes his prices on him, on the day when he senses that he has a hold over that boss or his children, the employee remembers and avenges himself. He is pitiless in his turn, he renders an eye for an eye and a tooth for a tooth. When a courtesan emerged from the people ruins a millionaire banker, it is an entire line of obscure ancestors that she is avenging, an entire atavism of rancor that she is satisfying in her appetite for futile and destructive luxury. In the maintainer subjected to sack she punishes an entire race of oppressors; she is an unconscious administrator of justice. A murderous weaver of ruination and scandal, the courtesan is almost a necessary evil; she repairs age-old injustices, suppresses arbitrarily established differences, puts ill-gotten gains into circulation, disseminates hoarded wealth and levels pride in the fashion of revolutions and wars, which are also leveling.

"The courtesan: scourge of God. Have you never thought of that?

"How can you expect the gigolo, the born associate of the courtesan, her equal in infamy and profession, to have any more pity for the daughter or the wife of the rich man than the rich man has for his sister, the courtesan? The bourgeoise or the granddame whom he has enticed by means of his plebeian strength and his provocative eye, his odor of the gutter and his perfume of the orgasm, by means of the very vice that he has acquired in the lower depths that have the Fate Money for despot, the tyrannical and cynical Money of the Exploiter, might be desirable in her youth and grace, her prettiness and freshness, but for him she is the Enemy, she is the caste that, for centuries, has weighed upon the existence and the tomb of his own kind; the privileged and abhorred class that made his old father sweat blood and his mother weep. Woe betide the poor; woe betide the rich! Sexual attraction has delivered the Enemy to him. So much the worse for her; he remembers and will remember. She will pay for the others.

"For him, she is what a princess of Egypt must have been for the Hebrew finally escaped from the Red Sea; she has held his race in captivity, she is the daughter of the Pharaoh, the daughter of the Rich, the woman of abominable Capital. He always awaits the opportunity for the catastrophe.

"Centuries devoid of generosity have prepared an epoch devoid of pity. The reign of Money has made us hateful mores. It is social war, and it is up to us to defend ourselves.

"So, my dear friend, when the attraction of sex has delivered one of our own to one of those wretches, and when the gigolo enslaves, exploits and degrades her, let us kill the man and save the sad creature ourselves; but let us only see that as the result of the conventions and codes of a bitter, ferocious and heavily armed society, and yet defenseless because without resource against the pressure of instinct.

"Where Christ no longer reigns, vulgar Venus triumphs without contest."

> *"Venus of the crossroads, circuses and hovels,*
> *Venus of matelots and urban coachmen,*
> *Venus of vagabonds and warmers of baths,*
> *Venus of brothels, catamites and whores*
> *Is also the Venus of the gods and Roman Caesars."*

quoted Gromentz, mangling a supplementary line with the beautiful sonnet by Robert d'Humières.[1] "It's that Venus who leads married women, mothers of families and respectable bouregoises into the furnished room of the bookmaker and pimp who exploits them and cuts their throats. It's that Venus, finally, who causes young misses, daughters of American billionaires, to swoon, their eyes capsized and theirs breast heaving, in the gloom of stables, in the sweating arms of palfreymen and lads. Yes, it's that Venus, for Messalina always descends to Suburra and nothing can resist the folly of the senses. Formidable and justice-administering Lust is at the bottom of everything; it animates, imprisons, grips and enlarges life, causes it to spring forth

---

1 The first four lines are from "À Vénus vulgaire" in *Du désir aux destinées* (1902) by Robert d'Humières.

and also suppresses it. Prejudices, conventions, laws, as many dikes and walls erected to dam the torrential flood, can only contain souls born to discipline, the souls of dream, devotion or faith."

"What you call the souls of servitude?"

"Exactly. I only admit liberated souls; only we are whole. Those who live their lives are the strong, for they are in the reality of the moment. They, in the surge of seed and sap, fly above human conventions . . ."

". . . Like the foam of the waves on the quays of a harbor, to end up in scandal and in the mud, like snowflakes in a squall amid the ignoble wastes and debris of a Mediterranean port."

But Gromentz did not give up for so little.

"Exactly, again, and that is another of the innumerable injustices of our society. Passion, whatever it might be, displaces and declasses. Prostitution alone consecrates it, because it enriches it, and fortune is the consideration and salvation of our average, official and bourgeois society. We receive millionaire courtesans ennobled by the infamy of an espouser, we welcome bankers fattened by bankruptcies, and even infidel accountants returned from abroad, but we close our doors pitilessly to the married woman who has fled the conjugal heath to follow the lover of her choice; we do not admit fault in the young woman. A surprise of the senses in a virgin is a crime; better still, we cease to know the man maladroit enough to have lost his fortune or allowed himself to be convicted of a futile vice, a ridiculous scandal or an inconvenient publicity coup. That is our morality, we modern people. Result: only honest men, or those esteemed as such, are blackmailed. The sentimental, whose principles are sufficiently routine-bound to have something to lose, are the only ones that are intimidated; but the liberated of conscience, the déclassé and the adventurers are above menaces of that genre; they defy with their cynicism the blackmailers, the species and other exploits.

"But there aren't only the ones who commit suicide, there are also women who kill. Sometimes, the sheep becomes rabid, and sinks its teeth into the wolf, and the victim becomes an executioner. There are women who are afraid and there are women who go mad. Again, that's something it has been given to me to see; here, in truth, is the denouement of a drama, which I witnessed two years ago, the year of the Exposition, at an auxiliary police station in the Trocadero quarter.

"It was ten o'clock in the evening. A traffic accident had forced me to go and make a statement there in favor of my own coachman. The fiacre that I had taken on leaving the Exposition had simply knocked over an unfortunate pedestrian, in spite of the warning cries and the whiplashes of the coachman trying to moderate his speed. It is also necessary to say that the man knocked down was deaf; in spite of the fellow standing up in his seat and shouting at the top of his voice, the passer-by didn't look round; the horse had struck him and the man had fallen under the fiacre's wheels. What a horrible sensation, of the carriage lifted up twice by the extended body, the consciousness of the elasticity of the spring as augmenting the crushing of flesh and bone! A crowd immediately gathered around us; men in blouses held the head of the horse. The man was picked up; he wasn't dead. Bewildered and dazed, he stammered vague words and didn't complain of any damage. The thing was inconceivable, inexplicable, but it was so.

"On the other hand, the woman whom I escorted back to her carriage, was struggling in an attack of nerves. She was transported to a pharmacy; she had thought that the man was dead, and a crisis of hysteria was twisting her like a vine-stock. But the crowd wouldn't let the coachman go. Strengthened by old rancor against the tyrants of the whip, they were threatening to do him a bad turn. The whole street was there, growling. Policemen intervened, putting the cab in the pound and taking the coachman to the station.

"I decided to go with them. After all, the coachman had shouted a warning and held his horses back; the pedestrian's deafness had caused the accident. They were all testifying against him; I owed it to the truth to defend the poor fellow. After all, I was the only one who had seen it clearly. My friend had returned home and I had put her in a closed fiacre, but as for having the sympathy of the crowd, no, I did not have the sympathy of the crowd. I went into the police station, literally booed.

"The argument that started there, and the chaos of contradictory depositions, the stupidity and the mumbling of people who had seen everything at first and, once interrogated, had seen nothing . . . only the pen of Henri Monnier could have retraced the idiocy of the Parisian street.

"We had been there for ten minutes battling against the ignorance and bad faith of witnesses when a curious crowd precipitated two new complainants, a man and a woman, into the station. The man, apprehended by the collar by agents, was darting around him the glances of a sly beast—a suffering beast, too, for his arm was in a sling and his livid pallor was aggravated by a blood-stained bandage. The man was wounded in the shoulder and the head. He was a robust fellow with a nasty face, a violent redness in the neck and angry eyes. A concentrated rage was shaking him with a tremor.

"The woman, a tall brunette with an opulent corsage, was in an evening gown, her shoulders bare. The ball-cape, and the diamonds in her ears and around her neck, were those of a woman of the well-to-do bourgeoisie. As white as a sheet under the savant undulations of her coiffure, she was silent, her entire face, of a rather vulgar model, rendered beautiful by tragedy and resolution. Motionless in the hands of agents, she was looking around with hallucinated eyes, and it was evident that her flesh did not have a frisson.

"The commissaire's secretary had stood up. No more attention was paid to the affair of the coachman and his fake victim. The crowd rushed behind the newcomer; the witnesses of my accident no longer had eyes for anything but the woman.

"'What is it? What's all this?'

"'It is, Monsieur le Commissaire, 'that Madame has fired two revolver shots at Monsieur in the street, outside the Gare de la Muette. Monsieur and Madame were arguing. Suddenly, Madame fired two revolver shots at Monsieur.'

"The woman stiffened, as if emerging from a dream, and in a clear and slow voice, said: "The agents refused to arrest Monsieur. The aid and protection I asked of them I was unable to obtain, so I fired; it was necessary to defend myself. I'm ready to respond.'

"The commissaire inclined slightly. 'Your name and forenames, Madame?'

"'Henriette-Isabelle X***. My age is forty-one years; my domicile here in Ranelagh, in the home of my husband.'"

"The commissaire raised his head, interested. Madame X*** had just pronounced one of the best-known names of high Parisian commerce. He turned toward the wounded man. 'Your name and forenames, Monsieur?'

"'Frédéric Burger, thirty-three years old.'

"'French?'

"'No, Luxembourgeois.'

"'Not naturalized?'

"'No.'

"'Domiciled?'

"'Paris, Rue des Epinettes, number 25.'

"'Your profession?'

"'Photography broker.'

"Addressing the woman, the commissaire said: 'You admit having fired two revolver shots at Monsieur and wounding him voluntarily?'

"'Indeed. It was a case of legitimate self-defense.'

"'Then it's you who are the complaintant? Strange! And you, Monsieur, do you want to make a complaint against Madame, who has wounded you?'

"The man, emerging from his silence, growled: 'That depends.'

"The commissaire enveloped the man with a searching gaze. 'That depends! The public ministry will pursue the affair; there are shots and wounds. You don't appear to want to have dealings with the law, Monsieur. Anyway, that's up to you.'

"And, addressing the woman, who was haughty and pale, again: 'I await your deposition, Madame.'

"Then, with a strangulation in her voice this time, she said: 'This man is my lover. I have been his mistress for two years; for two years Monsieur has been blackmailing me. I'm married; I have children; a situation; the thing was easy. I have everything to lose. The sums I have given Monsieur, the scandals with which he has threatened me, the apprehensions in which I have lived for two years, the martyrdom of every one of my hours, I shall spare you. I have cruelly expiated a moment of folly, and yet I supported it all in silence, without complaining, only too glad to be able to buy the tranquility of my family and spare my entourage the atrocious truth. But Monsieur is insatiable. My weakness emboldened him. It's my fault, I know, but I can do no more. Six months ago, I fell ill, my health destroyed, a nervous malady that kept me in bed for three months. Monsieur was relentless. He came to prowl under my windows, left letters with the concierge; I had to let my chambermaid in on the secret. Monsieur threatened to come up; I had been under his orders for eighteen months. With a word he made me run from one end of Paris to the other, but when I fell ill he immediately learned the road to my house. That was when my true torture began.'

"Madame X*** mopped her moist brow. She had become animated while speaking; her speech had become halting and clipped. Her face, devastated by relived horror, seemed to have aged ten years.

"'Pardon me, I'm being slow. A week ago, Monsieur fixed a rendezvous for me outside the Gare de la Muette, and I went to that rendezvous as to all the others. Monsieur talked about sea-baths and needed six hundred francs. I had to pay them

immediately; it was necessary for Monsieur to leave Paris immediately; Monsieur had got into trouble with the law.'

"'Bitch!' muttered the man between his teeth.

"Imperturbably, the commissaire wrote down the reply.
Madame X*** did not react to the insult. 'Those six hundred
francs I did not have, and those six hundred francs were
Monsieur's salvation. He promised to leave the next day and
leave me tranquil for a month, perhaps two. He had business in
Ostend, he said, and in the frightful argot that he always uses
now he explained a heap of things that I didn't understand, because I was mad with fear and felt ready for anything. In brief, I
told the man to wait. I went home and took from my husband's
safe six hundred francs that did not belong to me. In my distraction, however, a glimmer of composure still remained to me and
I made out a receipt to this man. I sat at a table in a restaurant
and I asked for a stamp of acquittal and I made monsieur sign
for the price of blood. That receipt I have. Then, Monsieur having gone, I breathed, saying: *Another month gained; between now
and then, I'll find something*—as if one ever gets free. Alas, no;
no the next day it was necessary for me to run to the lenders to
replace the six hundred francs.

"'Now, Monsieur le Commissaire'—and the poor woman
was biting and ripping her handkerchief between her teeth—'I
have a daughter, eighteen years old, and this evening was her
betrothal dinner. How did Monsieur know that? At any rate,
with three guests already in the dining room and me still in my
dressing room, my chambermaid came in, alarmed, to tell me
that Monsieur Frédéric was downstairs and wanted to talk to
me. And my guests were continuing to arrive and my daughter
was with me. It was impossible to quit my society. I scribbled
a note in haste asking Monsieur to wait, I told him to dine
in the quarter, and that I would attempt to get away at eleven
o'clock. But do these men ever wait? I only breathed when my
last guest arrived, for every ring of the bell made my heart lurch.
We finally sat down at table and then my torture began.

"'The bell rang every quarter of an hour. By the distressed face of my chambermaid, who appeared behind the waiters, I knew that it was him. She sent him away every time, but until when could she drive him away? He was a man to shove the girl out of the way and come straight to the apartment. And my daughter was smiling at her fiancé, and my husband was sitting opposite me, his face beaming. The family of the fiancé, the other guests, friends of twenty years, were all around me, and the ringing of the doorbell was attributed to suppliers, and my neighbor was making jokes. *What dessert have you reserved for us, Madame . . .*

"'I felt faint. *Are you suffering?* my husband said. The chambermaid handed me four notes written in pencil. Four coarse notes; worse, filled with filthy threats. The man was there waiting for me, ready for scandal, he said, since I wished it. I lost my head. I went to my bedroom, took this revolver, wrapped myself in a ball-cape, and went down into the street like a madwoman. I found the man outside the station.

"'*You're messing with me*, he said, rudely, *you know I don't like being taken for a mug. I've been hanging about for two hours.*

"'*And I've had enough*, I said. *This has gone on too long. You want money, you won't get it; for one thing, I haven't got any, and if I had, it would be the same thing.*

"'*Don't get carried away*, he drawled, in his mocking voice. *It's obvious that you've been drinking champagne this evening. I need a thousand francs, my petite.*

"'*A thousand francs. Here, this is all you can have.* And I aimed my revolver at him.

"'*Playthings, down paws*, and he tried to take the weapon away. I backed away abruptly and shouted for help. A crowd had formed around us; when I shouted, policemen intervened. *Arrest that man*, I shouted. *Take him to the station.*

"'*What's happening?*

"'Then the man said: *Pay no attention, Madame is drunk.* And there was laughter and jeers in the group of idlers; worse, someone murmured: *It's a whore and her pimp.* And the agents shrugged their shoulders. *Move on, move on!* and they said to Monsieur: *Take Madame away.* And he, already white with fear, said to the idlers, *Yes, she's my whore.* His whore, a prostitute, me! Then I saw red. *Arrest him, arrest him, or I'll do him harm.* And the agents continued to smile. Then I took aim at Monsieur's head and fired twice.'"

THOSE IN SOCIETY[1]

"IT'S necessary not to believe that only the street produces human predators; that would be an erroneous opinion. If the sidewalk, the café and the bar, the lawns of racecourses and the corridors of music halls are terrains ready prepared for the sprouting of exploiters of women, society also has its pirates of amour, the society of salons and the society of letters, and the societies of embassies too, and those maintained there, as avid for gain as their brethren of the street, certainly don't have their excuse, for the vulgar pimp is fighting for his bread, and the others are fighting for luxury. From the moral point of view, the arriviste, that ferocious product of our century, the arriviste at no matter what price, by way of marriage, by way of his mistress, by way of his protector, and always by way of lies, is as culpable as a burglar, and from the social point of view, just as dangerous.

"A man who sells himself is capable of anything. Dowry-hunters are as bad as prostitutes, and from the husband maintained by the actress, who accompanies his wife to the door of the brothel and has himself introduced, where he finds stirrers of money quoted on the boulevard in the wings of the theater or the stands of racecourses, to the espouser of a demoiselle who waited patient for the *spolia opima* of Vienna and Saint Petersburg to enrich his beloved in order to accord her his name and the sweetness of a home, all of them, plastered as they are

---

1 First published in *Le Journal* 14 August 1902 as "Ceux de monde."

with luxury and wellbeing, are at the immoral and social level of the courtiers of human flesh denounced in the *Traite des Blanches*.[1] It's the dynasty of Messieurs Betsy,[2] the innumerable family of suspect husbands, unknown or known to courtesans, the royal and the theatrical, the legitimate pimps, admirable in their insouciance and aplomb when they are forgotten, hateful, arrogant and devoured by bile when they are remembered.

"There are also the ambitious, the sharpers, the Rastignacs with cloven feet, who lie in wait for divorced women, the fat, widows indebted for millions, the resounding forty-somethings ripened by sin and exploitation, the demi-liberated of society and marriage, who parade their world-weariness and their curiosity for sensation through the spas and the stations of the Riviera. Those are the most dangerous, the boldest and the most obstinate, for they have latched on to the woman in order to edify their future. It's a situation that they seek above all, no matter what the cost, at the price of all lies and all infamies, and if the prey coveted slips through their fingers, they will stop at nothing to bring down the escaping game. Those avenge themselves cruelly; unable to obtain the millions they doom the woman, abort all the marriages that she might have sketched, mark her with their stain, and by virtue of having known them, the woman will be parked forever in shady society. It is those men who, by means of lassitude or disgust, eventually drive their victim to suicide.

"Unable to swim against the current, the pitiful woman prefers to finish it,

---

1 This phrase had been the subject of a sensational "exposé," *La Traite des blanches* (1877) by F. Tacussel, but had been in popular usage for some time even before then, echoed in the English phrase "the white slave trade." It refers to what is nowadays known as "sex-trafficking." Jules Clarétie, who had a regular fortnightly slot in *Le Journal*, published two fictional items there under that title on 23 July 1902 and 17 September 1902, and Lorrain presumably read the former shortly before writing his own story.
2 The reference is to the comedy *Monsieur Betsy* (1890) by Paul Alexis and Oscar Méténier.

"I have seen a victim of one of those predators on her deathbed.

"Madame Z*** had been one of the prettiest women of Jewish society. Tall, slender, admirably proportioned, with a profile of quasi-divine purity, Madame Z*** was one of those women who move gracefully and who, in a theater or in the street, immediately make all heads turn, as toward a living masterpiece. La Cavalieri and Caroline Otero are the only women to whom she could be compared.[2]

"Intellectual and haunted by a slightly naïve estheticism, Madame Z*** strove above all to resemble Gustave Moreau's creatures of dream and beauty. As she was rich, by virtue of adornments she sometimes contrived to evoke one of the painter's Salomes or Bathshebas, but it was necessary for her admirers to put something of their own into that, for, with all her research in the choice of gems and fabrics, Madame Z*** developed most of all her Oriental type, and more often had a delightful and unfortunate resemblance to La Belle Fatma.[3] She

---

1 The line is a slightly modified version of the last line of Lorrain's poem "Sapho" in the collection *L'Ombre ardente* (1897).

2 The references are to the Italian singer Lina Cavalieri (1874-1944) and the Spanish actress Carolina Otero (1868-1965), commonly known as "La Belle Otero." The former worked in Parisian café-concerts and music halls before becoming a famous opera singer, while the latter became a star of the Folies Bergère. Cavalieri also appeared at the Folies Bergère, filling in for Liane de Pougy in Lorrain's *L'Araignée d'or* when Pougy was indisposed. Otero notoriously claimed that six men had committed suicide over her and cited half a dozen kings—including the German emperor Wilhelm II—and Grand Dukes as her lovers; there is an oft-reproduced lithograph of a drawing by Sem made in Monte Carlo in which Otero appears with Lorrain and Liane de Pougy. Cavalieri and Otero evidently made some contribution of Lorrain's character studies of "theatresses."

3 "La Belle Fatma" (Rachel Ben-Eny) was an Algerian dancer who arrived in Paris as a child in the late 1870s, already performing in a family troupe, and became a star attraction in her own right, appearing regularly at the Folies

had her immobile physiognomy, her hieratic attitudes and her large dark velvet eyes floating in a blue-tinted sclerotic, lips as if carved in pink coral, and two lustrous black bands of hair pulled back over her temples like two crow's wings.

"Madame Z*** was a coquette and was pleased by the desires of men, but it was a cerebral coquetry, which did not descend any lower than the shoulders. She paraded them generously in society, but with the generosity of an idol. The very coldness of her nudity and her eternal smile protected her from covetousness even more than the ever-alert jealousy of her husband.

"No one admired Madame Z*** as much as she did herself; she hypnotized herself by means of her beauty like a fakir by his navel, and that perpetual narcissism had made her a kind of automaton. Artificial and theatrical, she walked with a constant preoccupation with her effects, and seemed to live her life before an invisible mirror.

"Provocative and bold, one sensed that she was honest. Passion would have disturbed the mystery of the smile and the harmony of the peignoir's pleats. 'She only has adultery in her hair,' a psychologist in quest of a lived adventure for a forthcoming novel had said of her. She had no lack of adorers, though; the conceit of men in regard to women found its count in the publicity organized around Madame Z***'s beauty. An amorous atmosphere reigned in her salon; words and manners were rather free there, but it was her friends who benefited from it; a few of them found serious maintainers there.

"At length, the incense burned at every minute of every hour to his wife ended up getting up Monsieur Z***'s nose, like mustard. He cleared the house, threw out the adorers and declared to his Olympia that she would have to change her ways; he had had enough of that *cour d'amour* installed in the conjugal hearth. Strong in her innocence, Madame Z*** rebelled. She played Caesar's wife, who could not be suspected; she had nothing for which to reproach herself, to submit to Monsieur Z***'s

Bergère in the late 1880s and 1890s.

will would have been to admit that she was culpable. The lack of simplicity doomed her. She became indignant, but before her mirror, and made the exit of an outraged empress, which the gallery applauded and flattered her self-respect.

"The divorce was pronounced against her; she emerged from the tribunal absolved by public opinion.

"In order to protest she threw herself into charity. The poor were insufficient for her need to give; she went to care for the sick and bandage the operated on in hospitals—or, rather, one hospital. She became the right arm, the muse and the sister of charity of a young surgeon, a very pretty man, very arriviste, who neglected nothing to make his personnel understand that Madame Z*** was his mistress. She followed his lectures at the Sorbonne, assisted in his operations, and paraded commiserations and sympathy learned in the theater from bed to bed and from ward to ward.

"There was talk about her.

"Disgusted by the malevolence of society, Madame Z*** departed for India. Her large fortune permitted that. She went to discover Ceylon and Benares, the Himalayas and the heroes of *The Jungle Book*. She was absent for two years.

"And then Paris saw her again. Madame Z*** had come back from distant Asia with a manuscript. Literary, obsessed with literature above all, the scientific ex-muse of Doctor B*** surrounded herself with litterateurs.

"Her apartment in the Rue de Lille, in the winter, and her installation on the Pré-Catelan, in the summer, where she played the Trianon queens, saw dinners of journalists. Her beauty, her millions, the perfume of exoticism that she brought back from abroad, soon enabled her to hypnotize the boulevard; the directors of great newspapers were seen in her house, academicians appeared alongside political men; the society of the Revues glided through her salons, and she penetrated into the Revues.

"Adventures were credited to her, but *L'Améthyste*, the most austere revue of the Faubourg Saint-Germain, published the account of the voyage of Ourida Balkis, the pseudonym of Madame Z***. Better than that, the rumor spread that Niollet, the dirty and omnipotent editor of *L'Améthyste*, an ex-schoolteacher arrived from the École des études sociales was madly in love with the beautiful voyager, a new Queen of Sheba before a modern Solomon.

"In order to marry Madame Z***, Niollet was going to break off a twenty-year relationship with his cook, and the authoress of *L'Inde des Bayadères* was about to become the directrice of *L'Améthyste*. Madame Z*** was approaching her goal. It was then that catastrophe struck.

"I was coming out of a rehearsal at the Français; my valet de chambre accosted me under the peristyle; he had an urgent letter for me. I opened it: *Madame Z*** is dead, come quickly if you want to see her again.* It was signed with the name of one of her friends.

"I leapt into a fiacre, paused to buy a spray at the florist's and arrived in the Rue de Lille. The entire house was in a stupor. 'She has killed herself,' Mademoiselle J***, the friend who had written to me told me as she greeted me on the threshold. 'Come and see how beautiful she is.'

"I followed her. In the brightly-lit room, a true *chapelle ardente* in the illumination of candles accumulated on all the items of furniture, Madame Z*** reposed in a white satin dress among the lace and silk pillows of a large bed strewn, piled, overwhelmed with flowers. She reposed in the black aureole of her undone hair, her shoulders and arms naked, like a wax statue; and the flames of the candles were almost reflected in the pallor of her flesh. All her rings on her fingers, a string of pearls around her neck, diamonds in her ears, ornamented like the saint of a reliquary, she seemed to be asleep, her face not at all dolorous, and beneath the shadow projected over her ivory cheeks by her long lustrous lashes, more like a work of art than a dead woman. A sheaf of white roses was shedding its petals between her joined hands; the same bright and candid roses were heaped under her bare feet.

"'She has killed herself,' Mademoiselle J** repeated, 'with a pistol shot to the heart. Oh, she knew the place, Doctor B*** had indicated it to her; she had asked him often enough when she assisted him at the hospital. Was she already thinking about suicide? She has killed herself because of a wretch, a man of letters—and that's certainly the name—who, furious at being unable to marry her, her and, above all, her millions, sent her intimate correspondence to the *Améthyste*. Then Monsieur Niollet wrote . . . and before her broken marriage, her crushed ambitions, the new life of which she dreamed destroyed forever, our friend no longer had the courage to live. What's the point of always recommencing a futile effort? She preferred to end it. I'll tell you the name of the man one day, so you can nail it to the pillory of a book.'"

EPILOGUE

To my friend Sem

THE TWO MORALITIES[1]

THAT evening, the hall of the Olympia was full. Two debuts in gallantry, that of Miss Toppett, a little discovery by the fat Ménard of the Baby Club, and the announcement in the program of that of the Marquise Hamburini, old Hamburini, had packed out the forestages, the orchestra stalls and the boxes with the special public of ceremonies of that sort. All the Acacias, all the Cythera overlooking the Rue des Champs-Élysées, Passy and Monceau were there, making the assault of costly excursions to the theater, enormous flowery hats, carcans of diamonds and pearl necklaces. A swarm of black coats had invaded the corridors and were poorly dissimulated behind the scenery, men who had come to see the debutants at closer range, and everywhere, in the hall and behind the curtain, there was the organized denigration of the two stars, the ordinary malevolence of women still overexcited by the displayed luxury of the silk muslins, painted batistes, insertions and Bruges lace of their combat frills.

Oh, those Parisian first nights and the unreal, almost nightmarish aspect of halls of spectators, seen from the stage, in the uniformity of the faces and garments of the men alongside the extravagant make-up of the women, their pallor and their rouge heightened by the multicolored tumult of boas and plumes.

---

1 First published in *Le Journal* in two parts as "Un Symbole" (20 July 1902) and "La Marquise Hamburini" (25 July 1902).

Under the pallid projections of electric light, there was the swirling and fluttering colors of a Goya *corrida*, the same dreary luminosity of a brighter face or hand under the inclined shadow of a coiffure or the flapping of a fan—but an anemiated Goya, as if dissolved and unified by the abuse of the neutral shades rife for two years in women's attire, the fashion that consecrates them all to creamy white, pale blue, straw yellow and flesh pink: insipid and monotonous hues.

It was the painter Marcel Hubert who pointed out those analogies and those poverties of fashion. Posted with us behind a panel of scenery, his opera-glasses raised, the portraitist in vogue observed while deploring it the laxity of our couturiers and the even slacker laxity of the Parisiennes, whose coquetry did not jib against that black and banal uniformity.

"I'm reduced to making them put on white and black dresses," Hubert told me. "It's the only means I have of having something to paint. The flesh fades away and liquefies in the midst of all those shades that aren't. People talk about Van Dyck and Velasquez, but what costumes they had and what models! All that society depicted by Sem and Forain . . ."

"And Hermann-Paul."[1]

"I'll stop you. Madame Humbert has never come here, and the fat Thérèse was the Midi in motion, the arriviste and ministerial Midi, the terrible Midi of Toulouse, the larded goose of the Capitol."

On stage, Miss Toppett presented in liberty three donkeys and a piglet. The bouffant culottes of her turquoise satin clown-suit tucked up to mid-thigh, a diamond bracelet around her left ankle, an enormous frieze of silver gauze further exaggerating the smallness of a thin, impertinent and bland face, the clowness arched her slenderness, tightened her loins, her hamstrings and all the rest. Her triangular smile illuminated with rouge and

---

1 The "intimiste" painter René Georges Hermann-Paul (1864-1940) worked extensively as an illustrator for Parisian newspapers and periodicals in the 1890s.

her oblique eyes underlined with blue in her plastered face, she wielded a pitiless whip over the three asses and the little pig. On the stage, gradually invaded, the black coats gave an ovation to the clowness with the head of a lizard.

"We hesitated for a long time between Miss Tranflute and Miss Toppett, but Bertrand, who knows what's what, advised Miss Toppett. She's nice, eh, the kid? And dispositions. She'll go far. She spent a fortnight training her beasts."

"And one evening lifting you up. Come on, we know that you bought her number at the Vaugirard fête; don't take us for another."

"But my dear friend, I assure you . . ."

"Get away! We'll talk about it again at the première to which she'll take you."

Miss Toppett withdrew, over a triple salvo of applause. The hall, amused by her aplomb, didn't spare the bravos or the recalls. Miss Toppett, delighted, broke herself in two and blew kisses with full hands, and bowed yet again, completely ridiculous. The public writhed; fat Ménard, who was the artiste's present proprietor, thought he ought to intervene. He precipitated himself toward the young woman and was called an idiot and an old fool by the animal-tamer, drunk on her success.

"Behold amour!" sniggered Hubert.

An acrobatic number followed with two American gymnasts, whose exercises were performed amid the indifference of the boxes, occupied in taking inventory of jewel-cases and denigrating them. Then the gymnasts retired and consulted programs caused heads to lift. Opera-glasses were aimed at the stage.

A similar curiosity excited the men and the women; groups of black coats formed and then dislocated in the perpetual back-and-forth movement from one corner to the other; there was the busy agitation of an anthill, and stifled laughter. The orchestra launched into the famous waltz from *Amoureuse* and, the conversations having suddenly fallen silent, the person expected appeared. A thunder of applause saluted her entrance.

Giant, obese, enormous, giving the impression of a Jane Bloch magnified by a tenth,[1] bloated, cubby-cheeked and big-breasted, her bosom bastioned, strapped up tightly to the point of strangulation, her abdomen swallowed up by a fashionable corset but her formidable thighs jutting all the more under the effort of an extravagant backside as broad as the rump of a hippopotamus, in the most garish yellow dress, amid the crazy flight of creases, boas, ruches and furbelows, there was a colossal ballooning Mère Gigogne, the extraordinary grotesquery of Footitt as the Marquise de Prétintaille,[2] a hilarious cardboard cut-out from the American circus of an ostrich crossed with a parrot, congestion made woman.

But of all the visions evoked, that of a chimerical Barnum animal was the truest, for the lady had the eruption of plumage and the sway of the hips, and amid the sprays of feathers and tulle floating around her it was the head of a parrot that the face displayed, with its round eyes and bulbous profile, posed like a blue fruit on the English lace and old Alençon of an immense Cherusque collar.

The heavy jowls of a collapsed, plastered, resurfaced and painted face, the flexed eyelids pulled toward the temples by invisible pincers hidden under the wig, the mask of that marionette—at least fifty years of active gallantry—advanced with little steps, inclined in a contorted waddle of her entire massive person, and in a lisping voice, simpering like a little girl, intoned the passionate request of the banal *degueulando*:

------

1 The café-concert singer and actress Jeanne Bloch (1858-1916) became rather stout in her later years, as evidenced by surviving photographs—the one in her Wikipedia entry is extremely unkind. She liked to perform Aristide Bruant's songs, and improvised a French adaptation of the English music hall classic "Ta-ra-ra-boom-de-ay." She was performing regularly at La Cigale in 1901-3.

2 "La Marquise de Prétintaille" was a popular song written by Pierre-Jean de Béranger in the early decades of the nineteenth century; the eponymous protagonist was adapted into vaudevilles as a stock character. George Foottit (1864-1921)—whose name was often rendered in France as Footitt, as it is here—was an English clown who became a star of the Parisian circus.

I love you, and yet I'm a coward!

And the electrified, transported hall applauded.

That evening, in the wheedling stutter of the old woman, in the swooning winks and roulades, in the offering of her cleavage and her rump, the manifestations of their sumptuous and empty lifestyle were revived for all the assembled fun-lovers, demoiselles and socialites: mornings in Armenonville, parades at the Acacias, dinners *in fiocchi* in fashionable cabarets, lunches and suppers in the hotels of Monte Carlo and the Réserves of the Riviera—and all of that, suppers, dinners, breakfasts, chaudfroids of snipe and bloody duck, Saint-Marceaux 1880 and refreshed fruits, always accompanied by the eternal gypsy waltz:

I love you, and yet I'm a coward!

And, swayed by the andante of the *Blue Danube* and the *Vie pour le Tsar*, hammered by the rhythm of czardas and Hungarian marches, there were, for all of them, the same depressing and weary memories, the same vision of exactly similar luxurious settings, when, in the midst of the coming and going of waiters, Boldi's[1] bow had launched at the same hour to the same eternal waltz, a subject of ready-made conversation between the woman extenuated by her late night and the man as anxious for his health as for his purse.

How much is she going to ask me for? Is she a ten-louis woman, a twenty-five or a fifty? Is she healthy? the diner meditates internally.

How much is he going to give me? Is he loaded or hard up? his companion is calculating secretly.

---

1 The Orchestre Boldi was a band of Hungarian tzigane [gypsy] musicians who played in many Parisian venues in the 1890s, including Maxim's and the Café de la Paix. La Belle Otero was very fond of them and often got her lovers to hire them.

But the music is there, which occupies the silences and gradually eases the malaise. The gypsy waltz, which exasperates the amorous and the talkers, is the supreme resource of snobs and demoiselles that the hazards of sports, professions and encounters have brought together; Boldi's bow causes stupidities to soften—what am I saying?—it melts them and unfreezes them; better, it makes them think of Rigo's bow.[1]

"Do you know the adventure of the princess?" That's a pretext ready-made for sounding out Monsieur's generosity. "Give the gypsies five louis, Chéri."

I love you, and yet I'm a coward!

The hall demanded an encore of the singer's waltz.

Bust forward, rump stuck out and swooning, the fat lady begins again. Her diamonds and her pearls, an entire steaming peddler's tray sparkling with necklaces, chains and pendant earrings, tinkle and glitter in droplets over her vast bosom.

"The *spolia opima* of Vienna, Berlin and Saint Petersburg," sniggers Hubert. "The lady has drained Europe. It's forty years of prostitution that her crumbling flesh and that luxury of jewels represents. A former waitress in a Ukraine inn, the lady now has millions, a small town house here, a villa in Monte Carlo, a château in Touraine. She has killed beneath her several banks, not to mention several bankers, ravaged foreign courts and slept in a few royal alcoves.

"Ten years ago, she was still the mistress and adviser of the financial backer of one of our most joyous hereditary princes, but she wasn't able to marry in time. She lacked the great seigneur, broke and déclassé, whose blazon regilds appropriately,

---

1 Boldi's great rival in the tzigane genre was Rigo Jancsi (1858-1927), who achieved the distinction of having a cake named after him after the American millionairess Clara Ward, then married to a Belgian prince, ran away with him in 1894. She joined him on stage, posing in a state of undress while he played, as his band toured Europe.

forces salutations and doors. Poor Zénobie—for her name is
Zénobie—as a princess of the Holy Empire or a German gra-
fina, would have been able to receive All Paris in her home, and
even a little of London in transit, and marry her daughters in
the purest faubourg. But Zénobie is a miser; she wasn't able to
make the necessary sacrifice; now she's old Hamburini, reduced
to coming to sing with the little whores on the music hall stage
at sixty! The most publicity-hungry gigolos refuse to be seen
with her. Even Monsieur de Montesquiou has not admitted her
to his Académie.

"Worse, Sem has disdained her, in spite of that frightful grotesquerie. She's Mère Hamburini, the joy, the scarecrow and the
living scandal of the Bois and the premières. Personally, I admire
her as a symbol, that of the high life; and that flaccid public of
snobs who are applauding her by derision doesn't suspect that
it's rendering homage to the old guard that never surrenders."

"For at our age, we still triumph," insinuated Albertine de
Cerizaie in her falsetto voice, having suddenly emerged behind
the two men.

"Gigolos have never prevented you from sleeping, Albertine,
have they? You're an orderly woman. It isn't you who would
have increased the print-run of *L'Orgueil du Mâle*."[1] And Marcel
Humbert drilled his little green eyes into the ballerina's somber
irises.

"Albertine has never had an exact notion of the sexes," insinuated Maxence Chottard, and nudged the painter's elbow slyly.

The dancer shrugged her shoulders. "You can talk, my lad. All
distastes are in nature, and you might have the shaven mouth of
a bad priest, but you've missed American chic. You just resemble
a flunkey. I certainly wouldn't march for your mug."

"Oh, everyone knows that you're only smitten with princesses."

---

1 *L'Orgueil du mâle* was a novel by the elusive and probably pseudonymous
Albert Juhellé published in 1902 and advertised in *Le Journal,* but presumably pornographic and now exceedingly hard to find.

"What do you expect, my lad? There are men of the world who are mad for whores; me, I'm a whore for women of the world."

"That's frankness."

"You don't say! I won't spare myself for you."

"They're still going, then, the little fêtes on the Île de la Grand-Jatte," sniggered Chottard.

To which the dancer riposted: "Be careful you don't go blind; you're mishandling the rod."

"Always the wit, Albertine."

"Oh, repartee at the most. Corridor wit, in the genre of yours. But I'm a good girl, That doesn't prevent me from giving you a good tip for the next Maisons-Lafitte. You're a mug when it comes to courses, my little Chottard."

The dancer aimed her opera-glasses at the dance-floor.

"Finally she's decided to cast off; that's not unfortunate. Now, Madame can be put to bed . . . and not alone. At her age! Oh, if anything could still disgust me about men it's what I can see there. Measure the scene for me. There it is, the punishment."

Marquise Hamburini retired.

Folded in two by the applause, as if kneeling in a reverential dive that put her hips higher than her head, the fat lady came offstage backwards. A frenetic joy shook the hall. An impeccable suit, thickset shoulders and hams jutting under the fabric, a pretty fellow with the mat pallor of a Sicilian, abundant slick black hair, the Marquise's sigisbeo collected the fat lady as she went past and threw an ample ball-wrap over her shoulder.

A low brow, a narrow nose in the same pane as the forehead, the willful advancement of a square chin with heavy jaws, the solidity of a marvelously constructed face and bright short teeth in a very red mouth gave the man the robust and healthy appearance of a fine animal. There was something of the bull and the ruffian in the neck, the gait and the attitude of the newcomer. Only the languorous softness of the gaze belied the brutality of the face: dark moist eyes whose caress attracted the attention of women.

Oh, how he contrasted with the bleak laxity of the others, the sigisbeo of the Marquise, and how that man of luxury and joy emphasized with his triumphant youth the professional lassitude and shored-up usury of that landslide!

"He'll kill her."

"Not even that. He'll rob her and move on to another."

"It's necessary to find another!"

"Oh, new beds! There are velodromes; they're seed-nurseries for old ladies."

"And then, the Marquise uses them up quickly. That mother of gigolos devours her children."

"In order to preserve them a mother."

"Madame Ugolino, then."

"More like Mount Peleus, because she's as bald as an egg underneath her wig. I saw her one morning at a spa two years ago."

"Without her curls?"

"Without her curls. The gigolo of the season had deserted her cup; he'd fled, taking her jewels, a few bonds and a bagatelle of twenty-five thousand francs. The bonds were sent to New York for a sum of ten thousand; they were nominative."

"Yes, the Rumper Agency!"

"And the victim?"

"Squealed like a guinea-fowl plucked alive. She went down to the hotel desk without her wig, The lover had taken everything, including the lady's luggage. It was an organized gang. Pardon me—he left her walking-stick."

"That was an attention."

"So, since then, the Marquise doesn't trust Italy. Her infidel was Neapolitan."

"This evening's then? Not Italian, with that type? Turkish?"

"Not even that. As French as you or me. Nature makes these errors."

"Where did Hamburini fish him up? In the Seine?"

"Better than that, in mid-Ocean."

"Naturally."

"On a transatlantic. He was a cook. The lady made two crossings in order to see him again and then abducted him from his ovens. Seasickness, rolling and pitching, there's nothing like sea air for giving you heart."

"And that master cook . . . ?"

"And the master chef has become the irreproachable gentleman who accompanies her."

"I'd rather have thought that he'd emerged from the abattoir."

"Yes, he's certainly the type to stun livestock."

"And he was only a cook. Hazard does well what it does, Messieurs. Who knows better than a cook what to do with leftovers?"

That was the tone of the conversations of the men in the wings of the music hall; the ferocity that men customarily have toward aged courtesans had something on which to exercise itself. It is a species of revenge that one sex takes on the other in the frenzied denigration of idols that have ceased to please; and we love to prove our independence by insulting what once caused us to tremble. The iconoclastic rage of renegade priests against their former objects of worship, or the simple cowardice of any human crowd, we were there, ten or fifteen black suits, tearing apart the marquise and her sigisbeo with sharp teeth, and we were all taking a real pleasure in it.

The handsome Lavarède was there, the lover of the Duchesse de Freneuse, who was a good ten years older than her; the Dameroys, two well-known sportsmen; Amand d'Harnache, the Punch cartoonist; Comte Berthold of the Automobile Club; Simpson, the rich banker of the Simpson, Fechter & Co. of London and Berlin; Thomas Somsett, the director of the Aquarium; Marcel Hubert the painter, and a few other seigneurs of lesser importance, all ardent in demolishing the lamentable ruin of the Marquise Hamburini.

A pantomime already seen too many times closed the evening. Most of us had already collected our coats, and, impatient to breathe a little pure air, an entire band, including Marcel Hubert, Maxence Chottard and me had quit the spectacle and reached the boulevard.

Chottard was obstinate in waiting to tell us a story about the marquise and an orthopedic net designed to lift up and sustain the poor woman's collapsing flesh, a saving bandage and buttock-sheath, the failure of which, in the middle of Auteuil racecourse, had caused an abrupt descent of her attire, to the great joy of the stands.

"Enough, Chottard, you're abusing her, and you're repeating yourself, my dear."

That was Amand d'Harnache, who lifted the session; Amand's judgments are peremptory.

"And then, it was stifling in that circus," said the stout Simpson. "Do you want to take a trip to the club before going home, Lavarède?"

"Impossible, my dear, I'm going to Comtesse Tcherkoff's."

"Oh, me too, I forgot. I've been invited. It's the evening of her daughter's contract."

"Are you going too, Berthold?"

"Indeed. All Paris will be in the Rue du Colisée this evening; the mass will be at the Nonciature. Our friend Vera is lucky, she's marrying her daughters well, her eldest to the Duc de Plaisance, the second to the Marquis de Merlfolk and the youngest to the young prince of the house of Illyria. That dear Archduke Stéphane, perhaps a trifle compromised in London, but such a handsome fellow. As long as he can give his wife a child . . ."

"You're being silly, my dear—Archduchesses always have little Archdukes."

"Are we taking a cab to the Rue du Colisée?"

"No, let's walk up the Boulevard Haussmann; we'll get there soon enough."

"Ah! In fact, unless we can fly . . ."

Our group broke up at the Madeleine. I remained alone with Marcel Hubert and Maxence. We went along the Faubourg Saint-Honoré, where the painter Hubert has his studio.

"Did you hear them? They didn't have enough filth to drool over that poor Hamburini, and they're making a glory out of going to Tcherkoff's. They want to be seen there, and yet, the two women are alike, and Paris isn't unaware of the past of either one of them, Paris and its unjust, frivolous and whimsical society, complaisant regarding the flaws of one and intractable regarding the weaknesses of another—for, looking at things at close range, the two women had the same debuts. If Zénobie was a waitress in an inn, Vera poured beers in a brasserie, and it's from one adventure to another and from one lover to another that they both made millions. Both of them have slept in royal alcoves and both of them have enriched themselves by bankruptcies and presided over crashes.

"It's for an operation of lands given to La Tcherkoff that the isthmus of Korea has been pierced. A colonial expedition was undertaken partly because of old Hamburini. Fifteen years ago she played a political role in a foreign country, and both of them have been, in the broadest acceptance of the word, cosmopolitan courtesans. But Tcherkoff has a few millions more and the advantage of sporting a husband. A Tcherkoff was found to make her a countess and recognize her eldest daughter. The marriage, moreover, didn't change anything. Vera continues to skim the spas and the capitals, but at triple and quadruple tariffs. Adultery is one spice more, and the fathers of her other daughters are easily cited. Tcherkoff hasn't even taken the trouble to have them recognized. You know as well as I do which rich merchant from Hamburg is endowing the one who's being married this evening. With Nadèje, it's German money that's returning to the court of Illyria.

"Zénobie and Vera! The same origins, the same debuts, the same adventures, the same vicissitudes of fortune, perhaps the same lovers—in any case, the same boards of exhibition. And one has gone to the purest Faubourg; her husband is in all the clubs and, already imposed by two sons-in-law on the aristocracy of Europe, she's almost entering today into an Imperial family. This evening, All Paris is in the Rue du Colisée and all the ambassadors. And Zénobie, who has done no more or less than Vera, has fallen into the basest coquetry, reduced to exhibiting her jewels and furbelows on the stage of a music hall. We chuckle merely in pronouncing her name, and don't have enough obscenities to pour on her back.

"You can see very clearly that there are two moralities."

APPENDIX

VICTIM

"**O**h, if we're talking about hysterics, we haven't finished laughing."

"Or weeping, for they're rather fatal to their entourage, those Our Ladies of Bromide and Valerian."

And Octave Vergy, who definitely held the record for anecdotes, put down the cards and, leaning his elbows on the table in a familiar fashion, said:

"In the matter of neurotics I knew one who was very interesting and very particular. Her name doesn't matter, she's run aground in marriage now and her identity isn't our business.

"She was also a painter, as if a woman isn't born to be a lover, wife and mother, art always disequilibrates her. It was Raymond Dutheuil, another painter who died of phthisis ten years ago, who took me to see her; I'd always suspected Dutheuil of a consumptive passion for his pretty colleague. As I mistrusted his enthusiasms I resisted for some time; I have an innate and justified suspicion of artistic bluestockings; before his persistence, however, I allowed myself to be taken to Sèvres one day to the home of the delightful pre-Raphaelite 'who was only guilty of having come after Ghirlandaio and Filippo Lippi'[1]—the phrase is Dutheuil's.

"On the way, under the tall trees of Saint-Cloud, Dutheuil sated me with his anthem; I would surely be impassioned by

---

1 The Florentine painters Domenico Ghirlandaio (1448-1494) and Fra Filippo Lippi (c1406-1469).

the plaintive bloodless faces that the young woman painted: the emaciated and transparent faces of murdered queens of martyred courtesans; that visionary art was entirely made for me, because the evocatrice of Sèvres was above all a painter of eyes: the gazes of ecstatic torture-victims, imploring and suffering; the resigned eyes of saints, the madly haggard eyes of exiled princesses or the faded and weary eyes of beggars; no one had magnified and rendered like her the morbid and terrifying enigma of eyes, the deceptive and penetrating charm of gazes; I would see from her faces crowned with thorns, meager *Ecce homos* with forgiving smiles, and supraterrestrial profiles of the elect or the possessed, evoked in maleficent landscapes . . .

"Then too, I would see her eyes, her eyes as blue as water, as green as waves and as milky as absinthe, those eyes changing with the dolor or pity that she inspired for her works, for it was herself that she painted, always and forever; she was such a strange woman . . .

"And I let Duthueil talk, while taking notes for the imminent article that I would consecrate to that unknown competitor of the likes of Filippo Lippi and Ghirlandaio.

"I came back from Sèvres astonished and charmed by my day, spent in the Lostein household—you'll permit me to name them thus. It was almost poverty, not even gilded mediocrity that I had found in that household of artists, but they appeared to love one another so much, and in such an atmosphere of great art!

"The man, a sculptor, and the woman, a painter, lived far from the century and the preoccupations of the boulevard, on that bank of the Seine. Whether it was their shared passion for the primitives or the reflection of their reading—they only read Saint Teresa, Saint Augustine and the admirable Ruysbroeck[1]—

---

1 The Flemish mystic John van Ruysbroeck (c1293-1381) was the author of a widely-read text known in English as *The Spiritual Espousals* or *The Adornment of the Spiritual Marriage* (he wrote in Dutch rather than Latin, but was translated into English in the early days of printing), as well as other languages.

the atmosphere created round them had ended up surrounding them with an aureole and making their eyes as luminous blue as Gozzoli's archangels.[1] The woman, especially, was extraordinary; I did not remain insensible to her charm. Dutheuil had not lied, she had the otherworldly gaze of her paintings, the heavenly and watery eyes of her sad and disconcerting works, simultaneously pious and perverse; and yet, did not the willfulness of the chin and the sensual and savage bestiality of the mouth belie adequately that elevated and mystical visage?

"Madame Lostein was red-haired, the warm and coppery red that I love; and like Dutheuil, I loved her pastels, their plaintive color and precious brushwork; like Dutheuil, I loved the heart-rending severed heads of martyrs that she painted, inevitably posed on a tray or bleeding, human cut flowers in the bloody water of an enormous calyx.

"The Lostein household! Such a perfume of simplicity and faith emanated from that interior. 'The man and the woman are certainly two complicated minds,' Dutheuil said, 'but their souls are so fresh!' Then too, the modest situation was so valiantly accepted by those two beings, such cleanliness and order reigned in their home, and with it such a love of beauty and good, revealed in every corner by some unexpected religious trinket, that I learned and retraced the road to that little house in Sèvres.

"That Bollandist[2] interior became a kind of haven for me, a harbor, a safe and salutary refuge in my moments of fever and ennui; I became a close friend of the Losteins.

"Whether it was because of the reproductions of Botticelli hanging on the walls, the Donatellos painted on faience in the antechamber, the old chasubles trailing on the divans or the church lamp and large altar-cross, whose bright silver apotheo-

---

1 The reference is to the Florentine painter Benozzo Gozzoli (c1420-1497).
2 The Bollandists were an association of scholars specializing in hagiography, founded in the early seventeenth century, named after the Flemish Jesuit Jean Bolland (1596-1665).

sized their mirror, I always returned from their house better, as if more serene, if not cured . . . oh, the fresh calm of their little studio, decorated with flowery old stoneware and varnished green pottery . . .

"The Losteins were poor; the wife's paintings did not sell well, and, ardent as the man was in his labor as a sculptor, the household had a great deal of trouble making both ends meet; and yet, in order to live, Lostein consented to make industrial art. Furthermore, paltry and thin, with the air of one of the ailing Christs that his wife painted, the poor fellow was shaken by a bad cough and seemed seriously afflicted.

"I took an interest in them. Enthusiastic articles consecrated to Madame Lostein's pastels opened a few exhibitions to her; I succeeded in attracting the attentions of art dealers and collectors to her; the society that buys paintings learned the road to Sèvres, and Madame Lostein obtained a few commissions. If she had been able to paint portraits, the wellbeing of the household would have been assured, but that strange young woman was only able to paint herself. To the few pastels that she succeeded in making of a few rich clients that I brought her she always lent the hallucinating liquid blue of her terrible eyes. I baptized her Narcissa; she smiled at the nickname and, resuming her mystical allegories, renounced portraits.

> *"Let us not force our talent,*
> *We would do nothing with grace.*[1]

"Such was the morality of the campaign undertaken by me to classify Madame Lostein with Madame Lemaire and Mademoiselle Abbéma.[2]

---

1 The quotation is from Jean de La Fontaine's verse fable "L'Âne et le petit chien."

2 The references are to Madeleine Lemaire, née Coll (1845-1928), a friend of Marcel Proust dubbed by Robert de Montesquiou "the Empress of Roses" (Lorrain would have been *persona non grata* at her salon in the Rue de Monceau), and Louise Abbéma (1853-1927), similarly wealthy, a close

"The painter had entirely taken possession of me; I was under her empire, but an empire more psychic than physical, a rather complex and bizarre state of mind, in which desire, initially very violent, for that blonde flesh and that voracious mouth, had gradually turned into the platonic adoration of her eyes. Her eyes! The extraordinary life that they appeared to live in that pale face, as if already marked by the expectation of death, I drank their anguish delectably; their presence had become necessary to me; there was witchcraft in the physical malaise that I experienced far away from them, and their emprise over me was so powerful that I rediscovered them everywhere, in the blue of a woman's dress, in the light azure of the sky, the profound blue of water or the vivacity of a flower; it was a sort of passionate and dolorous admiration for that woman, so frail and so pale, as if vowed to misfortune.

"Although very smitten with Madame Lostein, I always maintained a great reserve in her regard. The husband's illness, the mediocrity of the household and the great amour that the two beings seemed to have for one another protected me from myself, and I had always brought an extreme delicacy to making the young woman accept the various gifts, trinkets, jewels of art and fabrics, with which I loved to frame her beauty.

"It was, therefore, with an indignant amazement that I greeted Raymond Dutheuil when he took the most unexpected step in my regard. Truly, it was bad, and I was abusive. That I was smitten with Madame Lostein was perfectly natural; all those who approached her were the same; he had been subject to it himself for a long time, and charm had emanated from the young woman for a long time; but I had been unable to control my desire, and I had abused the authority given to me within the household by my prestige as a critic and the services rendered, in order to formulate that desire and trouble Madame Lostein's

---

friend of Sarah Bernhardt and a noted Parisian "amazon" who sported male attire and a masculine hairstyle, Lorrain wrote a sympathetic article about her work for the *Courrier français*.

repose with a request. No, that was unworthy of a gallant man, and he, Dutheuil, would never have believed me capable of such dastardly conduct.

"I sensed my temples tensing and my saliva drying up. Dutheuil's eyes were scintillating; he was speaking in a low, staccato voice, and the pallor of his poor tuberculosis-stricken face was frightfully injected over the cheekbones. I was ready to burst out laughing, but the devastation of that poor sick face commanded me to pity; I controlled myself.

"He continued his reproaches in a muffled voice. How had I dared to solicit the young woman? Madame Lostein had complained about it to him; she had struggled for a long time and hesitated to go to him, but there was her repose and that of her household to consider. In Lostein's condition, all emotion became a danger, and she was living in a perpetual tremor that the sculptor might discover something. What complications the slightest suspicion might cause that debilitated individual threatened by congestion. In brief, Madame Lostein had charged him, Dutheuil, to beg me to cease my pursuits; she could no longer receive me except on that condition.

"I did not even defend myself; I replied to Dutheuil that I would write to Madame Lostein to take my leave of her, and with a gesture, I invited him to retire. In a brief note I expressed my regrets and my astonishment to the painter for having been able to alarm her, and told her that henceforth, she would no longer have anything to fear from me, for that letter was an adieu. She would not see me again, and I assured her, in concluding, that she had mistaken my attentions.

"The next day, Madame Lostein was in my home. The sight of her brought me abruptly upright from my seat. Narcissa remained on the threshold, and in the suppliant and soft voice of a little girl caught at fault, she said: 'Forgive me, I'm a little crazy, and then, Dutheuil has also exaggerated a great deal. The poor fellow is so infatuated with me; I've deceived him, I know, I misinterpreted your attentions. You've been so good and so

generous that I misjudged you—which is to say that I judged
you like the others. O, if you knew, if you knew! I've been so
unhappy, I'm still so unhappy!'

"She had advanced toward me swiftly, had taken possession
of my hands, and now she was sobbing, her head abandoned on
my shoulder, her magnificent blue eyes filled with tears, looking
up at me from below. I had sat her down beside me and I tried
in vain to calm her down. 'Oh, if you knew, if you knew,' she
repeated, between two convulsive hiccups. 'If you knew the ignominy and the baseness of men as I do, of what attempts I have
been the objective, what steps have been taken in my regard and
what is still happening around me, perhaps you'd excuse me for
everything.'

"And, in a breathless rush, she launched into the atrocious
confession. She had not always been poor; she had been fifteen
years old when her father, X***, the famous art jeweler, had
died. Already orphaned of her mother, she had been left alone
in the world. Z***, the great critic, had been appointed as her
guardian; he had known her since she was a little child, he had
been her father's best friend and she had had every confidence in
him. On the very day of the interment, while returning from the
cemetery, in the mourning carriage that was taking them back to
the house, that man, while comforting and consoling her, had
strayed his caresses, and without her even being conscious of the
act, had deflowered and taken her—her, a poor little orphan,
disarmed and almost anesthetized by stupor.

"She had remained in that man's home for three years; the
relationship had continued between the ward and the guardian, until the day when Z*** had married her off, endowing her
quite richly, moreover, to Marcenay, a chemist at the Collège
de France, an alcoholic and an illuminate of science, who had
not even touched her on her wedding night and had always
respected her thereafter like a sister. That paternal husband had
not astonished her any more than the incestuous guardian; she
did not know anything!

"Marcenay left her alone in the house all day but in the evening he took her to an estaminet in the Rue des Écoles where he played games with other professors. She sat near the table and riffled through illustrated papers until half past eleven or midnight, in the midst of the tobacco smoke and the noise of the backgammon and dominoes of the customers. Her husband's friends had paid court to her, had found pretexts for coming to see her during the day and had taken her, poor unsuspicious creature; the café was frequented by students. Her eighteen years and her red hair had ignited covetousness, and Narcissa had satisfied some of them with that fresh candor of the *Fiancée du roi de Garbe*[1] fallen into the hands of pirates, and that had continued until the evening when she had met Lostein.

"Then there had been amour! Until then she had only been a passive little creature, complaisant and resigned; with Lostein, she had understood! The distress of her life had become apparent to her, and, penetrated by horror for her past, for her unworthy guardian, that impotent husband and all the men who had abused her, she had fled the conjugal home and gone to live with Lostein.

"Now there was a refuge, a haven after the storm. Poverty had been mild for her with the delightful individual that the sculptor was. He had embellished her soul and awakened within her the sacred flame of art. Marcenay had not held it against her. That debonair husband gave her the income from her dowry and added three thousand francs a year taken from his professorial salary; he came every month to spend a day with them at Sèvres, having lunch and dinner there, and they separated in the evening the best of friends, after a communal reading of the admirable Ruysbroeck or Saint Augustine.

"Only the unworthy guardian had borne a grudge; he had died having disinherited her; he had not forgiven her for Lostein,

---

1 "La Fiancée du roi de Garbe" is a *conte* by La Fontaine, which inspired an 1818 painting by Louis Hersent and an 1864 opera by Daniel Auber and Eugène Scribe; it is probably the painting that Lorrain has in mind.

and in spite of their mediocrity—for the dowry had been some-what eroded by Marcenay's neglect—Madame Lostein would have been happy but for the lust and filthy desires of men, al-ways after her skirts and unleashed like a pack of dogs on her heels. All her husband's friends paid court to her, she was forced to throw them out; the collectors caught fire in her presence like matches; the liquid of her eyes set them ablaze. Dutheuil was in-tolerable; in the street, men followed her; her life was poisoned by the carnal desire aroused in her wake. It was frightful, the conditions that editors of art proposed to her in order to exhibit her pastels.

"In brief, she had thought that I was like all the rest; mad-dened, her head turned by that endemic fever of covetousness, she had thought she divined in my gaze the desires that revolted her modesty . . .

"And with a long sob, like a wounded turtle-dove, the painter of emaciated Christs and dolorous saints extended her lips to me and fell into my arms."